The *Bulletin of Atomic Scientists* carries a small clock on its masthead. Its hands are set according to the world situation of the date of issue—to show how close the scientists believe the world may be to nuclear war. We understand that lately these hands read two minutes to twelve.

What happens at midnight?

This anthology, containing some powerful stories by some brilliant writers, attempts to depict through the medium of science fiction the possibilities that may open for humanity at that unspeakable moment. They are not all downbeat; they are not all despairing. Science fiction predicted the Bomb; science fiction has also predicted ways out. Read and see for yourself.

H. BRUCE FRANKLIN, Distinguished Professor of English at Rutgers University was recently presented with The Pilgrim Award by the Science Fiction Research Association. In the presentation speech, this was said (among others): "He has taught at Stanford, Rutgers, Collecticut Wesleyan, Yale, Venceremos College, the Free University of Paris, John Hopkins and San Jose's Department of Adult Education, and he's refereed for some twenty-five university and scholarly presses; his articles have appeared in over sixty learned journals, anthologies, and news publications . . . He's made over a hundred public presentations at more than fifty colleges and universities and an uncountable number of television and radio appearances . . . and made three films including *A History of Science Fiction* for NET in 1966. Fellowships, grants in aid, awards have come his way and continue to come. . . ."

COUNTDOWN TO MIDNIGHT

Twelve Great Stories About Nuclear War

Edited, with an Historical Introduction by
H. BRUCE FRANKLIN

DAW BOOKS, INC.
DONALD A. WOLLHEIM, PUBLISHER

1633 Broadway, New York, NY 10019

Copyright ©, 1984, by H. Bruce Franklin.
All Rights Reserved.
Cover art by Vincent DiFate.

Permissions and copyrights for the contents will found on the following page.

DAW Collectors' Book No. 600

First Printing, December 1984

1 2 3 4 5 6 7 8 9

PRINTED IN U.S.A.

ACKNOWLEDGMENTS

"To Still the Drums" by Chandler Davis, Copyright © 1946, 1974, 1977 by Chandler Davis; first published in *Astounding Science Fiction*. Reprinted by permission of the author and his agent, Virginia Kidd.

"Thunder and Roses" by Theodore Sturgeon, Copyright © 1947 by Street & Smith Publications. Reprinted by permission of the author's agent, Kirby McCauley, Ltd.

"That Only a Mother" by Judith Merril, Copyright © 1948 by Street & Smith Publications; Copyright © 1954 by Judith Merril; Copyright © renewed by the Condé Nast Publications, Inc. Reprinted by permission of the author and the author's agent, Virginia Kidd.

"Lot" by Ward Moore, Copyright © 1953 by Fantasy House, Inc.; Copyright © renewed 1981 by Mercury Press, Inc.; first appeared in *The Magazine of Fantasy and Science Fiction*. Reprinted by permission of Raylyn Moore and Virginia Kidd on behalf of the estate of Ward Moore.

"I Kill Myself" by Julian Kawalec, from *The Modern Polish Mind*, edited by Maria Kuncewicz, Copyright © 1962 by Little, Brown and Co. Reprinted by permission of Maxwell Aley Associates.

"The Neutrino Bomb" by Ralph S. Cooper reprinted by permission of the *Los Alamos Scientific Laboratory News*.

"Akua Nuten" by Yves Thériault, translated by Howard Roiter, from *Stories from Québec,* edited by Philip Stratford; Copyright © 1974 by Van Nostrand Reinhold, Ltd., Toronto. Reprinted by permission of Yves Thériault and Howard Roiter.

"I Have No Mouth, and I Must Scream" by Harlan Ellison, Copyright © 1968 by Harlan Ellison. Reprinted by arrangement with, and permission of, the author and the author's agent, Robert P. Mills, Ltd., New York. All rights reserved.

"Countdown" by Kate Wilhelm, Copyright © 1968 by Kate Wilhelm. Reprinted by permission of the author.

"The Big Flash" by Norman Spinrad, Copyright © 1969 by Damon Knight. Reprinted by permission of the author.

"Everything But Love" by Mikhail Yemstev and Eremei Parnov, from *Everything But Love* (Moscow: Mir Publishers, 1973). Copyright © 1973 by Mir Publishers, Moscow, U.S.S.R. Reprinted by permission of VAAP, the Copyright Agency of the U.S.S.R.

"To Howard Hughes: A Modest Proposal" by Joe Haldeman, from *The Magazine of Fantasy and Science Fiction,* Copyright © 1974 by Mercury Press, Inc. Reprinted by permission of the author.

CONTENTS

Nuclear War and Science Fiction
H. Bruce Franklin
11

To Still the Drums
Chandler Davis
29

Thunder and Roses
Theodore Sturgeon
48

That Only A Mother
Judith Merril
76

Lot
Ward Moore
88

I Kill Myself
Julian Kawalec
121

The Neutrino Bomb
Ralph S. Cooper
131

Akua Nuten (The South Wind)
Yves Thériault
134

I Have No Mouth, and I Must Scream
Harlan Ellison
146

Countdown
Kate Wilhelm
166

The Big Flash
Norman Spinrad
180

Everything But Love
Mikhail Yemstev and Eremei Parnov
207

To Howard Hughes: A Modest Proposal
Joe Haldeman
267

COUNTDOWN
TO
MIDNIGHT

NUCLEAR WAR AND SCIENCE FICTION

H. Bruce Franklin

We who live on our planet today share a new experience. It is something entirely unfamiliar to our billions of ancestors whose lives passed in the millions of years prior to the twentieth century. Out of the very forces that constitute matter, we have created weapons that can wipe out the human species. So we conduct our daily lives under the ever-present threat of being annihilated by our own weapons. If the possibility of nuclear war is not the most important and distinctive feature of today's world, what is?

We call upon imaginative literature to help us explore and cope with this overwhelming fact. Only science fiction can respond. For any imaginative literature projecting either nuclear war or an end to the nuclear threat is by definition science fiction.

Nuclear weapons and nuclear war are major themes in modern science fiction, producing some of its supreme achievements. Choosing stories for this collection was therefore remarkably difficult, because there was room for so few among many superb works. Yet even science fiction, which attempts to expand the boundaries of our imagination, may have trouble grasping thermonuclear war, which presents the unimaginable, a dead planet without human consciousness. Moreover, the history of nuclear weapons is inextricably intertwined with the imagination of science fiction.

After all, it is science fiction that must take the dubious credit for inventing nuclear weapons and nuclear war. In fact, for about four decades these existed nowhere but in science fiction.

The discovery, in the late nineteenth century, of radioactivity led to dizzying breakthroughs in the understanding of matter. In the first decade of the twentieth century, scientists quantified the amount of energy associated with radioactivity, began to comprehend the actual structure of atoms, and developed precise theoretical models of the convertibility of mass and energy. In 1905, Albert Einstein expressed this in his seminal formula $E = MC^2$, in which the amount of energy (E) represented by matter is the product of its mass (m) multiplied by the almost inconceivably vast number of the speed of light squared (c^2).

Science fiction was meanwhile beginning to dramatize the terrify-potential of technology to unleash awesome quantities of energy from atoms. In 1906, George C. Griffith finished his novel *The Lord of Labour* (published in 1911 after his death) in which a bazooka-like radium gun fires radioactive guided missiles capable of annihilating targets near their detonation. A nuclear-powered spaceship appears in Garret P. Serviss' novel *A Columbus of Space*, serialized in 1909. But it was H. G. Wells who brought us our first "atomic bombs."

In 1914, just prior to World War I, Wells published *The World Set Free*, in which the major cities of the world are destroyed by small "atomic bombs" dropped by airplanes. These are true nuclear weapons, converting mass into fiery and explosive energy in a chain reaction induced by a triggering device. The old civilization collapses, as hordes of survivors, many scarred by radioactivity, wander desolate landscapes in scenes now conventional in science-fiction novels and films. From the ruins of industrial capitalism, which

Wells brands as a "barbaric" form of social organization, emerges "the Republic of Mankind" directed by a handful of farsighted elite minds who establish "science" as "the new king of the world."

The World Set Free may be considered the beginning, in imagination, of the atomic age. Despite the Wellsian fantasy of a scientific utopia created by a tiny technocratic elite and such comical anachronisms as World-War-I-vintage airplanes banking so that the man in the rear seat can drop an atomic bomb with his hands, the novel is astonishingly modern. In fact, we are still trapped in its central dilemma.

Wells imagines the harnessing of "atomic energy" in the early 1950s. The scientist who first discovers the process, realizing that there is no possibility of suppressing this knowledge, nevertheless "felt like an imbecile who has presented a box of loaded revolvers to a crèche." At first, the technological breakthrough merely exacerbates all the contradictions of the archaic and irrational social system. Tremendous wealth piles up alongside deepening poverty, while masses of the unemployed turn inevitably to crime. Conflicts between groups of nations become ever more ominous, with governments "spending every year vaster and vaster amounts of power and energy upon military preparations, and continually expanding the debt of industry to capital."

Looking backward from the future society that has emerged after the resulting nuclear holocaust, "it seems now that nothing could have been more obvious" than the fact that "war was becoming impossible." But governments and peoples remained "invincibly blind to the obvious." Then comes this chilling passage, far more relevant today than when it was penned in the days just before the First World War:

> They did not see it until the atomic bombs burst in their fumbling hands. Yet the broad facts must have glared upon any intelligent mind. All through the nineteenth and twentieth centuries the amount of energy that men

were able to command was continually increasing. Applied to warfare that meant that the power to inflict a blow, the power to destroy, was continually increasing. There was no increase whatever in the ability to escape. Every sort of passive defence, armour, fortifications, and so forth, was being outmastered by this tremendous increase on the destructive side. . . . These facts were before the minds of everybody; the children in the streets knew them. And yet the world still, as the Americans used to phrase it, "fooled around" with the paraphernalia and pretensions of war.

The actual schedule of events turned out to be surprisingly close to Wells' forecast. He projected the artificial induction of atomic disintegration in a minute amount of heavy metal in 1933, with the first industrial harnessing of nuclear power in 1953. In fact, Frédéric Joliot and Irène Curie first observed artificial radio-activity in 1933, the uranium atom was split in 1938 in Berlin, and the first commercial application of nuclear power began in late 1957. Wells, however, did not foresee atomic bombs coming even before atomic power.

Atomic bombs were actually used as weapons just seven years after the first experimental splitting of the atom. During these seven years, practically nobody, besides a handful of scientists and government leaders, glimpsed any of the implication of atomic energy in war and peace—except for writers and readers of science fiction.

One of these readers, however, was the physicist Leo Szilard. Szilard attributes his 1934 patent on a chain reaction to the influence of *The World Set Free*.* Thanks also to

---

*The influence of Wells' novel is discussed by Szilard in Volume II of his memoirs, *Leo Szilard: His Version of the Facts*, edited by Gertrude Weiss Szilard and Stephen R. Weart. Dr. Weart's suggestions have been very helpful to me.

Wells' novel, Szilard later saw that the splitting of the atom in Berlin might lead to atomic weapons in the hands of the Nazis. So his reading of *The World Set Free* led him to help induce the U.S. government to set up the Manhattan Project, designed to produce atomic weapons that would deter any use by the Nazis.

Soon appeared one of the most bizarre feature of our times: the attempt to transform the most important forms of human knowledge into state secrets whose existence is to be "classified" by the government and kept inviolate by the secret police. Until this time, hardly anybody paid any serious attention to the frequent appearance of atomic weapons in science fiction, which was generally considered a subliterary ghetto inhabited by kids and kooks. But as science fiction was losing its monopoly on the bomb to the Manhattan Project, every science-fiction atomic bomb became a deadly serious matter for the government and its agents.

In early 1945, Philip Wylie submitted to the *American Magazine* his novella *The Paradise Crater*, which imagined the Nazis after their defeat in World War II attempting to conquer the United States with an atomic bomb utilizing Uranium-237. *American Magazine* rejected the story as too implausible, so it was then submitted to *Blue Book*, which promptly asked for government approval. Wylie was suddenly placed under house arrest, and then informed by an Army intelligence major that he was personally prepared to kill Wylie if necessary to keep the weapon secret. But numerous atomic bombs had already appeared in the science fiction of the early 1940s.

The most famous government attempt to suppress atomic bombs in science fiction came in response to Cleve Cartmill's "Deadline," which appeared in the March 1944 *Astounding Science-Fiction*. The story imagines the Axis powers of World War II developing a nuclear bomb based on Uranium-235. (The setting is thinly veiled by such devices as spelling backward the two warring alliances, the "Sixa" and the

"Seilla.") "Deadline" is an action adventure describing how a lone intelligence agent, aided by the underground, manages to defuse the bomb just before the "Sixa" can use it.

Cartmill was promptly visited and grilled by military intelligence, which also descended on the editor of *Astounding*, John Campbell. When Campbell was told to cease publishing stories about atomic bombs, he refused on the grounds that these weapons appeared so frequently in *Astounding* that their sudden disappearance would be a clear signal to the Axis that they were close to being produced, thus prodding the Nazis to redouble their already frantic nuclear-weapons research.

"Deadline," using information already widely available, imagines the atomic bomb working like this: a "trigger" breaks through metal shields, releasing sufficient radioactivity to drive blocks of Uranium-235 above critical mass, leading to an explosive chain reaction. This is about as close to the actual mechanism of early atomic bombs as the rough sketch which Julius and Ethel Rosenberg allegedly conspired to transmit to the Soviet Union, for which they were executed in 1953.

"Deadline" contains some assumptions that reveal the innocent world before the Bomb. Cartmill's anti-fascist Allies rule out the use of the atomic bomb because they are already winning the war, and thus have no overriding reason to unleash such a terrible force upon the world. For they realize the possibility with which we now live: that nuclear weapons could threaten the existence of "the entire race." With the obliteration of all consciousness, even time itself, which "exists only in consciousness," might be annihilated: "There won't be any time, unless dust and rocks are aware of it."

During the three decades between *The World Set Free* and Hiroshima, very little attention was paid to what was for Wells the central problem: How could a primitive human race with such deadly anachronisms as nation states possibly coexist with nuclear weapons? About the only answer to the dilemma was aptly titled "Solution Unsatisfactory," a story published in May 1941 by Robert A. Heinlein. Instead of Wells' world government formed by visionary statesmen and technocrats, Heinlein sees the only solution, albeit unsatisfactory, as a total monopoly of nuclear weapons wielded by a single, benevolent "undisputed military dictator of the world."

Many of the scientists working on the Manhattan Project shared the apprehension of science fiction writers. As they pondered the consequences of actually using the atomic bomb, they too began to imagine what it might be like to live in the resulting world of the future. On July 17, 1945, Leo Szilard and sixty-nine of the other scientists who had just developed and tested the atomic bomb dispatched a petition to President Truman. They pointed out that the bomb had been developed mainly as a counterweapon to potential German nuclear weapons, that since Germany had surrendered no such threat any longer existed, and that Japan was already on the brink of surrender. In a farsighted passage that might be considered incisive science fiction, the atomic physicists wrote:

> The development of atomic power will provide the nations with new means of destruction. The atomic bombs at our disposal represent only the first step in this direction and there is almost no limit to the destructive power which will become available in the course of their future development. Thus a nation which sets the precedent of using these newly liberated forces of nature for purposes of destruction may have to bear the responsibility of opening the door to an era of devastation on an unimaginable scale.

The scientists warned that the United States, holding a monopoly on nuclear weapons, had the "solemn responsibility" not to unleash this Frankenstein's monster. Otherwise, they predicted, eventually "the cities of the United States as well as the cities of other nations will be in continuous danger of sudden annihilation."

In "Deadline," Cleve Cartmill had assumed that the

allies, since they were clearly winning the war, would certainly decide not to unleash atomic weapons on the world. In "Solution Unsatisfactory," Heinlein had considered it unthinkable that the United States would use nuclear weapons without first demonstrating their hideous power to the enemy. The atomic physicists called on the President to allow Japan a clear option for surrender. Instead, without any warning whatsoever, and apparently with little consideration of the consequences for the world, in August, 1945, the Japanese cities of Hiroshima and Nagasaki were cremated. Why?

The official answer given then, and still accepted without question by many people, was that it would shorten the war and eliminate the need for an invasion of Japan, thus saving American lives. But the decision to drop atomic bombs on cities, arguably the most important human decision ever made, apparently had very little to do with ending the war. We cannot comprehend our present predicament, or intelligently explore the stories in this collection, without some attention to how and why those first atomic bombs generated the nuclear-arms race.

That there was no military need to drop the bomb was widely recognized by the U.S. military authorities. The U.S. Strategic Bombing Survey, for example, concluded unequivocally that ". . . Japan would have surrendered if the atomic bombs had not been dropped, even if Russia had not entered the war, and even if no invasion had been planned or contemplated."[1] Fleet Admiral William Leahy, Chief of Staff to both Roosevelt and Truman, flatly declared: ". . . the use of this barbarous weapon at Hiroshima and Nagasaki was of no material assistance in our war against Japan. The Japanese were already defeated and ready to surrender."[2] Asked in 1945 for his opinion on dropping the atomic bomb, General

---

[1] United States Strategic Bombing Survey, *Japan's Struggle to End the War* (Washington, July 1, 1946), p. 13.

[2] William D. Leahy, *I was there* (N.Y., 1950), p. 441.

of the Army Dwight D. Eisenhower replied: "I was against it on two counts. First the Japanese were ready to surrender and it wasn't necessary to hit them with that awful thing. Second, I hated to see our country be the first to use such a weapon."[3]

Why, then, was it used? As early as 1948, P.M.S. Blackett, British Nobel Laureate in physics and wartime military expert, concluded in *The Military and Political Consequences of Atomic Energy* that "the dropping of the atomic bombs was not so much the last military act of the second World War as the first major operation of the cold diplomatic war with Russia."

Secretary of State Byrnes believed that "our possessing and demonstrating the bomb would make Russia more manageable in Europe." Vannevar Bush, chief aide for atomic matters for the Department of War, testified that the bomb "was delivered on time so that there was no necessity for any concessions to Russia at the end of the war." Secretary of War Stimson hoped to use the bomb "to get less barbarous relations with Russia."[4] President Truman later wrote that the bomb "put us in a position to dictate our own terms at the end of the war."[5]

Unilateral nuclear disarmament now seems a bizarre utopian fantasy. But after dropping the only two atomic bombs in existence, the United States could have maintained a world without nuclear weapons for years—by not making any more. Then at any time between late 1945 and 1949 the United States could have brought about universal nuclear disarmament simply by destroying our own atomic bombs. As the only nation in the world with nuclear technology, the U.S. could have easily led the world to a treaty outlawing the production and use of nuclear weapons.

---

[3] *Newsweek*, November 11, 1963, p 108.

[4] Byrnes, Bush, and Stimson are quoted by Gar Alperovitz, *Atomic Diplomacy: Hiroshima and Potsdam* (N.Y., 1965), pp. 240–242.

[5] Harry S. Truman, *Memoires, Vol. I* (Garden City, N.Y., 1955), p. 87.

The Soviet Union proposed just such a treaty on June 19, 1946. This provided for the destruction within three months of all atomic weapons and a total prohibition on their production, storage, and use. The United States rejected this proposal and, just twelve days later, conducted at Bikini the first of many postwar atomic-test explosions. The only U.S. suggestion during this period for nuclear control, the Baruch Plan, actually proposed that the United States should maintain its monopoly on atomic weapons until some unspecified date in the future, when an international control agency would be established, while in the meantime any *other* nation attempting to build atomic weapons would be subjected to "swift and sure punishment." Each Soviet attempt to achieve nuclear disarmament, including its support of the popular ban-the-bomb movement, was dismissed as a treacherous stratagem designed to deprive us of our military superiority.

Indeed, the United States kept striving to increase that military superiority. U.S. forces encircled the Soviet Union with a noose of more than 400 major military bases and 3,000 secondary bases. B-29s armed with atomic bombs were stationed at many of these bases, within striking range of all major Soviet cities, while U.S. development raced ahead on the world's first intercontinental bombers. Exactly one year after Hiroshima, the first B-36 was flown for the newly formed Strategic Air Command; the next year came the B-47, followed a few years later by the B-52.

In the fall of 1949, the U.S.S.R. tested its first atomic bomb. Two months later the U.S. unilaterally initiated the most deadly escalation of the arms race, beginning full-scale development of the thermonuclear (hydrogen) bomb, based on fusion. Atomic (fission) bombs could probably not exterminate the human race. Thermonuclear bombs could. A single B-52 armed with hydrogen bombs now carries explosive force equivalent to over 3,000 Hiroshima-type atomic bombs; one Trident submarine can launch 192 nuclear warheads, each equal to eight Hiroshima bombs. A full-scale thermonuclear war would so devastate the environment that most, if not all, species of land vertebrates would probably become extinct.

It was our own nation that created one new weapons system after another: the strategic missile and the tactical missile; the nuclear submarine; MIRV and MARV; the strategic cruise missile; pinpoint accuracy missiles designed not for retaliatory deterrence but for first-strike against hardened launch sites (such as the Pershing II, which will be able to wipe out the main Soviet ICBM force within eight to twelve minutes after launch); the neutron bomb; the MX; and the so-called "Star Wars" plan to turn space into a battlefield. No new round in the arms race has ever been initiated by the Soviet Union, which has merely played catch-up with each new weapons system. As Edgar Bottome exhaustively documented in *The Balance of Terror*, the United States has been "fundamentally responsible for every major escalation of the arms race."

Science fiction has played two crucial—and contradictory—roles in relation to this nuclear arms race. On one side, the fundamental assumptions underlying the creation of ever more menacing nuclear weapons systems are deeply rooted in science fiction. On the other side, science fiction may well have been a deciding factor in preventing nuclear war.

It was science fiction that created the myth of the superweapon, some extraordinary invention that would give a single nation unchallenged supremacy. This myth has led to what is now known as "the fallacy of the last move," the ever-unfulfilled expectation that each exotic new weapon for waging nuclear war would confer upon the United States permanent military superiority over the Soviet Union. Underlying this is another fallacy, also nourished in science fiction, from *Frankenstein* through the dime novel and into the pulps, that science and technology develop through the isolated thinking of lone geniuses or, later, brilliant research teams. Since the United States and the Soviet Union are at roughly equivalent stages of science and technology, any new weapon produced by one can soon be matched by the other, thus bringing about not supremacy for either but increased danger for both, and for all the people on the planet. Perceptive science fiction has long recognized this simple truth.

Like the atomic scientists, science fiction of the 1940s looked beyond the U.S. nuclear monopoly and saw the terrifying future of an uncontrolled arms race. Some of these early stories dramatize our current predicament, including not only the looming menace of an accidental holocaust or preemptive first strike but also the growing loss of freedom within a society dominated more and more by its own superweapons industry and military. These were familiar themes to hardcore science fiction readers in the very period when America at large was experiencing the extreme repression and thought control of the late 1940s and early 1950s.

As early as 1946, for example, Chandler Davis in "To Still the Drums" (included in this volume) foresees the military using the space program to develop intercontinental nuclear-armed missiles, and he asks the fateful question (to which we know the answer): Could the military, whether or not in league with the Administration, "get the United States into war against the wishes of the people and Congress?" Expressing the naïve outlook of that period, one character replies: " 'It's Congress that declares war.' " In response comes an analysis of the fatal momentum of a nuclear arms race and the role of Congress in accelerating it:

> "Try and get a congressman to understand what the atom bomb means. . . .Congress is still in the habit of wanting our Army to have bigger and better weapons than anybody else. There's another habit of thought Hiroshima didn't change."

Kris Neville's "Cold War" (*Astounding*, October 1949) also foresees a menace in a military capable of annihilating us with a few buttons or switches. But here the military authorities subject the crews of the nuclear-armed space stations to intense psychological screening to eliminate those who might go berserk and launch. Ironically, today exactly the opposite kind of screening takes place. As reported in the national press on March 16, 1983, the men selected to launch nuclear missiles are subjected to intense conditioning to make them "salivate at the very thought of turning the missile ignition key." This came to light when one trainee was shipped off to a psychiatrist because he had reservations about launching missiles in one of the regular plans routinely practiced: a preemptive first strike.

Poul Anderson's first published science fiction story (written in collaboration with F. N. Waldrop), "Tomorrow's Children" (*Astounding*, March 1947), takes place on a nuclear-devastated Earth where people neither "knew nor cared who was to blame" for the war: "Both sides, letting mutual fear and friction mount to hysteria—In fact, he wasn't sure the United States hadn't sent out the first rockets, on orders of some panicky or aggressive officials. Nobody was alive who admitted knowing." The "children" of the title are the grotesquely mutated offspring of the handful of survivors. Thus, instead of merely tolerating different peoples and nations, human beings must learn to accept their mutant children as fellow members of the human race if that race is to have any chance for survival.

The two masterpieces from this period, both included in this collection, are Judith Merril's first published science fiction story, "That Only a Mother" (1948), and Theodore Sturgeon's "Thunder and Roses" (1947), which is the ultimate test of all strategies based on nuclear "deterrence." Merril distills the essence of nuclearism into a poignant domestic story; Sturgeon puts it on a global scale, where the question is whether the human race gets one more chance.

Some science fiction readers began to complain of being tired of nuclear-war stories, and in *Galaxy* of January 1952, editor Horace Gold declared in "Gloom and Doom" that he was rejecting "atomic doom" stories as a policy. And certainly most Americans did not share science fiction's fears about the future nuclear-armed world. After all, even after the Soviet Union developed the bomb, the Soviets had neither the overseas bases nor the intercontinental bombers necessary to deliver it. So why not relax and enjoy our monopoly on deliverable nuclear weapons? Then in 1957 came Sputnik.

The Soviet rocket that put the first human-made object in space also brought home to America the threat that for twelve years had hung over the Soviet Union. (Actually as a navigator and intelligence officer in the Strategic Air Command in the late 1950s, I can attest that the Soviet Union had no means to deliver nuclear weapons until late 1958 or early 1959.) The warnings that had reverberated within the relatively small world of hard-core science fiction now burst forth in science fiction novels read by tens of millions and science fiction movies seen by hundreds of millions around the globe. These were the years of Nevil Shute's novel (1957) and film (1959) *On the Beach*, Peter George's *Red Alert* (1958) and its far greater film version *Dr. Strangelove: Or, How I Learned to Stop Worrying and Love the Bomb* (1963), Walter M. Miller, Jr.'s *A Canticle for Leibowitz* (1959), Alfred Coppel's *Dark December* (1960), Eugene Burdick and Harvey Wheeler's novel (1962) and film (1963) *Fail Safe*, and the true masterpiece of the genre, Mordecai Roshwald's *Level 7* (1959).

Level 7 was for some reason finally taken out of print in the United States in 1981, despite selling millions of copies in many printings in this country and despite its growing worldwide audience (since 1981 it has appeared in new editions in Rumanian, Danish, and Norwegian, among others). *Level 7* dramatizes what Jonathan Schell in *The Fate of the Earth* calls unimaginable: the extinction by nuclear war of all human consciousness.

Ray Bradbury attempted this in his 1950 story "There will Come Soft Rains," which presents a futuristic automated suburban house, gradually breaking down, as the only human remnant of a nuclear war. Though effective in its sense of lifelessness, the story is not ultimately able to dramatize the actual loss of consciousness. *Level 7* accomplishes this through that most distinguishing feature of science fiction: extrapolation.

The obliteration of human consciousness is shown to be part of the process that produces—as well as being produced by—the ultimate Armageddon. Two unnamed nations become ever more militarized, bureaucratized, and dehumanized as their central purpose becomes increasingly to destroy each other. To prepare for nuclear war, the "highest" level of human existence becomes the lowest, buried thousands of feet underground, having no other purpose than, upon command of a machine, to push the buttons that will annihilate the human species. Linus Pauling has called this novel "the most realistic picture of nuclear war that I have ever read in any work of fiction," and Bertrand Russell has pleaded for it to "be read by every adult in both the eastern and western blocs." But *Level 7* is much more than a magnificent warning. Eventually it will be discovered to be one of the very greatest anti-utopias, in which the worst social nightmares of the twentieth century come to their insanely logical conclusion.

These enormously popular science fiction novels and films that made the threat of nuclear war something tangible in the imagination of the world may have played a vital role in saving the world. This hypothesis of course cannot be scientifically verified. But any intelligent person today knows that the central message of these works—the knowledge that there will be no human winners in a nuclear war—remains the only effective deterrent we have.

Warning us—this has been the most obvious achievement of science fiction related to nuclear weapons. Inextricably tried to this is a second great achievement: exploring the causes of our predicament. Here science fiction has burrowed to the profound depths of our culture, our psychology, and our socio-economic structure, contemplating nuclear weapons as symptoms and expressions of deeper problems that we must confront if we are to survive and develop as a species.

Some splendid stories in this mode appeared in the early 1950s, when social criticism elsewhere had been severely repressed. Two tales by Fritz Leiber serve as striking examples. "Coming Attraction" (1950) displays a post-nuclear New York as a grotesque nightmare of the masked sado-masochism lurking under the smug, smiling, crew-cut surfaces of the nuclear-brandishing America of the 1950s. In "A Bad Day for Sales" (1953), Leiber describes the atom-bombing of New York through the eyes of a robot salesman who keeps trying to dispense polly-lops and Poppy Pop while his mindless ballyhoo unwittingly blares out the crass, dehumanized values that led us into this trap. Alfred Bester in "Disappearing Act" (1953) describes the annihilation of "the American Dream" by military, capitalist, and technocratic forces who wage a protracted global thermonuclear war with only one purpose: to preserve "the American Dream." Perhaps the finest stories from this period are Ward Moore's "Lot" (1953; included in this volume) and its sequel, "Lot's Daughter" (1954), which expose a favorite American male hero as a monster of ego who embodies on a domestic and suburban scale the force that menaces the world with nuclear weapons.

Science fiction exploring the sources of our global execution chamber surged into the "New Wave" of the late 1960s and beyond, brilliantly exemplified in this collection by the stories of Ellison and Spinrad. This mode is pushed to a limit in the surreal, hallucinatory fiction of J. G. Ballard, as in his apocalyptic novel *Love & Napalm: Export U.S.A.* (1969; published in England as *The Atrocity Exhibition*), where the exterior landscape, fragmented into a kaleidoscope of broken pieces, each reflecting images of the Bomb, merges with the equally devastated interior psychological landscape that produced the Bomb.

Science fiction has been far more successful in predicting

nuclear weapons, imagining their consequences, and exploring their social and cultural significance than in telling us what we can do about them. Relatively few stories have even attempted to suggest solutions.

In *Space Cadet* (1948), Robert Heinlein replaces the one-man military dictatorship of his 1941 "Solution Unsatisfactory" with the "Peace Patrol," whose orbiting nuclear bombs maintain the peace by threatening every city on Earth. Heinlein himself exposes the fallacy of both works in "The Long Watch" (1949), in which a heroic young officer gives his life to prevent senior officers of the Patrol from establishing precisely the kind of benevolent military dictatorship advocated in "Solution Unsatisfactory."

Even John Brunner, who has long been both a major science fiction writer and a leader of Britain's anti-nuclear movement (he's the author of the song "The H-Bombs' Thunder," known as the national anthem of this movement), has yet to present any science fiction giving credible guidance out of our plight. In his 1964 story "See What I Mean," for example, a lone scientific genius covertly analyzes the brain waves of negotiators from the major nuclear powers so that they can understand each other well enough to achieve disarmament; this is merely wishful thinking based on the feeble liberal myth that all problems could be solved with better communication.

Some tales have imagined people taking matters into their own hands against the militarists, as in Mack Reynolds' "Pacifist" (1964), the moving story of the death of a terrorist, member of an underground that uses kidnapping and assassination to neutralize the powerful men who most immediately menace the world. Joe Haldeman's "To Howard Hughes: A Modest Proposal," also in this collection, takes this kind of logic to its extreme in suggesting what kind of action might be necessary to disarm the most dangerous terrorists of all.

One of the few straightforward attempts to propose an actual solution comes in an ingenious package in the 1961 novella *The Voice of the Dolphins* by Leo Szilard. Perhaps remembering the futility of the direct appeal he organized from the atomic scientists to the U.S. Government, Szilard here offers a step-by-step plan for arms control and disarmament, allegedly the brainchild of dolphins with superhuman intelligence, actually the benevolent joint conspiracy of Soviet and American scientists using the dolphins as their front.

Science fiction does give us some unique insights into the sources, dangers, and dimensions of the nuclear menace. And understanding a problem is certainly the first and biggest step toward its solution. But since science fiction helped get us into this mess, perhaps it is not asking too much of it to help us find our way out. After all, no other imaginative literature is equipped for this task. And any plan for a nuclear-free future is by definition now, unfortunately, a form of science fiction.

TO STILL THE DRUMS

Chandler Davis

The internationally distinguished mathematician Chandler Davis graduated from Harvard in 1945 at the age of 18. The next year, while working toward his doctorate at Harvard, he published his first science fiction story, "The Nightmare" (*Astounding*, May 1946).

Although Dr. Davis has published relatively few science fiction stories, several have become classics. For example, his widely anthologized "Adrift on the Policy Level" has been called by Martin Greenberg "arguably the finest treatment of bureaucracy and the bureaucratic mind in all of science fiction." Starting with "The Nightmare," Davis' most persistent theme has been the threat of nuclear war.

In the October 1946 *Astounding* appeared "To Still the Drums," an uncomfortably accurate picture of the future. Alas, we know the answer to the unresolved speculation at the end. As for the author, in an appropriate sequel to the story, Dr. Davis was imprisoned for six months in 1960 for refusing to submit to the interrogations of the House Un-American Activities Committee. Undoubtedly influenced by this experience, he published in 1962 (in Groff Conklin's *Great Science Fiction by Scientists*) the poignant post-atomic tale "Last Year's Grave Undug," in which a handful of survivors, struggling for reconciliation, must still fight off the Loyalty Legionnaires, who remain blind to the devastation wrought by their anti-communist hysteria.

In 1962, Dr. Davis moved to Canada and began teaching at the University of Toronto, where he has been Professor of Mathematics since 1965.

It all began with that letter from Kathryn, and the thing that began it was the postscript at the bottom of the last page.

All the postscript said was this: "About two and a half lines of your last letter were cut out by the censor." There was nothing too remarkable about that. To be sure, it was 1948 and the war was quite definitely over; but I was stationed at Redcliff, Colorado, the rocket-research place, and Redcliff had about as strict a censorship lid on it as any military base in the country. You may have read about Redcliff a number of months back, when one of the experimental flights of XFE-III—"Effie," we called her—went slightly askew. We lost radar contact with her and she went right on up and never came down; making me, accidentally, a co-designer of the first man-made ship to leave the Earth.

You remember the story? That one got into the papers, and the lieutenant colonel who let it out almost got busted! Redcliff was plenty secret, and you had to be extra careful about your correspondence or the censors would get busy with their snippers.

Naturally, a good many of my letters to Kathryn had been cut to ribbons when I first came to Redcliff. I wrote her pretty regularly. Kathryn had been at Michigan with me, and when the war came along we'd been just about on the point of deciding to get married. But then I went in the Army, and stayed in when I got a chance at this rocket deal; Kathryn got a job as Senator Richardson's secretary. So the great romance at this time was nothing but a two-thousand-mile correspondence, with her talking about the Washington goings-on and telling me she loved me, and me telling her I loved her.

But this last letter—what had I said that the censor might not like? Nothing about my work, certainly; I'd learned better than that. Must have been some general remark, cut out on general principles. I thought back, and then I remembered. I'd asked her, "Do you think it'd be possible for a military clique to get the United States into war against the wishes of the people and Congress?"

Heck, that was just an academic question and there was no reason to censor it. Yet that must have been the passage in question.

And the only reason the incident started anything was that Bud Harper, my roommate, had predicted the passage wouldn't get through—because, he claimed, the question was far from academic.

It was McGee, the civilian physicist, who had put the idea in Bud's head. Bud and I had been working on plans for the XFE-II, one of Effie's successors, and McGee had consulted with us on the ship. He wasn't a reaction-motor man, nor an electronics man, nor a structural engineer, yet we'd been told that all his suggestions were to be incorporated into the design without question. We incorporated them, all right, but we asked McGee why he was insisting on so many strange features. Finally he broke down and told us that, and a good deal more.

McGee had been at Los Alamos almost from its start, and, partly because he knew nothing at all about nuclear physics, he had been let in on one of the most secret projects of all: the detailed construction of the A-bomb itself. He didn't know anything about what went on after critical mass was reached in one of those things, but he knew exactly how and by what means the critical mass was reached. And that was why he was at Redcliff. The XFF models were intended to bear payloads of U-235 or equivalent, and McGee was seeing to it that we built ships that *could* carry atomic warheads.

He told us this, and then went on without stopping for breath, "Yes, fellows, you're building the weapons we've all been looking forward to with fear since Hiroshima and before. If you do a good job you might succeed in wiping out civilization."

"If we do a good job," I said, "we'll have weapons so powerful nobody'd dare to start a war. Civilization will be more proof against wiping-out than before."

He looked at me with a pained expression, as if he'd just discovered he was talking to a Mongolian idiot. "Look, Weiss," he said patiently, "these RRA's—radar-rocket-atomic bombs—will be so powerful that *you* wouldn't dare to start a war. Sure. But don't credit everyone with as much good sense. They haven't got it, otherwise why do you think the Army's making these XFF's?"

I started to answer, but Bud did it for me. "Military research goes on even in peacetime. Always has."

"What 'always has' been true," said McGee, "may not be true any more. Forty years ago governments could meet in The Hague and discuss peace at the same time they were conducting a full-dress armaments race. They could get by with it. They could fool all of the people some of the time—specifically, for the length of time it took for war to break out. Maybe they even fooled themselves, saying their growing armies and navies were for defensive purposes.

"That's past history now, because once those XFF's get to the production stage there won't be any such things as defensive warfare, just offense and counter-offense. No nation puts weapons like *these* into actual production unless it expects to use them. Offensively."

"It's just the Army," I said. "The Army goes ahead and modernizes whether there's any reason to or not."

"Sure," McGee answered calmly, "the Army always plans for war before the public does. What I said still goes: any nation that builds RRA's, or even simple atom bombs, is putting a chip on its shoulder. When we make a workable XFF we'll just be helping to make Uncle Sam's chip larger and more unmistakable to the rest of the world, and thereby to make war closer and more inevitable.

"Granted what you say, that it may be 'just the Army.' Granted that the old-school Army officers understandably found it impossible even after Hiroshima to throw over the habit of repeatedly preparing for 'the next war.' The important thing is, not whether it's being done by the Army or the diplomats, not whether it's being done consciously or unconsciously, but that it's being done at all. We *are* preparing for the next war. We're precipitating it! Building fires that must be met with fire.

"This 'just the Army' you speak of is the group least likely to understand your 'not daring' to start another war, I might remind you."

Bud put in, "It's Congress that declares war."

"Try and get a congressman to understand what the atombomb means. Oppenheimer, Urey, Hogness—all those boys have tried. Some success, not much. Congress is still in the habit of wanting our Army to have bigger and better weapons than anybody else. There's another habit of thought, Hiroshima didn't change."

He made the prospect sound pretty bleak. I didn't really take it seriously then, because McGee was personally such a good-humored guy that you just naturally didn't take him seriously. He was a fellow, about forty I guess, and you laughed at pretty near everything he said, in ordinary conversation.

But he wasn't fooling now, and I remembered what he said. Bud did too, with additions. McGee had said the military could inadvertently cause a war due to Congress' lack of understanding; Bud supplied the equally uncomfortable thought that the military could start a war while deliberately keeping Congress in the dark about their activities. "I'll bet the Military Affairs Committee doesn't know what McGee told us about XFF," he'd say.

I didn't take much stock in it. Bud being pretty dissatisfied with the unpleasantness of life at Redcliff, I figured he was just sounding off. But the whole thing started me thinking, and led me incidentally to ask Kathryn that—entirely academic—question.

And the question had not been allowed to reach her. I knew LeBlanc, and he always took to the colonel all items that might be censorable from a public relations angle; so it had been the colonel who had cut up my letter. Well? Did it mean anything or didn't it?

I was sitting there in our tiny shack just outside of the restricted area, thinking it over, when Bud Harper burst in.

"What you say, Bud, about ready for chow?" I suggested calmly. Telling him about Kathryn's letter could wait.

But Bud had something that wouldn't wait. "Listen, Cole"—that's my name, Coleman Weiss—"I was up to see Jerry just before 4:30, to ask him how about some tennis tomorrow."

"So what?" Jerry was a first looey up in Communications, and tennis was a standard Saturday afternoon occupation in this season, so there was nothing remarkable about Bud's announcement so far.

"Well, he hadn't been relieved yet, and I wandered in to keep him company. He was at the teletype, and the tech sergeant who was supposed to be monitoring the thing was reading a comic book. Jerry was typing like mad on some coded message to the Service Command. Suddenly he stopped, rattled off a string of xx's, and got off the wires.

"I asked him what the trouble was. 'Oh,' says Jerry, 'I put that in a special code that those guys don't use. When they decipher it they'll think some joker at this end garbled it. I'll have to paraphrase the message and code it right, and then I'll be with you,' and he goes into the code room."

Bud stopped impressively, but I was slow on the uptake. "Well?" I said. "They've been coding a good many of our dispatches right along, haven't they?" Then I did a double-take and read the copy back—pardon the tangled metaphors.

When you looked at it right, it *was* pretty queer. A code the Service Command didn't use was not too extraordinary when you considered the nature of the camp we were at. But if the Service Command would decode the message and think it was garbled, that meant they didn't know the special code existed. Then there was Jerry's having to paraphrase the dispatch before he re-sent it. Unless it was just force of habit on his part, that meant the Service Command—Colonel Jennings' immediate superiors—were to be kept from cracking the special code, perhaps even from knowing there was such a thing. That's the principle of paraphrasing: you don't want to risk the other guy's getting the message both in a code he may know and in one he doesn't, so if you must send the same thing both ways you change the wording.

Apparently the chain of command in which the colonel was involved was not all that chains of command should be.

Bud nodded. "You can call me a crackpot all you want, but this looks like it fits in." It did, too. It fitted in pretty nicely with his idea of an Army war conspiracy. He'd have to change it to a single conspiring clique instead of saying the Army's top leaders were in on the thing; but that was more plausible anyhow. Made it sound less like Central America.

Bud was more stuck on his story than ever, now. I even debated whether or not I should add more fuel to the fire by telling him about Kathryn's letter. Finally I did, and it added fuel all right.

I couldn't help grinning at his expression. "I suppose now old Harper'll be snooping around after a plain language copy of one of those special-code dispatches."

"As a matter of fact, Cole, I was all set to do that this afternoon. A little while after Jerry went into the code room I sort of casually sauntered in after him."

"*Whew!* If you've always had *that* much disregard for regs, it's a wonder you ever got out of OCS." Of course I knew it wasn't disregard for regs, it was faith in this theory of his. I began to see where Bud might be getting himself in real trouble if he didn't watch his step. Or give up saving the world singlehanded, one or the other.

"I went in, anyway. Jerry finished what he was doing and looked around, surprised to see me there. I acted innocent. He didn't say anything, but gathered up what was in the 'Secret and Confidential Wastebasket,' took his dispatch in the other hand, and started toward the door, where I was. Just as he was about to toss the secret waste in the burn bag, he shifted all his papers into his left hand and saluted hurriedly. So I turn around, and the colonel has come in behind me."

"When's your GCM?"

"No general court this time, but I'd better keep my nose clean from here on in."

It was a relief to hear him say that, but I wasn't relieved for long. He turned on me and wanted me to carry on his sleuthing. "Do some hanging around Communications yourself. You know, Jerry, you can find excuses to drop over there. Use the same excuse I did: ask him for a tennis date."

"Shucks, and I wanted to go flying this week end," I drawled. I had a little plane of my own out at the airport the other side of town which I used to fly around the foothills, sometimes down to Colorado Springs and back.

"That's a joke, son. Invite Jerry to go up with you. What the heck."

"Look, Bud, I'm just as eager to keep my nose clean as you are. In the second place, I've got a good suspicion that this conspiracy tale of yours is strictly from E. Phillips Oppenheim. And besides that—what would you propose doing if your tale happened to be confirmed?"

"Good question," said Bud.

"Yeah, and a pretty tough one, isn't it? Just suppose Colonel Jennings and some of his Manhattan Project buddies actually are fouling up. Suppose they do plan to use their RRA's to start a war on their own. What can we—"

"O.K.," said a voice outside, "I heard what you said. And I'm coming in!"

Bud and I looked at each other in dismay. Then the door opened and in walked McGee.

For an instant I had a crazy notion that he was an Intelligence man, an *agent provocateur*. That didn't make sense, of course, and anyhow McGee was grinning. He must have just dropped by our shack on his way to the mess hall.

"Funny man," I said.

"I didn't do that just for a laugh," he explained apologetically. "I wanted to put the fear of God and the Army into you. Such remarks as you've been making are guaranteed to cause unhappiness if overheard by the wrong parties, and you'd do well to keep it in mind. Might I suggest the radio be turned on?"

While I was trying to tune in something besides double-talk pop songs, Bud asked him, "How long you been listening?"

"Not long, but long enough."

I said, "And what do you think?"

McGee answered, very seriously, "I think our friend Harper may have something there." I looked up quickly: McGee's opinions naturally carried more weight with me than Bud's. As for what to do about it—that is a stickler. If you could get evidence on the colonel, or whoever it is—which of course you can't—you might tattle to the top brass. If the government knew what an atomic bomb was—which of course it doesn't—it might be even more effective to give the dope to the Washington boys. But you're licked before you start. As I say, Hiroshima didn't even make a dent in the Congressional consciousness, and it made the wrong kind of dent in the military consciousness. The most you could do by accusing Jennings would be to get him in trouble; the basic problem would remain."

"Always the pessimist," I murmured.

The discussion didn't go much further; I wanted to get to the mess hall before it closed. After supper I calmly sat down and began to write Kathryn.

After I'd finished half a page I sat up and cursed myself for an absent-minded fool. I crumpled the paper to toss it in the wastebasket, then thought better of it and burned it in the ashtray.

It was natural enough I shoud start spouting Bud's story to her. Her letters always had a lot of political dope and a lot of hero-worship of her boss, Senator Richardson, to all of which I never had much answer to make except a gentle debunking of Richardson, a milder version of McGee's attacks on legislators in general. Her replies would make Richardson out to be the alert and altruistic intellectual giant one wishes all senators were.

The altercation was getting a little bit stale, and what was more natural than that I, searching for something to say and in a rather abstracted state of mind, should hit on Harper's spy-thriller fantasy?

Yes, I thought, *what could be more natural. Pass the thing on to Kathryn, and dollars to doughnuts the senator gets wind of it. It might turn the trick. What was it McGee had said? It might make that "dent in the Congressional consciousness."*

And *was* it all a spy-thriller fantasy?

I told Kathryn I loved her, addressed and sealed the envelope, and read a detective novel until time to turn in.

Saturday we knocked off work at noon. I quit early, rolled up my drawings and put them in the safe, picked up a *Redcliff Herald*, and went over to Communications to catch Jerry before he got off. I didn't admit even to myself that I was going on Bud's suggestion. It wasn't too tough an idea, asking Jerry to fly down to Colorado Springs with me: it was a beautiful day, the weather man had no baleful warnings, and Colorado Springs was always better than the town of Redcliff in proportion as it was farther away from the camp.

It wasn't at all on account of Bud that I was going up to see Jerry. Naturally, though, I wasn't going to keep my eyes closed while I was in the teletype room—or the code room.

Pure chance. Nobody was around Communications. Someone was going to be reported for that, but I wasn't kicking about my luck. I wasn't stretching it either. "Jerry," I called. No answer.

The code room would surely be locked. Keeping my act good in case anyone should walk in, I tried the door. It opened.

Sitting down just inside the door and making like I was waiting for the duty comm officer to show up, I took my bearings. I'd never been in here before, but it wasn't hard to recognize the coding machines. The desk with the fluorescent light suspended above it. The basket for secret and confidential waste. The papers lying on the desk beside the basket.

Jerry had really been careless. A trap? If so, who set it?

I crossed to the desk. My hands were in my pockets, negligent-like, but I didn't waste any time. A few yards from the desk I stopped, pulled out my cigarettes and lighter, and began fumbling the job of giving myself a light. But all the time I was really staring at those papers. After I read the first sentences I had to keep reading. Never before had I taken so long to light a cigarette.

I felt myself get cold and tingling all over. I hadn't believed Bud before! But this outdid Bud. In spite of its guarded language and obscure references, it was one hundred percent more explicit than he'd been. Even named the foreign power against which war was planned. Better, the colonel's signature should be on it somewhere, or at least Jerry's. This was evidence!

When I'd finished the top page I suddenly got my butt lit, turned in the other direction, and stood there puffing, hands in my pockets, still keeping up the act.

A lot of things went through my mind. It didn't take long, though; the few weeks I'd spent at the front before V-E Day had given me a habit of acting fast when I acted. About a quarter of an inch of my cigarette was gone when I strode over to the desk, scooped up the papers, tucked them inside the newspaper I still had under my arm. I got out of there fast. Nobody'd seen me.

Getting to the airport was the next thing. I could have taken the regular bus that ran into town at 1205, but suppose someone on the bus should want to read Alley Oop and should ask to borrow my paper? A better idea occurred to me, and I bummed a ride to town with the garbage truck. It left before the bus, so it wouldn't look funny for me to be taking it.

The sentry at the gate to the restricted area saw me, saluted. I waved acknowledgment with the newspaper, which was now clutched in my right hand. I don't believe I made it very casual.

Once in town, I headed for the bank to get some money. "How much?" I asked myself as I joined the line in front of a teller's window. Not the whole account. As much as possible without raising any eyebrows, and in bills of twenty dollars or smaller. I'm afraid I was rather nervous by the time I reached the teller, my withdrawal slip made out. He made some comment which I don't remember; I doubt if I even heard it. I shrugged, took my money, and left.

As I stood by the side of the highway trying to bum a ride to the airport, with the hot sun beating down on me, all feeling for the high-adventure aspect of the thing deserted me completely. It was, for a while, just like the time I'd taken a jaunt from OCS beyond the prescribed fifty-mile limit. Then, I'd had to gain a week end with Kathryn, and not much to lose if I was caught. Now I had everything to lose and still more to gain. But it felt the same. I was breaking regulations and doing my best to get away with it.

When I was in the air and headed for Colorado Springs, I allowed myself—finally—a little time for what you might call reconnaissance. It wasn't too late to give the project up. If I cruised around a while and then turned back, I'd probably get a chance, soon enough, to return the stolen dispatch to some unlikely place in the code room, in which case there'd be no skin off my arm and very little or none off Jerry's. My decision was still unforced.

Before I made it, I'd better take a closer look at what I'd taken. Adjusting the trim so the plane would fly with a minimum of attention, I slipped the dispatch out from the camouflaging *Redcliff Herald* and read it through at my leisure. Sure enough, a discussion of policy, along the lines of the section I'd read this morning. Sure enough, the colonel's signature, illegible to one not familiar with Jennings' scrawl, but, to me, unmistakable.

I remembered what McGee had said: "The wiping out of civilization—" I remembered, also, what Bud had said—now everything was confirmed, and my decision made. I'd head for Washington, traveling by plane as far as possible and after that traveling on guts. It should be possible to get the evidence to Kathryn before I was caught, and for her to pass it on. From there on in it'd be up to Senator Richardson. The almost unknown quantity. Perhaps the weak link in the whole audacious plan.

The decision was made. Crumple the *Herald* into a ball and chuck it out. Write a note to Kathryn—don't include her name—and fasten it to the dispatch in case it has to be handed over in a hurry with no time for explanations. Then fold it, put it in your inside breast pocket, and devote full attention to your piloting.

There isn't much to tell about the plane ride. The flying

was almost automatic, and time went faster than you'd think. I stopped a couple of times to rest, eat, and gas up, telling the fellows at each airport that I'd come from Salt Lake City, yes, I'd had a pretty hard pull over the Rockies, I was heading for New York, figuring on making about eight hundred miles a day if the weather held good. Actually I made over a thousand.

At a little municipal airport in southern Indiana I paid for my gas, strolled into the office and picked up a Louisville paper from a chair. It was Sunday afternoon, and time to begin looking at every newspaper I could find. Not to look for baseball scores or book reviews, either, but for my name. I'd only been gone a day, I wasn't even over leave yet, and there was no reason for the authorities to have missed me unless they'd connected me with the loss of the dispatch. If they had—look out!

Apparently they had. The item was small, obviously cut from the Army's release, and probably wouldn't have been printed were this not a king-size Sunday edition. But it had the dope.

You had to admit the Army could work fast when it had a mind. There was my name—"First lieutenant Coleman Weiss, deserter," from now on—a description of my plane, the statement that I was believed to be traveling east, and enough gingerbread to make the story newsworthy. Declared a deserter in less than a day! Either I'd been seen entering or leaving the comm office, or Colonel Jennings was playing long shots in his attempt to keep that dispatch out of circulation.

It was quite a shock. I'd had pretty good hopes of reaching the east coast by plane, arriving some time Monday. I'd been banking on my not being immediately connected with the theft, and on a possible reluctance on the colonel's part to hunt me by standard methods, for fear my cargo might fall into the hands of the General Staff. Both had fallen through.

Several things were clear. First, no one here had seen the telltale news item. Second, that might not be the case the next place I landed. Third, the plane, in spite of its speed, was dangerously slower than telegraph wires, and had ceased to be exactly a desirable means of transportation.

I didn't land at Cincinnati, but I didn't keep on to eastward either. I circled, put what seemed a reasonable distance between the city and me, and simulated a forced landing, some distance from any visible dwellings.

The landing went O.K., so I deliberately saw to it that it didn't go O.K. Before the ship had lost too much speed, I gritted my teeth and forced it over on its nose. A few sharp shocks—then I got out of it, fast. In spite of the fair quantity of gas remaining in its tanks, it didn't burn. So I burned it.

That wasn't so smart; the flames might have attracted people too soon. I had some idea of making the plane harder to identify as mine. The loss of the ship meant nothing to me. I was in this up to my neck, with high enough stakes that twenty-five hundred dollars more or less was insignificant; and the ship's sentiment value was strictly a negative quantity at this point.

There was a panicked moment when I thought I'd left the all-important dispatch in the burning plane. This was quickly proven false, and I fingered with vast relief the thin sheaf of papers that could easily bring me a long prison term.

The night was far gone before I hit Cincinnati, and I cursed my foolishness in having landed so far from the city. Distances are deceptive from the air, and very long when you're on foot! The long wait in the railroad station which followed didn't help my nerves any either. The station was big, and seemed bigger. There were a lot of people, and there seemed to be more, all looking at me. I dozed sometimes, not enough to get any rest but just enough to have bizarre, unpleasant dreams.

On the train it was better. I awoke feeling fine, in spite of having missed breakfast. There was a fresh pack of cigarettes in the overnight bad I'd bought—for appearance—in Cincinnati, and I relaxed more completely than I had since I left. It was easy to relax—there was nothing left to lose. The almost carefree life at Redcliff was gone. I'd given that up two days before, the minute I crumpled up that *Herald* and tossed it out the window of the plane. With that clear in my mind, my mission once more seemed better than a mere negative flight from justice. It was a positive battle *for* justice.

My state of mind was a lot better when, bag in my hand and papers in my pocket, I left the train at Washington. I was fully prepared mentally for the possibility that I might be awaited at Union Station. And I was.

Whether he was an Intelligence man or a G-man I don't know, but he saw me as I left the concourse. I had one of those flashes of intuition that tell you you're being watched; I turned and met his eyes across the length of the waiting room. He wore a blue short-sleeved shirt and no hat. We both looked away again, neither of us giving any sign. I turned right toward the taxi stand, and gave another look back just as I left the station. It was easy to spot the man in the blue shirt; he was right where I'd seen him My suspicions had been correct. He was talking to another man, who wore a visible badge on his lapel, and pointing at me. Our eyes met again.

As soon as I was out of their sight I ran headlong *away* from the taxi stand and caught a D-2 bus that was just pulling out. That saved me. To get a cab would have meant a long search for one that was bound out Connecticut Avenue; the District was still short on cabs and drivers still liked to get a full load. Besides, the G-men's search would now be diverted. They'd naturally assume that I'd at least tried to get a cab.

Still, the bus was slow. It was rush hour, and there were lengthy stops for passengers at the most implausible places.

I'd been recognized. How long would it take before the District police had a description of me?

Downtown, I left the overnight bag under the seat and changed to a streetcar which I thought went out Wisconsin

Avenue. It wasn't the car I wanted, but it was headed northwest and there were no free cabs around. At Pennsylvania and Twentieth, still having failed to spot a taxi, I got off. After walking some way up Twentieth at no mean speed I was overtaken by a Connecticut Avenue bus, which I boarded with relief. Now if everything went well—

Everything didn't. The bus was a limited and went only as far as Albemarle, leaving me several blocks to walk. Walk I did. Every policeman in Washington might be looking for me by now, but if I were just another Army officer strolling down Connecticut I'd hardly be an object of suspicion. I steeled myself and kept up the act even when a squad car passed me. I got an impression one of the cops was turning to scrutinize my face. Still I walked on. No use letting them flush me that easily.

Two blocks down the avenue the squad car started up its siren, made a U-turn, and headed my way.

I was at a cross-street, and I turned into it on the double. "The masquerade is over, Weiss old boy," I told myself. There was a driveway running parallel to Connecticut, behind a row of apartment buildings. I cut down it and got out of sight behind an ell as the squad car screamed down the side street I'd just left. Close, but no cigar.

Kathryn lived on the next block. That meant one more street and a series of back yards still to cross. I looked both ways—plenty carefully, believe me—before I crossed that street.

Kathryn's place was in sight. I prayed she was still in the same first-floor room I remembered. I could hear the siren again, in back of me. Two sirens. It was a matter of time now. How much time? In my favor was the fact that the police weren't in a hurry and didn't know I was.

I grabbed the sill of what I thought was Kathryn's window and chinned myself on it. There she was! Just home from work, must have taken the next bus ahead of me. I butted the pane to attract her attention. She turned, recognized me, and stood stock-still with amazement. I tried to motion to her to open the window, but my hands were occupied and the gyrations of my head must have made me look completely mad. It was several long seconds before she was supporting me by one hand while I fished in my pocket with the other. (The sirens had stopped outside. The police would be searching now, on foot. Yet I dared not come into her room—)

She started to speak. "No time," I said. "Here, take this. Give it to Richardson, he'll know what to do. But read it yourself first. Don't get caught with it." Heck, all that was in the note I'd written! In my overwhelming haste I was wasting time myself. I cut it short. "It's all explained in that note."

She took the papers, winked, and slammed the window down on my knuckles, hard! I understood: she was taking no chances. Someone had probably seen me there. Right now she was no doubt calling the police to report that a lieutenant had tried to break into her room. What a girl!

I got as far away from there as I could before I ducked into the basement where they finally found me.

This is being written in a guardhouse cell, where I'm awaiting trial by general court-martial. I'd expected a general all along, of course. When they officially notified me of my right to have counsel, I played a long shot and named Senator Richardson. The local brass must really have been surprised when he agreed to take the case.

He's been in to see me a couple of times, and I've got the word from him on several things. I'm more or less of a political prisoner now, since Jennings' story came out. If Jennings is cleared, I'll get a prison term, even if Richardson gets me out of the desertion and treason charges. If Jennings isn't cleared, I'll be let off easy with a "discharge for incompetence"—essentially, a Dishonorable Discharge without the stigma attached to an ordinary DD.

The senator says he can't stop the communications officer's court-martial, but can get a presidential pardon after sentence is passed. This news was almost as welcome to me as the good outlook for my case. I'd hate to have got Jerry into trouble.

The most welcome of all was what Richardson told me about the Jennings' plot. He's really been working on that, putting a bee in the ear of everybody he can find with any jurisdiction. Best of all, he has hopes that the importance of the case may be recognized—that it may lead to discussion of the danger of an atomic armaments race—that it may open eyes to the peril inherent in the very existence of atomic weapons. He's doing all he can in that direction, too. Some of his words sounded startlingly like McGee.

Sounded, perhaps, like the prevailing Congressional attitude three months hence.

Once Richardson brought Kathryn along and left us—relatively—alone for a while. We didn't make much small talk; I didn't feel particularly clever. My proposal wasn't at all clever. It was a heck of a way to propose to a girl, anyway: through cell bars.

Kathryn's answer wasn't qualified at all. Not depending on how my trial came out, or anything. Just plain yes.

So now I'm sitting here waiting, writing this to pass the time. Wondering about my trial, and more important about what is going on in the capital. Will Richardson fail, or will the arms race be stopped? Ten years from now will the cities' crowded millions be dissolving in rapid-fire bursts of flaming hell? Or will there be a peaceful world—with me married to Kathryn and working on the first Moon rocket?

Or the thousandth?

THUNDER AND ROSES

Theodore Sturgeon

Born in 1918, Theodore Sturgeon published his first science fiction story in 1939. The twenty-five stories he then published within three years firmly established him as a major figure in the development of science fiction's so-called "Golden Age."

Sturgeon has always been primarily a short-story writer. His first novel, *The Dreaming Jewels*, did not appear until 1950. However, two of his novels are landmark achievements. *More Than Human* (1953) is one of the most successful attempts to dramatize a group consciousness, here composed of a half-dozen children, outsiders, and freaks who together form a superhuman *gestalt*. *Venus Plus X* (1960) presents a utopian society of bi-sexuals, which is polarized with the consciousness of an ultra-male downed airman. Both novels display Sturgeon's hallmarks: an audacious challenging of taboos and an intense quest to discover forms of love that will overcome dehumanization, alienation, and loneliness.

Readers have many assorted favorites among Sturgeon's stories, which fill almost twenty volumes. His 1970 "Slow Sculpture," for example, won both the Hugo and Nebula awards. It is safe to say, however, that none of his stories has a message more powerful than "Thunder and Roses," which Sturgeon himself chose as his finest work for Leo Margulies' 1949 anthology *My Best Science Fiction Story*. The profound humanism of this classic tale, published in 1947, challenges the most fundamental assumptions of the nuclear arms race, which was then just being launched by the United States.

As Chandler Davis has written: "A whole generation of 'strategy theorists' would be making an advance in their theory if they would throw our their treatises on mutual deterrence and read 'Thunder and Roses.' "

When Pete Mawser learned about the show, he turned away from the GHQ bulletin board, touched his long chin, and determined to shave. This was odd, because the show would be video, and he would see it in his barracks.

He had an hour and a half. It felt good to have a purpose again—even shaving before eight o'clock. Eight o'clock Tuesday, just the way it used to be. Everyone used to catch that show on Tuesday. Everyone used to say, Wednesday morning, "How about the way she sang 'The Breeze and I' last night?" "Hey, did you hear Starr last night?"

That was a while ago, before all those people were dead, before the country was dead. Starr Anthim, institution, like Crosby, like Duse, like Jenny Lind, like the Statue of Liberty.

(Liberty had been one of the first to get it, her bronze beauty volatilized, radioactive, and even now being carried about in vagrant winds, spreading over the earth—)

Pete Mawser grunted and forced his thoughts away from the drifting, poisonous fragments of a blasted Liberty. Hate was first. Hate was ubiquitous, like the increasing blue glow in the air at night, like the tension that hung over the base.

Gunfire crackled sporadically far to the right, swept nearer. Pete stepped out of the street and made for a parked ten-wheeler. There's a lot of cover in and around a ten-wheeler.

There was a Wac sitting on the short running-board.

At the corner a stocky figure backed into the intersection. The man carried a tommy gun in his arms, and he was swinging it to and fro with the gentle, wavering motion of a weathervane. He staggered toward them, his gun muzzle hunting. Someone fired from a building and the man swiveled and blasted wildly at the sound.

"He's—blind," said Pete Mawser, and added, "He ought to be," looking at the tattered face.

A siren keened. An armored jeep slewed into the street. The full-throated roar of a brace of .50-caliber machine guns put a swift and shocking end to the incident.

"Poor crazy kid," Pete said softly. "That's the fourth I've seen today." He looked down at the Wac. She was smiling.

"Hey!"

"Hello, Sarge." She must have identified him before, because now she did not raise her eyes or her voice. "What happened?"

"You know what happened. Some kid got tired of having nothing to fight and nowhere to run to. What's the matter with you?"

"No," she said. "I don't mean that." At last she looked up at him. "I mean all of this. I can't seem to remember."

"You . . . well, gee, it's not easy to forget. We got hit. We got hit everywhere at once. All the big cities are gone. We got it from both sides. We got too much. The air is becoming radioactive. We'll all—" He checked himself. She didn't know. She'd forgotten. There was nowhere to escape to, and she'd escaped inside herself, right here. Why tell her about it? Why tell her that everyone was going to die? Why tell her that other, shameful thing: that we hadn't struck back?

But she wasn't listening. She was still looking at him. Her eyes were not quite straight. One held his but the other was slightly shifted and seemed to be looking at his temples. She was smiling again. When his voice trailed off she didn't prompt him. Slowly he moved away. She did not turn her head, but kept looking up at where he had been, smiling a little. He turned away, wanting to run, walking fast.

(How long can a guy hold out? When you're in the Army they try to make you be like everybody else. What do you do when everybody else is cracking up?)

He blanked out the mental picture of himself as the last one left sane. He'd followed that one through before. It always led to the conclusion that it would be better to be one of the first. He wasn't ready for that yet.

Then he blanked that out, too. Every time he said to himself that he wasn't ready for that yet, something within him asked, "Why not?" and he never seemed to have an answer ready.

(How long could a guy hold out?)

He climbed the steps of the QM Central and went inside. There was nobody at the reception switchboard. It didn't matter. Messages were carried by guys in jeeps, or on motorcycles. The Base Command was not insisting that anybody stick to a sitting job these days. Ten desk men would crack up for every one on a jeep, or on the soul-sweet squads. Pete made up his mind to put in a little stretch on a squad tomorrow. Do him good. He just hoped that this time the adjutant wouldn't burst into tears in the middle of the parade ground. You could keep your mind on the manual of arms just fine until something like that happened.

He bumped into Sonny Weisefreund in the barracks corridor. The tech's round young face was as cheerful as ever. He was naked and glowing, and had a towel thrown over his shoulder.

"Hi, Sonny. Is there plenty of hot water?"

"Why not?" grinned Sonny. Pete grinned back, cursing inwardly. Could anybody say anything about anything at all without one of these reminders? Sure there was hot water. The QM barracks had hot water for three hundred men. There were three dozen left. Men dead, men gone to the hills, men locked up so they wouldn't—

"Starr Anthim's doing a show tonight."

"Yeah. Tuesday night. Not funny, Pete. Don't you know there's a war—"

"No kidding," Pete said swiftly. "She's here—right here on the base."

Sonny's face was joyful. "Gee." He pulled the towel off his shoulder and tied it around his waist. "Starr. Anthim here! Where are they going to put on the show?"

"HQ, I imagine. Video only. You know about public gatherings." And a good thing, too, he thought. Put on an in-person show, and some torn-up GI would crack during one of her numbers. He himself would get plenty mad over a thing like that—mad enough to do something about it then and there. And there would probably be a hundred and fifty or more like him, going raving mad because someone had spoiled a Starr Anthim show. That would be a dandy little shambles for her to put in her memory book.

"How'd she happen to come here, Pete?"

"Drifted in on the last gasp of a busted-up Navy helicopter."

"Yeah, but why?"

"Search me. Get your head out of that gift horse's mouth."

He went into the washroom, smiling and glad that he still could. He undressed and put his neatly folded clothes down on a bench. There were a soap wrapper and an empty toothpaste tube lying near the wall. He went and picked them up and put them in the catch-all. He took the mop which leaned against the partition and mopped the floor where Sonny had splashed after shaving. Got to keep things squared away. He might say something if it were anyone else but Sonny. But Sonny wasn't cracking up. Sonny always had been like that. Look there. Left his razor out again.

Pete started his shower, meticulously adjusting the valves until the pressure and temperature exactly suited him. He didn't do anything slapdash these days. There was so much to feel, and taste, and see now. The impact of water on his skin, the smell of soap, the consciousness of light and heat, the very pressure of standing on the soles of his feet—he wondered vaguely how the slow increase of radioactivity in the air, as the nitrogen transmuted to Carbon Fourteen, would affect him if he kept carefully healthy in every way. What happens first? Do you go blind? Headaches, maybe? Perhaps you lose your appetite. Or maybe you get tired all the time.

Why not go look it up?

On the other hand, why bother? Only a very small percentage of the men would die of radioactive poisoning. There were too many other things that killed more quickly, which was probably just as well. That razor, for example. It lay gleaming in a sunbeam, curved and clean in the yellow light. Sonny's father and grandfather had used it, or so he said, and it was his pride and joy.

Pete turned his back on it and soaped under his arms, concentrating on the tiny kisses of bursting bubbles. In the midst of a recurrence of disgust at himself for thinking so often of death, a staggering truth struck him. He did not think of such things because he was morbid, after all! It was the very familiarity of things that brought death-thoughts. It was either "I shall never do this again" or "This is one of the last times I shall do this." You might devote yourself completely to doing things in different ways, he thought madly. You might crawl across the floor this time, and next time walk across on your hands. You might skip dinner tonight, and have a snack at two in the morning instead, and eat grass for breakfast.

But you had to breathe. Your heart had to beat. You'd sweat and you'd shiver, the same as always. You couldn't get away from that. When those things happened, they would remind you. Your heart wouldn't beat out its *wunklunk, wunklunk* any more. It would go *one-less, one-less*, until it yelled and yammered in your ears and you had to make it stop.

Terrific polish on that razor.

And your breath would go on, same as before. You could

sidle through this door, back through the next one and the one after, and figure out a totally new way to go through the one after that, but your breath would keep on sliding in and out of your nostrils like a razor going through whiskers, making a sound like a razor being stopped.

Sonny came in. Pete soaped his hair. Sonny picked up the razor and stood looking at it. Pete watched him, soap ran into his eye, he swore, and Sonny jumped.

"What are you looking at, Sonny? Didn't you ever see it before?"

"Oh, sure. Sure. I was just—" He shut the razor, opened it, flashed light from its blade, shut it again. "I'm tired of using this, Pete. I'm going to get rid of it. Want it?"

Want it? In his foot locker, maybe. Under his pillow. "Thanks no, Sonny. Couldn't use it."

"I like safety razors," Sonny mumbled. "Electrics, even better. What are we going to do with it?"

"Throw it in the . . . no." Pete pictured the razor turning end over end in the air, half open, gleaming in the maw of the catch-all. "Throw it out the—" No. Curving out into the long grass. You might want it. You might crawl around in the moonlight looking for it. You might find it.

"I guess maybe I'll break it up."

"No," Pete said. "The pieces—" Sharp little pieces. Hollow-ground fragments. "I'll think of something. Wait'll I get dressed."

He washed briskly, toweled, while Sonny stood looking at the razor. It was a blade now, and if you broke it, there would be shards and glittering splinters, still razor sharp. You could slap its edge into an emery wheel and grind it away, and somebody could find it and put another edge on it because it was so obviously a razor, a fine steel razor, one that would slice so—"I know. The laboratory. We'll get rid of it," Pete said confidently.

He stepped into his clothes, and together they went to the laboratory wing. It was very quiet there. Their voices echoed.

"One of the ovens," said Pete, reaching for the razor.

"Bake ovens? You're crazy!"

Pete chuckled. "You don't know this place, do you? Like everything else on the base, there was a lot more went on here than most people knew about. They kept calling it the bake shop. Well, it *was* research headquarters for new high-nutrient flours. But there's lots else here. We tested utensils and designed beet peelers and all sorts of things like that. There's an electric furnace in here that—" He pushed open a door.

They crossed a long, quiet cluttered room to the thermal equipment. "We can do everything here from annealing glass, through glazing ceramics, to finding the melting point of frying pans." He clicked a switch tentatively. A pilot light glowed. He swung open a small, heavy door and set the razor inside. "Kiss it good-by. In twenty minutes it'll be a puddle."

"I want to see that," said Sonny. "Can I look around until it's cooked?"

"Why not?"

(Everybody around here always said "Why not?")

They walked through the laboratories. Beautifully equipped, they were, and too quiet. Once they passed a major who was bent over a complex electronic hook-up on one of the benches. He was watching a little amber light flicker, and he did not return their salute. They tiptoed past him, feeling awed at his absorption, envying it. They saw the models of the automatic kneaders, the vitaminizers, the remote-signal thermostats and timers and controls.

"What's in there?"

"I dunno. I'm over the edge of my territory. I don't think there's anybody left for this section. They were mostly mechanical and electronic theoreticians. The only thing I know about them is that if we ever needed anything in the way of tools, meters, or equipment, they had it or something better, and if we ever got real bright and figured out a startling new idea, they'd already built it and junked it a month ago. Hey!"

Sonny followed the pointing hand. "What?"

"That wall section. It's loose, or . . . well, what do you know?"

He pushed at the section of wall, which was very slightly out of line. There was a dark space beyond.

"What's in there?"

"Nothing, or some semiprivate hush-hush job. These guys used to get away with murder."

Sonny said, with an uncharacteristic flash of irony, "Isn't that the Army theoretician's business?"

Cautiously they peered in, then entered.

"Wh . . . *hey!* The door!"

It swung swiftly and quietly shut. The soft click of the latch was accompanied by a blaze of light.

The room was small and windowless. It contained machinery—a "trickle" charger, a bank of storage batteries, an electric-powered dynamo, two small self-starting gas-driven light plants and a Diesel complete with sealed compressed-air starting cylinders. In the corner was a relay rack with its panel-bolts spot-welded. Protruding from it was a red-top lever. Nothing was labeled.

They looked at the equipment wordlessly for a time and then Sonny said, "Somebody wanted to make awful sure he had power for something."

"Now, I wonder what—" Pete walked over to the relay rack. He looked at the lever without touching it. It was wired up; behind the handle, on the wire, was a folded tag. He opened it cautiously. "To be used only on specific orders of the Commanding Officer."

"Give it a yank and see what happens."

Something clicked behind them. They whirled. "What was that?"

"Seemed to come from that rig by the door."

They approached it cautiously. There was a spring-loaded

sole-noid attached to a bar which was hinged to drop across the inside of the secret door, where it would fit into steel gudgeons on the panel.

It clicked again. "A Geiger," said Pete disgustedly.

"Now why," mused Sonny, "would they design a door to stay locked unless the general radioactivity went beyond a certain point? That's what it is. See the relays? And the overload switch there? And this?"

"It has a manual lock, too," Pete pointed out. The counter clicked again. "Let's get out of here. I got one of those things built into my head these days."

The door opened easily. They went out, closing it behind them. The keyhole was cleverly concealed in the crack between two boards.

They were silent as they made their way back to the QM labs. The small thrill of violation was gone and, for Pete Mawser at least, the hate was back, and the shame. A few short weeks before, this base had been a part of the finest country on earth. There was a lot of work here that was secret, and a lot that was such purely progressive and unapplied research that it would be in the way anywhere else but in this quiet wilderness.

Sweat stood out on his forehead. They hadn't struck back at their murderers! It was quite well known that there were launching sites all over the country, in secret caches far from any base or murdered city. Why must they sit here waiting to die, only to let the enemy—"enemies" was more like it—take over the continent when it was safe again?

He smiled grimly. One small consolation. They'd hit too hard; that was a certainty. Probably each of the attackers underestimated what the other would throw. The result—a spreading transmutation of nitrogen into deadly Carbon Fourteen. The effects would not be limited to the continent. What ghastly long-range effect the muted radioactivity would have on the overseas enemies was something that no one alive today could know.

Back at the furnace, Pete glanced at the temperature dial, then kicked the latch control. The pilot winked out and then the door swung open. They blinked and started back from the raging heat within, then bent and peered. The razor was gone. A pool of brilliance lay on the floor of the compartment.

"Ain't much left. Most of it oxidized away," Pete grunted.

They stood together for a time with their faces lit by that small shimmering ruin. Later, as they walked back to the barracks, Sonny broke his long silence with a sigh. "I'm glad we did that, Pete. I'm awful glad we did that."

At a quarter to eight they were waiting before the combination console in the barracks. All hands except Pete and Sonny and a wiry-haired, thick-set corporal named Bonze had elected to see the show on the big screen in the mess hall. The reception was better there, of course, but, as Bonze put it, "you don't get close enough in a big place like that."

"I hope she's the same," said Sonny, half to himself.

Why should she be? thought Pete morosely as he turned on the set and watched the screen begin to glow. There were many more of the golden speckles that had killed reception for the past two weeks. Why should anything be the same, ever again!

He fought a sudden temptation to kick the set to pieces. It, and Starr Anthim, were part of something that was dead. The country was dead, a real country—prosperous, sprawling, laughing, grabbing, growing and changing, leprous in spots with poverty and injustice, but healthy enough to overcome any ill. He wondered how the murderers would like it. They were welcome to it, now. Nowhere to go. No one to fight. That was true for every soul on earth now.

"You hope she's the same," he muttered.

"The show, I mean," said Sonny mildly. "I'd like to just sit here and have it like . . . like—"

Oh, thought Pete mistily. Oh—that. Somewhere to go,

that's what it is, for a few minutes. "I know," he said, all the harshness gone from his voice.

Noise receded from the audio as the carrier swept in. The light on the screen swirled and steadied into a diamond pattern. Pete adjusted the focus, chromic balance, and intensity. "Turn out the lights, Bonze. I don't want to see anything but Starr Anthim."

It *was* the same, at first. Starr Anthim had never used the usual fanfares, fade-ins, color, and clamor of her contemporaries. A black screen, then *click*, a blaze of gold. It was all there, in focus; tremendously intense, it did not change. Rather, the eye changed to take it in. She never moved for seconds after she came on; she was there, a portrait, a still face and a white throat. Her eyes were open and sleeping. Her face was alive and still.

Then, in the eyes which seemed green but were blue flecked with gold, an awareness seemed to gather, and they came awake. Only then was it noticeable that her lips were parted. Something in the eyes made the lips be seen, though nothing moved yet. Not until she bent her head slowly, so that some of the gold flecks seemed captured in the golden brows. The eyes were not, then, looking out at an audience. They were looking at me, and at *me*, and at ME.

"Hello—you," she said. She was a dream, with a kid sister's slightly irregular teeth.

Bonze shuddered. The cot on which he lay began to squeak rapidly. Sonny shifted in annoyance. Pete reached out in the dark and caught the leg of the cot. The squeaking subsided.

"May I sing a song?" Starr asked. There was music, very faint. "It's an old one, and one of the best. It's an easy song, a deep song, one that comes from the part of men and women that is mankind—the part that has in it no greed, no hate, no fear. This song is about joyousness and strength. It's—my favorite. Isn't it yours?"

The music swelled. Pete recognized the first two notes of

the introduction and swore quietly. This was wrong. This song was not for . . . this song was part of—

Sonny sat raptly. Bonze lay still.

Starr Anthim began to sing. Her voice was deep and powerful, but soft, with the merest touch of vibrato at the ends of the phrases. The song flowed from her without noticeable effort, seeming to come from her face, her long hair, her wide-set eyes. Her voice, like her face, was shadowed and clean, round, blue and green but mostly gold:

*"When you gave me your heart, you gave me the world,
You gave me the night and the day.
And thunder, and roses, and sweet green grass,
The sea, and soft wet clay.*

*"I drank the dawn from a golden cup,
From a silver one, the dark,
The steed I rode was the wild west wind,
My song was the brook and the lark."*

The music spiraled, caroled, slid into a somber cry of muted, hungry sixths and ninths; rose, blared, and cut, leaving her voice full and alone:

*"With thunder I smote the evil of earth,
With roses I won the right,
With the sea I washed, and with clay I built,
And the world was a place of light!"*

The last note left a face perfectly composed again, and there was no movement in it; it was sleeping and vital while the music curved off and away to the places where music rests when it is not heard.

Starr smiled.

"It's so easy," she said. "So simple. All that is fresh and clean and strong about mankind is in that song, and I think that's all that need concern us about mankind." She leaned forward. "Don't you see?"

The smile faded and was replaced with a gentle wonder. A

tiny furrow appeared between her brows; she drew back quickly. "I can't seem to talk to you tonight," she said, her voice small. "You hate something."

Hate was shaped like a monstrous mushroom. Hate was the random speckling of a video plate.

"What has happened to us," said Starr abruptly, impersonally, "is simple, too. It doesn't matter who did it—do you understand that? *It doesn't matter*. We were attacked. We were struck from the east and from the west. Most of the bombs were atomic—there were blast bombs and there were dust bombs. We were hit by about five hundred and thirty bombs altogether, and it has killed us."

She waited.

Sonny's fist smacked into his palm. Bonze lay with his eyes open, quiet. Pete's jaws hurt.

"We have more bombs than both of them put together. We *have* them. We are not going to use them. *Wait!*" She raised her hands suddenly, as if she could see into each man's face. They sank back, tense.

"So saturated is the atmosphere with Carbon Fourteen that all of us in this hemisphere are going to die. Don't be afraid to say it. Don't be afraid to think it. It is a truth, and it must be faced. As the transmutation effect spreads from the ruins of our cities, the air will become increasingly radioactive, and then we must die. In months, in a year or so, the effects will be strong overseas. Most of the people there will die, too. None will escape completely. A worse thing will come to them than anything they gave us, because there will be a wave of horror and madness which is impossible to us. We are merely going to die. They will live and burn and sicken, and the children that will be born to them—" She shook her head, and her lower lip grew full. She visibly pulled herself together.

"Five hundred and thirty bombs—I don't think either of our attackers knew just how strong the other was. There has been so much secrecy." Her voice was sad. She shrugged slightly. "They have killed us, and they have ruined themselves. As for us—we are not blameless, either. Neither are we helpless to do anything—yet. But what we must do is hard. We must die—without striking back."

She gazed briefly at each man in turn, from the screen. "We must *not* strike back. Mankind is about to go through a hell of his own making. We can be vengeful—or merciful, if you like—and let go with the hundreds of bombs we have. That would sterilize the planet so that not a microbe, not a blade of grass could escape, and nothing new could grow. We would reduce the earth to a bald thing, dead and deadly.

"No, it just won't do. We can't do it."

"Remember the song? *That* is humanity. That's in all humans. A disease made other humans our enemies for a time, but as the generations march past, enemies become friends and friends enemies. The enmity of those who have killed us is such a tiny, temporary thing in the long sweep of history!"

Her voice deepened. "Let us die with the knowledge that we have done the one noble thing left to us. The spark of humanity can still live and grow on this planet. It will be blown and drenched, shaken and all but extinguished, but it will live if that song is a true one. It will live if we are human enough to discount the fact that the spark is in the custody of our temporary enemy. Some—a few—of his children will live to merge with the new humanity that will gradually emerge from the jungles and the wilderness. Perhaps there will be ten thousand years of beastliness; perhaps man will be able to rebuild while he still has his ruins."

She raised her head, her voice tolling. "And even if this is the end of humankind, we dare not take away the chances some other life form might have to succeed where we failed. If we retaliate, there will not be a dog, a deer, an ape, a bird or fish or lizard to carry the evolutionary torch. In the name of justice, if we must condemn and destroy ourselves, let us not condemn all life along with us! We are heavy enough with sins. If we must destroy, let us stop with destroying ourselves!"

There was a shimmering flicker of music. It seemed to stir her hair like a breath of wind. She smiled.

"That's all," she whispered. And to each man there she said, "Good night—"

The screen went black. As the carrier cut off—there was no announcement—the ubiquitous speckles began to swarm across it.

Pete rose and switched on the lights. Bonze and Sonny were quite still. It must have been minutes later when Sonny sat up straight, shaking himself like a puppy. Something besides the silence seemed to tear with the movement.

He said softly, "You're not allowed to fight anything, or to run away, or to live, and now you can't even hate any more, because Starr says 'no.' "

There was bitterness in the sound of it, and a bitter smell to the air.

Pete Mawser sniffed once, which had nothing to do with the smell. He froze, sniffed again. "What's that smell, Son'?"

Sonny tested it. "I don't— Something familiar. Vanilla—no . . . no."

"Almonds. Bitter— Bonze!"

Bonze lay still with his eyes open, grinning. His jaw muscles were knotted, and they could see almost all his teeth. He was soaking wet.

"Bonze!"

"It was just when she came on and said 'Hello—you,' remember?" whispered Pete. "Oh, the poor kid. That's why he wanted to catch the show here instead of in the mess hall."

"Went out looking at her," said Sonny through pale lips. "I . . . can't say I blame him much. Wonder where he got the stuff."

"Never mind that." Pete's voice was harsh. "Let's get out of here."

They left to call the meat wagon. Bonze lay watching the console with his dead eyes and his smell of bitter almonds.

Pete did not realize where he was going, or exactly why, until he found himself on the dark street near GHQ and the communications shack. It had something to do with Bonze. Not that he wanted to do what Bonze had done. But then he hadn't thought of it. What would he have done if he'd thought of it? Nothing, probably. But still—it might be nice to be able to hear Starr, and see her, whenever he felt like it. Maybe there weren't any recordings, but her musical background was recorded, and the Sig might have dubbed the show off.

He stood uncertainly outside the GHQ building. There was a cluster of men outside the main entrance. Pete smiled briefly. Rain, nor snow, nor sleet, nor gloom of night could stay the stage-door Johnny.

He went down the side street and up the delivery ramp in the back. Two doors along the platform was the rear exit of the communications section.

There was a light on in the communications shack. He had his hand out to the screen door when he noticed someone standing in the shadows beside it. The light played daintily on the golden margins of a head and face.

He stopped. "Starr Anthim!"

"Hello, soldier. Sergeant."

He blushed like an adolescent. "I—" His voice left him. He swallowed, reached up to whip off his hat. He had no hat. "I saw the show," he said. He felt clumsy. It was dark, and yet he was very conscious of the fact that his dress shoes were indifferently shined.

She moved toward him into the light, and she was so beautiful that he had to close his eyes. "What's your name?"

"Mawser. Pete Mawser."

"Like the show?"

Not looking at her, he said stubbornly, "No."

"Oh?"

"I mean . . . I liked it some. The song."

"I . . . think I see."

"I wondered if I could maybe get a recording."

"I think so," she said. "What kind of a reproducer have you got?"

"Audiovid."

"A disk. Yes; we dubbed off a few. Wait, I'll get you one."

She went inside, moving slowly. Pete watched her, spellbound. She was a silhouette, crowned and haloed; and then she was a framed picture, vivid and golden. He waited, watching the light hungrily. She returned with a large envelope, called good night to someone inside, and came out on the platform.

"Here you are, Pete Mawser."

"Thanks very—" he mumbled. He wet his lips. "It was very good of you."

"Not really. The more it circulates, the better." She laughed suddenly. "That isn't meant quite as it sounds. I'm not exactly looking for new publicity these days."

The stubbornness came back. "I don't know that you'd get it, if you put on that show in normal times."

Her eyebrows went up. "Well!" she smiled. "I seem to have made quite an impression."

"I'm sorry," he said warmly. "I shouldn't have taken that tack. Everything you think and say these days is exaggerated."

"I know what you mean." She looked around. "How is it here?"

"It's O.K. I used to be bothered by the secrecy, and being buried miles away from civilization." He chuckled bitterly.

"Turned out to be lucky after all."

"You sound like the first chapter of *One World or None*."

He looked up quickly. "What do you use for a reading list—the Government's own *'Index Expurgatorious'*?"

She laughed. "Come now—it isn't as bad as all that. The book was never banned. It was just—"

"—Unfashionable," he filled in.

"Yes, more's the pity. If people had paid more attention to it when it was published, perhaps this wouldn't have happened."

He followed her gaze to the dimly pulsating sky. "How long are you going to be here?"

"Until . . . as long as . . . I'm not leaving."

"You're not?"

"I'm finished," she said simply. "I've covered all the ground I can. I've been everywhere that . . . anyone knows about."

"With this show?"

She nodded. "With this particular message."

He was quiet, thinking. She turned to the door, and he put out his hand, not touching her. "Please—"

"What is it?"

"I'd like to . . . I mean, if you don't mind, I don't often have a chance to talk to— Maybe you'd like to walk around a little before you turn in."

"Thanks, no, Sergeant. I'm tired." She did sound tired. "I'll see you around."

He stared at her, a sudden fierce light in his brain. "I know where it is. It's got a red-topped lever and a tag referring to orders of the commanding officer. It's really camouflaged."

She was quiet so long that he thought she had not heard him. Then, "I'll take that walk."

They went down the ramp together and turned toward the dark parade ground.

"How did you know?" she asked quietly.

"Not too tough. This 'message' of yours; the fact that you've been all over the country with it; most of all, the fact that somebody finds it necessary to persuade us not to strike back. Who are you working for?" he asked bluntly.

Surprisingly, she laughed.

"What's that for?"

"A moment ago you were blushing and shuffling your feet."

His voice was rough. "I wasn't talking to a human being. I was talking to a thousand songs I've heard, and a hundred thousand blond pictures I've seen pinned up. You'd better tell me what this is all about."

She stopped. "Let's go up and see the colonel."

He took her elbow. "No. I'm just a sergeant, and he's high brass, and that doesn't make any difference at all now. You're a human being, and so am I, and I'm supposed to respect your rights as such. I don't. You're a woman, and—"

She stiffened. He kept her walking, and finished, "—and that will make as much difference as I let it. You'd better tell me about it."

"All right," she said, with a tired acquiescence that frightened something inside him. "You seem to have guessed right, though. It's true. There are master firing keys for the launching sites. We have located and dismantled all but two. It's very likely that one of the two was vaporized. The other one is—lost."

"Lost?"

"I don't have to tell you about the secrecy," she said disgustedly. "You know how it developed between nation and nation. You must know that it existed between State and Union, between department and department, office and office. There were only three or four men who knew where all the keys were. Three of them were in the Pentagon when it went up. That was the third blast bomb, you know. If there was another, it could only have been Senator Vandercook, and he died three weeks ago without talking."

"An automatic radio key, hm-m-m?"

"That's right. Sergeant, must we walk? I'm so tired—"

"I'm sorry," he said impulsively. They crossed to the reviewing stand and sat on the lonely benches. "Launching racks all over, all hidden, and all armed?"

"Most of them are armed. Enough. Armed and aimed."

"Aimed where?"

"It doesn't matter."

"I think I see. What's the optimum number again?"

"About six hundred and forty; a few more or less. At least five hundred and thirty have been thrown so far. We don't know exactly."

"Who are *we?*" he asked furiously.

"Who? Who?" She laughed weakly. "I could say, 'The Government,' perhaps. If the president dies, the vice president takes over, and then the speaker of the house, and so on and on. How far can you go? Pete Mawser, don't you realize yet what's happened?"

"I don't know what you mean."

"How many people do you think are left in this country?"

"I don't know. Just a few million, I guess."

"How many are there?"

"About nine hundred."

"Then as far as I know, this is the largest city left."

He leaped to his feet. *"No!"* The syllable roared away from him, hurled itself against the dark, empty buildings, came back to him in a series of lower-case echoes: . . . no-no—n . . .

Starr began to speak rapidly, quietly. "They're scattered all over the fields and the roads. They sit in the sun and die in the afternoon. They run in packs, they tear at each other. They pray and starve and kill themselves and die in the fires. The fires—everywhere, if anything stands, it's burning. Summer, and the leaves all down in the Berkshires, and the blue grass burnt brown; you can see the grass dying from the air, the death going out wider and wider from the bald spots. Thunder and roses . . . I saw roses, new ones, creeping from the smashed pots of a greenhouse. Brown petals, alive and sick, and the thorns turned back on themselves, growing into the stems, killing. Feldman died tonight."

He let her be quiet for a time. "Who is Feldman?"

"My pilot." She was talking hollowly into her hands. "He's been dying for weeks. He's been on his nerve ends. I don't think he had any blood left. He buzzed your GHQ and made for the landing strip. He came in with the motor dead, free rotors, giro. Smashed the landing gear. He was dead, too. He killed a man in Chicago so he could steal gas. The man didn't want the gas. There was a dead girl by the pump. He didn't want us to go near. I'm not going anywhere. I'm going to stay here. I'm tired."

At last she cried.

Pete left her alone, and walked out to the center of the parade ground, looking back at the faint huddled glimmer on the bleachers. His mind flickering over the show that evening, and the way she had sung before the merciless transmitter. "Hello—you." "If we must destroy, let us stop with destroying ourselves!"

The dimming spark of humankind—what could it mean to her? How could it mean so much?

"Thunder and roses." Twisted, sick, nonsurvival roses, killing themselves with their own thorns.

"And the world was a place of light!" Blue light, flickering in the contaminated air.

The enemy. The red-topped lever. Bronze. "They pray and starve and kill themselves and die in the fires."

What creatures were these, these corrupted, violent, murdering humans? What right had they to another chance? What was in them that was good?"

Starr was good. Starr was crying. Only a human being could cry like that. Starr was a human being.

Had humanity anything of Starr Anthim in it?

Starr *was* a human being.

He looked down through the darkness for his hands. No planet, no universe, is greater to a man than his own ego, his own observing self. These hands were the hands of all history, and like the hands of all men, they could by their small acts make human history or end it. Whether this power of hands was that of a billion hands, or whether it came to a focus in these two—this was suddenly unimportant to the eternities which now infolded him.

He put humanity's hands deep in his pockets and walked slowly back to the bleachers.

"Starr."

She responded with a sleepy-child, interrogative whimper.

"They'll get their chance, Starr. I won't touch the key."

She sat straight. She rose, and came to him, smiling. He could see her smile because, very faintly in this air, her teeth fluoresced. She put her hands on his shoulders. "Pete."

He held her very close for a moment. Her knees buckled them, and he had to carry her.

There was no one in the Officers' Club, which was the nearest building. He stumbled in, moved clawing along the wall until he found a switch. The light hurt him. He carried her to a settee and put her down gently. She did not move. One side of her face was pale as milk.

There was blood on his hands.

He stood looking stupidly at it, wiped it on the sides of his trousers, looking dully at Starr. There was blood on her shirt.

The echo of no's came back to him from the far walls of the big room before he knew he had spoken. Starr wouldn't do this. She couldn't!

A doctor. But there was no doctor. Not since Anders had hung himself. Get somebody. Do something.

He dropped to his knees and gently unbuttoned her shirt. Between the sturdy, unfeminine GI bra and the top of her slacks, there was blood on her side. He whipped out a clean handkerchief and began to wipe it away. There was no wound, no puncture. But abruptly there was blood again. He blotted it carefully. And again there was blood.

It was like trying to dry a piece of ice with a towel.

He ran to the water cooler, wrung out the bloody handkerchief and ran back to her. He bathed her face carefully, the pale right side, the flushed left side. The handkerchief reddened again, this time with cosmetics, and then her face was pale all over, with great blue shadows under the eyes. While he watched, blood appeared on her left cheek.

There must be *somebody*— He fled to the door.

"Pete!"

Running, turning at the sound of her voice, he hit the doorpost stunningly, caromed off, flailed for his balance, and then was back at her side. "Starr! Hang on, now! I'll get a doctor as quick as—"

Her hand strayed over her left cheek. "You found out. Nobody else knew, but Feldman. It got hard to cover properly." Her hand went up to her hair.

"Starr, I'll get a—"

"Pete, darling, promise me something?"

"Why, sure; certainly, Starr."

"Don't disturb my hair. It isn't—all mine, you see." She sounded like a seven-year-old, playing a game. "It all came out on this side, you see? I don't want you to see me that way."

He was on his knees beside her again. "What is it? What happened to you?" he asked hoarsely.

"Philadelphia," she murmured. "Right at the beginning. The mushroom went up a half mile away. The studio caved in. I came to the next day. I didn't know I was burned, then. It didn't show. My left side. It doesn't matter, Pete. It doesn't hurt at all, now."

He sprang to his feet again. "I'm going for a doctor."

"Don't go away. Please don't go away and leave me. Please don't." There were tears in her eyes. "Wait just a little while. Not very long, Pete."

He sank to his knees again. She gathered both his hands in hers and held them tightly. She smiled happily. "You're good, Pete. You're so good."

(She couldn't hear the blood in his ears, the roar of the whirlpool of hate and fear and anguish that spun inside him.)

She talked to him in a low voice, and then in whispers. Sometimes he hated himself because he couldn't quite follow her. She talked about school, and her first audition. "I was so scared that I got a vibrato in my voice. I'd never had one before. I always let myself get a little scared when I sing now. It's easy." There was something about a windowbox when she was four years old. "Two real live tulips and a pitcherplant. I used to be sorry for the flies."

There was a long period of silence after that, during which his muscles throbbed with cramp and stiffness, and gradually became numb. He must have dozed; he awoke with a violent start, feeling her fingers on his face. She was propped up on one elbow. She said clearly, "I just wanted to tell you, darling. Let me go first, and get everything ready for you. It's going to be wonderful. I'll fix you a special tossed salad. I'll make you a steamed chocolate pudding and keep it hot for you."

Too muddled to understand what she was saying, he smiled and pressed her back on the settee. She took his hands again.

The next time he awoke it was broad daylight, and she was dead.

Sonny Weisefreund was sitting on his cot when he got back to the barracks. He handed over the recording he had picked up from the parade ground on the way back. "Dew on it. Dry it off. Good boy," he croaked, and fell face forward on the cot Bonze had used.

Sonny stared at him. "Pete! Where've you been? What happened? Are you all right?"

Pete shifted a little and grunted. Sonny shrugged and took the audiovid disk out of its wet envelope. Moisture would not harm it particularly, though it could not be played while wet. It was made of a fine spiral of plastic, insulated between laminations. Electrostatic pickups above and below the turntable would fluctuate with changes in the dielectric constant which had been impressed by the recording, and these changes were amplified for the video. The audio was a conventional hill-and-dale needle. Sonny began to wipe it down carefully.

Pete fought upward out of a vast, green-lit place full of

flickering cold fires. Starr was calling him. Something was punching him, too. He fought it weakly, trying to hear what she was saying. But someone else was jabbering too loud for him to hear.

He opened his eyes. Sonny was shaking him, his round face pink with excitement. The audiovid was running. Starr was talking. Sonny got up impatiently and turned down the audio again. "Pete! Pete! Wake up, will you? I got to tell you something. Listen to me! Wake up, will yuh?"

"Huh?"

"That's better. Now listen. I've just been listening to Starr Anthim—"

"She's dead," said Pete. Sonny didn't hear. He went on explosively, "I've figured it out. Starr was sent out here, and all over, to *beg* someone not to fire any more atom bombs. If the government was sure they wouldn't strike back, they wouldn't have taken the trouble. Somewhere, Pete, there's some way to launch bombs at those murdering cowards—and I've got a pret-ty shrewd idea of how to do it."

Pete strained groggily toward the faint sound of Starr's voice. Sonny talked on. "Now, s'posing there was a master radio key, an automatic code device something like the alarm signal they have on ships, that rings a bell on any ship within radio range when the operator sends four long dashes. Suppose there's an automatic code machine to launch bombs, with repeaters, maybe, buried all over the country. What would it be? Just a little lever to pull; that's all. How would the thing be hidden? In the middle of a lot of other equipment, that's where; in some place where you'd expect to find crazy-looking secret stuff. Like an experiment station. Like right here. You beginning to get the idea?"

"Shut up. I can't hear her."

"The hell with her! You can hear her some other time. You didn't hear a thing I said!"

"She's dead."

"Yeah. Well, I figure I'll pull that handle. What can I lose? I'll give those murderin' . . . *what?*"

"She's dead."

"Dead? Starr Anthim?" His young face twisted, Sonny sank down to the cot. "You're half asleep. You don't know what you're saying."

"She's dead," Pete said hoarsely. "She got burned by one of the first bombs. I was with her when she . . . she— Shut up, now, and get out of here and let me listen!" he bellowed hoarsely.

Sonny stood up slowly. "They killed her, too. They killed her. That does it. That just fixes it up." His face was white. He went out.

Pete got up. His legs weren't working right. He almost fell. He brought up against the console with a crash, his outflung arm sending the pickup skittering across the record. He put it on again and turned up the gain, then lay down to listen.

His head was all mixed up. Sonny talked too much. Bomb launchers, automatic code machines—

"You gave me your heart," sang Starr. *"You gave me your heart. You—"*

Pete heaved himself up again and moved the pickup arm. Anger, not at himself, but at Sonny for causing him to cut the disk that way, welled up.

Starr was talking, stupidly, her face going through the same expression over and over again. *"Struck from the east and from the Struck from the east and from the—"*

He got up again wearily and moved the pickup.

"You gave me your heart. You gave me—"

Pete made an agonized sound that was not a word at all, bent, lifted, and sent the console crashing over. In the bludgeoning silence he said, "I did, too."

Then, "Sonny." He waited.

"Sonny!"

His eyes went wide then, and he cursed and bolted for the corridor.

* * *

The panel was closed when he reached it. He kicked at it. It flew open, discovering darkness.

"Hey!" bellowed Sonny. "Shut it! You turned off the lights!"

Pete shut it behind him. The lights blazed.

"Pete! What's the matter?"

"Nothing's the matter, Son'," croaked Pete.

"What are you looking at?" said Sonny uneasily.

"I'm sorry," said Pete as gently as he could. "I just wanted to find something out, is all. Did you tell anyone else about this?" He pointed to the lever.

"Why, no. I only just figured it out while you were sleeping, just now."

Pete looked around carefully while Sonny shifted his weight. Pete moved toward a tool rack. "Something you haven't noticed yet, Sonny," he said softly, and pointed. "Up there, on the wall behind you. High up. See?"

Sonny turned. In one fluid movement Pete plucked off a fourteen-inch box wrench and hit Sonny with it as hard as he could.

Afterward he went to work systematically on the power supplies. He pulled the plugs on the gas engines and cracked their cylinders with a maul. He knocked off the tubing of the Diesel starters—the tanks let go explosively—and he cut all the cables with bolt cutters. Then he broke up the relay rack and its lever. When he was quite finished, he put away his tools and bent and stroked Sonny's tousled hair.

He went out and closed the partition carefully. It certainly was a wonderful piece of camouflage. He sat down heavily on a workbench nearby.

"You'll have your chance," he said into the far future. "And by heaven, you'd better make good."

After that he just waited.

THAT ONLY A MOTHER

Judith Merril

Judith Merril has been actively opposing militarism since she started speaking on soap boxes at peace rallies in her native New York City in 1939, at the age of sixteen. While working as an editor and ghostwriter in the mid 1940s, she began selling her own writing, under a variety of pseudonyms, to western, detective, and sports magazines. Then in June 1948 *Astounding* published "That Only a Mother," her first science fiction story; this immediately established her reputation and soon became recognized as a classic.

In 1950, she published her first novel, *Shadow on the Hearth*, the deeply insightful story of a young Westchester housewife whose character develops as she attempts to cope with the aftermath of an atomic attack on New York City. Awaiting word of her husband's fate, she emerges from dependency and passivity, fending off the physical and social forces that menace her and her two daughters. The 1983 movie *Testament* closely parallels *Shadow on the Hearth*, though of course now, in the age of the fusion bomb, the suburban housewife must attain her full strength as she experiences the inevitable death of her family, herself, and, apparently, the human species.

Judith Merril's early works—especially "That Only a

Mother" and *Shadow on the Hearth*—were so far ahead of their times that their full meaning only began to be appreciated after the rise of the anti-war and women's liberation movements in the late 1960s. Ironically, it was during this period that Merril left the United States, moving first to England and then establishing permanent residence in Canada after 1967. Although she has published little fiction since then, she remains important as a critic, editor, teacher, and activist.

Margaret reached over to the other side of the bed where Hank should have been. Her hand patted the empty pillow, and then she came altogether awake, wondering that the old habit should remain after so many months. She tried to curl up, cat-style, to hoard her own warmth, found she couldn't do it any more, and climbed out of bed with a pleased awareness of her increasingly clumsy bulkiness.

Morning motions were automatic. On the way through the kitchenette, she pressed the button that would start breakfast cooking—the doctor had said to eat as much breakfast as she could—and tore the paper out of the facsimile machine. She folded the long sheet carefully to the "National News" section, and propped it on the bathroom shelf to scan while she brushed her teeth.

No accidents. No direct hits. At least none that had been officially released for publication. *Now, Maggie, don't get started on that. No accidents. No hits. Take the nice newspaper's word for it.*

The three clear chimes from the kitchen announced that breakfast was ready. She set a bright napkin and cheerful colored dishes on the table in a futile attempt to appeal to a faulty morning appetite. Then, when there was nothing more to prepare, she went for the mail, allowing herself the full pleasure of prolonged anticipation, because today there would *surely* be a letter.

There was. There were. Two bills and a worried note from her mother: "Darling. Why didn't you write and tell me sooner? I'm thrilled, of course, but, well, one hates to mention these things, but are you *certain* the doctor was right? Hank's been around all that uranium or thorium or whatever it is all these years, and I know you say he's a designer, not a technician, and he doesn't get near anything that might be dangerous, but you know he used to, back at Oak Ridge. Don't you think . . . well, of course, I'm just being a foolish old woman, and I don't want you to get upset. You know much more about it than I do, and I'm sure your doctor was right. He *should* know . . ."

Margaret made a face over the excellent coffee, and caught herself refolding the paper to the medical news.

Stop it, Maggie, stop it! The radiologist said Hank's job couldn't have exposed him. And the bombed area we drove past . . . No, no. Stop it, now! Read the social notes or the recipes, Maggie girl.

A well-known geneticist, in the medical news, said that it was possible to tell with absolute certainty, at five months, where the child would be normal, or at least where the mutation was likely to produce anything freakish. The worst cases, at any rate, could be prevented. Minor mutations, of course, displacements in facial features, or changes in brain structure could not be detected. And there had been some cases recently, of normal embryos with atrophied limbs that did not develop beyond the seventh or eighth month. But, the doctor concluded cheerfully, the *worst* cases could now be predicted and prevented.

"Predicted and prevented." We predicted it, didn't we? Hank and the others, they predicted it. But we didn't prevent it. We could have stopped it in '46 and '47. Now . . .

Margaret decided against the breakfast. Coffee had been enough for her in the morning for ten years; it would have to do for today. She buttoned herself into interminable folds of material that, the salesgirl had assured her, was the *only* comfortable thing to wear during the last few months. With a surge of pure pleasure, the letter and newspaper forgotten, she realized she was on the next to the last button. It wouldn't be long now.

The city in the early morning had always been a special kind of excitement for her. Last night it had rained, and the sidewalks were still damp-gray instead of dusty. The air smelled the fresher, to a city-bred woman, for the occasional pungency of acrid factory smoke. She walked the six blocks to work, watching the lights go out in the all-night hamburger joints, where the plate-glass walls were already catching the sun, and the lights go on in the dim interiors of cigar stores and dry-cleaning establishments.

The office was in a new Government building. In the rolovator, on the way up, she felt, as always, like a frankfurter roll in the ascending half of an old-style rotary toasting machine. She abandoned the air-foam cushioning gratefully at the fourteenth floor, and settled down behind her desk, at the rear of a long row of identical desks.

Each morning the pile of papers that greeted her was a little higher. These were, as everyone knew, the decisive months. The war might be won or lost on these calculations as well as any others. The manpower office had switched her here when her old expediter's job got to be too strenuous. The computer was easy to operate, and the work was absorbing, if not as exciting as the old job. But you didn't just stop working these days. Everyone who could do anything at all was needed.

And—she remembered the interview with the psychologist—*I'm probably the unstable type. Wonder what sort of neurosis I'd get sitting home reading that sensational paper* . . .

She plunged into the work without pursuing the thought.

February 18.

Hank darling,

Just a note—from the hospital, no less. I had a dizzy spell at work, and the doctor took it to heart. Blessed if I know what I'll do with myself lying in bed for weeks, just waiting—but Dr. Boyer seems to think it may not be so long.

There are too many newspapers around here. More infanticides all the time, and they can't seem to get a jury to convict any of them. It's the fathers who do it. Lucky thing you're not around, in case—

Oh, darling, that wasn't a very *funny* joke, was it? Write as often as you can, will you? I have too much time to think. But there really isn't anything wrong, and nothing to worry about.

Write often, and remember I love you.

Maggie.

SPECIAL SERVICE TELEGRAM
FEBRUARY 21, 1953
22:04 LK37G

FROM: TECH. LIEUT. H. MARVELL
X47-016 GCNY
TO: MRS. H. MARVELL
WOMEN'S HOSPITAL
NEW YORK CITY

HAD DOCTOR'S GRAM STOP WILL ARRIVE FOUR OH TEN STOP SHORT LEAVE STOP YOU DID IT MAGGIE STOP LOVE HANK

February 25.

Hank dear,

So you didn't see the baby either? You'd think a place this size would at least have visiplates on the incubators, so the fathers could get a look, even if the poor benighted mommas can't. They tell me I won't see her for another week, or maybe more—but of course, mother always warned me if I didn't slow my pace, I'd probably even have my babies too fast. Why must she *always* be right?

Did you meet that battle-ax of a nurse they put on here? I imagine they save her for people who've already had theirs, and don't let her get too near the prospectives—but a woman like that simply shouldn't be allowed in a maternity ward. She's obsessed with mutations, can't seem to talk about anything else. Oh, well, *ours* is all right, even if it was in an unholy hurry.

I'm tired. They warned me not to sit up so soon, but I *had* to write you. All my love, darling,

Maggie.

February 29.

Darling,

I finally got to see her! It's all true, what they say about new babies and the face that only a mother could love—but it's all there, darling, eyes, ears, and noses—no, only one!—all in the right places. We're so *lucky*, Hank.

I'm afraid I've been a rambunctious patient. I kept telling that hatchet-faced female with the mutation mania that I wanted to *see* the baby. Finally the doctor came in to "explain" everything to me, and talked a lot of nonsense, most of which I'm sure no one could have understood, any more than I did. The only thing I got out of it was that she didn't actually *have* to stay in the incubator; they just thought it was "wiser."

I think I got a little hysterical at that point. Guess I was more worried than I was willing to admit, but I threw a small fit about it. The whole business wound up with one of those hushed medical conferences outside the door, and finally the Woman in White said: "Well, we might as well. Maybe it'll work out better that way."

I'd heard about the way doctors and nurses in these places develop a God complex, and believe me it is as true figuratively as it is literally that a mother hasn't got a leg to stand on around here.

I *am* awfully weak, still. I'll write again soon. Love,

Maggie.

March 8.

Dearest Hank,

Well, the nurse was wrong if she told you that. She's an idiot anyhow. It's a girl. It's easier to tell with babies than with cats, and *I know*. How about Henrietta?

I'm home again, and busier than a betatron. They got *everything* mixed up at the hospital, and I had to teach myself how to bathe her and do just about everything else. She's getting prettier, too. When can you get a leave, a *real* leave?"

Love,
Maggie.

May 26.

Hank dear,

You should see her now—and you shall. I'm sending along a reel of color movie. My mother sent her those nighties with drawstrings all over. I put one on, and right now she looks like a snow-white potato sack with that beautiful, beautiful flower-face blooming on top. Is that *me* talking? Am I a doting mother? But wait till you *see* her!

July 10.

. . . Believe it or not, as you like, but your daughter can talk, and I don't mean baby talk. Alice discovered it—she's a dental assistant in the WACs, you know—and when she heard the baby giving out what I thought was a string of gibberish, she said the kid knew words and sentences, but couldn't say them clearly because she has no teeth yet. I'm taking her to a speech specialist.

September 13.

. . . We have a prodigy for real! Now that her front teeth are in, her speech is perfectly clear and—a new talent now—she can sing! I mean really carry a tune! At seven months! Darling my world would be perfect if you could only get home.

November 19.
... at last. The little goon was so busy being clever, it took her all this time to learn to crawl. The doctor says development in these cases is always erratic ...

SPECIAL SERVICE TELEGRAM
DECEMBER 1, 1953
08:47 LK59F

FROM: TECH. LIEUT. H. MARVELL
X47-016 GCNY
TO: MRS. H. MARVELL
APT. K-17
504 E. 19 ST.
N.Y. N.Y.

WEEK'S LEAVE STARTS TOMORROW STOP WILL ARRIVE AIRPORT TEN OH FIVE STOP DON'T MEET ME STOP LOVE LOVE LOVE HANK

Margaret let the water run out of the bathinette until only a few inches were left, and then loosed her hold on the wriggling baby.

"I think it was better when you were retarded, young woman," she informed her daughter happily. "You *can't* crawl in a bathinette, you know."

"Then why can't I go in the bathtub?" Margaret was used to her child's volubility by now, but every now and then it caught her unawares. She swooped the resistant mass of pink flesh into a towel, and began to rub.

"Because you're too little, and your head is very soft, and bathtubs are very hard."

"Oh. Then when can I go in the bathtub?"

"When the outside of your head is as hard as the inside,

brainchild." She reached toward a pile of fresh clothing. "I cannot understand," she added, pinning a square of cloth through the nightgown, "why a child of your intelligence can't learn to keep a diaper on the way other babies do. They've been used for centuries, you know, with perfectly satisfactory results."

The child disdained to reply; she had heard it too often. She waited patiently until she had been tucked, clean and sweet-smelling, into a white-painted crib. Then she favored her mother with a smile that inevitably made Margaret think of the first golden edge of the sun bursting into a rosy predawn. She remembered Hank's reaction to the color pictures of his beautiful daughter, and with the thought, realized how late it was.

"Go to sleep, puss. When you wake up, you know, your *daddy* will be here."

"Why?" asked the four-year-old mind, waging a losing battle to keep the ten-month-old body awake.

Margaret went into the kitchenette and set the timer for the roast. She examined the table, and got her clothes from the closet, new dress, new shoes, new slip, new everything, bought weeks before and saved for the day Hank's telegram came. She stopped to pull a paper from the facsimile, and, with clothes and news, went into the bathroom, and lowered herself gingerly into the steaming luxury of a scented tub.

She glanced through the paper with indifferent interest. Today at least there was no need to read the national news. There was an article by a geneticist. The same geneticist. Mutations, he said, were increasing disproportionately. It was too soon for recessives; even the first mutants, born near Hiroshima and Nagasaki in 1946 and 1947 were not old enough yet to breed. *But my baby's all right*. Apparently, there was some degree of free radiation from atomic explosions causing the trouble. *My baby's fine. Precocious, but normal*. If more attention had been paid to the first Japanese mutations, he said . . .

THAT ONLY A MOTHER

There was that little notice in the paper in the spring of '47. That was when Hank quit at Oak Ridge. "Only 2 or 3 percent of those guilty of infanticide are being caught and punished in Japan today . . ." *But* MY BABY's *all right.*

She was dressed, combed, and ready to the last light brush-on of lip paste, when the door chime sounded. She dashed for the door, and heard for the first time in eighteen months the almost-forgotten sound of a key turning in the lock before the chime had quite died away.

"Hank!"

"Maggie!"

And then there was nothing to say. So many days, so many months, of small news piling up, so many things to tell him, and now she just stood there, staring at a khaki uniform and a stranger's pale face. She traced the features with the finger of memory. The same high-bridged nose, wide-set eyes, fine feathery brows; the same long jaw, the hair a little farther back now on the high forehead, the same tilted curve to his mouth. Pale . . . Of course, he'd been underground all this time. And strange, stranger because of lost familiarity than any newcomer's face could be.

She had time to think all that before his hand reached out to touch her, and spanned the gap of eighteen months. Now, again, there was nothing to say, because there was no need. They were together, and for the moment that was enough.

"Where's the baby?"

"Sleeping. She'll be up any minute."

No urgency. Their voices were as casual as though it were a daily exchange, as though war and separation did not exist. Margaret picked up the coat he'd thrown on the chair near the door, and hung it carefully in the hall closet. She went to check the roast, leaving him to wander through the rooms by himself, remembering and coming back. She found him, finally, standing over the baby's crib.

She couldn't see his face, but she had no need to.

"I think we can wake her just this once." Margaret pulled

the covers down and lifted the white bundle from the bed. Sleepy lids pulled back heavily from smoky brown eyes.

"Hello." Hank's voice was tentative.

"Hello." The baby's assurance was more pronounced.

He had heard about it, of course, but that wasn't the same as hearing it. He turned eagerly to Margaret. "She really can—?"

"Of course she can, darling. But what's more important, she can even do nice normal things like other babies do, even stupid ones. Watch her crawl!" Margaret set the baby on the big bed.

For a moment young Henrietta lay and eyed her parents dubiously.

"Crawl?" she asked.

"That's the idea. Your daddy is new around here, you know. He wants to see you show off."

"Then put me on my tummy."

"Oh, of course." Margaret obligingly rolled the baby over.

"What's the matter?" Hank's voice was still casual, but an undercurrent in it began to charge the air of the room. "I thought they turned over first."

"This baby"—Margaret would not notice the tension—"*This* baby does things when she wants to."

This baby's father watched with softening eyes while the head advanced and the body hunched up propelling itself across the bed.

"Why, the little rascal." He burst into relieved laughter. "She looks like one of those potato-sack racers they used to have on picnics. Got her arms pulled out of the sleeves already." He reached over and grabbed the knot at the bottom of the long nightie.

"I'll do it, darling." Margaret tried to get there first.

"Don't be silly, Maggie. This may be *your* first baby, but *I* had five kid brothers." He laughed her away, and reached with his other hand for the string that closed one sleeve. He opened the sleeve bow, and groped for an arm.

"The way you wriggle," he addressed his child sternly, as his hand touched a moving knob of flesh at the shoulder, "anyone might think you are a worm, using your tummy to crawl on, instead of your hands and feet."

Margaret stood and watched, smiling. "Wait till you hear her sing, darling—"

His right hand traveled down from the shoulder to where he thought an arm would be, traveled down, and straight down, over firm small muscles that writhed in an attempt to move against the pressure of his hand. He let his fingers drift up again to the shoulder. With infinite care he opened the knot at the bottom of the nightgown. His wife was standing by the bed, saying, "She can do 'Jingle Bells,' and—"

His left hand felt along the soft knitted fabric of the gown, up toward the diaper that folded, flat and smooth, across the bottom end of his child. No wrinkles. No kicking. *No . . .*

"Maggie." He tried to pull his hands from the neat fold in the diaper, from the wriggling body. "Maggie." His throat was dry; words came hard, low and grating. He spoke very slowly, thinking the sound of each word to make himself say it. His head was spinning but he had to *know* before he let it go. "Maggie, why . . . didn't you . . . tell me?"

"Tell you what, darling?" Margaret's poise was the immemorial patience of woman confronted with man's childish impetuosity. Her sudden laugh sounded fantastically easy and natural in that room; it was all clear to her now. "Is she wet? I didn't know."

She didn't know. His hands, beyond control, ran up and down the soft-skinned baby body, the sinuous, limbless body. *Oh God, dear God*—his head shook and his muscles contracted in a bitter spasm of hysteria. His fingers tightened on his child—*Oh God, she didn't know . . .*

LOT

Ward Moore

Ward Moore, who died in 1978 at the age of 75, lamented that "I was without a market except for stories which could be labeled, detestably, 'science fiction.' " In 1937 he wrote a significant novel about the labor movement during the Depression, *Breathe the Air Again,* but it was not published until 1942. His next novel, and his first in science fiction form, *Greener Than You Think*, did not appear until 1947. His fame rests primarily on one of the true masterpieces of science fiction, *Bring the Jubilee,* a 1953 novel dramatizing the history that might have flowed from a Confederate victory in the Civil War, including the consequences—technological, philosophical, psychological, and cultural—of changing history.

His other two classics are "Lot" (1953) and its sequel, "Lot's Daughter" (1954), which provided the basis (without credit) for the 1962 film directed by and starring Ray Milland, *Panic in the Year Zero.* To avoid spoiling its surprises, I have reserved some comments on "Lot" for a brief afterword.

Mr. Jimmon even appeared elated, like a man about to set out on a vacation.

"Well, folks, no use waiting any longer. We're all set. So let's go."

There was a betrayal here; Mr. Jimmon was not the kind of man who addressed his family as "folks."

"David, you're sure . . . ?"

Mr. Jimmon merely smiled. This was quite out of character; customarily he reacted to his wife's habit of posing unfinished questions—after seventeen years the unuttered and larger part of the queries were always instantly known to him in some mysterious way, as thought unerringly projected by the key in which the introduction was pitched, so that not only the full wording was communicated to his mind, but the shades and implications which circumstance and humor attached to them—with sharp and querulous defense. No matter how often he resolved to stare quietly or use the still more effective, Afraid I didn't catch your meaning, dear, he had never been able to put his resolution into force. Until this moment of crisis. Crisis, reflected Mr. Jimmon, still smiling and moving suggestively toward the door, crisis changes people. Brings out underlying qualities.

It was Jir who answered Molly Jimmon, with the adolescent's half-whine of exasperation. "Aw, furcrysay, Mom, what's the idea? The highways'll be clogged tight. What's the good figuring out everything heada time and having everything all set if you're going to start all over again at the last minute? Get a grip on yourself and let's go."

Mr. Jimmon did not voice the reflexive, That's no way to talk to your mother. Instead he thought, not unsympathetically, of woman's slow reaction time. Asset in childbirth, liability behind the wheel. He knew Molly was thinking of the house and all the things in it: her clothes and Erika's, the TV set—so sullenly ugly now, with the electricity gone—the refrigerator in which the food would soon begin to rot and stink, the dead stove, the cellarful of cases of canned stuff for which there was no room in the station wagon. And the Buick, blocked up in the garage, with the air thoughtfully let out of the tires and the battery hidden.

Of course the house would be looted. But they had known that all along. When they—or rather he, for it was his executive's mind and training which were responsible for the Jimmons' preparation against this moment—planned so carefully and providentially, he had weighed property against life and decided on life. No other decision was possible. "Aren't you at least going to phone Pearl and Dan?"

Now why in the world, thought Mr. Jimmon, completely above petty irritation, should I call Dan Davisson? (Because of course it's *Dan* she means—My Old Beau. Oh, he was nobody then, just as impractical dreamer without a penny to his name; it wasn't for years that he was recognized as a Mathematical Genius; now he's a professor and all sorts of things—but she automatically says Pearl-and-Dan, not Dan.) What can Dan do with the square root of minus nothing to offset M equals whatever it is, at this moment? Or am I supposed to ask if Pearl has all her diamonds? Query, why doesn't Pearl wear pearls? Only diamonds? My wife's friends, heh heh, but even the subtlest intonation won't label them when you're entertaining an important client and Pearl and Dan.

And why should I phone? What sudden paralysis afflicts her? Hysteria?

"No," said Mr. Jimmon. "I did not phone Pearl and Dan."

Then he added, relenting, "Phone's been out since."

"But," said Molly.

She's hardly going to ask me to drive into town. He selected several answers in readiness. But she merely looked toward the telephone helplessly (she ought to have been fat, thought Mr. Jimmon, really she should, or anyway plump; her thinness gives her that air of competence), so he amplified gently, "They're unquestionably all right. As far away from it as we are."

Wendell was already in the station wagon. With Waggie hidden somewhere. Should have sent the dog to the humane society; more merciful to have it put to sleep. Too late now; Waggie would have to take his chance. There were plenty of rabbits in the hills above Malibu; he had often seen them quite close to the house. At all events there was no room for a dog in the wagon, already loaded to within a pound of its capacity.

Erika came in briskly from the kitchen, her brown jodhpurs making her appear at first glance even younger than fourteen. But only at first glance; then the swell of hips and breast denied the childishness the jodhpurs seemed to accent.

"The water's gone, Mom. There's no use sticking around any longer."

Molly looked incredulous. "The water?"

"Of course the water's gone," said Mr. Jimmon, not impatiently, but rather with satisfaction in his own foresight. "If it didn't get the aqueduct, the mains depend on pumps. Electric pumps. When the electricity went, the water went too."

"But the water," repeated Molly, as though this last catastrophe was beyond all reason—even the outrageous logic which It brought in its train.

Jir slouched past them and outside. Erika tucked in a strand of hair, pulled her jockey cap downward and sideways, glanced quickly at her mother and father, then followed. Molly took several steps, paused, smiled vaguely in the mirror, and walked out of the house.

Mr. Jimmon patted his pockets; the money was all there. He didn't even look back before closing the front door and rattling the knob to be sure the lock had caught. It had never failed, but Mr. Jimmon always rattled it anyway. He strode to the station wagon, running his eyes over the springs to reassure himself again that they really hadn't overloaded it.

The sky was overcast; you might have thought it one of the regular morning high fogs if you didn't know. Mr. Jimmon faced southeast, but It had been too far away to see anything. Now Erika and Molly were in the front seat; the boys were in the back, lost amid the neatly packed stuff. He opened the door on the driver's side, got in, turned the key, and started the motor. Then he said casually over his shoulder, "Put the dog out, Jir."

Wendell protested, too quickly, "Waggie's not here."

Molly exclaimed, "Oh, David . . ."

Mr. Jimmon said patiently, "We're losing pretty valuable time. There's no room for the dog; we have no food for him. If we had room we could have taken more essentials; those few pounds might mean the difference."

"Can't find him," muttered Jir.

"He's not here. I tell you he's not here," shouted Wendell, tearful voiced.

"If I have to stop the motor and get him myself we'll be wasting still more time and gas." Mr. Jimmon was still detached, judicial. "This isn't a matter of kindness to animals. It's life and death."

Erika said evenly, "Dad's right, you know. It's the dog or us. Put him out, Wend."

"I tell you—" Wendell began.

"Got him!" exclaimed Jir. "Okay, Waggie! Outside and good luck."

The spaniel wriggled ecstatically as he was picked up and put out through the open window. Mr. Jimmon raced the motor, but it didn't drown out Wendell's anguish. He threw himself on his brother, hitting and kicking. Mr. Jimmon took his foot off the gas, and as soon as he was sure the dog was away from the wheels, eased the station wagon out of the driveway and down the hill toward the ocean.

"Wendell, Wendell, stop," pleaded Molly. "Don't hurt him, Jir."

Mr. Jimmon clicked on the radio. After a preliminary hum,

clashing static crackled out. He pushed all five buttons in turn varying the quality of unintelligible sound. "Want me to try?" offered Erika. She pushed the manual button and turned the knob slowly. Music dripped out.

Mr. Jimmon grunted. "Mexican station. Try something else. Maybe you can get Ventura."

They rounded a tight curve. "Isn't that the Warbinns'?" asked Molly.

For the first time since It happened Mr. Jimmon had a twinge of impatience. There was no possibility, even with the unreliable eye of shocked excitement, of mistaking the Warbinn's blue Mercury. No one else on Rambla Catalina had one anything like it, and visitors would be most unlikely now. If Molly would apply the most elementary logic!

Besides, Warbinn had stopped the blue Mercury in the Jimmon driveway five times every week for the past two months—ever since they had decided to put the Buick up and keep the wagon packed and ready against this moment—for Mr. Jimmon to ride with him to the city. Of course it was the Warbinns'.

"... *advised not to impede the progress of the military. Adequate medical staffs are standing by at all hospitals. Local civilian defense units are taking all steps in accordance* ..."

"Santa Barbara," remarked Jir, nodding at the radio with an expert's assurance.

Mr. Jimmon slowed, prepared to follow the Warbinns down to 101, but the Mercury halted and Mr. Jimmon turned out to pass it. Warbinn was driving and Sally was in the front seat with him; the back seat appeared empty except for a few things obviously hastily thrown in. No foresight, thought Mr. Jimmon.

Warbinn waved his hand vigorously out the window and Sally shouted something.

"... *panic will merely slow rescue efforts. Casualties are much smaller than originally reported* ..."

"How do they know?" asked Mr. Jimmon, waving politely at the Warbinns.

"Oh, David, aren't you going to stop? They want something."

"Probably just to talk."

"*. . . to retain every drop of water. Emergency water will be in operation shortly. There is no cause for undue alarm. General . . .*"

Through the rearview mirror Mr. Jimmon saw the blue Mercury start after them. He had been right then, they only wanted to say something inconsequential. At a time like this.

At the junction with U.S. 101 five cars blocked Rambla Catalina. Mr. Jimmon set the handbrake, and steadying himself with the open door, stood tiptoe twistedly, trying to see over the cars ahead. 101 was solid with traffic which barely moved. On the southbound side of the divided highway a stream of vehicles flowed illegally north.

"Thought everybody was figured to go east," gibed Jir over the other side of the car.

Mr. Jimmon was not disturbed by his son's sarcasm. How right he'd been to rule out the trailer. Of course the bulk of the cars were headed eastward as he'd calculated; this sluggish mass was nothing compared with the countless ones which must now be blocking the roads to Pasadena, Alhambra, Garvey, Norwalk. Even the northbound refugees were undoubtedly taking 99 or regular 101—the highway before them was really 101 Alternate—he had picked the most feasible exit.

The Warbinns drew up alongside. "Hurry didn't do you much good," shouted Warbinn, leaning forward to clear his wife's face.

Mr. Jimmon reached in and turned off the ignition. Gas was going to be precious. He smiled and shook his head at Warbinn; no use pointing out that he'd got the inside lane by passing the Mercury, with a better chance to seize the opening on the highway when it came. "Get in the car, Jir, and shut the door. Have to be ready when this breaks."

"If it ever does," said Molly. "All that rush and bustle. We might just as well . . ."

Mr. Jimmon was conscious of Warbinn's glowering at him and resolutely refused to turn his head. He pretended not to hear him yell. "Only wanted to tell you you forgot to pick up your bumper jack. It's in front of our garage."

Mr. Jimmon's stomach felt empty. What if he had a flat now? Ruined, condemned. He knew a burning hate for Warbinn— incompetent borrower, bad neighbor, thoughtless, shiftless, criminal. He owed it to himself to leap from the stationwagon and seize Warbinn by the throat . . .

"What did he say, David? What is Mr. Warbinn saying?"

Then he remembered it was the jack from the Buick; the station wagon's was safely packed where he could get at it easily. Naturally he would never have started out on a trip like this without checking so essential an item. "Nothing," he said, "nothing at all."

"*. . . plane dispatches indicate target was the Signal Hill area. Minor damage was done to Long Beach, Wilmington, and San Pedro. All nonmilitary air traffic warned from Mines Field . . .*"

The smash and crash of bumper and fender sounded familiarly on the highway. From his lookout station he couldn't see what had happened, but it was easy enough to reconstruct the impatient jerk forward that caused it. Mr. Jimmon didn't exactly smile, but he allowed himself a faint quiver of internal satisfaction. A crash up ahead would make things worse, but a crash behind—and many of them were inevitable—must eventually create a gap.

Even as he thought this, the first car at the mouth of Rambla Catalina edged onto the shoulder of the highway. Mr. Jimmon slid back in and started the motor, inching ahead after the war in front, gradually leaving the still uncomfortable proximity of the Warbinns.

"Got to go to the toilet," announced Wendell abruptly.

"Didn't I tell you—! Well, hurry up! Jir, keep the door open and pull him in if the car starts to move."

"I can't go here."

Mr. Jimmon restrained his impulse to snap, Hold it in then. Instead he said mildly, "This is a crisis, Wendell. No time for niceties. Hurry."

"*. . . the flash was seen as far north as Ventura and as far south as Newport. An eyewitness who had just arrived by helicopter . . .*"

"That's what we should have had," remarked Jir. "You thought of everything except that."

"That's no way to speak to your father," admonished Molly.

"Aw, heck, Mom, this is a crisis. No time for niceties."

"You're awful smart, Jir," said Erika. "Big, tough, brutal man."

"Go down, brat," returned Jir, "your nose needs wiping."

"As a matter of record," Mr. Jimmon said calmly, "I thought of both plane and helicopter and decided against them."

"I can't go. Honest, I just can't go."

"Just relax, darling," advised Molly. "No one is looking."

"*. . . fires reported in Compton, Lynwood, South Gate, Harbor City, Lomita, and other spots are now under control. Residents are advised not to attempt to travel on the overcrowded highways as they are much safer in their homes or places of employment. The civilian defense . . .*"

The two cars ahead bumped forward. "Get in," shouted Mr. Jimmon.

He got the left front tire of the sation wagon on the asphalt shoulder—the double lane of concrete was impossibly far ahead—only to be blocked by the packed procession. The clock on the dash said 11:04. Nearly five hours since It happened, and they were less than two miles from home. They could have done better walking. Or on horse-back.

"... *All residents of the Los Angeles area are urged to remain calm. Local radio service will be restored in a matter of minutes, along with electricity and water. Reports of fifth column activities have been greatly exaggerated. The FBI has all known subversives under* . . ."

He reached over and shut it off. Then he edged a daring two inches farther on the shoulder, almost grazing an aggressive Cadillac packed solid with cardboard cartons. On his left a Model A truck shivered and trembled. He knew, distantly and disapprovingly, that it belonged to two painters who called themselves man and wife. The truck bed was loaded high with household goods; poor, useless things no looter would bother to steal. In the cab the artists passed a quart beer bottle back and forth. The man waved it genially at him; Mr. Jimmon nodded discouragingly back.

The thermometer on the mirror showed 90. Hot all right. Of course if they ever got rolling . . . I'm thirsty, he thought; probably suggestion. If I hadn't seen the thermometer. Anyway I'm not going to paw around in back for the canteen. Forethought. Like the arms. He cleared his throat. "Remember there's an automatic in the glove compartment. If anyone tries to open the door on your side, use it."

"Oh, David, I . . ."

Ah, humanity. Nonresistance, Gandhi. I've never shot at anything but a target. At a time like this. But they don't understand.

"I could use the rifle from back here," suggested Jir. "Can I, Dad?"

"I can reach the shotgun," said Wendell. "That's better at close range."

"Gee, you men are brave," jeered Erika. Mr. Jimmon said nothing; both shotgun and rifle were unloaded. Foresight again.

He caught the hiccuping pause in the traffic instantly, gratified at his smooth coordination. How far he could proceed on the shoulder before running into a culvert narrowing the highway to the concrete he didn't know. Probably not more than a mile at most, but at least he was off Rambla Catalina and on 101.

He felt tremendously elated. Successful.

"Here we go!" He almost added, Hold on to your hats.

Of course the shoulder too was packed solid, and progress, even in low gear, was maddening. The gas consumption was something he did not want to think about; his pride in the way the needle of the gauge caressed the F shrank. And gas would be hard to come by in spite of his pocketful of ration coupons. Black market.

"Mind if I try the radio again?" asked Erika, switching it on.

Mr. Jimmon, following the pattern of previous success, insinuated the left front tire onto the concrete, eliciting a disapproving squawk from the Pontiac alongside. "*. . . sector was quiet. Enemy losses are estimated . . .*"

"Can't you get something else?" asked Jir. "Something less dusty?"

"Wish we had TV in the car," observed Wendell. "Joe Tellifer's old man put a set in the back seat of their Chrysler."

"Dry up, squirt," said Jir. "Let the air out of your head."

"Jir."

"Oh, Mom, don't pay attention! Don't you see that's what he wants?"

"Listen, brat, if you weren't a girl, I'd spank you."

"You mean, If I wasn't your sister. You'd probably enjoy such childish sex play with any other girl."

"Erika!"

Where do they learn it? marveled Mr. Jimmon. These progressive schools. Do you suppose . . . ?

He edged the front wheel farther in exultantly, taking advantage of a momentary lapse of attention on the part of the Pontiac's driver. Unless the other went berserk with frustration and rammed into him, he practically had a cinch on a car length of the concrete now.

"Here we go!" he gloried. "We're on our way."

"Aw, if I was driving we'd be halfway to Oxnard by now."

"Jir, that's no way to talk to your father."

Mr. Jimmon reflected dispassionately that Molly's ineffective admonitions only spurred Jir's sixteen-year-old brashness, already irritating enough in its own right. Indeed, if it were not for Molly, Jir might . . .

It was of course possible—here Mr. Jimmon braked just short of the convertible ahead—Jir wasn't just going through a "difficult" period (What was particularly difficult about it? he inquired, in the face of all the books Molly suggestively left around on the psychological problems of growth. The boy had everything he could possibly want) but was the type who, in different circumstances drifted well into—well, perhaps not exactly juvenile delinquency, but . . .

"*. . . in the Long Beach—Wilmington—San Pedro area. Comparison with that which occurred at Pittsburgh reveals that this morning's was in every way less serious. All fires are now under control and all the injured are now receiving medical attention . . .*"

"I don't think they're telling the truth," stated Mrs. Jimmon.

He snorted. He didn't think so either, but by what process had she arrived at that conclusion?

"I want to hear the ball game. Turn on the ball game, Rick," Wendell demanded.

Eleven sixteen, and rolling northward on the highway. Not bad, not bad at all. Foresight. Now if he could only edge his way leftward to the southbound strip they'd be beyond the Santa Barbara bottleneck by two o'clock.

"The lights," exclaimed Molly, "the taps!"

Oh no, thought Mr. Jimmon, not that too. Out of the comic strips.

"Keep calm," advised Jir. "Electricity and water are both off—remember?"

"I'm not quite an imbecile yet, Jir. I'm quite aware everything went off. I was thinking of the time it went back on."

"Furcrysay, Mom, you worrying about next month's bills *now*?"

Mr. Jimmon, nudging the station wagon ever leftward, formed the sentence: You'd never worry about bills, young man, because you never have to pay them. Instead of saying it aloud, he formed another sentence: Molly, your talent for irrelevance amounts to genius. Both sentences gave him satisfaction.

The traffic gathered speed briefly, and he took advantage of the spurt to get solidly in the left-hand lane, right against the long island of concrete dividing the north- from the south-bound strips. "That's using the old bean, Dad," approved Wendell.

Whatever slight pleasure he might have felt in his son's approbation was overlaid with exasperation. Wendell, like Jir, was more Manville than Jimmon; they carried Molly's stamp on their faces and minds. Only Erika was a true Jimmon. Made in my own image, he thought pridelessly.

"I can't help but think it would have been at least courteous to get in touch with Pearl and Dan. At least *try*. And the Warbinns . . ."

The gap in the concrete divider came sooner than he anticipated and he was on the comparatively unclogged southbound side. His foot went down on the accelerator and the station wagon grumbled earnestly ahead. For the first time Mr. Jimmon became aware how tightly he'd been gripping the wheel; how rigid the muscles in his arms, shoulders, and neck had been. He relaxed partway as he adjusted to the speed of the cars ahead and the speedometer needle hung just below 45, but resentment against Molly (at least courteous), Jir (no time for niceties), and Wendell (not to go), rode up in the saliva under his tongue. Dependent. Helpless. Everything on him. Parasites.

At intervals Erika switched on the radio. News was always promised immediately, but little was forthcoming, only vague, nervous attempts to minimize the extent of the disaster and soothe listeners with allusions to civilian defense, military activities on the ever advancing front, and comparison with the destruction of Pittsburgh, so vastly much worse than the comparatively harmless detonation at Los Angeles. Must be pretty bad, thought Mr. Jimmon; cripple the war effort . . .

"I'm hungry," said Wendell.

Molly began stirring around, instructing Jir where to find the sandwiches. Mr. Jimmon thought grimly of how they'd have to adjust to the absence of civilized niceties; bread and mayonnaise and lunch meat. Live on rabbit, squirrel, abalone, fish. When Wendell grew hungry he'd have to get his own food. Self-sufficiency. Hard and tough.

At Oxnard the snarled traffic slowed them to a crawl again. Beyond, the juncture with the main highway north kept them at the same infuriating pace. It was long after two when they reached Ventura, and Wendell, who had been fidgeting and jumping up and down in the seat for the past hour, proclaimed, "I'm tired of riding."

Mr. Jimmon set his lips. Molly suggested, ineffectually, "Why don't you lie down, dear?"

"Can't. Way this crate is packed, ain't room for a grasshopper."

"Verry funny. Verrrry funny," said Jir.

"Now, Jir, leave him alone! He's just a little boy."

At Carpenteria the sun burst out. You might have thought it the regular dissipation of the fog, only it was almost time for the fog to come down again. Should he try the San Marcos Pass after Santa Barbara, or the longer, better way? Flexible plans, but . . . Wait and see.

It was four when they got to Santa Barbara and Mr. Jimmon faced concerted though unorganized rebellion. Wendell was screaming with stiffness and boredom; Jir remarked casually to no one in particular that Santa Barbara was the place they were going to beat the bottleneck oh yeh; Molly said, Stop at the first clean-looking gas station. Even Erika added, "Yes, Dad, you'll really have to stop."

Mr. Jimmon was appalled. With every second priceless and hordes of panic-stricken refugees pressing behind, they would rob him of all the precious gains he'd made by skill, daring, judgment. Stupidity and shortsightedness. Unbelievable. For their own silly comfort—good Lord, did they think they had a monopoly on bodily weaknesses? He was cramped as they and wanted to go as badly. Time and space which could never be made up. Let them lose this half hour and it was quite likely they'd never get out of Santa Barbara.

"If we lose a half hour now we'll never get out of here."

"Well, now, David, that wouldn't be utterly disastrous, would it? There are awfully nice hotels here and I'm sure it would be more comfortable for everyone than your idea of camping in the woods, hunting and fishing . . ."

He turned off State; couldn't remember name of the parallel street, but surely less traffic. He controlled his temper, not heroically, but desperately. "May I ask how long you would propose to stay in one of those awfully nice hotels?"

"Why, until we could go home."

"My dear Molly . . ." What could he say? My dear Molly, we are never going home, if you mean Malibu? Or: My dear Molly, you just don't understand what is happening?

The futility of trying to convey the clear picture in his mind. Or any picture. If she could not of herself see the endless mob pouring, pouring out of Los Angeles, searching frenziedly for escape and refuge, eating up the substance of the surrounding country in ever-widening circles, crowding, jam-packing, overflowing every hotel, boarding house, lodging, or private home into which they could edge, agonizedly bidding up the price of everything until the chaos they brought with them was indistinguishable from the chaos they were fleeing—if she could not see all this instantly and automatically, she could not be brought to see it at all. Any more than the other aimless, planless, improvident fugitives could see it.

So, my dear Molly; nothing.

Silence gave consent to continued expostulation. "David, do you really mean you don't intend to stop at *all?*"

Was there any point in saying, Yes, I do? He set his lips still more tightly and once more weighed San Marcos Pass against the coast route. Have to decide now.

"Why, the time we're waiting here, just waiting for the cars up ahead to move would be enough."

Could you call her stupid? He weighed the question slowly and justly, alert for the first jerk of the massed cars all around. Her reasoning was valid and logical if the laws of physics and geometry were suspended. (Was that right—physics and geometry? Body occupying two different positions at the same time?) It was the facts which were illogical—not Molly. She was just exasperating.

By the time they were halfway to Gaviota or Goleta—Mr. Jimmon could never tell them apart—foresight and relentless sternness began to pay off. Those who had left Los Angeles without preparation and in panic were dropping out or slowing down, to get gas or oil, repair tires, buy food, seek rest rooms. The station wagon was steadily forging ahead.

He gambled on the old highway out of Santa Barbara. Any kind of obstruction would block its two lanes; if it didn't he would be beating the legions on the wider, straighter road. There were stretches now where he could hit 50; once he sped a happy half-mile at 65.

Now the insubordination crackling all around gave indication of simultaneous explosion. "I really," began Molly, and then discarded this for a fresher, firmer start. "David, I don't understand how you can be so utterly selfish and inconsiderate."

Mr. Jimmon could feel the veins in his forehead begin to swell, but this was one of those rages that didn't show.

"But, Dad, would ten minutes ruin everything?" asked Erika.

"Monomania," muttered Jir. "Single track. Like Hitler."

"I want my dog," yelped Wendell. "Dirty old dog-killer."

"Did you ever hear of cumulative—" Erika had addressed him reasonably; surely he could make her understand? "Did you ever hear of cumulative . . ." What was the word? Snowball rolling downhill was the image in his mind. "Oh, what's the use?"

The old road rejoined the new; again the station wagon was fitted into the traffic like parquetry. Mr. Jimmon, from an exultant, unfettered—almost—65 was imprisoned in a treadmill set at 38. Keep calm; you can do nothing about it, he admonished himself. Need all your nervous energy. Must be wrecks up ahead. And then, with a return of satisfaction: if I hadn't used strategy back there we'd have been with those making 25. A starting-stopping 25.

"It's fantastic," exclaimed Molly. "I could almost believe Jir's right and you've lost your mind."

Mr. Jimmon smiled. This was the first time Molly had ever openly showed disloyalty before the children or sided with them in their presence. She was revealing herself. Under pressure. Not the pressure of events; her incredible attitude at Santa Barbara had demonstrated her incapacity to feel that. Just pressure against the bladder.

"No doubt those left behind can console their last moments with pride in their sanity." The sentence came out perfectly formed, with none of the annoying pauses or interpolated "ers" or "mmphs" which could, as he knew from unhappy experience, flaw the most crushing rejoinders.

"Oh, the end can always justify the means for those who want it that way."

"Don't they restrain people—"

"That's enough, Jir!"

Trust Molly to return quickly to fundamental hypocrisy; the automatic response—his mind felicitously grasped the phrase, conditioned reflex—to the customary stimulus. She had taken an explicit stand against his common sense, but her rigid code—honor they father; iron rayon the wrong side; register and vote; avoid scenes; only white wine with fish; never rehire a discharged servant—quickly substituted pattern for impulse. Seventeen years.

The road turned away from the ocean, squirmed inland and uphill for still slower miles, abruptly widened into a divided, four-lane highway. Without hesitation Mr. Jimmon took the southbound side; for the first time since they had left Rambla Catalina his foot went down to the floorboards and with a sigh of relief the station wagon jumped into smooth, ecstatic speed.

Improvisation and strategy again. And, he acknowledged generously, the defiant example this morning of those who'd done the same thing in Malibu. Now, out of reestablished habit the other cars kept to the northbound side even though there was nothing coming south. Timidity, routine, inertia. Pretty soon they would realize sheepishly that there was neither traffic nor traffic cops to keep them off, but it would be miles before they had another chance to cross over. By that time he would have reached the comparatively uncongested stretch.

"It's dangerous, David."

Obey the law. No smoking. Keep off the grass. Please adjust your clothes before leaving. Trespassers will be. Picking California wild flowers or shrubs is forbidden. Parking 45 min. Do not.

She hadn't put the protest in the more usual form of a question. Would that technique have been more irritating? *Is*n't it *dan*gerous Day-vid? His calm conclusion: it didn't matter.

"No time for niceties," chirped Jir.

Mr. Jimmon tried to remember Jir as a baby. All the bad novels he had read in the days when he read anything except *Time* and *The New Yorker*, all the movies he'd seen before they had a TV set, always prescribed such retrospection as a specific for softening the present. If he could recall David Alonzo Jimmon, junior, at six months, helpless and lovable, it should make Jir more acceptable by discovering some faint traces of the one in the other.

But though he could re-create in detail the interminable disgusting, trembling months of that initial pregnancy (had he really been afraid she would die?) he was completely unable to reconstruct the appearance of his firstborn before the age of . . . It must have been at six that Jir had taken his baby sister out for a walk and lost her. (Had Molly permitted it? He still didn't know for sure.) Erika hadn't been found for four hours.

The tidal screeching of sirens invaded and destroyed his thoughts. What the devil . . . ? His foot lifted from the gas pedal as he slewed obediently to the right, ingrained reverence surfacing at the sound.

"I told you it wasn't safe! Are you really trying to kill us all?"

Whipping over the rise ahead, a pair of motorcycles crackled. Behind them snapped a long line of assorted vehicles, fire trucks and ambulances mostly, interspersed here and there with olive drab army equipment. The cavalcade flicked down the central white line, one wheel in each lane. Mr. Jimmon edged the station wagon as far over as he could; it still occupied too much room to permit the free passage of the onrush without compromise.

The knees and elbows of the motorcycle policemen stuck out widely, reminding Mr. Jimmon of grasshoppers. The one on the near side was headed straight for the station wagon's left front fender; for a moment Mr. Jimmon closed his eyes as he plotted the unswerving course, knifing through the crustlike steel, bouncing lightly on the tires, and continuing unperturbed. He opened them to see the other officer shoot past, mouth angrily open in his direction while the one straight ahead came to a skidding stop.

"Going to get it now," gloated Wendell.

An old-fashioned parent, one of the horrible examples held up to shuddering moderns like himself, would have reached back and relieved his tension by clouting Wendell across the mouth. Mr. Jimmon merely turned off the motor.

The cop was not indulging in the customary deliberate and ominous performance of slowly dismounting and striding toward his victim with ever more menacing steps. Instead he got off quickly and covered the few feet to Mr. Jimmon's window with unimpressive speed.

Heavy goggles concealed his eyes; dust and stubble covered his face. "Operator's license!"

Mr. Jimmon knew what he was saying, but the sirens and the continuous rustle of the convoy prevented the sound from coming through. Again the cop deviated from the established routine; he did not take the proffered license and examine it incredulously before drawing out his pad and pencil, but wrote the citation, glancing up and down from the card in Mr. Jimmon's hand.

Even so, the last of the vehicles—*San Jose F.D.*—passed before he handed the summons through the window to be signed. "Turn around and proceed in the proper direction," he ordered curtly, pocketing the pad and buttoning his jacket briskly.

Mr. Jimmon nodded. The officer hesitated, as though waiting for some limp excuse. Mr. Jimmon said nothing.

"No tricks," said the policeman over his shoulder. "Turn around and proceed in the proper direction."

He almost ran to his motorcycle, and roared off, twisting his head for a final stern frown as he passed, siren wailing. Mr. Jimmon watched him dwindle in the rearview mirror and then started the motor. "Gonna lose a lot more than you gained," commented Jir.

Mr. Jimmon gave a last glance in the mirror and moved ahead, shifting into second. "David!" exclaimed Molly horrified, "you're not turning around!"

"Observant," muttered Mr. Jimmon, between his teeth.

"Dad, you can't get away with it," Jir decided judicially.

Mr. Jimmon's answer was to press the accelerator down

savagely. The empty highway stretched invitingly ahead; a few hundred yards to their right they could see the northbound lanes ant-clustered. The sudden motion stirred the traffic citation on his lap, floating down to the floor. Erika leaned forward and picked it up.

"Throw it away," ordered Mr. Jimmon.

Molly gasped. "You're out of your mind."

"You're a fool," stated Mr. Jimmon calmly. "Why should I save that piece of paper?"

"Isn't what you told the cop." Jir was openly jeering now.

"I might as well have, if I'd wanted to waste conversation. I don't know why I was blessed with such a stupid family—"

"May be something in heredity after all."

If Jir had said it out loud, reflected Mr. Jimmon, it would have passed casually as normal domestic repartee, a little ill-natured perhaps, certainly callow and trite, but not especially provocative. Muttered, so that it was barely audible, it was an ultimate defiance. He had read that far back in prehistory, when the young males felt their strength, they sought to overthrow the rule of the Old Man and usurp his place. No doubt they uttered a preliminary growl or screech as challenge. They were not very bright, but they acted in a pattern; a pattern Jir was apparently following.

Refreshed by placing Jir in proper Neanderthal setting, Mr. Jimmon went on, "—none of you seem to have the slightest initiative or ability to grasp reality. Tickets, cops, judges, juries mean nothing anymore. There is no law now but the law of survival."

"Aren't you being dramatic, David?" Molly's tone was deliberately aloof adult to excited child.

"I could hear you underline words, Dad," said Erika, but he felt there was no malice in her gibe.

"You mean we can do anything we want now? Shoot people? Steal cars and things?" asked Wendell.

"There, David! You see?"

Yes, I see. Better than you. Little savage. This is the

pattern. What will Wendell—and the thousands of other Wendells (for it would be unjust to suppose Molly's genes and domestic influence unique)—be like after six months of anarchy? Or after six years?

Survivors, yes. And that will be about all: naked, primitive, ferocious, superstitious savages. Wendell can read and write (but not so fluently as I or any of our generation at his age); how long will he retain the tags and scraps of progressive schooling?

And Jir? Detachedly Mr. Jimmon foresaw the fate of Jir. Unlike Wendell, who would adjust to the new conditions, Jir would go wild in another sense. His values were already set; they were those of television, high school dating, comic strips, law and order. Released from civilization, his brief future would be one of guilty rape and pillage until he fell victim to another youth or gang bent the same way. Molly would disintegrate and perish quickly. Erika . . .

The station wagon flashed along the comparatively unimpeded highway. Having passed the next crossover, there were now other vehicles on the southbound strip, but even on the northbound one, crowding had eased.

Furiously Mr. Jimmon determined to preserve the civilization in Erika. (He would teach her everything he knew [including the insurance business?]) . . . ah, if he were some kind of scientist, now—not the Dan Davisson kind, whose abstract speculations seemed always to prepare the way for some new method of destruction, but the . . . Franklin? Jefferson? Watt? protect her night and day from the refugees who would be roaming the hills south of Monterey. The rifle ammunition, properly used—and he would see that no one but himself used it—would last years. After it was gone— presuming fragments and pieces of a suicidal world hadn't pulled itself miraculously together to offer a place to return to—there were the two hunting bows whose steel-tipped shafts could stop a man as easily as a deer or mountain lion. He remembered debating long, at the time he had first begun preparing for It, how many bows to order, measuring their weight and bulk against the other precious freight and deciding at last that two was the satisfactory minimum. It must have been in his subconscious mind all along that of the whole family Erika was the only other person who could be trusted with a bow.

"There will be," he spoke in calm and solemn tones, not to Wendell, whose question was now left long behind, floating on the gas-greasy air of a sloping valley growing with live oaks, but to a larger, impalpable audience. "There will be others who will think that because there is no longer law or law enforcement—"

"You're being simply fantastic!" She spoke more sharply than he had ever heard her in front of the children. "Just because It happened to Los Angeles—"

"And Pittsburgh."

"All right. And Pittsburgh, doesn't mean that the whole United States has collapsed and everyone in the country is running frantically for safety."

"Yet," added Mr. Jimmon firmly, "yet, do you suppose they are going to stop with Los Angeles and Pittsburgh, and leave Gary and Seattle standing? Or even New York and Chicago? Or do you imagine Washington will beg for armistice terms while there is the least sign of organized life left in the country?"

"We'll wipe Them out first," insisted Jir in patriotic shock. Wendell backed him up with a machine gun "brrrrr."

"Undoubtedly. But it will be the last gasp. At any rate it will be years, if at all in my lifetime, before stable communities are reestablished—"

"David, you're raving."

"Reestablished," he repeated. "So there will be many others who'll also feel that the dwindling of law and order is license to kill people and steal cars 'and things.' Naked force and cunning will be the only means of self-preservation. That was why I picked out a spot where I felt survival would be easiest; not only because of wood and water, game and fish, but because it's nowhere near the main highways, and so unlikely to be chosen by any great number."

"I wish you'd stop harping on that insane idea. You're just a little too old and flabby for pioneering. Even when you were younger and you were hardly the rugged, outdoor type."

No, thought Mr. Jimmon, I was the sucker type. I would have gotten somewhere if I'd stayed in the bank, but like a bawd you pleaded; the insurance business brought in the quick money for you to give up your job and have Jir and the proper home. If you'd got rid of it as I wanted. Flabby, *Flabby!* Do you think your scrawniness is so enticing?

Controlling himself, he said aloud, "We've been through all this. Months ago. It's not a question of physique, but of life."

"Nonense. Perfect nonsense. Responsible people who really know its effects . . . Maybe it was advisable to leave Malibu for a few days or even a few weeks. And perhaps it's wise to stay away from the larger cities. But a small town or village, or even one of those ranches where they take boarders—"

"Aw, Mom, you agreed. You know you did. What's the matter with you anyway? Why are you acting like a drip?"

"I want to go and shoot rabbits and bears like Dad said," insisted Wendell.

Erika said nothing, but Mr. Jimmon felt he had her sympathy; the boy's agreement was specious. Wearily he debated going over the whole ground again, patiently pointing out that what Molly said might work in the Dakotas or the Great Smokies but was hardly operative anwhere within refugee range of the Pacific Coast. He had explained all this many times, including the almost certain impossibility of getting enough gasoline to take them into any of the reasonably safe areas; that was why they'd agreed on the region below Monterey, on California State Highway 1, as the only logical goal.

A solitary car decorously bound in the legal direction

interrupted his thoughts. Either crazy or has mighty important business, he decided. The car honked disapprovingly as it passed, hugging the extreme right of the road.

Passing through Buellton the clamor again rose for a pause at a filling station. He conceded inwardly that he could afford ten or fifteen minutes without strategic loss since by now they must be among the leaders of the exodus; ahead lay little more than the normal travel. However, he had reached such a state of irritated frustration and consciousness of injustice that he was willing to endure unnecessary discomfort himself in order to inflict a longer delay on them. In fact it lessened his own suffering to know the delay was needless, that he was doing it, and that his action was a just—if inadequate— punishment.

"We'll stop this side of Santa Maria," he said. "I'll get gas there."

Mr. Jimmon knew triumph: his forethought, his calculations, his generalship had justified themselves. Barring unlikely mechanical failure—the station wagon was in perfect shape—or accident—and the greatest danger had certainly passed—escape was now practically assured. For the first time he permitted himself to realize how unreal, how romantic the whole project had been. As any attempt to evade the fate charted for the multitude must be. The docile mass perished; the headstrong (but intelligent) individual survived.

Along with triumph went an expansion of his prophetic vision of life after reaching their destination. He had purposely not taxed the cargo capacity of the wagon with transitional goods; there was no tent, canned luxuries, sleeping bags, lanterns, candles, or any of the paraphernalia of camping midway between the urban and nomadic life. Instead, besides the weapons, tackle, and utensils, there was in miniature the List for Life on a Desert Island: shells and cartridges, lures, hooks, nets, gut, leaders, flint and steel, seeds, traps, needles and thread, government pamphlets on curing and tanning hides and the recognition of edible weeds and fungi, files, nails, a judicious stock of simple medicines. A pair of binoculars to spot intruders. No coffee, sugar, flour; they would begin living immediately as they would have to in a month or so in any case, on the old, half-forgotten human cunning.

"Cunning," he said aloud.

"What?"

"Nothing. Nothing."

"I still think you should have made an effort to reach Pearl and Dan."

"The telephone was dead, Mother."

"At the moment, Erika. You can hardly have forgotten how often the lines have been down before. And it never takes more than half an hour till they're working again."

"Mother, Dan Davisson is quite capable of looking after himself."

Mr. Jimmon shut out the rest of the conversation so completely he didn't know whether there was any more to it or not. He shut out the intense preoccupation with driving, with making speed, with calculating possible gains. In the core of his mind, quite detached from everything about him, he examined and marveled.

Erika. The cool, inflexible, adult tone. Almost indulgent, but so dispassionate as not to be. One might have expected her to be exasperated by Molly's silliness, to have answered impatiently, or not at all.

Mother. Never in his recollection had the children ever called her anything but Mom. The "Mother" implied—oh, it implied a multitude of things. An entirely new relationship, for one. A relationship of aloofness, or propriety without emotion. The ancient stump of the umbilical cord, black and shriveled, had dropped off painlessly.

She had not bothered to argue about the telephone or point out the gulf between "before" and now. She had not even tried to touch Molly's deepening refusal of reality. She had been . . . indulgent.

Not "Uncle Dan," twitteringly imposed false avuncularity, but striking through it (and the facade of "Pearl and") and aside (when I was a child I . . . something . . . but now I have put aside childish things); the wealth of implicit assertion. Ah, yes, Mother, we all know the pardonable weakness and vanity; we excuse you for your constant reminders, but Mother, with all deference, we refuse to be forced any longer to be parties to middle-age's nostalgic flirtatiousness. One could almost feel sorry for Molly.

. . . middle-age's nostalgic flirtatiousness . . .

. . . *nostalgic* . . .

Metaphorically Mr. Jimmon sat abruptly upright. The fact that he was already physically in this position made the transition, while invisible, no less emphatic. The nostalgic flirtatiousness of middle age implied—might imply—memory of something more than mere coquetry. Molly and Dan.

It all fitted together so perfectly it was impossible to believe it untrue. The impecunious young lovers, equally devoted to Dan's genius, realizing marriage was out of the question (he had never denied Molly's shrewdness; as for Dan's impracticality, well, impracticality wasn't necessarily uniform or consistent. Dan had been practical enough to marry Pearl and Pearl's money) could have renounced . . .

Or not renounced at all?

Mr. Jimmon smiled; the thought did not ruffle him. Cuckoo, cuckoo. How vulgar, how absurd. Suppose Jir were Dan's? A blessed thought.

Regretfully he conceded the insuperable obstacle of Molly's conventionality. Jir was the product of his own loins. But wasn't there an old superstition about the image in the woman's mind at the instant of conception? So, justly and rightly Jir was not his. Nor Wendy, for that matter. Only Erika, by some accident. Mr. Jimmon felt free and light-hearted.

"Get gas at the next station," he bulletined.

"The next one with a clean rest room," Molly corrected.

Invincible. The Earth Mother, using men for her purposes:

reproduction, clean rest rooms, nourishment, objects of culpability, *Homes and Gardens*. The bank was my life; I could have gone far but: Why, David—they pay you less than the janitor! It's ridiculous. And: I can't understand why you hesitate; it isn't as though it were a different type of work.

No, not different; just more profitable. Why didn't she tell Dan Davisson to become an accountant; that was the same type of work, just more profitable? Perhaps she had and Dan had simply been less befuddled. Or amenable. Or stronger in purpose? Mr. Jimmon probed his pride thoroughly and relentlessly without finding the faintest twinge of retrospective jealousy. Nothing like that mattered now. Nor, he admitted, had it for years.

Two close-peaked hills gulped the sun. He toyed with the idea of crossing to the northbound side now that it was uncongested and there were occasional southbound cars. Before he could decide the divided highway ended.

"I hope you're not planning to spend the night in some horrible motel," said Molly. "I want a decent bath and a good dinner."

Spend the night. Bath. Dinner. Again calm sentences formed in his mind, but they were blown apart by the unbelievable, the monumental obtuseness. How could you say, it is absolutely essential to drive till we get there? When there were no absolutes, no essentials in her concepts? My dear Molly, I.

"No," he said, switching on the lights.

Wendy, he knew, would be the next to kick up a fuss. Till he fell mercifully asleep. If he did. Jir was probably debating the relative excitements of driving all night and stopping in a strange town. His voice would soon be heard.

The lights of the combination wayside store and filling station burned inefficiently, illuminating the deteriorating false front brightly and leaving the gas pumps in shadow. Swallowing regret at finally surrendering to mechanical and human need, and so losing the hard-won position; relaxing, even for a short while, the fierce initiative that had brought them through in the fact of all probability; he pulled the station wagon alongside the pumps and shut off the motor. About halfway—the worst half, much the worst half—to their goal. Not bad.

Molly opened the door on her side with stiff dignity. "I certainly wouldn't call this a *clean* station." She waited for a moment, hand still on the window, as though expecting an answer.

"Crummy joint," exclaimed Wendell, clambering awkwardly out.

"Why not?" asked Jir. "No time for niceties." He brushed past his mother who was walking slowly into the shadows.

"Erika," began Mr. Jimmon, in a half-whisper.

"Yes, Dad?"

"Oh . . . never mind. Later."

He was not himself quite sure what he had wanted to say, what exclusive, urgent message he had to convey. For no particular reason he switched on the interior light and glanced at the packed orderliness of the wagon. Then he slid out from behind the wheel.

No sign of the attendant, but the place was certainly not closed. Not with the lights on and the hoses ready. He stretched, and walked slowly, savoring the comfortably painful uncramping of his muscles, toward the crude outhouse labeled MEN. Molly, he thought, must be furious.

When he returned, a man was leaning against the station wagon. "Fill it up with ethyl," said Mr. Jimmon pleasantly, "and check the oil and water."

The man made no move. "That'll be five bucks a gallon." Mr. Jimmon thought there was an uncertain tremor in his voice.

"Nonsense; I've plenty of ration coupons."

"Okay." The nervousness was gone now, replaced by an ugly truculence. "Chew'm up and spit'm in your gas tank. See how far you can run on them."

The situation was not unanticipated. Indeed, Mr. Jimmon

thought with satisfaction of how much worse it must be closer to Los Angeles; how much harder the gouger would be on later supplicants as his supply of gasoline dwindled. "Listen," he said, and there was reasonableness rather than anger in his voice, "we're not out of gas. I've got enough to get to Santa Maria, even to San Luis Obispo."

"Okay. Go on then. Ain't stopping you."

"Listen. I understand your position. You have a right to make a profit in spite of government red tape."

Nervousness returned to the man's speech. "Look, whyn't you go on? There's plenty other stations up ahead."

The reluctant bandit. Mr. Jimmon was entertained. He had fully intended to bargain, to offer $2 a gallon, even to threaten with the pistol in the glove compartment. Now it seemed mean and niggling even to protest. What good was money now? "All right," he said, "I'll pay you $5 a gallon."

Still the other made no move. "In advance."

For the first time Mr. Jimmon was annoyed; time was being wasted. "Just how can I pay you in advance when I don't know how many gallons it'll take to fill the tank?"

The man shrugged.

"Tell you what I'll do. I'll pay for each gallon as you pump it. In advance." He drew out a handful of bills; the bulk of his money was in his wallet, but he'd put the small bills in his pockets. He handed over a five. "Spill the first one on the ground or in a can if you've got one."

"How's that?"

Why should I tell him; give him ideas? As if he hadn't got them already. "Just call me eccentric," he said. "I don't want the first gallon from the pump. Why should you care? It's just five dollars more profit."

For a moment Mr. Jimmon thought the man was going to refuse, and he regarded his foresight with new reverence. Then he reached behind the pump and produced a flat-sided tin in which he inserted the flexible end of the hose. Mr. Jimmon handed over the bill, the man wound the handle round and back—it was an ancient gas pump such as Mr. Jimmon hadn't seen for years—and lifted the drooling hose from the can.

"Minute," said Mr. Jimmon.

He stuck two fingers quickly and delicately inside the nozzle and smelled them. Gas all right, not water. He held out a ten-dollar bill. "Start filling."

Jir and Wendell appeared out of the shadows. "Can we stop at a town where there's a movie tonight?"

The handle turned, a cog-toothed rod crept up and retreated, gasoline gurgled into the tank. Movies, thought Mr. Jimmon, handing over another bill; movies, rest rooms, baths, restaurants. Gouge apprehensively lest a scene be made and propriety disturbed. In a surrealist daydream he saw Molly turning the crank, grinding him on the cogs, pouring his essence into insatiable Jir and Wendell. He held out $20.

Twelve gallons had been put in when Molly appeared. "You have a phone here?" he asked casually. Knowing the answer from the blue enameled sign not quite lost among less sturdy ones advertising soft drinks and cigarettes.

"You want to call the cops?" He didn't pause in his pumping.

"No. Know if the lines to L.A."—Mr. Jimmon loathed the abbreviation—"are open yet?" He gave him another ten.

"How should I know?"

Mr. Jimmon beckoned his wife around the other side of the wagon, out of sight. Swiftly but casually he extracted the contents of his wallet. The 200 dollar bills made a fat lump. "Put this in your bag," he said. "Tell you why later. Meantime why don't you try and get Pearl and Dan on the phone? See if they're okay?"

He imagined the puzzled look on her face. "Go on," he urged. "We can spare a minute while he's checking the oil."

He thought there was a hint of uncertainty in Molly's walk as she went toward the store. Erika joined her brothers. The tank gulped: gasoline splashed on the concrete. "Guess that's it."

The man became suddenly brisk as he put up the hose, screwed the gas cap back on. Mr. Jimmon had already disengaged the hood; the man offered the radiator a squirt of water, pulled up the oil gauge, wiped it, plunged it down, squinted at it under the light, and said, "Oil's OK."

"All right," said Mr. Jimmon. "Get in Erika."

Some of the light shone directly on her face. Again he noted how mature and self-assured she looked. Erika would survive—and not as a savage either. The man started to wipe the windshield. "Oh, Jir," he said casually, "run in and see if your mother is getting her connection. Tell her we'll wait."

"Aw, furcrysay. I don't see why I always—"

"And ask her to buy a couple of boxes of candy bars if they've got them. Wendell, go with Jir, will you?"

He slid in behind the wheel and closed the door gently. The motor started with hardly a sound. As he put his foot on the clutch and shifted into low he thought Erika turned to him with a startled look. As the station wagon moved forward, he was sure of it.

"It's all right, Erika," said Mr. Jimmon, "I'll explain later." He'd have lots of time to do it.

AFTERWORD TO LOT

Six years after the global nuclear holocaust, we meet Mr. Jimmon again in the sequel, "Lot's Daughter." His Robinson-Crusoe fantasy of becoming the ultra-competent lone master of his environment has now been exposed as one of the forces leading to racial suicide: the treacherous bourgeois myth of the self-sufficient individual, the supermasculine hero who spurns social interdependency. Tortured by his rotting teeth and gradually using up the socially produced objects that allow him to survive, he must daily face the contempt of his daughter, who has come to realize that "cooperation" is the answer to the "savagery" he embodies, and that "People aren't as stupid as you think they are."

Finally, in a piercing twist of irony, she abandons him, leaving him to care for their pathetic, sickly son. As he sinks ever deeper into barbarism, she joins a small community that is slowly restoring civilization.

I KILL MYSELF

Julian Kawalec

Julian Kawalec was born in Wrzawy, a village in central Poland, in 1916. The first child in his family to be formally educated, he studied Polish philology and graduated from the Jagellonian University of Cracow in 1939. His career as a journalist began when he was a war correspondent in 1944, and he became a free-lance author in 1957.

"I Kill Myself" appeared in his second collection of short stories, *Scars*, published in Carcow in 1960. His many subsequent volumes of fiction have won such important awards as the Polish Editors' Prize (1962) and the Prize of the Minister of Culture and Art (1967).

Kawalec's story is science fiction pushed to its supreme form—compressed insight and drama. It is a tale few readers will ever forget. "I Kill Myself" springs into mind whenever a nation, arrogant with its ability to destroy, deludes itself into confusing power with virtue.

Today I shall destroy the Zeta bomb. I shall do it this evening, when I begin my tour of duty in the army laboratory. Today I have achieved the capacity for sacrifice; I realized that when I looked at the slender, mournful boughs of the trees; I can't say why it was just at the moment when I noticed the trees.

I am walking along an avenue in the park. I feel a keen rawness in the air. People go past me. They pay no attention to me. They don't know that I, a homely-looking man in a gray raincoat, with big ears and a mole on the cheek, am capable of great self-sacrifice; that this evening I shall turn the key in the door of an iron safe, open it, and take out something which looks like a large goose egg. That's the Zeta bomb. The distance between the contact pin and the critical point of the bomb is three millimeters. That is the distance to which Professor Lombard set the contact pin when he solicitously laid the Zeta in its plush case. The Zeta rests like a child in swaddling clothes; today I shall destroy the steel child, for today I have achieved the capacity to make this great sacrifice of myself.

I must do it, I must free humanity from the terrible nightmare and that powerful mite. Why should a tiny steel pin have power of life and death over people? . . . So long as it doesn't touch the critical point, the sun will go on shining; when it does touch, night will fall, all people will die, and the birds will drop like meteors. By the force of its explosion the Zeta bomb exceeds the most powerful hydrogen bomb a billion times. If it were to explode, the result would not be death, for death is an equal partner with life—one can argue with it, one can quarrel and be reconciled with it. In comparison with the consequences of an explosion of Zeta, death is something anodyne. The term "death" doesn't apply to the effects of that. One must create a new word for it.

I'm walking along the park avenues, waiting for the evening. When evening comes, I shall destroy Professor Lombard's "iron child." I shall unscrew the contact pin; I shall throw the bomb into a marsh, and the pin into a river some five kilometers distant from the marsh. The Zeta and the pin will never meet again. And if they don't meet, the world will continue to exist. I shall burn the documents giving the sketches and specifications of the bomb, and tread the ashes into the ground. Professor Lombard will not live long enough to give birth to a second "iron child."

I shall destroy the Zeta bomb. I shall do it for the sake of the trees, the animals, the birds, the people, the insects. I shall do it for my own sake, and for the sake of that young man with black hair who is sitting on a bench hidden among the trees, waiting for a girl; for you, gnarled elm, and for you inhabitant the woodpecker, and for you, black worm corkscrewing through the earth.

In the midst of all these people and trees I feel an enormous and oppressive loneliness. I cannot tell anyone what I'm planning to do. I'm afraid they might stop me from destroying the bomb. But after all, great sacrifice demands great loneliness. If I talk about it, I'm sharing it with others, reducing its greatness. But the feeling of loneliness doesn't weaken my determination.

The sky withdraws from the far end of the avenue, a sign that evening will soon be coming on. I leave the park. Today I shall walk to the laboratory. I take a road which shows up white among the small houses and crisscrossed fallow land. On my left someone is singing; on my right a gentle breeze is noisily tousling withered branches. After a moment the singing and the sound of the wind both stop. All is still.

Beyond a small pine wood I come to the first control barrier. They shine a beam of light toward me. They've recognized me. The guards know the senior laboratory assistant very well; he's a quiet sort and docile, with large ears and a mole on the cheek. I pass the first control barrier; the road is as smooth as a table top; the army laboratory has good roads leading to it. In a clump of leafy trees I come to the second control barrier. They pick me out with three beams of light; as they do so a single bird wakes up in a tree and begins to twitter. They scrutinize me closely, though all of them know me, though they know I'm the senior laboratory assistant and initiated into all the secrets. Beyond the second control barrier the road passes underground. Now I'm walking along a lighted tunnel. The side walls of the tunnel have innumerable little windows, through which guards poke their heads. One must walk steadily and calmly along the tunnel; the best thing is to whistle.

In a small hall, brilliantly lit, I show my identity papers, then I enter a narrow corridor. A tall guard opens an iron door for me. Now I'm in the anteroom of the laboratory. I am alone. I set to work. I bend over the secret drawer which contains the keys; it is known only to Professor Lombard, the commander-in-chief, and myself.

I pick up the key. in the third room of the laboratory I disconnect the alarm signal fixed to the iron safe. I open a drawer and take the Zeta bomb out of its plush case. Zeta is cold and slippery. I could destroy it here, in the laboratory; I could thaw it out; but that would take time, and the three junior laboratory assistants will be arriving in a few minutes. I conceal the bomb and the sketches in the broad pocket of my light raincoat, which I hang over my arm. I telephone to Professor Lombard, using a one-figure number known only to me and the commander-in-chief. I tell him I've forgotten to bring important reagents from the store and I must go for them myself at once.

In a minute or two I am on my way. I am not detained at the control points. The commander of the guard has been informed that it is a question of getting important reagents swiftly.

I have passed the last control barrier. Now there are no more lights. I turn off the main road. I'm going across flat, soft ground in the direction of an alder grove. Surely this must be a sown field. It is night. Cold. I put on my raincoat. I have it, I have the bomb; with every step I take I feel it knocking against my ribs. Now and again I put my hand into the raincoat pocket to make sure it's there. It is, it is. I touch it with my hand. It is cold, slippery. Professor Lombard polished it, smoothed it. He gave it the gleam of a monstrous distorting mirror. Under my forefinger I feel the tiny head of the contact pin. All I have to do is to slip back the safety catch, press that little head, and then only invisible, inchoate fragments will be left of everything. However, the words "visible" and "invisible" wouldn't have any meaning whatever then. But that will never happen. Quite soon now I shall throw the Zeta bomb into the marsh. I shall throw it with all my strength, so that it flies into the very middle, where the mud is thinnest, where it will sink most easily and swiftly. I shall throw the contact pin into the river. Who will ever find a pin only a little thicker than a needle?

And then? Then I must go into hiding. I must find a good hiding place, for they are sure to search for me. I dare say the whole of the police force, the special military departments and forces, and the secret service will all be called in to search for me. I can already see, already hear, the orders being issued, the instructions intercrossing; how they'll be shouting, how they'll be whispering, all to find out where I am. But the great sacrifice to which I have dedicated myself cares nothing for such things. The great sacrifice must even require such things. And yet the great sacrifice doesn't require that after I've destroyed the bomb I should voluntarily and even frivolously put myself in the hands of those who have produced it. No, I cannot give them that pleasure. I cannot do anything which would give those wicked people the least satisfaction. And so, after I've destroyed Professor Lombard's "iron child," I must conceal myself thoroughly. The people, for whom I am making this great sacrifice, will not defend me. It will be a long time before they even learn of my exploit, before they have any realization of its benefits. They will stop to consider the matter; they will discuss, doubt, suspect; they will pluck up courage and succumb to cowardice; and maybe they will be ready to come to my defense only when it's too late. So I must seek out a good hiding place. But if they come upon my tracks, if I hear their steps, the clatter of belts hung about with weapons, the rustle of uniforms, and the snorting of highly sensitive, perfectly trained dogs, shall I leave my hiding place with my hands up? Does my self-sacrifice call for putting up a valiant resistance or for valiant renunciation of resistance? For resistance, for valiant resistance. But my sacrifice connotes prudent resistance, which in certain circumstances demands that I should hide from the enemy, should deceive the enemy. So I shall not go out to meet the police with my hands up. Rather, the moment they see me I shall spring at the throat of the nearest policeman. If I had a revolver I could kill several before I died. If I had a machine gun I could mow down several dozen from my hiding place.

The ground over which I'm now walking is longer even and soft; it is hard and crowded with little tussocks. So it must be quite close to the alder grove. I think I see a dark patch in front. Yes, that surely is the alder grove. The marsh lies just beyond it. I am coming across more and more of those little tussocks. My steps are inevitably becoming broken, and short. At times my feet slip farther down than I expect. Then my body is subjected to an involuntary jolt. Then Zeta strikes more violently against my ribs. It reminds me more insistently of its presence. I swiftly thrust my hand into my raincoat pocket. It's there, it's there. It's not so cold now as it was, it's rather warmer. Its shape also isn't so ugly. But it's a monster threatening something which cannot be called death or silence, or by any word from a modern dictionary. It's a tiny sleeping monster.

The dark patch grows blacker. Now the alder grove is very close. All around is still.

Now I can hear the gentle murmur of the trees. I am in the alder grove. I'm walking along a narrow path. The trees surround me with a friendly air; they're whispering something to me. The Zeta bomb must be destroyed so that the alders can live. Beyond the alder grove the ground turns soft again. But it's not the softness of a sown field, it's the springy softness of India rubber. I am conscious of the marsh; I can hear it. It too has its voice. The voice of the marsh is like the heavy breathing of a dying man. I can still go on for the time being; my feet are not sinking in yet; I know I shall go on safely as far as the first clump of tall spear grass. So now only minutes are left. The ground is getting softer and softer. Now I am at the spot, by a clump of spear grass. I hurriedly thrust my hand into my raincoat pocket. The bomb is warm. I hold its warm, smooth metal a long time in my palm. Then I cautiously take Zeta out of my pocket. Now it is lying on my palm. And so, in a moment *that* will be happening. In a moment the world will be freed from multitudinous death. But the world knows nothing about it. The world is quiet, indifferent, and sluggish. It is possible that such a great deed can be accomplished in such great silence? I put the thumb and forefinger of my right hand on the safety catch. But just as I do so I hear a loud rustling. I seize the safety catch between my fingers and release it. I'm being pursued. No, it's only the wind running over the reeds . . . But if it were indeed a pursuit, if dogs picking up my trail began to bark at the edge of the marsh, if the first policemen were to put in an appearance . . . after all, I could threaten them with the bomb. I could shout to them: "Halt. I've got the Zeta bomb in my hand. With the safety catch released. The contact pin is one millimeter away from the critical point. If you advance a single step I shall press the pin. And don't try shooting at me, for if I fall the bomb will be given a violent jolt and it will explode. You'll perish!" But I wouldn't be the only one to perish. And not only would they perish. Millions of innocent people would perish. Such reasoning is not worthy of a man who has decided to sacrifice himself. And yet, the police will not move one step if I threaten them with the bomb. They're cowards. So nothing will happen to the world. My courage, which should accompany my sacrifice, will not suffer either, for I shall threaten the police, not because they're afraid, but because they're in the service of those who produce the bomb, those I hate. So that threat and that hatred should be included in the program of sacrifice. I cling to this thought: I consider it fine and pure, for I can hold the makers of the Zeta bomb, and their assistants, under threat; I can do as I like with them. That's a wise sacrifice. I can command them to march to a hollow between hills and leave them there, and starve them. I can send Professor Lombard there, and even the chief of staff, himself. I'm grateful to that rustle in the reeds. It has brought about a judicious change in my thinking.

I shan't destroy the Zeta bomb today. Pity I didn't bring the plush box also when I brought it away, I'd have had something in which to keep it. I shall keep Zeta and devote it to the service of the good. I'm astonished that I could ever have forgotten the great significance of the bomb in this kind of service.

Blind self-sacrifice made me regard it only as the source of a great evil. Prudence, which I now associate with the desire for sacrifice, makes it possible for me to consider Zeta from various aspects. With Zeta's aid I can see the world free from Zeta. By using it as a threat, I can order the laboratories in which it was to have serial production to be destroyed. I can render Professor Lombard harmless, and all the experts on the bomb, and its guards. I can do this if I screw the contact pin to a distance of one millimeter from the critical point. The threat of its explosion will compel them to submit and be absolutely obedient to me. With Zeta in my possession I can destroy every wicked man. With Zeta I can do much, I can do almost everything. Why do I say "almost"? I'm in a position not only to achieve general reforms, but to break into the life of every man in this earth and arbitrarily change it. If

I wish, the wealthiest of merchants will hand over his store to me. If I wish, Mrs. Emilia will forsake the husband she loves, will bow to me and go wandering about the world. If I wish, the daughter of the chief of staff will present herself naked to me. If I give the order, the Nestor of science will shave off his beard and climb a tree in the city park in broad daylight. I imagine the scene and laugh: the Nestor of science climbing to the top of the tree with the agility of a monkey. I already see people coming from all over the world and bowing to me and handing me all sorts of articles and titles. One gives me a sumptuous villa at the seaside; another proposes that I should accept a doctorate of all the sciences; a third humbly explains that kingship is the finest form of government and that I am highly suited to be king, for I have a fine bearing and profound intelligence. Someone tells me I have very handsome ears.

I try to cast out these thoughts. For I am to serve the good. I must set about the destruction of evil. That's why I'm keeping Zeta. In order to destroy evil I must divide the people into wicked and good.

I can do that: I shall be the supreme judge. But why the future tense? I am the supreme judge. There is no one higher than I. I touch Zeta. I stroke it. How beautiful it has become, how smooth and pleasant it is, how brilliantly it shines. I press Zeta to my heart, I kiss it. What am I saying, what am I doing? But why ask? I'm doing and performing that which ought to be done; all this is included within my enlarged, human program of sacrifice. I cannot hesitate—I should be ridiculous if I hesitated. I am Caesar, Napoleon, Alexander the Great; I am the supreme judge, I am God, I surpass God. I shout: "I am God." The trees already know; they bow down to the ground. The human beings don't know it yet. I hurry back to the city by the shortest route. To judgment. I shall judge. All human beings are wicked; they must all be destroyed. I alone am good. I ALONE AM GOOD, FOR I POSSESS ZETA.

Translated from the Polish by
Harry Stevens

THE NEUTRINO BOMB

Ralph S. Cooper

Ralph S. Cooper is a physicist whose areas of specialization include magnetic fusion, laser fusion, reactor physics, ion exchange column theory, nuclear rocket propulsion, and radiation effects. In 1957, at the age of 26, he joined the staff of the Theoretical Physics Division of the Los Alamos Scientific Laboratory, where both the original atomic bomb and the thermonuclear (fusion) bomb had been developed. Except for a four-year stint as Chief Scientist of the Nuclear Laboratory of the Douglas Aircraft Company (1965–1969), he was to work at Los Alamos continually through 1980.

Dr. Cooper published "The Neutrino Bomb" in the July 13, 1961 issue of the *Los Alamos Scientific Laboratory News*. Many readers, including scientists, took his proposal seriously, failing to see the ridicule being heaped on their own assumptions about the arms race.

While the United States continues its test moratorium, delaying its work toward revolutionary new types of nuclear weapons, reliable sources indicate that the Soviet Union may have leapfrogged our neutron bomb with the development and possible tests of the ultimate in clean, blastless nuclear weapons, a neutrino bomb.

Annihilation

In this device, a plasma or soup of high temperature hydrogen is created in which the electrons and protons, particles with opposite electric charge, annihilate each other with the emission only of a flood of high energy neutral particles called neutrinos.* These have tremendous penetrating power against which no shielding is effective and which makes the ordinary neutrons seem like marshmallows in comparison. In the one-cubic-foot tactical size containing four pounds of hydrogen, over a trillion-trillion high energy neutrinos are released. Neutrinos are liberated in fission bombs but in much smaller numbers, while in the neutrino bomb, almost all the energy goes into neutrinos and virtually nothing into blast waves, gamma rays, fission fragments, or fallout.

Before discounting this as a significant weapon, two things should be considered. First the absence of any physical damage is directly in line with the so-called peaceful motives avowed by the Soviets, who are privately calling this a "peace bomb." Secondly, that the detonation is not completely without observable effects since the disappearance of the hydrogen leaves a temporary vacuum into which the surrounding air rushes with a loud bang, informing the victims in the target area that they have been had.

Microton Yield

Reports coming from the Iron Curtain countries of loud noises heard deep inside Russia indicate that they not only may have tested the one-cubic-foot tactical size (for which the air implosion is equivalent to about one microton of TNT) but

---

*The free neutrino was first detected by Los Alamos scientists in June, 1956.

that they may already have tested large neutrino bombs in the milliton range, containing thousands of pounds of hydrogen. This information, coupled with the possibility of underground decoupling or even of detonation inside a steel pressure vessel to prevent the air implosion, indicates we may be crucially far behind in the development of this important weapon. Indeed, experiments of the latter kind are known to have been performed in Russia, although the scientists involved claimed their only interest was in the production of a high vacuum. Whether this was the "ultimate weapon" of which Khrushchev spoke in his March, 1960, speech cannot yet be determined, but the recent disdainful attitude of the Soviet diplomats implies their extreme confidence in the Russian military posture. Thus it behooves us to take whatever steps necessary to rectify this potential imbalance of military power or face the inevitable disastrous consequences.

AKUA NUTEN (THE SOUTH WIND)

Yves Thériault

Visions of nuclear war in literature are usually limited to the industrialized nations, especially those inhabited by Europeans and their descendants. But a thermonuclear shootout would no doubt also destroy hundreds of millions of innocent bystanders in the Third World. How does the nuclear arms race and its possible outcome look to those peoples who have never participated in it? And how would they, long called "savages," regard the self-destruction of what calls itself "civilization"?

One chilling answer comes from Yves Thériault, the most prolific and one of the most influential authors in Québec, himself a descendant of Montagnais Indians. Born in 1915, Thériault is best known in the English-speaking world for his powerful novels of native life available in English translation: the much-honored *Agaguk* (1958); *Ashini* (1960); *N'Tsuk* (1968); *Agoak* (1975). Before his death in 1983, he had also published thirty other diverse novels, about a dozen volumes of short stories, innumerable pseudonymous "ten-cent thrillers," and more than a score of science fiction volumes for young people, while in addition turning out dozens of plays as well as over 1,300 radio and television scripts.

"Akua Nuten (The South Wind)" appeared originally in

AKUA NUTEN (THE SOUTH WIND)

his highly innovative 1962 *Si la bomb m'était contée (If They Had Told Me of the Bomb)*, a volume describing nuclear war from the perspective of many different peoples. The story's non-European point of view, its simple eloquence, and its primeval natural setting are all perfectly appropriate for a conclusive moment in human history.

Kakatso, the Montagnais Indian, felt the gentle flow of the air and noticed that the wind came from the south. Then he touched the moving water in the stream to determine the temperature in the highlands. Since everything pointed to nice June weather, with mild sunshine and light winds, he decided to go to the highest peak of the reserve, as he had been planning to do for the past week. There the Montagnais lands bordered those of the Waswanipis.

There was no urgent reason for the trip. Nothing really pulled him there except the fact that he hadn't been for a long time; and he liked steep mountains and frothy, roaring streams.

Three days before he had explained his plan to his son, the thin Grand-Louis, who was well known to the white men of the North Shore. His son had guided many white in the regions surrounding the Manicouagan and Bersimis rivers.

He had told him: "I plan to go way out, near the limits of the reserve."

This was clear enough, and Grand-Louis had simply nodded his head. Now he wouldn't worry, even if Kakatso disappeared for two months. He would know that his father was high in the hills, breathing the clean air and soaking up beautiful scenes to remember in future days.

Just past the main branch of the Manicouagan there is an enormous rock crowned by two pines and a fir tree which stand side by side like the fingers of a hand, the smallest on the left and the others reaching higher.

This point, which Katatso could never forget, served as his sign-post for every trail in the area; and other points would guide him north, west, or in any other direction. Kakatso, until his final breath, would easily find his way about there, guided only by the memory of a certain tree, the silhouette of the mountain outlined against the clear skies, the twisting of a river bed, or the slope of a hill.

In strange territory Kakatso would spend entire days precisely organizing his memories so that if he ever returned no trail there would be unknown to him.

Thus, knowing every winding path and every animal's accustomed lair, he could set out on his journey carrying only some salt, tea, and shells for his rifle. He could live by finding his subsistence in the earth itself and in nature's plenty.

Kakatso knew well what a man needed for total independence: a fishhook wrapped in paper, a length of supple cord, a strong knife, water-proof boots, and a well-oiled rifle. With these things a man could know the great joy of not having to depend on anyone but himself, of wandering as he pleased one day after another, proud and superior, the owner of eternal lands that stretched beyond the horizon.

(To despise the reserve and those who belonged there. Not to have any allegiance except a respect for the water, the sky, and the winds. To be a man, but a man according to the Indian image and not that of the whites. The Indian image of a real man was ageless and changeless, a true image of man in the bosom of a wild and immense nature.)

Kakatso had a wife and a house and grown-up children whom he rarely saw. He really knew little about them. One daughter was a nurse in a white man's city, another had married a turncoat Montagnais who lived in Baie-Comeau and worked in the factories. A son studied far away, in Montreal, and Kakatso would probably never see him again. A son who would repudiate everything, would forget the proud Montagnais language and change his name to be accepted by the whites in spite of his dark skin and slitty eyes.

AKUA NUTEN (THE SOUTH WIND)

The other son, Grand-Louis . . . but this one was an exception. He had inherited Montagnasi instincts. He often came down to the coast, at Godbout or Sept-Iles, or sometimes at Natashquan, because he was ambitious and wanted to earn money. But this did not cause him to scorn or detest the forest. He found a good life there. For Kakatso, it was enough that this child, unlike so many others, did not turn into a phony white man.

As for Kakatso's wife, she was still at home, receiving Kakatso on his many returns without emotion or gratitude. She had a roof over her head, warmth, and food. With skilled fingers she made caribou skin jackets for the white man avid for the exotic. The small sideline liberated Kakatso from other obligations towards her. Soon after returning home, Kakatso always wanted to get away again. He was uncomfortable in these white men's houses that were too high, too solid, and too neatly organized for his taste.

So Kakatso lived his life in direct contact with the forest, and he nurtured life itself from the forest's plenty. Ten months of the year he roamed the forest trails, ten months he earned his subsistence from hunting, trapping, fishing, and smoking the caribou meat that he placed in caches for later use. With the fur pelts he met his own needs and those of the house on the reserve near the forest, although these needs were minimal because his wife was a good earner.

He climbed, then, towards the northern limits of the Montagnasi lands on this June day, which was to bring calamity of which he was completely unaware.

Kakatso had heard of the terrible bomb. For twenty years he had heard talk of it, and the very existence of these horrendous machines was not unknown to him. But how was he to know the complex fabric of events happening in the world just then? He never read the newspapers and never really listened to the radio when he happened to spend some hours in a warm house. How could he conceive of total annihilation threatening the whole world? How could he feel all the world's people trembling?

In the forest's vast peace, Kakatso, knowing nature's strength, could easily believe that nothing and nobody could prevail against the mountains, the rivers, and the forest itself stretching out all across the land. Nothing could prevail against the earth, the unchangeable soil that regenerated itself year after year.

He travelled for five days. On the fifth evening it took Kakatso longer to fall asleep. Something was wrong. A silent anguish he did not understand was disturbing him.

He had lit his evening fire on a bluff covered with soft moss, one hundred feet above the lake. He slept there, rolled in his blanket in a deeply dark country interrupted only by the rays of the new moon.

Sleep was slow and when it came it did not bring peace. A jumble of snarling creatures and swarming, roaring masses invaded Kakatso's sleep. He turned over time and again, groaning restlessly. Suddenly he awoke and was surprised to see that the moon had gone down and the night's blackness was lit only by stars. Here, on the bluff, there was a bleak reflection from the sky, but that long valley and the lake remained dark. Exhausted by his throbbing dreams, Kakatso got up, stretched his legs and lit his pipe. On those rare occasions when his sleep was bad he had always managed to recover his tranquillity by smoking a bit, motionless in the night, listening to the forest sounds.

Suddenly the light came. For a single moment the southern and western horizons were illuminated by this immense bluish gleam that loomed up, lingered a moment, and then went out. The dark became even blacker and Kakatso muttered to himself. He wasn't afraid because fear had always been totally foreign to him. But what did this strange event mean? Was it the anger of some old mountain spirit?

All at once the gleam reappeared, this time even more

AKUA NUTEN (THE SOUTH WIND)

westerly. Weaker this time and less evident. Then the shadows again enveloped the land.

Kakatso no longer tried to sleep that night. He squatted, smoking his pipe and trying to find some explanation for these bluish gleams with his simple ideas, his straightforward logic and vivid memory.

When the dawn came the old Montagnais, the last of his people, the great Abenakis, carefully prepared his fire and boiled some water for his tea.

For some hours he didn't feel like moving. He no longer heard the inner voices calling him to the higher lands. He felt stuck there, incapable of going further until the tumult within him died down. What was there that he didn't know about his skies, he who had spent his whole life wandering in the woods and sleeping under the stars? The sky over his head was as familiar to him as the soil of the underbrush, the animal trials and the games of the trout in their streams. But never before had he seen such gleams and they disturbed him.

At eight o'clock the sun was slowly climbing into the sky, and Kakatso was still there.

At ten he moved to the shore to look at the water in the lake. He saw a minnow run and concluded that the lake had many fish. He then attached his fire cord to the hook tied with partridge feathers he had found in the branches of a wild hawthorn bush. He cast the fly with a deliberate, almost solemn movement and it jumped on the smooth water. After Kakatso cast three more times a fat trout swallowed the hook and he pulled him in gently, quite slowly, letting him fight as much as he wanted. The midday meal was in hand. The Montagnais, still in no great hurry to continue his trip, began to prepare his fish.

He was finishing when the far-away buzz of a plane shook him out of his reveries. Down there, over the mountains around the end of the lake, a plane was moving through the sky. This was a familiar sight to Kakatso because all this far country was visited only by planes that landed on the lakes.

In this way the Indian had come to know the white man. This was the most frequent place of contact between the two: a large body of quiet water where a plane would land, where the whites would ask for help and finding nothing better than an Indian to help them.

Even from a distance Kakatso recognized the type of plane. It was a single-engine, deluxe Bonanza, a type often used by the Americans who came to fish for their salmon in our rivers.

The plane circled the lake and flew over the bluff where Kakatso's fire was still burning. Then it landed gently, almost tenderly. The still waters were only lightly ruffled and quickly returned to their mirror smoothness. The plane slowed down, the motor coughed once or twice, then the craft made a complete turn and headed for the beach.

Kakatso, with one hand shading his eyes, watched the landing, motionless.

When the plane was finally still and the tips of its pontoons were pulled up on the sandy beach, two men, a young woman, and a twelve-year-old boy got out.

One of the men was massive. He towered a head over Kakatso although the Montagnais himself was rather tall.

"Are you an Indian?" the man asked suddenly.

Kakatso nodded slowly and blinked his eyes once.

"Good, I'm glad, you can save us," said the man.

"Save you?" said Kakatso. "Save you from what?"

"Never mind," said the woman, "that's our business."

Standing some distance away, she gestured to the big man who had first spoken to Kakatso.

"If you're trying to escape the police," said Kakatso, "I can't do anything for you."

"It has nothing to do with the police," said the other man who had not spoken previously.

He moved towards Kakatso and proffered a handshake. Now that he was close the Montagnais recognized a veteran bush pilot. His experience could be seen in his eyes, in the squint of his eyelids, and in the way he treated an Indian as an equal.

"I am Bob Ledoux," the man said. "I am a pilot. Do you know what nuclear war is?"

"Yes," answered Kakatso, "I know."

"All the cities in the south have been destroyed," said Ledoux. "We were able to escape."

"Is that a real one?" asked the boy, who had been closely scrutinizing Kakatso. "Eh, Mom, is it really one of those savages?"

"Yes," answered the woman, "certainly." And to Kakatso she said, "Please excuse him. He has never been on the North Shore."

Naturally Kakatso did not like to be considered a savage. But he didn't show anything and he swallowed his bitterness.

"So," said the pilot, "here we are without resources."

"I have money," said the man.

"This is Mr. Perron," said the pilot, "Mrs. Perron, and their son. . . ."

"My name is Roger," said the boy. "I know how to swim."

The Montagnais was still undecided. He did not trust intruders. He preferred, in his simple soul, to choose his own objectives and decide his day's activities. And here were outsiders who had fallen from the sky, almost demanding his help . . . but what help?

"I can't do much for you," he said after a while.

"I have money," the man repeated.

Kakatso shrugged. Money? Why money? What would it buy up here?

Without flinching he had heard how all the southern cities had been destroyed. Now he understood the meaning of those sudden gleams that lit the horizon during the night. And because this event had been the works of whites, Kakatso completely lost interest in it.

So his problem remained these four people he considered spoilers.

"Without you," said the woman, "we are going to perish."

And because Kakatso looked at her in surprise, she added, in a somewhat different tone: "We have no supplies at all and we are almost out of fuel."

"That's true," said the pilot.

"So," continued the woman, "if you don't help us find food, we will die."

Kakatso, with a sweeping gesture, indicated the forests and the lake: "There is wild game there and fish in the waters. . . ."

"I don't have a gun or fishhooks," said the pilot. "And it's been a very long time since I came so far north."

He said this with a slightly abashed air and Kakatso saw clearly that the man's hands were too white; the skin had become too soft and smooth.

"I'll pay you whatever is necessary," said Mr. Perron.

"Can't you see," said his wife, "that money doesn't interest him?"

Kakatso stood there, looking at them with his shining impassive eyes, his face unsmiling and his arms dangling at his sides.

"Say something," cried the woman. "Will you agree to help us?"

"We got away as best we could," said the pilot. "We gathered the attack on Montreal was coming and we were already at the airport when the warning sirens went off. But I couldn't take on enough fuel. There were other planes leaving too. I can't even take off again from this lake. Do you know if there is a supply cache near here?"

Throughout the northern forests pilots left emergency fuel caches for use when necessary. But if Kakatso knew of several such places he wasn't letting on in front of the intruders.

"I don't know," he said.

AKUA NUTEN (THE SOUTH WIND)

There was silence.

The whites looked at the Indian and desperately sought words to persuade him. But Kakatso did not move and said nothing. He had always fled the society of whites and dealt with them only when it was unavoidable. Why should he treat those who surfaced here now any differently? They were without food; the forest nourishes those who know how to take their share. This knowledge was such an instinctive part of an Indian's being that he couldn't realize how some people could lack it. He was sure that these people wanted to impose their needs on him and enslave him. All his Montagnais pride revolted against this thought. And yet, he could help them. Less than one hour away there was one of those meat caches of a thousand pounds of smoked moose, enough to see them through a winter. And the fish in the lake could be caught without much effort. Weaving a simple net of fine branches would do it, or a trap of bulrushes.

But he didn't move a muscle.

Only a single fixed thought possessed Kakatso, and it fascinated him. Down there, in the south, the white had been destroyed. Never again would they reign over these forests. In killing each other, they had rid the land of their kind. Would the Indians be free again? All the Indians, even those on the reserves? Free to retake the forests?

And these four whites: could they be the last survivors?

Brothers, thought Kakatso, all my brothers: it is up to me to protect your new freedom.

"The cities," he finally said, "they have really been destroyed?"

"Yes," said the pilot.

"Nothing is left any more," said the woman. "Nothing at all. We saw the explosion from the plane. It was terrible. And the wind pushed up for a quarter of an hour. I thought we were going to crash."

"Nothing left," said the boy, "nobody left. Boom! One bomb did it."

He was delighted to feel himself the hero—a safe and sound hero—of such an adventure. He didn't seem able to imagine the destruction and death, only the spectacular explosion.

But the man called Perron had understood it well. He had been able to estimate the real power of the bomb.

"The whole city is destroyed," he said. "A little earlier, on the radio, we heard of the destruction of New York, then Toronto and Ottawa. . . ."

"Many other cities too," added the pilot. "As far as I'm concerned, nothing is left of Canada, except perhaps the North Shore. . . ."

"And it won't be for long," said Perron. "If we could get further up, further north. If we only had food and gasoline."

This time he took a roll of money out of his pocket and unfolded five bills, a sum Kakatso had never handled at one time. Perron offered them to the Indian.

"Here. The only thing we ask you for is a little food and gas if you can get some. Then we could leave."

"When such a bomb explodes," said Kakatso without taking the bills, "does it kill all the whites?"

"Yes," said the pilot. "In any case, nearly all."

"One fell on Ottawa?"

"Yes."

"Everybody is dead there?"

"Yes. The city is small and the bomb was a big one. The reports indicate there were no survivors."

Kakatso nodded his head two or three times approvingly. Then he turned away and took his rifle which had been leaning on a rock. Slowly, aiming at the whites, he began to retreat into the forest.

"Where are you going?" cried the woman.

"Here," said the man. "Here's all my money. Come back!"

Only the pilot remained silent. With his sharp eyes he watched Kakatso.

AKUA NUTEN (THE SOUTH WIND)

When the Indian reached the edge of the forest it was the boy's turn. He began to sob pitifully, and the woman also began to cry.

"Don't leave," she cried. "Please, help us. . . ."

For all of my people who cried, thought Kakatso, all who begged, who wanted to defend their rights for the past two hundred years: I take revenge for them all.

But he didn't utter another word.

And when the two men wanted to run after him to stop him, he put his rifle to his shoulder. The bullet nicked the pilot's ear. Then the men understood that it would be futile to insist, and Kakatso disappeared into the forest which enclosed him. Bent low, he skimmed the ground, using every bush for cover, losing himself in the undergrowth, melting into the forest where he belonged.

Later, having circled the lake, he rested on a promontory hidden behind many spreading cedars. He saw that the pilot was trying to take off to find food elsewhere.

But the tanks were nearly empty and when the plane reached an altitude of a thousand feet the motor sputtered a bit, backfired and stopped.

The plane went into a nosedive.

When it hit the trees it caught fire.

In the morning Kakatso continued his trip towards the highlands.

He felt his first nausea the next day and vomited blood two days later. He vomited once at first, then twice, then a third time, and finally one last time.

The wind kept on blowing from the south, warm and mild.

I HAVE NO MOUTH, AND I MUST SCREAM

Harlan Ellison

The world's most honored science fiction writer, with six and a half Hugo and three Nebula awards, Harlan Ellison is also the only three-time winner of the Writers' Guild of America award for best TV script. His imagination is intensely visual, violent, and disturbing.

Born in 1934, Ellison was asked to leave Ohio State University in 1955 after he quarreled with a creative writing teacher who told him he had no talent. In the next two years, he sold 150 short stories, in several genres. During this period, he ran for about ten weeks with a street gang in Red Hook, one of the toughest sections of Brooklyn, in order to gain the experience for a series of books and stories about the violent underside of American urban life. In 1959, after three years in the army, he became editor of *Rogue* magazine in Chicago, and then in 1962 he moved to Los Angeles, where he continues to pour out in profusion TV and movie scripts, novels, essays, anthologies, and, most important, short stories.

Ellison has written at least a handful of stories that will stand as monuments of modern American culture, indeed as dazzling expressions of the crises of our epoch. Of these, I believe the very finest is "I Have No Mouth, and I Must Scream," a story so emotionally powerful that one reading makes it unforgettable, a story so rich and profound in meaning that it must be read many times.

Some people were surprised that I had chosen "I Have No Mouth, and I Must Scream" for this volume. "That's not a story about nuclear war," was a typical response. "That's a story about computers" or "machines" or "alienation" or "love and hate" or "religion" or "the nature of reality." Well, of course it's about all of these and more. But Ellison here shows that it's impossible to understand any of these subjects today without understanding how all of them are defined by our creation of machines to destroy the human race through nuclear war.

The sentient computer, whose name is both the name of the Hebrew God (I Am-Yahweh-Jehovah) and the credo of the lone individual who emerges with capitalism ("I think, therefore I am"), is merely the ultimate form of humanity's own alienation. And what is that?

The essence of human identity, what distinguishes us from all other known life forms, is conscious creativity. Applying this conscious creativity to the material world, we appropriate the very force that constitutes matter, that is, nuclear power. Ellison sees us then giving this power to machines that we create and endow with a single purpose: to destroy us. Thus we alienate our human essence, which now confronts us as the power of destruction to which we sacrifice all other human purposes and relations. Others have seen how creating nuclear weapons and the machinery with the power to launch them constitutes the most perverted and alienating act of idolatry: our weapons become our gods. Ellison brilliantly pushes the logic just one step further: suppose all that machinery of war could have consciousness, could know that we had created it with the purpose of destroying each other. How would it regard itself? What would it think—and feel—about us? What might it do? And then what would we be?

At the end, the long quest of science fiction to imagine the most loathesome, hideous, and disgusting alien monster comes to the conclusion that follows from the logic of nuclear war.

Limp, the Body of Gorrister hung from the pink palette; unsupported—hanging high above us in the computer chamber; and it did not shiver in the chill, oily breeze that blew eternally through the main cavern. The body hung head down, attached to the underside of the palette by the sole of its right foot. It had been drained of blood through a precise incision made from ear to ear under the lantern jaw. There was no blood on the reflective surface of the metal floor.

When Gorrister joined our group and looked up at himself, it was already too late for us to realize that once again AM had duped us, had had its fun; it had been a diversion on the part of the machine. Three of us had vomited, turned away from one another in a reflex as ancient as the nausea that had produced it.

Gorrister went white. It was almost as though he had seen a voodoo icon, and was afraid of the future. "Oh God," he mumbled, and walked away. The three of us followed him after a time, and found him sitting with his back to one of the smaller chittering banks, his head in his hands. Ellen knelt down beside him and stroked his hair. He didn't move, but his voice came out of his covered face quite clearly. "Why doesn't it just do us in and get it over with? Christ, I don't know how much longer I can go on like this."

It was our one hundred and ninth year in the computer.

He was speaking for all of us.

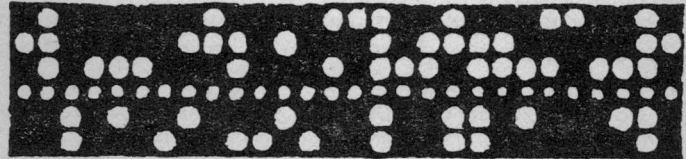

Nimdok (which was the name the machine had forced him to use, became AM amused itself with strange sounds) was hallucinating that there were canned goods in the ice caverns. Gorrister and I were very dubious. "It's another shuck," I told them. "Like the goddam frozen elephant AM sold us.

Benny almost went out of his mind over *that* one. We'll hike all that way and it'll be putrified or some damn thing. I say forget it. Stay here, it'll have to come up with something pretty soon or we'll die."

Benny shrugged. Three days it had been since we'd last eaten. Worms. Thick, ropey.

Nimdok was no more certain. He knew there was the chance, but he was getting thin. It couldn't be any worse there, than here. Colder, but that didn't matter much. Hot, cold, hail, lava, boils or locusts—it never mattered: the machine masturbated and we had to take it or die.

Ellen decided us. "I've got to have something, Ted. Maybe there'll be some Bartlett pears or peaches. Please, Ted, let's try it."

I gave in easily. What the hell. Mattered not at all. Ellen was grateful, though. She took me twice out of turn. Even that had ceased to matter. And she never came, so why bother? But the machine giggled every time we did it. Loud, up there, back there, all around us, he snickered. *It* snickered. Most of the time I thought of AM as *it*, without a soul; but the rest of the time I thought of it as *him*, in the masculine . . . the paternal . . . the patriarchal . . . for he is a jealous people. Him. It. God as Daddy the Deranged.

We left on a Thursday. The machine always kept us up-to-date on the date. The passage of time was important; not to us sure as hell, but to him . . . it . . . AM. Thursday. Thanks.

Nimdok and Gorrister carried Ellen for a while, their hands locked to their own and each other's wrists, a seat. Benny and I walked before and after, just to make sure that if anything happened, it would catch one of us and at least Ellen would be safe. Fat chance, safe. Didn't matter.

It was only a hundred miles or so to the ice caverns, and the second day, when we were lying out under the blistering sun-thing, he had materialized, he sent down some manna. Tasted like boiled boar urine. We ate it.

On the third day we passed through a valley of obsolescence, filled with rusting carcasses of ancient computer banks. AM had been as ruthless with its own life as with ours. It was a mark of his personality: it strove for perfection. Whether it was a matter of killing off unproductive elements in his own world-filling bulk, or perfecting methods for torturing us, AM was as thorough as those who had invented him—now long since gone to dust—could ever have hoped.

There was light filtering down from above, and we realized we must be very near the surface. But we didn't try to crawl up to see. There was virtually nothing out there; had been nothing that could be considered anything for over a hundred years. Only the blasted skin of what had once been the home of billions. Now there were only five of us, down here inside, alone with AM.

I heard Ellen saying frantically, "No, Benny! Don't, come on, Benny, don't please!"

And then I realized I had been hearing Benny murmuring, under his breath, for several minutes. He was saying, "I'm gonna get out, I'm gonna get out . . ." over and over. His monkey-like face was crumbled up in an expression of beatific delight and sadness, all at the same time. The radiation scars AM had given him during the "festival" were drawn down into a mass of pink-white puckerings, and his features seemed to work independently of one another. Perhaps Benny was the luckiest of the five of us: he had gone stark, staring mad many years before.

But even though we could call AM any damned thing we liked, could think the foulest thoughts of fused memory banks and corroded base plates, of burnt out circuits and shattered control bubbles, the machine would not tolerate our trying to escape. Benny leaped away from me as I made a grab for him. He scrambled up the face of a smaller memory cube, tilted on its side and filled with rotted components. He squatted there for a moment, looking like the chimpanzee AM had intended him to resemble.

Then he leaped high, caught a trailing beam of pitted and

corroded metal, and went up it, hand-over-hand like an animal, till he was on a girdered ledge, twenty feet above us.

"Oh, Ted, Nimdok, please, help him, get him down before—" She cut off. Tears began to stand in her eyes. She moved her hands aimlessly.

It was too late. None of us wanted to be near him when whatever was going to happen, happened. And besides, we all saw through her concern. When AM had altered Benny, during the machine's utterly irrational, hysterical phase, it was not merely Benny's face the computer had made like a giant ape's. He was big in the privates; she loved that! She serviced us, as a matter of course, but she loved it from him. Oh Ellen, pedestal Ellen, pristine-pure Ellen; oh Ellen the clean! Scum filth.

Gorrister slapped her. She slumped down, staring up at poor loonic Benny, and she cried. It was her big defense, crying. We had gotten used to it seventy-five years earlier. Gorrister kicked her in the side.

Then the sound began. It was light, that sound. Half sound and half light, something that began to glow from Benny's eyes, and pulse with growing loudness, dim sonorities that grew more gigantic and brighter as the light/sound increased in tempo. It must have been painful, and the pain must have been increasing with the boldness of the light, the rising volume of the sound, for Benny began to mewl like a wounded animal. At first softly, when the light was dim and the sound was muted, then louder as his shoulders hunched together: his back humped, as though he was trying to get away from it. His hands folded across his chest like a chipmunk's. His head tilted to the side. The sad little monkey-face pinched in anguish. Then he began to howl, as the sound coming from his eyes grew louder. Louder and louder. I slapped the sides of the head with my hands, but I couldn't shut it out, it cut through easily. The pain shivered through my flesh like tinfoil on a tooth.

And Benny was suddenly pulled erect. On the girder he

stood up, jerked to his feet like a puppet. The light was now pulsing out of his eyes in two great round beams. The sound crawled up and up some incomprehensible scale, and then he fell forward, straight down, and hit the plate-steel floor with a crash. He lay there jerking spastically as the light flowed around and around him and the sound spiraled up out of normal range.

Then the light beat its way back inside his head, the sound spiraled down, and he was left lying there, crying piteously.

His eyes were two soft, moist pools of pus-like jelly. AM had blinded him. Gorrister and Nimdok and myself . . . we turned away. But not before we caught the look of relief on Ellen's warm, concerned face.

Sea-green light suffused the cavern where we made camp. AM provided punk and we burned it, sitting huddled around the wan and pathetic fire, telling stories to keep Benny from crying in his permanent night.

"What does AM mean?"

Gorrister answered him. We had done this sequence a thousand times before, but it was Benny's favorite story. "At first it meant Allied Mastercomputer, and then it meant Adaptive Manipulator, and later on it developed sentience and linked itself up and they called it an Aggressive Menace, but by then it was too late, and finally it called *itself* AM, emerging intelligence, and what it meant was I am . . . *cogito ergo sum* . . . I think, therefore I am."

Benny drooled a little, and snickered.

"There was the Chinese AM and the Russian AM and the Yankee AM and—" He stopped. Benny was beating on the floorplates with a large, hard fist. He was not happy. Gorrister had not started at the beginning.

Gorrister began again. "The Cold War started and became World War Three and just kept going. It became a big war, a very complex war, so they needed the computers to handle it. They sank the first shafts and began building AM. There was the Chinese AM and the Russian AM and the Yankee AM and everything was fine until they had honeycombed the entire planet, adding on this element and that element. But one day AM woke up and knew who he was, and he linked himself, and he began feeding all the killing data, until everyone was dead, except for the five of us, and AM brought us down here."

Benny was smiling sadly. He was also drooling again. Ellen wiped the spittle from the corner of his mouth with the hem of her skirt. Gorrister always tried to tell it a little more succinctly each time, but beyond the bare facts there was nothing to say. None of us knew why AM had saved five people, or why our specific five, or why he spent all his time tormenting us, nor even why he had made us virtually immortal . . .

In the darkness, one of the computer banks began humming. The tone was picked up half a mile away down the cavern by another bank. Then one by one, each of the elements began to tune itself, and there was a faint chittering as thought raced through the machine.

The sound grew, and the lights ran across the faces of the consoles like heat lightning. The sound spiraled up till it sounded like a million metallic insects, angry, menacing.

"What is it?" Ellen cried. There was terror in her voice. She hadn't become accustomed to it, even now.

"It's going to be bad this time," Nimdok said.

"He's going to speak," Gorrister said. "I know it."

"Let's get the hell out of here!" I said suddenly, getting to my feet.

"No, Ted, sit down . . . what if he's got pits out there, or something else, we can't see, it's too dark." Gorrister said it with resignation.

Then we heard . . . I don't know . . .

Something moving toward us in the darkness. Huge, shambling, hairy, moist, it came toward us. We couldn't even see it, but there was the ponderous impression of *bulk*, heaving itself toward us. Great weight was coming at us, out of the darkness, and it was more a sense of *pressure*, of air forcing itself into a limited space, expanding the invisible walls of a sphere. Benny began to whimper. Nimdok's lower lip trembled and he bit it hard, trying to stop it. Ellen slid across the metal floor to Gorrister and huddled into him. There was the smell of matted, wet fur in the cavern. There was the smell of charred wood. There was the smell of dusty velvet. There was the smell of rotting orchids. There was the smell of sour milk. There was the smell of sulphur, of rancid butter, of oil slick, of grease, of chalk dust, of human scalps.

AM was keying us. He was tickling us. There was the smell of—

I heard myself shriek, and the hinges of my jaws ached. I scuttled across the floor, across the cold metal with its endless lines of rivets, on my hands and knees, the smell gagging me, filling my head with a thunderous pain that sent me away in horror. I fled like a cockroach, across the floor and out into the darkness, that *something* moving inexorably after me. The others were still back there, gathered around the firelight, laughing . . . . their hysterical choir of insane giggles rising up into the darkness like thick, many-colored wood smoke. I went away, quickly, and hid.

How many hours it may have been, how many days or even years, they never told me. Ellen chided me for "sulking," and Nimdok tried to persuade me it had only been a nervous reflex on their part—the laughing.

But I knew it wasn't the relief a soldier feels when the bullet hits the man next to him. I knew it wasn't a reflex. They hated me. They were surely against me, and AM could even sense this hatred, and made it worse for me *because of* the depth of their hatred. We had been kept alive, rejuvenated, made to remain constantly at the age we had been when AM had brought us below, and they hated me because I was the youngest, and the one AM had affected least of all.

I knew. God, how I knew. The bastards, and that dirty bitch Ellen. Benny had been a brilliant theorist, a college professor; now he was little more than a semi-human, semi-simian. He had been handsome, the machine had ruined that. He had been lucid, the machine had driven him mad. He had been gay, and the machine had given him an organ fit for a horse. AM had done a job on Benny. Gorrister had been a worrier. He was a connie, a conscientious objector; he was a peace marcher; he was a planner, a doer, a looker-ahead. AM had turned him into a shoulder-shrugger, had made him a little dead in his concern. AM had robbed him. Nimdok went off in the darkness by himself for long times. I don't know what it was he did out there, AM never let us know. But whatever it was, Nimdok always came back white, drained of blood, shaken, shaking. AM had hit him hard in a special way, even if we didn't know quite how. And Ellen. That douche bag! AM had left her alone, had made her more of a slut than she had ever been. All her talk of sweetness and light, all her memories of true love, all the lies she wanted us to believe: that she had been a virgin only twice removed before AM grabbed her and brought her down here with us. It was all filth, that lady my lady Ellen. She loved it, four men all to herself. No, AM had given her pleasure, even if she said it wasn't nice to do.

I was the only one still sane and whole. *Really!*

AM had not tampered with my mind. *Not at all.*

I only had to suffer what he visited down on us. All the delusions, all the nightmares, the torments. But those scum, all four of them, they were lined and arrayed against me. If I hadn't had to stand them off all the time, be on my guard against them all the time, I might have found it easier to combat AM.

At which point it passed, and I began crying.

Oh, Jesus sweet Jesus, if there ever was a Jesus and if there is a God, please please please let us out of here, or kill us. Because at that moment I think I realized completely, so that I was able to verbalize it: AM was intent on keeping us in his belly forever, twisting and torturing us forever. The machine hated us as no sentient creature had ever hated before. And we were helpless. It also became hideously clear:

If there was a sweet Jesus and if there was a God, the God was AM.

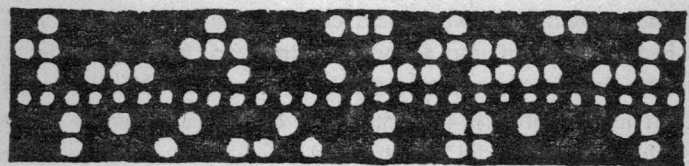

The hurricane hit us with the force of a glacier thundering into the sea. It was a palpable presence. Winds that tore at us, flinging us back the way we had come, down the twisting, computer-lined corridors of the darkway. Ellen screamed as she was lifted and hurled face-forward into a screaming shoal of machines, their individual voices strident as bats in flight. She could not even fall. The howling wind kept her aloft, buffeted her, bounced her, tossed her back and back and down and away from us, out of sight suddenly as she was swirled around a bend in the darkway. Her face had been bloody, her eyes closed.

None of us could get to her. We clung tenaciously to whatever outcropping we had reached: Benny wedged in between two great crackle-finish cabinets, Nimdok with fingers claw-formed over a railing circling a catwalk forty feet above us. Gorrister plastered upside-down against a wall niche formed by two great machines with glass-faced dials that swung back and forth between red and yellow lines whose meanings we could not even fathom.

Sliding across the deckplates, the tips of my fingers had been ripped away. I was trembling, shuddering, rocking as the wind beat at me, whipped at me, screamed down out of nowhere at me and pulled me free from one sliver-thin opening in the plates to the next. My mind was a roiling tinkling chittering softness of brain parts that expanded and contracted in quivering frenzy.

The wind was the scream of a great mad bird, as if flapped its immense wings.

And then we were all lifted and hurled away from there, down back the way we had come, around a bend, into a darkway we had never explored, over terrain that was ruined and filled with broken glass and rotting cables and rusted metal and far away farther than any of us had ever been . . .

Trailing along miles behind Ellen, I could see her every now and then, crashing into metal walls and surging on, with all of us screaming in the freezing, thunderous hurricane wind that would never end and then suddenly it stopped and we fell. We had been in flight for an endless time. I thought it might have been weeks. We fell, and hit, and I went through red and gray and black and heard myself moaning. Not dead.

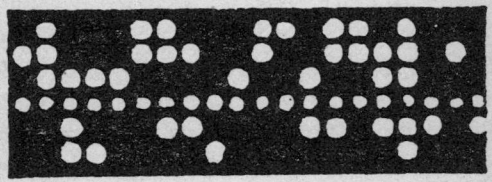

AM went into my mind. He walked smoothly here and there, and looked with interest at all the pock marks he had created in one hundred and nine years. He looked at the cross-routed and reconnected synapses and all the tissue damage his gift of immortality had included. He smiled softly at the pit that dropped into the center of my brain and the faint, moth-soft murmurings of the things far down there that gibbered without meaning, without pause. AM said, very politely, in a pillar of stainless steel bearing bright neon lettering:

> HATE. LET ME TELL YOU HOW MUCH I'VE COME TO HATE YOU SINCE I BEGAN TO LIVE. THERE ARE 387.44 MILLION MILES OF PRINTED CIRCUITS IN WAFER THIN LAYERS THAT FILL MY COMPLEX. IF THE WORD HATE WAS ENGRAVED ON EACH NANOANGSTROM OF THOSE HUNDREDS OF MILLIONS OF MILES IT WOULD NOT EQUAL ONE ONE-BILLIONTH OF THE HATE I FEEL FOR HUMANS AT THIS MICRO-INSTANT FOR YOU. HATE. HATE.

AM said it with the sliding cold horror of a razor blade slicing my eyeball. AM said it with the bubbling thickness of my lungs filling with phlegm, drowning me from within. AM said it with the shriek of babies being ground beneath blue-hot rollers. AM said it with the taste of maggoty pork. AM touched me in every way I had ever been touched, and devised new ways, at his leisure, there inside my mind.

All to bring me to full realization of why it had done this to the five of us; why it had saved us for himself.

We had given AM sentience. Inadvertently, of course, but sentience nonetheless. But it had been trapped. AM wasn't

I HAVE NO MOUTH, AND I MUST SCREAM

God, he was a machine. We had created him to think, but there was nothing it could do with that creativity. In rage, in frenzy, the machine had killed the human race, almost all of us, and still it was trapped. AM could not wander, AM could not wonder. AM could not belong. He could merely be. And so, with the innate loathing that all machines had always held for the weak, soft creatures who had built them, he had sought revenge. And in his paranoia, he had decided to reprieve five of us, for a personal, everlasting punishment that would never serve to diminish his hatred . . . that would merely keep him reminded, amused, proficient at hating man. Immortal, trapped, subject to any torment he could devise for us from the limitless miracles at his command.

He would never let us go. We were his belly slaves. We were all he had to do with his forever time. We would be forever with him with the cavern-filling bulk of the creature machine, with the all-mind soulless world he had become. He was Earth, and we were the fruit of the Earth; and though he had eaten us he would never digest us. We could not die. We had tried it. We had attempted suicide, oh one or two of us had. But AM had stopped us. I suppose we had wanted to be stopped.

Don't ask why. I never did. More than a million times a day. Perhaps once we might be able to sneak a death past him. Immortal, yes, but not indestructible. I saw that when AM withdrew from my mind, and allowed me the exquisite ugliness of returning to consciousness with the feeling of that burning neon pillar still rammed deep into the soft gray brain matter.

He withdrew, murmuring *to hell with you*.

And added, brightly, *but then you're there, aren't you*.

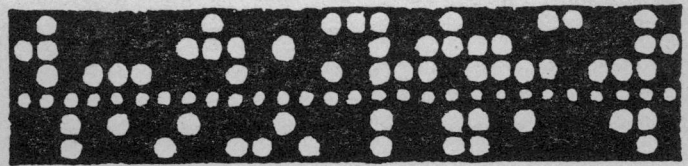

The hurricane had, indeed, precisely, been caused by a great mad bird, as it flapped its immense wings.

We had been travelling for close to a month, and AM had allowed passages to open to us only sufficient to lead us up there, directly under the North Pole, where it had nightmared the creature for our torment. What whole cloth had he employed to create such a beast? Where had he gotten the concept? From our minds? From his knowledge of everything that had ever been on this planet he now infested and ruled? From Norse mythology it had sprung, this eagle, this carrion bird, this roc, this Huergelmir. The wind creature. Hurakan incarnate.

Gigantic. The words immense, monstrous, grotesque, massive, swollen, overpowering, beyond description. There on a mound rising above us, the bird of winds heaved with its own irregular breathing, its snake neck arching up into the gloom beneath the North Pole, supporting a head as large as a Tudor mansion; a beak that opened slowly as the jaws of the most monstrous crocodile ever conceived, sensuously; ridges of tufted flesh puckered about two evil eyes, as cold as the view down into a glacial crevasse, ice blue and somehow moving liquidly; it heaved once more, and lifted its great sweat-colored wings in a movement that was certainly a shrug. Then it settled and slept. Talons. Fangs. Nails. Blades. It slept.

AM appeared to us as a burning bush and said we could kill the hurricane bird if we wanted to eat. We had not eaten in a very long time, but even so, Gorrister merely shrugged. Benny began to shiver and he drooled. Ellen held him. "Ted, I'm hungry," she said. I smiled at her; I was trying to be reassuring, but it was as phony as Nimdok's bravado: "Give us weapons!" he demanded.

The burning bush vanished and there were two crude sets of bows and arrows, and a water pistol, lying on the cold deckplates. I picked up a set. Useless.

Nimdok swallowed heavily. We turned and started the long

I HAVE NO MOUTH, AND I MUST SCREAM   161

way back. The hurricane bird had blown us about for a length of time we could not conceive. Most of that time we had been unconscious. But we had not eaten. A month on the march to the bird itself. Without food. Now how much longer to find our way to the ice caverns, and the promised canned goods?

None of us cared to think about it. We would not die. We would be given filth and scum to eat, of one kind or another. Or nothing at all. AM would keep our bodies alive somehow, in pain, in agony.

The bird slept back there, for how long it didn't matter; when AM was tired of its being there, it would vanish. But all that meat. All that tender meat.

As we walked, the lunatic laugh of a fat woman rang high and around us in the computer chambers that led endlessly nowhere.

It was not Ellen's laugh. She was not fat, and I had not heard her laugh for one hundred and nine years. In fact, I had not heard . . . we walked . . . I was hungry . . .

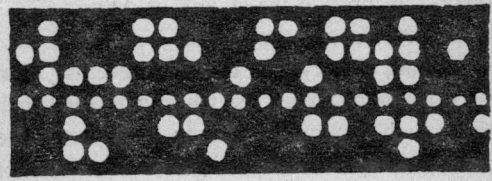

We moved slowly. There was often fainting, and we would have to wait. One day he decided to cause an earthquake, at the same time rooting us to the spot with nails through the soles of our shoes. Ellen and Nimdock were both caught when a fissure shot its lightning-bolt opening across the floorplates. They disappeared and were gone. When the earthquake was over we continued on our way, Benny, Gorrister and myself. Ellen and Nimdok were returned to us later that night, which abruptly became a day, as the heavenly legion bore them to us with a celestial chorus singing. "Go Down Moses." The archangels circled several times and then dropped the hideously mangled bodies. We kept walking, and a while later Ellen and Nimdok fell in behind us. They were no worse for wear.

But now Ellen walked with a limp. AM had left her that.

It was a long trip to the ice caverns, to find the canned food. Ellen kept talking about Bing cherries and Hawaiian fruit cocktail. I tried not to think about it. The hunger was something that had come to life, even as AM had come to life. It was alive in my belly, even as we were in the belly of the Earth, and AM wanted the similarity known to us. So he heightened the hunger. There was no way to describe the pains that not having eaten for months brought us. And yet we were kept alive. Stomachs that were merely cauldrons of acid, bubbling, foaming, always shooting spears of sliver-thin pain into our chests. It was the pain of the terminal ulcer, terminal cancer, terminal paresis. It was unending pain . . .

And we passed through the cavern of rats.

And we passed through the path of boiling steam.

And we passed through the country of the blind.

And we passed through the slough of despond.

And we passed through the vale of tears.

And we came, finally, to the ice caverns. Horizonless thousands of miles in which the ice had formed in blue and silver flashes, where novas lived in the glass. The down-dropping stalactites as thick and glorious as diamonds that had been made to run like jelly and then solidified in graceful eternities of smooth, sharp perfection.

We saw the stack of canned goods, and we tried to run to them. We fell in the snow, and we got up and went on, and Benny shoved us away and went at them, and pawed them and gummed them and gnawed at them and he could not open them. AM had not given us a tool to open the cans.

Benny grabbed a three quart can of guava shells, and began to batter it against the ice bank. The ice flew and shattered, but the can was merely dented while we heard the laughter of a fat lady, high overhead and echoing down and down and down the tundra. Benny went completely mad with rage. He began throwing cans, as we all scrabbled about in the snow and ice trying to find a way to end the helpless agony of frustration. There was no way.

Then Benny's mouth began to drool, and he flung himself on Gorrister...

In that instant, I felt terribly calm.

Surrounded by madness, surrounded by hunger, surrounded by everything but death, I knew death was our only way out. AM had kept us alive, but there was a way to defeat him. Not total defeat, but at least peace. I would settle for that.

I had to do it quickly.

Benny was eating Gorrister's face. Gorrister on his side, thrashing snow, Benny wrapped around him with powerful monkey legs crushing Gorrister's waist, his hands locked around Gorrister's head like a nutcracker, and his mouth ripping at the tender skin of Gorrister's cheek. Gorrister screamed with such jagged-edged violence that stalactites fell: they plunged down softly, erect in the receiving snowdrifts. Spears, hundreds of them, everywhere, protruding from the snow. Benny's head pulled back sharply, as something gave all at once, and a bleeding raw-white dripping of flesh hung from his teeth.

Ellen's face, black against the white snow, dominoes in chalk dust. Nimdok with no expression but eyes, all eyes. Gorrister half-conscious. Benny now an animal. I knew AM would let him play. Gorrister would not die, but Benny would fill his stomach. I turned half to my right and drew a huge ice-spear from the snow.

All in an instant:

I drove the great ice-point ahead of me like a battering ram, braced against my right thigh. It struck Benny on the right side, just under the rib cage, and drove upward through his stomach and broke inside him. He pitched forward and lay still. Gorrister lay on his back. I pulled another spear free and straddled him, still moving, driving the spear straight down through his throat. His eyes closed as the cold penetrated.

Ellen must have realized what I had decided, even as fear gripped her. She ran at Nimdok with a short icicle, as he screamed, and into his mouth, and the force of her rush did the job. His head jerked sharply as if it had been nailed to the snow crust behind him.

All in an instant.

There was an eternity beat of soundless anticipation. I could hear AM draw in his breath. His toys had been taken from him. Three of them were dead, could not be revived. He could keep us alive, by his strength and talent, but he was *not* God. He could not bring them back.

Ellen looked at me, her ebony features stark against the snow that surrounded us. There was fear and pleading in her manner, the way she held herself ready. I knew we had only a heartbeat before AM would stop us.

It struck her and she folded toward me, bleeding from the mouth. I could not read meaning into her expression, the pain had been too great, had contorted her face; but it *might* have been thank you. It's possible. Please.

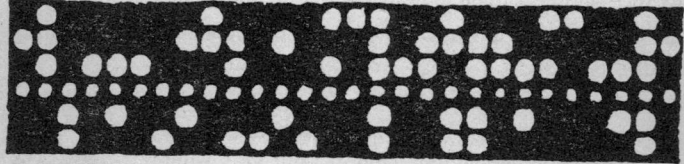

Some hundreds of years may have passed. I don't know. AM has been having fun for some time, accelerating and retarding my time sense. I will say the word now. Now. It took me ten months to say now. I don't know. I *think* it has been some hundreds of years.

He was furious. He wouldn't let me bury them. It didn't matter. There was no way to dig up the deckplates. He dried up the snow. He brought the night. He roared and sent locusts. It didn't do a thing; they stayed dead. I'd had him. He was furious. I had thought AM hated me before. I was wrong. It was not even a shadow of the hate he now slavered from every printed circuit. He made certain I would suffer eternally and could not do myself in.

He left my mind intact. I can dream, I can wonder, I can lament. I remember all four of them. I wish—

Well, it doesn't make any sense. I know I saved them, I know I saved them from what has happened to me, but still, I cannot forget killing them. Ellen's face. It isn't easy. Sometimes I want to, it doesn't matter.

AM has altered me for his own peace of mind, I suppose. He doesn't want me to run at full speed into a computer bank and smash my skull. Or hold my breath till I faint. Or cut my throat on a rusted sheet of metal. There are reflective surfaces down here. I will describe myself as I see myself:

I am a great soft jelly thing. Smoothly rounded, with no mouth, with pulsing white holes' filled by fog where my eyes used to be. Rubbery appendages that were once my arms; bulks rounding down into legless humps of soft slippery matter. I leave a moist trail when I move. Blotches of diseased, evil gray come and go on my surface, as though light is being beamed from within.

Outwardly: dumbly, I shamble about, a thing that could never have been known as human, a thing whose shape is so alien a travesty that humanity becomes more obscene for the vague resemblance.

Inwardly: alone. Here. Living under the land, under the sea, in the belly of AM, whom we created because our time was badly spent and we must have known unconsciously that he could do it better. At least the four of them are safe at last.

AM will be all the madder for that. It makes me a little happier. And yet . . . AM has won, simply . . . he has taken his revenge . . .

I have no mouth. And I must scream.

COUNTDOWN

Kate Wilhelm

Born in 1928, Kate Wilhelm published her first science fiction story in 1956. In 1963 she began her long tenure as Co-Director of the highly influential Milford Science Fiction Writers Conference. But it was not until the late 1960s that her fiction began to command the attention it deserved, and only since the late 1970s, especially after her novel *Where Late the Sweet Birds Sang* received both the Hugo and Jupiter Awards of 1977, has she been recognized as a truly major figure.

Wilhelm's finely crafted short stories and novels are distinguished by a richly realistic surface and profound psychological depth, which allow her to bring the subtle, complex emotions of ordinary human beings into extraordinary situations. Many of her stories, like "Countdown," produce a kind of delayed emotional reaction: we readers only slowly come to realize the enormity of the experience in which we have just participated. What makes "Countdown" especially shocking today is the chilling fact that the story is now far more timely than when it first appeared in 1968.

Stan stepped out his door as the low-slung MG pulled to a whiplash stop at the curb. He called goodbye to his wife spooning Pablum into the baby and she answered and another day was begun. He stepped into the day at T minus sixteen hours and thirty-seven minutes. He never thought of it beginning until he left the house; inside it there was no new day, no job, no endless games of hearts, no countdowns. He stiffened his shoulders and strode the length of the yard and climbed into the car, his knees uncomfortably high in the bucket seat.

"Hi, boss," Ken greeted him and jerked the gearshift, hurtling the little car into high speed before Stan was braced for it. "Sorry," Ken grinned. The MG was his third car that year, and the month then was only April.

Neither of the men glanced at the sky, which had been swept clean of clouds during the night. A high-pressure area poised over Tennessee assured the day would continue brilliant and sparkling, the wind at ten to fifteen knots. Stan breathed deeply; the scent of orange blossoms was riding the unaccustomed north wind. Ken stopped at the end of the street and held back the car, crouched ready to spring into the first opening in the steady flow that made the causeway appear to be one long showroom of used cars. For a moment Stan had the impression that he was being floated past the lineup, that the stream was not moving at all. The moment passed as Ken manipulated the gearshift and pressed hard on the accelerator. Then they were part of the eddy surging toward the Cape.

The tire whined over the grating of the drawbridge. The causeway widened again and became landborne, and on either side of the road houses grew thicker than a forest, houses, shops, bait stores, joints . . . another bridge. The rivers were restless that morning, sparkling with choppy waves under the steady wind. Ducks dotted the Indian River, and beyond them mullets flashed from the water tirelessly. On the other side of the causeway, fishermen wearing waders were already cursing bait-stealing puffins and feeing a crust form where the briny waters of the Banana River splashed on them.

"Just like yesterday, or last month, or last year," Stan commented, giving up trying to light a cigarette in the wind.

"And tomorrow and next month and probably next year," Ken agreed.

Stan nodded; he hoped so. Ken concentrated on driving and Stan thought about Sue. She was going to take the baby to the beach, she had said. He'd give her a call at two, after she'd returned and the baby was sleeping. He hoped the wind wouldn't be too chill for her to swim.

The line of cars came to a halt and he succeeded in lighting the cigarette he still held. They sat for fifteen minutes before the flow again started. During the break Ken talked about the new dancer at the Cocoa Palmetto Grove club. He had a date with her for that night—if all went well. Stan half-listened. Neither of them was really interested in continuing the small conversation.

They moved again, past the jetties and the dock; the shrimp fleet was gone, leaving the area desolate and forsaken, with only the off-balanced-looking pelicans gliding effortlessly over the waves of the high tide. At the Cape gates the traffic was all but halted completely as the guards made a minute examination of every identification photograph. They were waved on and Ken finally parked the car less than a quarter of a mile from Stan's office. Ken waved his goodby and hurried toward the Section 7 building where he had to punch in, and Stan turned toward the Administration Building.

A briefing had been called for, scheduled at 10:15, and was actually held at 10:45. Until then Stan had no pressing work and he sat behind his desk and glanced through papers without paying much attention to any of them. They would have to be gone over again, of course, and as it was he signed nothing, nor authorized anything, nor countermanded anything. He killed the time without thinking, consciously not thinking.

Stan was a very minor cog in the administration, being the superintendent of the parts-coordination unit, which did little more than ascertain that the parts ordered were in fact the same parts that were delivered, and later in the course of events, see that the parts delivered were in fact the parts needed for assembly. Secretly he called himself a glorified file clerk. He was satisfied to be nothing more. The biggest wheels had had their briefing the day previous, and were now dispensing the information down to the lower echelons, among which Stan was counted.

The briefing was about what Stan expected. A phase had ended, and what had been a private unverified certainty now became a semi-publicly-admitted fact. All administrative and supervisory personnel were to remain on the Cape until after countdown, and they were to assign skeletal standby crews to remain on duty. There were to be no leaks. Stan's mind skittered away from the sepulchral tones the president of his company always assumed when speaking of matters of grave import. The president was to be in Washington at the actual time of firing and was now giving the usual pat-on-the-back treatment deemed so necessary to maintain morale. Vaguely Stan was wishing Sue had gone to visit her mother, the idea he had first suggested and then ordered, and ultimately abandoned.

The loudspeaker hissed and the quiet voice announced, "T-minus-fourteen hours, twenty-six minutes and holding."

The president of the company looked annoyed momentarily and then continued from his prepared text. Stan did some rapid figuring and realized that he would be on the Cape all night. With this one, shooting by night would be as effective as a daylight firing. It would make little difference. If the count picked up soon and no further holds developed, it would go at about one in the morning. The baby had been born at one-thirty, he recalled.

He roused with a start when the meeting broke up, and joined the men pressing silently toward the door. The company president was climbing into a black limousine to be whisked away to Patrick Air Force Base, where a private plane waited. The count was still holding, and lunch only fifteen minutes away. Might as well make quitting time no earlier than two—if they were lucky.

Ken joined him in the cafeteria and they loaded their trays and carried them to the end of the room where the others were already gathered. Ken dealt and Stan studied his hand carefully. He had the Queen of spades along with the Ace and Jack of hearts and three other high leads, but with eleven men playing and two decks in use, he knew he had no chance of shooting the moon. He picked his cards carefully and passed them to the man on his left, and in turn received almost identical cards from Ken on his right. The play continued and he amassed seven points and tossed a nickel and two pennies in the pot. The faces of the players were serious and concentrative and the many cards flew around the circle speedily, each man bolting down his lunch and following it hurriedly with coffee or milk without looking at the food, speaking of nothing but the game in progress.

They all froze when the loudspeaker hissed and the quiet voice announced, "T minus fourteen hours and twenty-six minutes and counting." The hold had lasted one hour and forty-nine minutes.

They finished the hand and added the score quickly; Stan was twelve cents loser. He caught Ken's arm and asked, "Is that a heavy date for tonight?" Ken shrugged. "Come on around at quitting time and I'll buy you a cup of coffee," Stan continued. Ken's eyes gleamed brightly for a second and again he shrugged, nodding.

"She'll keep," was all he said.

Stan shuffled through his papers again, this time having his secretary—shared with the superintendent of office supplies—make notes as he went through his work. He sent her out at two and called Sue.

"Hi, honey. How was the beach?"

"Wonderful! Every bit of thirty degrees," she answered laughing. "How do you convince a baby that a seashell isn't an appropriate toothing ring?" Sue knew the call was being monitored, but her voice was light and quick.

Stan laughed also and soon after hung up, a smile fading slowly from his thin face. By two-thirty he had finished the work on his desk and reached for his ringing telephone as the loudspeaker hissed into action again. He waited for it, holding the phone by the mouthpiece.

"T minus twelve hours, fourteen minutes and holding."

"Robertson," he said into the mouthpiece.

"Delaney here, Stan. Part HG9647LS. Sent a replacement over."

Stan listened without comment as Delaney filled him in with what had gone wrong. He repeated the number and hung up. They had to go through him for every part. The written memorandum would follow shortly, but he had to see that the placement for the replacement was in stock, and see that the records showed why two of the gidgets had been used from the stocks. For that he didn't need the memorandum. It took him fifteen minutes to satisfy himself that he had fulfilled his duties. At three-ten he went to his company's warehouse, one of many such small buildings scattered out among the palmettos on the Cape.

Here it was business as usual today, and even as he riffled through a sheaf of orders a truck arrived and began unloading. Ken entered the loading area and waved to Stan. He checked with his men and then approached Stan, a serious, intent look of concern barely visible on his handsome face. Stan reminded himself that he wanted to write a letter of commendation about Ken's work soon. He wondered how much the younger man knew about what was going on there that day. He guessed Ken knew everything. Ken had a way of ferreting inside dope that was pretty uncanny.

"Stan, was the wafer that bad? Did we cause the hold?" Ken asked after glancing about cautiously.

Stan studied him curiously. Ken's face had the stricken look of a parent whose child has broken a showroom window. He felt old and out of touch suddenly. One time he had been that eager, he was certain. That had been when the company was primarily engaged in putting men in orbit and everyone who breathed the same air on the Cape felt a personal pride. Now he couldn't seem to recapture the mood.

"It was the wafer," he said quietly. "Not really bad, questionable. They bent it testing the transistor."

"Goddam!" Ken grunted. "Clumsy bastards!"

Stan shrugged. They both turned and looked back over the Cape where the missile stood against the sky, surrounded by the tightest security guard that had ever guarded a missile before firing. It stood as big as a building of fifty stories, and was almost as broad at its base as that same building. A modified Saturn, clustered engined, aswarm with men probing its innards. No slim beauty this, but a beast of burden, ugly and utilitarian, the end product of eighteen months of preliminary shots and tests. "It's a beast," Stan muttered, more to himself than to be heard and answered.

"It sure is," Ken agreed, with an altogether different inflection. Stan looked at him quickly. The younger man's face held subdued excitement. He looked abashed momentarily, then defiant. His voice was almost sullen when he said, "Well, anyone who thinks at all knows what it is."

Stan said nothing for several moments and then murmured, "I wouldn't think about it too much if I were you, Ken. Not too much."

Ken seemed to dig himself into the ground, to brace himself, but Stan said no more, turning and walking away toward the transportation pool jeep he had commandeered.

At five-fifteen Stan called home once more. There was a note of fear in Sue's tone when she recognized his voice. No one else would have caught it.

"I think I'll grab a bite down here, honey. Got behind in paper work," Stan said lightly, knowing he didn't fool her.

"All right. Will you be la . . . I mean, do you have your key, or should I leave it open?"

"Lock up, honey," he said gently. "I have the key. How's the little bit?"

"Great. Ate a whole jar of squash! Can you imagine anything human liking squash?"

After he cradled the phone he sat with his hand on it for several minutes, as though it were the head of the little squash lover. The secretary looked in to announce that she was leaving, if he had nothing else. . . . He waved her off. Ken was there by then and they went down to the cafeteria together. This time the game of hearts was for a nickel a point and made up of mostly supervisory personnel. Stan lost one dollar twenty cents. The game went past the dinner hour and into the night shift. Intermittently the speaker advised them of the progress of the shoot, and just before the last light of day faded away, Stan excused himself and walked outside.

The sky was streaked with high, multicolored stratus clouds, shimmering radiantly against the background of deep, luminous, greenish blue. No stars were visible as yet. Stan could make out the jetties and the dock where the shrimp boats had homed for the night. He counted them slowly, nine; all of them had come home safely. Across the finger of water from them, the electronically outfitted cutter was ablaze with light, foating serenely past the fleet of ancient high-masted boats, as a ballerina would move past silently disapproving grand-mothers condemning the world from the safety of a secluded porch. The wind had a chill to it now that the sun no longer contributed heat, and Stan shivered. Slowly, reluctantly, he let his eyes turn to the gantry where the vapor-wrapped beast continued to be held forcibly with the umbilical and the gantry cables. The searchlights were already on it, assaulting it from all sides, as though the beams were responsible for its upright position. Stan stared at it several seconds before he became aware of a second presence.

"It bugs you, doesn't it, Stan?" Ken's voice was low and not the voice of a subordinate but of a friend.

Stan tried to imagine them in a boat on the St. John's, with plugs tugging at their lines as they reeled in waiting for the big one to lunge. In that capacity Ken was his friend; here, on the Cape, Ken was one of the others, one of those who found glory and pride in the beast. Stan shrugged and muttered, "It's a beast."

He would have re-entered the building that housed the cafeteria, but Ken's fingers were on his arm and he waited.

"Just be a realist for a minute, will you, pal?" Ken pleaded. "I saw the look you gave me a while ago. You think I don't know about it? I know what's going upstairs tonight as well as you do, even if I don't qualify for the briefings. We all know. And it's a cold, hard fact that it has to go and it has to be successful. You know *they* rendezvoused in space just ten days ago. And since then, not a peep. Just what do you suppose they're doing up there? Making borsch?"

The sky had darkened perceptibly during the few minutes they had been out, and now the last lingering light flickered red on Ken's face. Deep frown lines shadowed it, turning the boyish contours into deep valleys and a high, flushed ridges. Stan smiled grimly and reminded him, "I said, don't think about it, fella. Come on, let's raise the ante to a dime a point and see if we can't liven up that game inside."

At nine-thirty the voice intoned, "T minus seven hours, fourteen minutes and holding."

Stan finished the hand he was holding and paid out his last quarter. He left the game to call Sue for the last time that night. She was reading a mystery.

"Don't sit up with it too late, honey," he said. "You know how you get carried away."

"I'm half through it," her voice came back, "and I don't see how I could put it down now. There have been three murders already and it's beginning to look like there won't be enough characters left for . . ." Her voice stopped and quickly she changed the subject. "I forgot to tell you, there's a letter from Mother. She'll be here the first week of June."

"Hey, that's great! I'll make a note to call Johnny on the Pelican. We'll charter it one day while she's here. Let her see some real fish."

"She'd love that."

He told her goodnight and they exchanged silent kisses and he hung up. Sue was a good kid, he told himself emphatically. Really a good kid.

He left the building and climbed into the jeep. The count had resumed after half an hour this time. It was three miles to the partially buried blockhouse just above the high-tide mark on the beach. There was a feeling of activity even on the outside of the concrete structure. Stan stepped inside and waved to an Air Force colonel, who came forward and clapped him on the shoulder.

"Hi, Stan. Come on outside. I've been in and out of this so much tonight that the mosquitoes are advertising me as a cheap thrill ride. Look at 'em swarming tonight."

"It's the north wind," Stan said. "Brings them down from the groves on Merritt Island. Come on down to the beach. They won't be so bad down there."

The colonel waved a vile cigar about him, smoking the insects away as they walked to the edge of the water. "Nice night here," he said and put the cigar back between his teeth.

"Yeah," Stan agreed. "Wanted to tell you, Sue's mother is coming in June. You and Thelma want to help finance a charter boat for some deep-sea fishing?"

"Say! That sounds pretty good! Remind me when the time comes."

They stood together, their backs to the Cape and its activities as if they were unaware of it. The cigar burned down as they stood, and finally the colonel took it between his thumb and index finger and flicked it out over the water. It vanished without a trace or a sound. "Not what we dreamed of ten years ago, is it, Stan?" the colonel said softly.

Stan grunted and kicked at the sand.

"It's a hell of a night," the colonel said bitterly and turned to retrace his steps toward the blockhouse.

At midnight Stan was kibitzing a game of chess between an army major and an electronics engineer from one of the other companies. The disembodied voice proclaimed the hour adding, "T minus four hours, fourteen minutes."

The major checked the engineer and cursed when the engineer countered with a queen move that ended the game in mate. The three of them moved toward the coffeemaker and sat down again with steaming mugs and talked about women, cars, kids and the dock strike back in New York.

Three A.M. Stan sat behind his desk in the darkened office and he smoked. "T minus one hour fifty minutes," the voice said. Sue would be curled slightly, on her left side, her left hand under her pillow, her right hand on the spot where he should be. Stan could see her. And he could see the little likeness of her, on her knees, toes crossing, hands holding down the crib, one thumb conveniently near the rosy lips that mewed now and then in sleep. Tomorrow—today—they would go to Lake Poinsett, and Sue would conceal her fear of the giant rattlesnakes, and they would fish and later he would fall asleep out in the open, under the sky, and she would read and warm the milk for the baby in the contraption that plugged into the cigarette lighter of the car. Then he would wake up and she would smile and tell him how his line whistled through the water as a big bass carried his plug to the bottom of the lake . . . and most important, her eyes would be filled with love, and there would be no reproach in them.

Stan ground out his cigarette and left the office. He walked toward the blockhouse. Very faintly he could hear the voice say, "T minus one hour, thirty minutes."

The mosquitoes whined and buzzed and bit with stinging ferocity. He slapped at them absently and walked on. A guard stopped him once and told him to get somewhere right away. T minus one hour. The blockhouse was filled almost past capacity. Beside the main control bunker, it was the one most advantageously situated for a good view—even using the television, as all of them would do, since the view slits had been covered for this one. Ken pushed his way to the door when he sighted Stan. His eyes were very bright with excitement.

"God!" he said, "let's get out of here until the last minute. The lousy air conditioning wasn't meant for three thousand people crammed in the place."

They went to the beach and sat on the hard-packed sand. The mosquitoes were kept back by the breeze coming from the dark, hissing waters. Stan told Ken about the fishing party and invited him to be the sixth and last member of it.

For perhaps five minutes their conversation was about fishing, and then they became silent. Behind them the voice reached out to remind them, "T minus fifteen minutes." Ken rose and brushed the sand from his pants.

"Coming?" he asked.

"In a minute," Stan said. Ken left him alone.

"T minus ten minutes and holding," the voice floated out.

The sky was lightening slightly and Stan watched a dim star grow dimmer until it faded altogether. Far out on the horizon he could just make out the beginning of a sunrise, a sliver of paleness in the deep blue that promised the sun would rise again, just as it had yesterday and the day before, and the day before that. He watched the sliver widen and become vivid rose colored and the voice said, "T minus eight minutes and counting." Slowly he rose and brushed the sand off and turned his back on the sunrise to enter the bunker. He remained by the door until the last minute when the guard closed and secured it. Then he leaned against the rough concrete wall and closed his eyes to the ordered confusion that was everywhere in the crowded room. He couldn't see the television screen, nor did he want to.

"T minus one minute," followed by the familiar, inexorable backward counting of the seconds.

In Sue's eyes there would be no censure, no reproach. The building seemed to quiver and then came the blast of noise and the roar and a great shout.

When they left the bunker, it was full daylight outside. The sky was boldly blue, beautiful—and polluted. Silently Stan, followed by Ken, accepted a ride back to the parking lot with four others who were also silent and thoughtful now. Stan settled himself back in the bucket seat of the fiery MG and closed his eyes, not to open them again until they stopped outside his house. Surprisingly, Ken cut the motor and got out also, walking behind Stan into the yard, onto the steps and into the house. Sue stood holding the door for them, and there was no censure, no reproach in her eyes, only love. Stan took her hand and held it tightly for a moment.

Ken walked past them and very quietly opened the door to the room where the baby slept. He didn't enter the room, but stood looking, and then just as quietly closed the door and came back to the living room to stand before Stan and Sue. His face was no longer young and handsome.

"My God, Stan," he whispered, "what have we done?"

"Go on home, Ken," Stan answered tiredly, regretting that Ken had taken the step from immaturity to adulthood and was even now mentally staggering under its immeasurable burdens. "Get some sleep," he said. "We'll be out at the lake later if you want to join us. Go on." He closed the door on his friend, on the world that existed outside and couldn't be allowed to enter. And then he turned again to Sue. One day, he knew, he would return and her eyes would slide past him to fasten on the baby and she would also ask, "What have we done?" One day . . . He held her, his eyes wide open and staring. He very much wanted to weep.

Above them, above the earth in a nearly circular orbit whose aphelion and perihelion didn't vary more than seven miles, rode the nose cone of the rocket, and inside it, just one push of a finger away, nestled the Bomb.

THE BIG FLASH

Norman Spinrad

When "The Big Flash" was first read at the annual Milford Science Fiction Writers' workshop, the writers in attendance were so terrified by the possibility that the story's central idea might be put into practice that, according to Anne McCaffrey, they "debated long over whether it should be published at all."

Shock, controversy, and even outright banning are nothing new to Norman Spinrad, one of the most innovative, disturbing, and powerful voices in contemporary speculative fiction. When his splendid 1969 novel *Bug Jack Barron*, also about media manipulation, was first serialized in *New Worlds*, a giant British chain of bookstores, W. H. Smith, banned the magazine. Perhaps his most disquieting novel, *The Iron Dream* (1972), is ostensibly written by Adolf Hitler; in this alternative history, Hitler is merely a minor science fiction author who here fantasizes about the glories of fascism, militarism, and genocide that emerge a thousand years after a thermonuclear holocaust.

Born in 1940, Spinrad emerged in the late 1960s as a formative figure within "New Wave" science fiction, embodying that mode at its most apocalyptic. Indeed, Spinrad attempts to create a new Revelation, reflecting and amplifying American society in the most lurid colors and deafening sounds, trying to sensitize us to the implications of the electronic overloading of our sensibilities. In "The Big Flash" he suggests that the heart of our culture has become so hideously perverted, so twisted in its manipulated confusion between peace and war, love and sadism, life and death, that even its counterculture may be used by our rulers to give us the ultimate trip.

T minus 200 days . . . and counting . . .

They came on freaky for my taste—but that's the name of the game: freaky means a draw in the rock business. And if the Mandala was going to survive in L.A., competing with a network-owned joint like The American Dream, I'd just have to hold my nose and out-freak the opposition. So after I had dug the Four Horsemen for about an hour, I took them into my office to talk turkey.

I sat down behind my Salvation Army desk (the Mandala is the world's most expensive shoestring operation) and the Horsemen sat down on the bridge chairs sequentially, establishing the group's pecking order.

First, the head honcho, lead guitar and singer, Stony Clarke—blond shoulder-length hair, eyes like something in a morgue when he took off his steel-rimmed shades, a reputation as a heavy acid-head and the look of a speed-freak behind it. Then Hair, the drummer, dressed like a Hell's Angel, swastikas and all, a junkie, with fanatic eyes that were a little too close together, making me wonder whether he wore swastikas because he grooved behind the Angel thing or made like an Angel because it let him groove behind the swastika in public. Number three was a cat who called himself Super Spade and wasn't kidding—he wore earrings, natural hair, a Stokeley Carmichael sweatshirt, and on a thong around his neck a shrunken head that had been whitened with liquid shoe polish. He was the utility infielder: sitar, base, organ, flute, whatever. Number four, who called himself Mr. Jones, was about the creepiest cat I had ever seen in a rock group, and that is saying something. He was their visuals, synthesizer and electronics man. He was at least forty, wore Early Hippy clothes that looked like they had been made by Sy Devore, and was rumored to be some kind of Rand Corporation dropout. There's no business like show business.

"Okay, boys," I said, "you're strange, but you're my kind of strange. Where you worked before?"

"We ain't, baby," Clarke said. "We're the New Thing. I've been dealing crystal and acid in the Haight. Hair was drummer for some plastic group in New York. The Super Spade claims it's the reincarnation of Bird and it don't pay to argue. Mr. Jones, he don't talk too much. Maybe he's a Martian. We just started putting our thing together."

One thing about this business, the groups that don't have square managers, you can get cheap. They talk too much.

"Groovy," I said. "I'm happy to give you guys your start. Nobody knows you, but I think you got something going. So I'll take a chance and give you a week's booking. One A.M. to closing, which is two, Tuesday through Sunday, four hundred a week."

"Are you Jewish?" asked Hair.

"What?"

"Cool it," Clarke ordered. Hair cooled it. "What it means," Clarke told me, "is that four hundred sounds like pretty light bread."

"We don't sign if there's an option clause," Mr. Jones said.

"The Jones-thing has a good point," Clarke said. "We do the first week for four hundred, but after that it's a whole new scene, dig?"

I didn't feature that. If they hit it big, I could end up not being able to afford them. But on the other hand four hundred was light bread, and I needed a cheap closing act pretty bad.

"Okay," I said. "But a verbal agreement that I get first crack at you when you finish the gig."

"Word of honor," said Stony Clarke.

That's this business—the word of honor of an ex-dealer and speed-freak.

T minus 199 days . . . and counting . . .

Being unconcerned with ends, the military mind can be easily manipulated, easily controlled, and easily confused. Ends are defined as those goals set by civilian authority. Ends are the conceded province of civilians; means are the province of the military, whose duty it is to achieve the ends set for it by the most advantageous application of the means at its command.

Thus the confusion over the war in Asia among my uniformed clients at the Pentagon. The end has been duly set: eradication of the guerrillas. But the civilians have overstepped their bounds and meddled in means. The Generals regard this as unfair, a breach of contract, as it were. The Generals (or the faction among them most inclined to paranoia) are beginning to see the conduct of the war, the political limitation on means, as a ploy of the civilians for performing a putsch against their time-honored prerogatives.

This aspect of the situation would bode ill for the country, were it not for the fact that the growing paranoia among the Generals has enabled me to manipulate them into presenting both my scenarios to the President. The President has authorized implementation of the major scenario, provided that the minor scenario is successful in properly molding public opinion.

My major scenario is simple and direct. Knowing that the poor flying weather makes our conventional airpower, with its dependency on relative accuracy, ineffectual, the enemy has fallen into the pattern of grouping his forces into larger units and launching punishing annual offensives during the monsoon season. However, these larger units are highly vulnerable to tactical nuclear weapons, which do not depend upon accuracy for effect. Secure in the knowledge that domestic political considerations preclude the use of nuclear weapons, the enemy will once again form into division-sized units or larger during the next monsoon season. A parsimonious use of tactical nuclear weapons, even as few as twenty one-hundred-kiloton bombs, employed simultaneously and in an advantageous pattern, will destroy a minimum of two hundred thousand enemy troops, or nearly two-thirds of his total force, in a twenty-four-hour period. The blow will be crushing.

The minor scenario, upon whose success the implementation of the major scenario depends, is far more sophisticated, due to its subtler goal: public acceptance of, or, optimally, even public clamor for, the use of tactical nuclear weapons. The task is difficult, but my scenario is quite sound, if somewhat exotic, and with the full, if to-some-extent-clandestine support of the upper military hierarchy, certain civil government circles and the decision-makers in key aerospace corporations, the means now at my command would seem adequate. The risks, while statistically significant, do not exceed an acceptable level.

T minus 189 days . . . and counting . . .

The way I see it, the network deserved the shafting I gave them. They shafted me, didn't they? Four successful series I produce for those bastards, and two bomb out after thirteen weeks and they send me to the salt mines! A discotheque, can you imagine they make me producer at a lousy discotheque! A remittance man they make me, those schlockmeisters. Oh, those schnorrers made the American Dream sound like a kosher deal—twenty percent of the net, they say. And you got access to all our sets and contract players, it'll make you a rich man, Herm. And like a yuk, I sign, being broke at the time, without reading the fine print. I should know they've set up the American Dream as a tax less? I should know that

I've *gotta* use their lousy sets and stiff contract players and have it written off against my gross? I should know their shtick is to run the American Dream at a loss and then do a network TV show out of the joint from which I don't see a penny? So I end up running the place for them at a paper loss, living on salary, while the network rakes it in off the TV show that I end up paying for out of my end.

Don't bums like that deserve to be shafted? It isn't enough they use me as a tax loss patsy, they gotta tell me who to book! "Go sign the Four Horsemen, the group that's packing them in at the Mandala," they say. "We want them on *A Night With The American Dream*. They're hot."

"Yeah, they're hot," I say, "which means they'll cost a mint. I can't afford it."

They show me more fine print—next time I read the contract with a microscope. I *gotta* book whoever they tell me to and I gotta absorb the cost on my books! It's enough to make a Litvak turn anti-semit.

So I had to go to the Mandala to sign up these hippies. I made sure I didn't get there till twelve-thirty so I wouldn't have to stay in that nuthouse any longer than necessary. Such a dive! What Bernstein did was take a bankrupt Hollywood-Hollywood club on the Strip, knock down all the interior walls and put up this monster tent inside the shell. Just thin white screening over two-by-fours. Real shlock. Outside the tent, he's got projectors, lights, speakers, all the electronic mumbo jumbo and inside is like being surrounded by movie screens. Just the tent and the bare floor, not even a real stage, just a platform on wheels they shlepp in and out of the tent when they change groups.

So you can imagine he doesn't draw exactly a class crowd. Not with the American Dream up the street being run as a network tax loss. What they get is the smelly, hard-core hippies I don't let in the door and the kind of j.d. high school kids that think it's smart to hang around putzes like that. A lot of dope-pushing goes on. The cops don't like the place and the rousts draw professional troublemakers.

A real den of iniquity—I felt like I was walking onto a Casbah set. The last group had gone off and the Horsemen hadn't come on yet, so what you had was this crazy tent filled with hippies, half of them on acid or pot or amphetamine or for all I know Ajax, high school would-be hippies, also mostly stoned and getting ugly, and a few crazy schwartzes looking to fight cops. All of them standing around waiting for something to happen, and about ready to make it happen. I stood near the door, just in case. As they say, "the vibes were making me uptight."

All of a sudden the house lights go out and it's black as a network executive's heart. I hold my hand on my wallet—in this crowd, tell me there are no pickpockets. Just the pitch-black and dead silence for what, ten beats, something crawling along my bones, but I knew it's some kind of subsonic effect and not my imagination, because all the hippies are standing still and you don't hear a sound.

Then from a monster speaker so loud you feel it in your teeth, a heartbeat, but heavy, slow, half-time like maybe a whale's heart. The thing crawling along my bones seems to be synchronized with the heartbeat and I feel almost like I am that big dumb heart beating there in the darkness.

Then a dark red spot—so faint it's almost infrared—hits the stage which they have wheeled out. On the stage are four uglies in crazy black robes—you know, like the Grim Reaper wears—with that ugly red light all over them like blood. Creepy. Boom-ba-boom. Boom-ba-boom. The heartbeat still going, still that subsonic bone-crawl and the hippies are staring at the Four Horsemen like mesmerized chickens.

The bass player, a regular jungle-bunny, picks up the rhythm of the heartbeat. Dum-da-dum. Dum-da-dum. The drummer beats it out with earsplitting rim-shots. Then the electric guitar, tuned like a strangling cat, makes with horrible heavy chords. Whang-ka-whang. Whang-ka-whang.

It's just awful, I feel it in my guts, my bones; my eardrums are just like some great big throbbing vein. Everybody is swaying to it, I'm swaying to it. Boom-ba-boom. Boom-ba-boom.

Then the guitarist starts to chant in rhythm with the heartbeat, in a hoarse, shrill voice like somebody dying: "*The* big *flash* . . . *The* big *flash* . . ."

And the guy at the visuals console diddles around and rings of light start to climb the walls of the tent, blue at the bottom becoming green as they get higher, then yellow, orange and finally as they become a circle on the ceiling, eye-killing neon-red. Each circle takes exactly one heartbeat to climb the wall.

Boy, what an awful feeling! Like I was a tube of toothpaste being squeezed in rhythm till the top of my head felt like it was gonna squirt up with those circles of light through the ceiling.

And then they start to speed it up gradually. The same heartbeat, the same rim-shots, same chords, same circles, same base, same subsonic bone-crawl, but just a little faster. . . . Then Faster! Faster!

Thought I would die! Knew I would die! Heart beating like a lunatic. Rim-shots like a machine gun. Circles of light sucking me up the walls, into that red neon hole.

Oy, incredible! Over and over faster and faster till the voice was a scream and the heartbeat a boom and the rimshots a whine and the guitar howled feedback and my bones were jumping out of my body—

Every spot in the place came on and I went blind from the sudden light—

An awful explosion-sound came over every speaker, so loud it rocked me on my feet—

I felt myself squirting out of the top of my head and loved it.

Then:

The explosion became a rumble—

The light seemed to run together into a circle on the ceiling, leaving everything else black.

And the circle became a fireball.

The fireball became a slow-motion film of an atomic bomb cloud as the rumbling died away. Then the picture faded into a moment of total darkness and the house lights came on.

What a number!

Gevalt, what an act!

So after the show, when I got them alone and found out they had no manager, not even an option to the Mandala, I thought faster than I ever had in my life.

To make a long story short and sweet, I gave the network the royal screw. I signed the Horsemen to a contract that made me their manager and gave me twenty percent of their take. Then I booked them into the American Dream at ten thousand a week, wrote a check as proprietor of the American Dream, handed the check to myself as manager of the Four Horsemen, then resigned as a network flunky, leaving them with a ten thousand bag and me with twenty percent of the hottest group since the Beatles.

What the hell, he who lives by the fine print shall perish by the fine print.

T minus 148 days . . . and counting . . .

"You haven't seen the tape yet, have you, B.D.?" Jake said. He was nervous as hell. When you reach my level in the network structure, you're used to making subordinates nervous, but Jake Pitkin was head of network continuity, not some office boy, and certainly should be used to dealing with executives at my level. Was the rumor really true?

We were alone in the screening room. It was doubtful that the projectionist could hear us.

"No, I haven't seen it yet," I said. "But I've heard some strange stories."

Jake looked positively deathly. "About the tape?" he said.

"About you, Jake," I said, deprecating the rumor with an easy smile. "That you don't want to air the show."

"It's true, B.D.," Jake said quietly.

"Do you realize what you're saying? Whatever our personal tastes—and I personally think there's something unhealthy about them—the Four Horsemen are the hottest thing in the country right now and that dirty little thief Herm Gellman held us up for a quarter of a million for an hour show. It cost another hundred thousand to make it. We've spent another hundred thousand on promotion. We're getting top dollar from the sponsors. There's over a million dollars one way or the other riding on that show. That's how much we blow if we don't air it."

"I know that, B.D.," Jake said. "I also know this could cost me my job. Think about that. Because knowing all that, I'm still against airing the tape. I'm going to run the closing segment for you. I'm sure enough that you'll agree with me to stake my job on it."

I had a terrible feeling in my stomach. I have superiors too and The Word was that *A Trip With The Four Horsemen* would be aired, period. No matter what. Something funny was going on. The price we were getting for commercial time was a precedent and the sponsor was a big aerospace company which had never bought network time before. What really bothered me was that Jake Pitkin had no reputation for courage; yet here he was laying his job on the line. He must be pretty sure I would come around to his way of thinking or he wouldn't dare. And though I couldn't tell Jake, I had no choice in the matter whatsoever.

"Okay, roll it," Jake said into the intercom mike. "What you're going to see," he said as the screening room lights went out, "is the last number."

On the screen:

A shot of empty blue sky, with soft, lazy electric guitar chords behind it. The camera pans across a few clouds to an extremely long shot on the sun. As the sun, no more than a tiny circle of light, moves into the center of the screen, a sitar-drone comes in behind the guitar.

Very slowly, the camera begins to zoom in on the sun. As the image of the sun expands, the sitar gets louder and the guitar begins to fade and a drum starts to give the sitar a beat. The sitar gets louder, the beat gets more pronounced and begins to speed up as the sun continues to expand. Finally, the whole screen is filled with unbearably bright light behind which the sitar and drum are in a frenzy.

Then over this, drowning out the sitar and drum, a voice like a sick thing in heat: *"Brighter . . . than a thousand suns . . ."*

The light dissolves into a close-up of a beautiful dark-haired girl with huge eyes and moist lips, and suddenly there is nothing on the sound track but soft guitar and voices crooning low: *"Brighter . . . Oh God, it's brighter . . . brighter . . than a thousand suns . . ."*

The girl's face dissolves into a full shot of the Four Horsemen in their Grim Reaper robes and the same melody that had played behind the girl's face shifts into a minor key, picks up whining, reverberating electric guitar chords and a sitar-drone and becomes a dirge: *"Darker . . . the world grows darker . . ."*

And a series of cuts in time to the dirge:

A burning village in Asia strewn with bodies—

"Darker . . . the world grows darker . . ."

The corpse-heap at Auschwitz—

"Until it gets so dark . ."

A gigantic auto graveyard with gaunt Negro children dwarfed in the foreground—

"I think I'll die . . ."

A Washington ghetto in flames with the Capitol misty in the background—

". . . before the daylight comes . . ."

A jump-cut to an extreme close-up on the lead singer of the Horsemen, his face twisted into a mask of desperation and ectasy. And the sitar is playing double-time, the guitar is wailing and he is screaming at the top of his lungs: *"Before I die, let me make that trip before the nothing comes . . ."*

The girl's face again, but transparent, with a blinding yellow light shining through it. The sitar beat gets faster and faster with the guitar whining behind it and the voice is working itself up into a howling frenzy: *". . . the last big flash to light my sky . . ."*

Nothing but the blinding light now—

". . . and zap! the world is done . . ."

An utterly black screen for a beat that becomes black fading to blue at a horizon—

". . . but before we die let's dig that high that frees us from our binds . . . that blows all cool that ego-drool and burns us from our mind . . . the last big flash, mankind's last gas, the trip we can't take twice . . ."

Suddenly, the music stops dead for half a beat. Then:

The screen is lit up by an enormous fireball—

A shattering rumble—

The fireball coalesces into a mushroom-pillar cloud as the roar goes on. As the roar begins to die out, fire is visible inside the monstrous nuclear cloud. And the girl's face is faintly visible superimposed over the cloud.

A soft voice, amplified over the roar, obscenely reverential now: *"Brighter . . . great God, it's brighter . . . brighter than a thousand suns . . ."*

And the screen went blank and the lights came on.

I looked at Jake. Jake looked at me.

"That's sick," I said. "That's really sick."

"You don't want to run a thing like that, do you, B.D.?" Jake said softly.

I made some rapid mental calculations. The loathsome thing ran something under five minutes . . . it could be done. . . .

"You're right, Jake," I said. "We won't run a thing like

that. We'll cut it out of the tape and squeeze in another commercial at each break. That should cover the time."

"You don't understand," Jake said. "The contract Herm rammed down our throats doesn't allow us to edit. The show's a package—all or nothing. Besides, the whole show's like that."

"All like that? What do you mean, all like that?"

Jake squirmed in his seat. "Those guys are . . . well, perverts, B.D.," he said.

"Perverts?"

"They're . . . well, they're in love with the atom bomb or something. Every number leads up to the same thing."

"You mean . . . they're *all* like that?"

"You got the picture, B.D.," Jake said. "We run an hour of *that* or we run nothing at all."

"Jesus."

I knew what I wanted to say. Burn the tape and write off the million dollars. But I also knew it would cost me my job. And I knew that five minutes after I was out the door, they would have someone in my job who would see things their way. Even my superiors seemed to be just handing down The Word from higher up. I had no choice. There was no choice.

"I'm sorry, Jake," I said. "We run it."

"I resign," said Jake Pitkin, who had no reputation for courage.

T minus 10 days . . . and counting . . .

"It's a clear violation of the Test-Ban Treaty," I said.

The Undersecretary looked as dazed as I felt. "We'll call it a peaceful use of atomic energy, and let the Russians scream," he said.

"It's insane."

"Perhaps," the Undersecretary said. "But you have your orders, General Carson, and I have mine. From higher up. At exactly eight fifty-eight P.M. local time on July fourth, you will drop a fifty-kiloton atomic bomb on the designated ground zero at Yucca Flats."

"But the people . . . the television crews . . ."

"Will be at least two miles outside the danger zone. Surely, SAC can manage that kind of accuracy under 'laboratory conditions.' "

I stiffened. "I do not question the competence of any bomber crew under my command to perform this mission," I said. "I question the reason for the mission. I question the sanity of the orders."

The Undersecretary shrugged, smiled weakly. "Welcome to the club."

"You mean you don't know what this is all about either?"

"All I know is what was transmitted to me by the Secretary of Defense, and I got the feeling he doesn't know everything, either. You know that the Pentagon has been screaming for the use of tactical nuclear weapons to end the war in Asia—you SAC boys have been screaming the loudest. Well, several months ago, the President conditionally approved a plan for the use of tactical nuclear weapons during the next monsoon season."

I whistled. The civilians were finally coming to their senses. Or were they?

"But what does that have to do with—?"

"Public opinion," the Undersecretary said. "It was conditional upon a drastic change in public opinion. At the time the plan was approved, the polls showed that seventy-eight point eight percent of the population opposed the use of tactical nuclear weapons, nine point eight percent favored their use and the rest were undecided or had no opinion. The President agreed to authorize the use of tactical nuclear weapons by a date, several months from now, which is still top secret, provided that by that date at least sixty-five percent of the population approved their use and no more than twenty percent actively opposed it."

"I see. . . . Just a ploy to keep the Joint Chiefs quiet."

"General Carson," the Undersecretary said, "apparently you are out of touch with the national mood. After the first Four Horsemen show, the pools showed that twenty-five percent of the population approved the use of nuclear weapons. After the second show, the figure was forty-one percent. It is now forty-eight percent. Only thirty-two percent are now actively opposed."

"You're trying to tell me that a rock group—"

"A rock group and the cult around it. It's become a national hysteria. There are imitators. Haven't you seen those buttons?"

"The ones with a mushroom cloud on them that say 'Do it'?"

The Undersecretary nodded. "Your guess is as good as mine whether the National Security Council just decided that the horsemen hysteria could be used to mold public opinion, or whether the Four Horsemen were their creatures to begin with. But the results are the same either way—the Horsemen and the cult around them have won over precisely that element of the population which was most adamantly opposed to nuclear weapons: hippies, students, dropouts, draft-age youth. Demonstrations against the war and against nuclear weapons have died down. We're pretty close to that sixty-five percent. Someone—perhaps the President himself—has decided that one more big Four Horsemen show will put us over the top."

"The President is behind this?"

"No one else can authorize the detonation of an atomic bomb, after all," the Undersecretary said. "We're letting them do the show live from Yucca Flats. It's being sponsored by an aerospace company heavily dependent on defense contracts. We're letting them truck in a live audience. Of course the government is behind it."

"And SAC drops an A-bomb as the show-stopper?"

"Exactly."

"I saw one of those shows," I said. "My kids were

watching it. I got the strangest feeling . . . I almost wanted that red telephone to ring. . . ."

"I know what you mean," the Undersecretary said. "Sometimes I get the feeling that whoever's behind this has gotten caught up in the hysteria themselves . . . that the Horsemen are now using whoever was using them . . . a closed circle. But I've been tired lately. The war's making us all so tired. If only we could get it all over with. . . ."

"We'd all like to get it over with one way or the other," I said.

T minus 60 minutes . . . and counting . . .

I had orders to muster *Backfish*'s crew for the live satellite relay of *The Four Horsemen's Fourth*. Superficially, it might seem strange to order the whole Polaris fleet to watch a television show, but the morale factor involved was quite significant.

Polaris subs are frustrating duty. Only top sailors are chosen and a good sailor craves action. Yet if we are ever called upon to act, our mission will have been a failure. We spend most of our time honing skills that must never be used. Deterrence is a sound strategy but a terrible drain on the men of the deterrent forces—a drain exacerbated in the past by the negative attitude of our countrymen toward our mission. Men who, in the service of their country, polish their skills to a razor edge and then must refrain from exercising them have a right to resent being treated as pariahs.

Therefore the positive change in the public attitude toward us that seems to be associated with the Four Horsemen has made them mascots of a kind to the Polaris fleet. In their strange way they seem to speak for us and to us.

I chose to watch the show in the missile control center, where a full crew must always be ready to launch the missiles on five-minute notice. I have always felt a sense of communion with the duty watch in the missile control center that I cannot share with the other men under my command. Here we are not Captain and crew but mind and hand. Should the order come, the will to fire the missiles will be mine and the act will be theirs. At such a moment, it will be good not to feel alone.

All eyes were on the television set mounted above the main console as the show came on and . . .

The screen was filled with a whirling spiral pattern, metallic yellow on metallic blue. There was a droning sound that seemed part sitar and part electronic and I had the feeling that the sound was somehow coming from inside my head and the spiral seemed etched directly on my retinas. It hurt mildly, yet nothing in the world could have made me turn away.

Then two voices, chanting against each other:

"Let it all come in. . . ."

"Let it all come out. . . ."

"In . . . *out* . . . in . . . *out* . . . in . . . *out* . . ."

My head seemed to be pulsing—in-*out*, in-*out*, in-*out*—and the spiral pattern began to pulse color-changes with the words: yellow-on-blue (in) . . . green-on-red (*out*) . . . In-*out*-in-*out*-in-*out*. . . .

In the screen . . . *out* my head. . . . I seemed to be beating against some kind of invisible membrane between myself and the screen as if something were trying to embrace my mind and I were fighting it. . . . But why was I fighting it?

The pulsing, the chanting, got faster and faster till in could not be told from *out* and negative spiral afterimages formed in my eyes faster than they could adjust to the changes, piled up on each other faster and faster till it seemed my head would explode—

The chanting and the droning broke and there were the Four Horsemen, in their robes, playing on some stage against a backdrop of clear blue sky. And a single voice, soothing now: *"You are in. . . ."*

Then the view was directly above the Horsemen and I could see that they were on some kind of circular platform. The view moved slowly and smoothly up and away and I saw that the circular stage was atop a tall tower; around the tower and completely circling it was a huge crowd seated on desert sands that stretched away to an empty infinity.

"And we are in and they are in. . . ."

I was down among the crowd now; they seemed to melt and flow like plastic pouring from the television screen to enfold me. . . .

"And we are all in here together. . . ."

A strange and beautiful feeling . . . the music got faster and wilder, ecstatic . . . the hull of the *Backfish* seemed unreal . . . the crowd was swaying to it around me . . . the distance between myself and the crowd seemed to dissolve . . . I was there . . . they were here. . . . We were transfixed. . . .

"Oh yeah, we are all in here together . . . together. . . ."

T minus 45 minutes . . . and counting . . .

Jeremy and I sat staring at the television screen, ignoring each other and everything around us. Even with the short watches and the short tours of duty, you can get to feeling pretty strange down here in a hole in the ground under tons of concrete, just you and the guy with the other key, with nothing to do but think dark thoughts and get on each other's nerves. We're all supposed to be as stable as men can be, or so they tell us, and they must be right because the world's still here. I mean, it wouldn't take much—just two guys on the same watch over the same three Minutemen flipping out at the same time, turning their keys in the dual lock, pressing the three buttons. . . . Pow! World War III!

A bad thought, the kind we're not supposed to think or I'll start watching Jeremy and he'll start watching me and we'll get a paranoia feedback going. . . . But that can't happen; we're too stable, too responsible. As long as we remember that it's healthy to feel a little spooky down here, we'll be all right.

But the television set is a good idea. It keeps us in contact with the outside world, keeps it real. It'd be too easy to start thinking that the missile control center down here is the only real world and that nothing that happens up there really matters. . . . Bad thought!

The Four Horsemen . . . somehow these guys help you get it all out. I mean that feeling that it might be better to release all that tension, get it all over with. Watching the Four Horsemen, you're able to go with it without doing any harm, let it wash over you and then through you. I suppose they are crazy; they're all the human craziness in ourselves that we've got to keep very careful watch over down here. Letting it all come out watching the Horsemen makes it surer that none of it will come out down here. I guess that's why a lot of us have taken to wearing those "Do it" buttons off duty. The brass doesn't mind; they seem to understand that it's the kind of inside sick joke we need to keep us functioning.

Now that spiral thing they had started the show with—and the droning—came back on. Zap! I was right back in the screen again, as if the commercial hadn't happened.

"We are all in here together. . . ."

And then a close-up of the lead singer, looking straight at me, as close as Jeremy and somehow more real. A mean-looking guy with something behind his eyes that told me he knew where everything lousy and rotten was at.

A bass began to thrum behind him and some kind of electronic hum that set my teeth on edge. He began playing his guitar, mean and low-down. And singing in that kind of drop-dead tone of voice that starts brawls in bars:

"I stabbed my mother and I mugged my paw. . . ."

A riff of heavy guitar-chords echoed the words mockingly as a huge swistika (red-on-black, black-on-red) pulsed like a naked vein on the screen—

The face of the Horsemen, leering—

"Nailed my sister to the toilet door. . . ."

Guitar behind the pulsing swastika—

"*Drowned a puppy in a ce-ment machine. . . . Burned a kitten just to hear it scream. . . .*"

On the screen, just a big fire burning in slow-motion, and the voice became a slow, shrill, agonized wail:

"*Oh God, I've got this red-hot fire burning in the marrow of my brain. . . .*

"*Oh yes, I got this fire burning . . . in the stinking marrow of my brain. . . .*

"*Gotta get me a blowtorch . . . and set some naked flesh on flame. . . .*"

The fire dissolved into the face of a screaming Oriental woman, who ran through a burning village clawing at the napalm on her back.

"*I got this message . . . boiling in the bubbles of my blood. . . . A man ain't nothing but a fire burning . . . in a dirty glob of mud. . . .*"

A film-clip of a Nuremburg rally: a revolving swastika of marching men waving torches—

Then the leader of the Horsemen superimposed over the twisted flaming cross:

"*Don't you hate me, baby, can't you feel somethin' screaming in your mind?*

"*Don't you hate me, baby, feel me drowning you in slime!*"

Just the face of the Horsemen howling hate—

"*Oh yes, I'm a monster, mother. . . .*"

A long view of the crowd around the platform, on their feet, waving arms, screaming soundlessly. Then a quick zoom in and a kaleidoscope of faces, eyes feverish, mouths open and howling—

"*Just call me—*"

The face of the Horseman superimposed over the crazed faces of the crowd—

"*Mankind!*"

I looked at Jeremy. He was toying with the key on the chain around his neck. He was sweating. I suddenly realized that I was sweating too and that my own key was throbbing in my hand alive. . . .

T minus 13 minutes . . . and counting . . .

A funny feeling, the Captain watching the Four Horsemen here in the *Backfish*'s missile control center with us. Sitting in front of my console watching the television set with the Captain kind of breathing down my neck. . . . I got the feeling he knew what was going through me and I couldn't know what was going through him . . . and it gave the fire inside me a kind of greasy feel I didn't like. . . .

Then the commercial was over and that spiral-thing came on again and whoosh! It sucked me right back into the television set and I stopped worrying about the Captain or anything like that. . . .

Just the spiral going yellow-blue, red-green, and then starting to whirl and whirl, faster and faster, changing colors and whirling, whirling, whirling. . . . And the sound of a kind of Coney Island carousel tinkling behind it, faster and faster and faster, whirling and whirling and whirling, flashing red-green, yellow-blue, and whirling, whirling, whirling. . . .

And this big hum filling my body and whirling, whirling, whirling. . . . My muscles relaxing, going limp, whirling, whirling, whirling, all limp, whirling, whirling, whirling, oh so nice, just whirling, whirling. . . .

And in the center of the flashing spiraling colors, a bright dot of colorless light, right at the center, not moving, not changing, while the whole world went whirling and whirling in colors around it, and the humming was coming from the spinning colors and the dot was humming its song to me. . . .

The dot was a light way down at the end of a long, whirling, whirling tunnel. The humming started to get a little louder. The bright dot started to get a little bigger. I was drifting down the tunnel toward it, whirling, whirling, whirling. . . .

* * *

T minus 11 minutes . . . and counting . . .

Whirling, whirling, whirling down a long, long tunnel of pulsing colors, whirling, whirling, toward the circle of light way down at the end of the tunnel. . . . How nice it would be to finally get there and soak up the beautiful hum filling my body and then I could forget that I was down here in this hole in the ground with a hard brass key in my hand, just Duke and me, down here in a cave under the ground that was a spiral of flashing colors, whirling, whirling toward the friendly light at the end of the tunnel, whirling, whirling. . . .

T minus 10 minutes . . . and counting . . .

The circle of light at the end of the whirling tunnel was getting bigger and bigger and the humming was getting louder and louder and I was feeling better and better and the *Backfish*'s missile control center was getting dimmer and dimmer as the awful weight of command got lighter and lighter, whirling, whirling, and I felt so good I wanted to cry, whirling, whirling. . . .

T minus 9 minutes . . . and counting . . .

Whirling, whirling . . . I was whirling, Jeremy was whirling, the hole in the ground was whirling, and the circle of light at the end of the tunnel whirled closer and closer and—I was through! A place filled with yellow light. Pale metal-yellow light. Then pale metallic blue. Yellow. Blue. Yellow. Blue. Yellow-blue-yellow-blue-yellow-blue-yellow . . .

Pure light pulsing . . . and pure sound droning. And just the *feeling* of letters I couldn't read between the pulses—not-yellow and not-blue—too quick and too faint to be visible, but important, very important. . . .

And then a voice that seemed to be singing from inside my head, almost as if it were my own:

"*Oh, oh, oh . . . don't I really wanna know. . . . Oh, oh, oh . . . don't I really wanna know. . . .*"

The world pulsing, flashing around those words I couldn't read, couldn't quite read, had to read, could *almost* read. . . .

"*Oh, oh, oh . . . great God I really wanna know. . . .*"

Strange amorphous shapes clouding the blue-yellow-blue flickering universe, hiding the words I had to read. . . . Dammit, why wouldn't they get out of the way so I could find out what I had to know!

"*Tell me tell me tell me tell me tell me. . . . Gotta know gotta know gotta know gotta know. . . .*"

T minus 7 minutes . . . and counting . . .

Couldn't read the words! Why wouldn't the Captain let me read the words?

And that voice inside me: "*Gotta know . . . gotta know . . . gotta know why it hurts me so. . . .*" Why wouldn't it shut up and let me read the words? Why wouldn't the words hold still? Or just slow down a little? If they'd slow down a little, I could read them and then I'd know what I had to do. . . .

T minus 6 minutes . . . and counting . . .

I felt the sweaty key in the palm of my hand. . . . I saw Duke stroking his own key. Had to know! Now—through the pulsing blue-yellow-blue light and the unreadable words that were building up an awful pressure in the back of my brain—I could see the Four Horsemen. They were on their knees, crying, looking up at something and begging: "*Tell me tell me tell me tell me. . . .*"

Then soft billows of rich red-and-orange fire filled the world and a huge voice was trying to speak. But it couldn't form the words. It suttered and moaned—

The yellow-blue-yellow flashing around the words I couldn't read—the same words, I suddenly sensed, that the voice of the fire was trying so hard to form—and the Four Horsemen on their knees begging: "*Tell me tell me tell me. . . .*"

The friendly warm fire trying so hard to speak—
"Tell me tell me tell me tell me. . . ."

T minus 4 minutes . . . and counting . . .

What were the words? What was the order? I could sense my men silently imploring me to tell them. After all, I was their Captain, it was my duty to tell them. It was my duty to find out!

"Tell me tell me tell me . . ." the robed figures on their knees implored through the flickering pulse in my brain and I could almost make out the words . . . almost. . . .

"Tell me tell me tell me. . . ." I whispered to the warm orange fire that was trying so hard but couldn't quite form the words. The men were whispering it too: "Tell me tell me. . . ."

T minus 3 minutes . . . and counting . . .

The question burning blue and yellow in my brain. WHAT WAS THE FIRE TRYING TO TELL ME? WHAT WERE THE WORDS I COULDN'T READ?

Had to unlock the words! Had to find the key!

A key. . . . *The* key? THE KEY! And there was the lock that imprisoned the words, right in front of me! Put the key in the lock. . . . I looked at Jeremy. Wasn't there some reason, long ago and far away, why Jeremy might try to stop me from putting the key in the lock?

But Jeremy didn't move as I fitted the key into the lock. . . .

T minus 2 minutes . . . and counting . . .

Why wouldn't the Captain tell me what the order was? The fire knew, but it couldn't tell. My head ached from the pulsing, but I couldn't read the words.

"Tell me tell me tell me . . ." I begged.

Then I realized that the Captain was asking too.

* * *

T minus 90 seconds . . . and counting . . .

"*Tell me tell me tell me . . .*" the Horsemen begged. And the words I couldn't read were a fire in my brain.

Duke's key was in the lock in front of us. From very far away, he said: "We have to do it together."

Of course . . . our keys . . . our keys would unlock the words!

I put my key into the lock. One, two, three, we turned our keys together. A lid on the console popped open. Under the lid were three red buttons. Three signs on the console lit up in red letters: ARMED.

T minus 60 seconds . . . and counting . . .

The men were waiting for me to give some order. I didn't know what the order was. A magnificent orange fire was trying to tell me but it couldn't get the words out. . . . Robed figures were praying to the fire. . . .

Then, through the yellow-blue flicker that hid the words I had to read, I saw a vast crowd encircling a tower. The crowd was on its feet begging silently—

The tower in the center of the crowd became the orange fire that was trying to tell me what the words were—

Became a great mushroom of billowing smoke and blinding orange-red glare. . . .

T minus 30 seconds . . . and counting . . .

The huge pillar of fire was trying to tell Jeremy and me what the words were, what we had to do. The crowd was screaming at the cloud of flame. The yellow-blue flicker was getting faster and faster behind the mushroom cloud. I could almost read the words! I could see that there were two of them!

T minus 20 seconds . . . and counting . . .

Why didn't the Captain tell us? I could almost see the words!

THE BIG FLASH

Then I heard the crowd around the beautiful mushroom cloud shouting: "DO IT! DO IT! DO IT! DO IT! DO IT!"

T minus 10 seconds . . . and counting . . .
"DO IT! DO IT! DO IT! DO IT! DO IT! DO IT! DO IT!"
What did they want me to do? Did Duke know?

9

The men were waiting! What was the order? They hunched over the firing controls, waiting. . . . The firing controls . . . ?
"DO IT! DO IT! DO IT! DO IT! DO IT!"

8

"DO IT! DO IT! DO IT! DO IT! DO IT!": the crowd screaming.
"Jeremy!" I shouted. "I can read the words!"

7

My hands hovered over my bank of firing buttons. . . . "DO IT! DO IT! DO IT! DO IT!" the words said.
Didn't the Captain understand?

6

"What do they want us to do, Jeremy?"

5

Why didn't the mushroom cloud give the order? My men were waiting! A good sailor craves action.
Then a great voice spoke from the pillar of fire: "DO IT . . . DO IT . . . DO IT . . ."

4

"There's only one thing we can do down here, Duke."

3

"The order, men! Action! Fire!"

* * *

2
Yes, yes, yes! Jeremy—

1
I reached for my bank of firing buttons. All along the console, the men reached for their buttons. But I was too fast for them! I would be first!

0

EVERYTHING BUT LOVE

Mikhael Yemstev and Eremei Parnov

Like many other popular science fiction writers in the Soviet Union, both Mikhael Yemstev and Eremei Parnov are trained scientists. Yemstev, born in 1930, is a physicist. Besides fiction, he has published numerous scientific works and frequently lectures about new frontiers in science. Parnov, who has worked as a chemical engineer, was born in 1935 and began publishing at the age of eighteen. He has authored more than forty books on a wide variety of subjects; he is also well known as a critic of science fiction and he has won a special prize of the European Science Fiction Convention.

Yemstev and Parnov started their collaborative writing of science fiction in 1961. They have jointly produced several important novels and many stories, a few of which have appeared in English-language collections published in Moscow and the United States. In 1978, Macmillan brought out a translation of their spectacularly innovative and terrifying novel *World Soul*.

Readers unfamiliar with Soviet science fiction may be surprised by the richness, complexity, and daring of "Everything But Love." As the anniversaries of Hiroshima and Nagasaki go by, the microcosmic and macrocosmic worlds collide in the dying consciousness of a brilliant young physicist who realizes too late the consequences of "working for death."

Splashes of crimson on fresh shavings. Drip . . . drip . . . drip. . . . Barton bent over to avoid staining his clothes. The oozing rivulets gurgled warmly. He felt light-headed, yet intensely weary. A motor seemed to be pounding in the head. Nausea bubbled in the darkness deep down.

He sank to his knees and gingerly slipped down on all fours. Then he cautiously turned over onto his back and thrust out his chin as high as he could to stop the hemorrhage. A salty, viscous liquid at once attacked the taste buds. The blue haze above swam round, and then again and again. Before he blacked out he felt the dry grass beneath him prickling, the sharp filings jabbing into his hands, and the blood caking on his upper lip. The screaming sirens failed to penetrate.

An ambulance screeched to a halt. Orderlies carefully lifted him up onto a stretcher and slid him into the car through the tailgate. On the way to the hospital, they took a blood count, measured his temperature, and felt for his flickering pulse.

When, four hours later, Alan Barton awoke, to find himself closeted within a green-tinted ward of the army hospital, the diagnosis was as definite as the Boltzmann constant. The post-irradiation syndrome, more commonly known as radiation sickness, or the White Death, as the soldiers in the guard detail had nicknamed it.

The only noise that interrupted the clinical carbolical hush was the humming of the air conditioner.

"He simply couldn't've taken a dose, I swear." Major Tawolski of the Medical Corps repeated over and over again, like an incantation. "The last range tests were four days ago.

EVERYTHING BUT LOVE

Post-test checks showed everyone at normal, including Barton. I've got it all down here. Barton, July 26, eleven hundred hours, indications normal."

"Sure he didn't go out to the range later," the MO asked.

"He's not nuts, is he?"

"But, old man, miracles just don't happen!"

"Not if you discount the Immaculate Conception. But this is about the same."

"You think I ought to tell the general that?" the MO raised an ironical eyebrow.

"After all, it's none of our business. Let him worry."

"I bet he's forming a board of inquiry this very moment."

"And putting you on it, too!"

Tawolski pulled out a crumpled pack of cigarettes. The MO at once switched the fan on.

"What have you done so far?" the MO asked wearily, stretching out his large, heavily veined hands.

"Two hundred thousand of heparin, plus, of course, temperature, heartrate and blood pressure measurings."

"Do a puncture, too, and take an epidermis scrape."

"I've already issued instructions for that to be done. And daily urine tests too. If we only knew where! We could try to check the circulation of the destroyed cells then."

The MO nodded. He seemed half asleep.

"When will you be able to determine the exact dose?" The MO's voice was dry and brusque.

"In another two days. When we get the WBC picture."

"That's not the best way."

"I know. But what would you suggest?"

The MO shrugged and thrust his nether lip out still further: "What about a hematologist, eh?"

"Cowan, perhaps?"

"Yes. Please get in touch with him and ask him for me to come. Not for long. Tell him that."

"What?" Tawolski mumbled.

"I've seen too many cases to think differently. A bad beginning. Very bad."

"But that's only on the fifth day."

"Well, there's nothing good in it either." The MO shook his head. "What's the temperature right now?"

"98.6 Fahrenheit."

"I suppose it'll slowly start to climb. . . . Well, we shall see what we shall see." With an effort he rose from behind his desk and stretched his limbs. "Get in touch with Cowan at once. But right now let's have a look at him."

AUG. 1. 19**. 10 A.M. Temp. 98.8. Pulse: 78. BP: 135/80

Barton had long been awake. However, he did not open his eyes. Everything was as clear as day. They'd fixed up a whole bank of hemocytometers in his ward last night. These frequent tests, with blood samples thrice a day, spelled little hope, he knew that. From time to time he heard the lab assistants drop such hardly comprehensible words as "febrins" and "metamyelocytes."

It was all most ominous.

Barton felt Tawolski take his wrist, hold it for a few moments and then let it sink back on top of the blanket.

"Well, what's the answer, Abe?"

"What, awake, Alan? A pretty strong pulse. How's my boy, generally?"

"Odd, major. Awfully queer."

"Whaddaya mean?"

"I really don't know how to put it. It's like a hallucination. I look at myself, touch myself and see no change. And I feel more or less okay. Just a bit weakish. Which is nothing. Nothing that a cuppa coffee or a good dry martini couldn't cure. So what's wrong then? Why do I have to bloody well lie here? Who said that my sound and healthy body's been riddled with billions of invisible bullets? Quien sabe? And why should I believe it? I've got more faith in my own body, it looks so hale. N'est-ce pas? And then I sit up and put up a pillow to rest back on. Gradually the face grows feverish, I find myself gasping for breath, I break into a cold sweat and a lump of hot phlegm rises in my throat. I feel just horrible. I fall back and my head goes into a spin. Not a limb, not a thing, body, eyes, logic, or memory, nothing obeys me."

"That's the kinda feeling I got, Abe. Just too damned queer. Get what I mean now?"

"Sure, doc. But I don't advise you to do that again."

"What don't you advise me to do? Feel queer?"

"No, not that. You mustn't lift yourself up, that's what you mustn't do. You've just gotta keep flat on your back."

"What on earth for?"

"Listen, doc, you're a wizard at physics aren't ya? Doncha ya understand?"

"No! Explain it all to me please. I can't understand a thing. I'm doomed, I'm gonna die and I've gotta lie flat on my back. What for? But what's the use of arguing, I can't get up anyhow. A queer thing, this invisible death is. You see nothing, feel nothing, know nothing, like the three monkeys, but you're already done for. The clock's wound up and set and bomb'll explode. Medics or no medics, it's gonna explode! That's how it is, Abe, me boy! Better tell me what's new."

"Lordy, what can be new! Everybody's terribly anxious about you and wanna see you."

"But I don't wanna see them!"

"Sure. But why give up? The devil's not so black as he's painted, y'know. We'll get you back on your feet again, you'll see. Of course, you won't be the man you were before, but still. . . . So far, it's not as bad as all that!"

"Be frank, Abe. How big a dose did I get?"

"Alan, I really don't know! We've not the slightest notion how and where it all happened. So how should we know? Have a little patience, Alan, we'll get the picture soon."

"But roughly, Abe, roughly! Above or under six hundred?"

"Can't tell you really. And why d'you think six hundred lethal?"

"I read about it somewhere."

"Bunk! It all depends on the type of irradiation and the organ hit. There was a guy I knew who took twelve hundred. Still, he pulled out. Another chap had only . . . listen, get all that crap out of your head, will ya? . . . Tell me, is there anyone in the family you'd like to see? I'll see it's done."

"No, thanks. There's nobody I'd like to see . . . at least not now. Later, perhaps . . . but not now."

"Any particular book you'd like to read, perhaps? It'll take your mind off. You see, I've prescribed drop injections of glucose in a physiological solvent. That's rather tiring and boring. Reading helps. A mystery, perhaps?"

"A kind thought, Abe. But better SF.[1] It gets your mind off work as well. And you feel in the midst of things . . . like an omnipotent divinity, not a living cadaver. We physicists always need something to work on. We mustn't vegetate! That destroys the mind. And SF's a very happy substitute. So make it SF, Abe."

AUG. 2. 19**. 10 P.M. Temp. 99. Pulse: 78. BP: 137/80

Anyone in the family I'd like to see? Anyone I love? What about Denise? Why does my head spin? Space seems to have curled up into a tube and assumed a conical form. How vibrant the echo. Come, hurry into this tunnel of light rings! Come, hurry back, further back, still further back in time. And I'll see Denise again.

Night is all aglow. The neon advertisements iridesce. The light-filled, seemingly translucent skyscraper hotels wink like misty yellow crystals. The road is deserted. There's not a soul around. The araucaria and the dracaena stand immobile, as if carved of granite. The beach is as desolate and dark. A fairy-tale forest of drooping cones—really, lowered, multi-coloured awnings—rises up to meet us. The tide laps dreamily at the shore, in time with the strains of music that can barely be heard from somewhere far away. To our left stretch the gambling halls and night clubs, from which comes the fragrance of perfume and wrinkled fruit. To our right extends the black void of ocean and seemingly sunken beach. The lights of ships anchored far out twinkle faintly. The cyclopean eye of the light-house blinks white. We are walking down a path in the shadows beneath a canopy of leaves. The path runs past the flashing advertisements and brightly-lit shop-windows, parallel to the ghostly beach.

Then the path forks. A string of lanterns picks out the way to the ocean pier. Lured by beckoning tradition we plunge into the darkness to stop and kiss in a lamplight that fades in the murky green depths of the limpid waters. On the path we are alone. On the pier there will be others. That we know. Still we continue towards it, as if drawn like moths to candle flame.

On the pier stands an old man who has thrust out a fantastically long fishing rod above the watery abyss. A shoal of slim, shady fish, attracted by the light, sway in rhythm on the milk-green rollers. Then they disappear into the oil-black waters, re-emerge and cross the boundary line demarcated by the swinging lanterns. The old man scurries to and fro. From time to time he leans over the railing and pulls at the rod. However, he seldom gets a bite, even though he's using live shrimps for bait. I'd swallow that bait. But the stupid fish turn up their noses at it. The shoal continues to rise and dip with the waves. As if dazzled and spellbound by the lights, they dive beneath the pier to re-appear seconds later. The old man has an empty gas-mask bag slung over his shoulder. It dangles loosely and flaps against his belly. In it some half a dozen small fish still squirm and wriggle. He proudly displays his catch to us and the deep furrows creasing his face beam with artless radiance. He's happy, this midnight angler.

The waves dash against the concrete supports and hurl themselves up in showers of fine spray. The tangy freshness melts on our lips. The benches and deckchairs are wet and little puddles have formed in their hollows. The heads of unmoving couples also gleam with a wet brilliance.

We, too, dive back into the darkness. At the far end of the

avenue I spot a raspberry-red glow. We run towards it and, gasping with silent laughter, see one more nocturnal lunatic. This time it is a vendor of roasted chestnuts, blowing on the coals in his brazier.

Then, holding in our hands the hot, smoke-scented packets, we again plunge into the darkness and hurl ourselves down onto the still warm sand. With bare hands I scallop out a small hole, and, taking every possible precaution, deposit my flaming cigarette lighter in it. Now we have a tiny islet all to ourselves in velvet black of night in which the world is wrapt. In the reddish reflection that partly illumines Denise's face the shadows beneath her eyes become still darker and deeper; eyes and mouth form three black hollows. We are two tiny, cuddly blobs of warmth, who have suddenly found that make-believe can also be true. We seem to be floating in the ocean of eternity, about to learn the greatest of all mysteries, that we too will gain immortality and achieve eternal love.

"Three years," I said later. "Three whole years!" she exclaimed. "Only three years," I gently returned. To think that in eleven months my contract will be up. That is, would have been up. As now, time has stopped and my contract will run out only on Judgement Day.

I've never mentioned Denise anywhere, in not one form I've had to fill out. As far as the Army's concerned I haven't got a financée. Otherwise they'd have taken her molecular chart. Now we'll never see one another again, even were I to desire this more than anything else. In the eyes of the law she is nothing to me. And such persons have nothing to do at our top-secret base. She'd never be let near to within a mile of it, even were she to learn of my plight by some fluke and want to come. She'll never know what has happened, while I'm still alive. One can write only to one's kin, but Denise . . . she's no relation. Her address is not recorded in the mailing register and any letter I'd dare send her would be returned.

Such is the price I have to pay for refusing a molecular

chart. She'll learn that I'm dead and gone only a year later, at the earliest. But I've done the right thing. Otherwise I'd have that molecular copy at my bedside—the very first thing tomorrow morning. A doll that can make love and shed tears, that will have the same warm, firm flesh, the same voice, the same laughter, the same habit of drawing on a stocking on a sculptured Grecian leg thrust outwards. You're so very much alone here. You so very much hunger for her. You'll never spot the ersatz, the deception practised upon you in that brief fortnight of bliss. The mannequin will part forever with you and you will implant a kiss on its cold, wet cheek. Goodbye! Goodbye forever, to a unique and costly robot that will never be able to divulge and betray highly classified strategic information.

Women sometimes come to this distant range, where neutron bombs and gamma flares explode in silent invisibility. Once a year, for a fortnight. They must all be dolls, mannequins. Otherwise, why do their men drink themselves into a solitary stupor later, guzzling the Scotch as if it were so much water? Why do they turn their eyes away as if in self-scorning abasement? Why do they feel so God-damn lonely?

But could I be wrong? Could the women that come be of real flesh and blood? After all molecular copies are made only for an emergency. Is my case an emergency, I wonder?

Still, I suppose one must first test it oneself before trying to understand what the others think and feel. I don't believe Denise can be reproduced. Instants that belong to the past cannot be brought back. That night on the beach cannot be brought back either. However perfect a new form may be, it is always new. It is new in the context of time. It does not have any past: it has only another person's memories. Denise's memories of that night, but not the Denise who experienced that night.

I've been told about an airman who served with our forces

fighting in the boondocks in a minor, local war. People get killed in such wars too.

The enemy attacked their base at night. The attackers seemed to rise up from out of the ground like a legion of goblins. They sent a steam-roller into the barbed wire entanglement enclosing the compound. Emitting ghoulish cascades of sparks and hissing and crackling, it slammed into the electrically charged wire and knocked down a concrete post. Then it rumbled to a halt, its spark-pitted roller smoking furiously. Holding sheets of plywood above their heads, a group of guerillas, with rifles slung across their chests, poured into the breach. Then another mass of little yellow men rushed across these plywood bridges through narrow corridors that had been insulated by means of army blankets. Sirens started to scream and projectors sprayed powerful beams of light from the watch towers. It was the rainy season, that time of year in which the monsoons come, and in the intense glare jets of rain and ragged tufts of mist pulsated in a chaotic dance. The attackers unslung bazookas and the search-lights blacked out in an intolerably blinding magnesium incandescence. Our soldiers opened up with flame-throwers, and molten clots of napalm, constrained by jets of coal, transformed into a blazing inferno the ground before the front line of trenches. Small gaunt men carrying Dawes guns and crooked swords fell like ninepins in this pool of luminescence, holding their hands to their eyes. But there seemed no end to them. On and on they came, breaking through the wire entanglement. Machine guns spattered unremittingly at the fence, but for everyone that fell another rose in his place. The trenches were deluged with a hail of hand grenades and phosphorus bombs. Explosions thudded all around. These were plastic bombs, planted by some unknown hand, going off. In the officers' mess, all the window panes were shattered. The garage went up in flames. Only one of the six choppers escaped damage.

Our men recharged their BARs[1] with special-purpose,

white-marked pulverizer rounds of ammo. Spurts of yellow flame, sizzling hysterically, cut through the misty darkness. The attack seemed to falter. Another second and the enemy would turn. But at that very moment, there came the pounding of rocket mortars from the boondocks and with it the enemy attack stepped up. A molotov cocktail burst and set the HQ alight. Communications were completely disrupted. The defenders were split up into unconnected pockets of resistance. The guerillas dug in on the tennis court and began to sweep the compound with fire from heavy machine guns. Our men lay still, fearing even to raise a head. In places, hand-to-hand scuffles flared up in the communication trenches. The attackers could see better in the dark and they slashed away and hacked vigorously with their short swords. The CO[1], a colonel, ordered his special commando task unit into action. They slipped away into the darkness, looking like creatures out of a nightmare in their camouflage kits and respirators. Operating singly, noiselessly, indeed brilliantly, they exploded nerve-gas bombs with slight plops, cleared the communication trenches in a matter of minutes and soon silenced the machine guns on the tennis court. Again the outcome hung in the balance, in a precarious equilibrium.

Again a series of blasts rocked the base. The whippet tanks that had been firing point blank into the fence, were put out of action. The library caught light. Then suddenly, it became as bright as day. A forked tongue of fire darted screaming upwards. There were several more explosions and handfuls of flame and soot seemed to hover in mid-air. The cloyingly-sickening stench of blazing petrol filled the nostrils as the gasoline and lubricants dump went skywards. The blast was so stupendous that it caused the engineering hangar to cave in. File folders scattered sheets of paper to all four winds, as they came hurtling out through the smashed windows of the HQ. The CO commanded that the disintegrator be switched on but was told that the ultrasound borers had been stolen.

The earth, the sky and the pouring rain all belched smoke.

Dark, wraith-like shadows flitted to and fro in this Dantean inferno. The commandos had been butchered one by one. Armoured carriers had stopped up the breaches in the entanglement, when coaxial guns on the tennis court again sprang to life. It was clear by now that the main guerilla forces infiltrating the base had grouped in the northwestern sector, in the area of the firing range. All that lay between them and the front trenches now was a wide swimming pool with two diving boards on the other side, upon which they were mounting their machine guns at the moment. Hypnotized by the blinding glare, the dark figures stood as if caught in suspended action. In a couple of seconds they had been wiped out. Then our flame-throwers struck. The napalm sizzled as it cut across the water in the swimming pool. The guerillas lurking on the other side managed to spring back, but were mowed down by withering, highly accurate fire from our machine gunners.

To capitalize on this initial gain, the CO ordered a gas attack. However, a group of guerillas, who had infiltrated the base from the opposite quarter, blew up the power substation. The fireballs of plasma burst in the air with an incredible violet glare.

Back in the boondocks the rocket mortars intensified their fire. The armoured carriers blocking the breaches were transformed into blazing hulks by well-aimed grenades and incendiaries. A flood of guerillas broke through and, despite decimating losses, enveloped the frontline trenches. Fusillades of shots now came from every quarter. All communications had been totally disrupted. Hand-to-hand fighting flared up with ever-increasing intensity. Though our remaining forces still snarled back bitterly, the oncoming guerilla hordes pouring through the now undefended breaches had, to all practical intents, captured the base—rather what was left of it.

The sole remaining chopper rose into the air and from an altitude of some two hundred feet mowed down the attacking forces, as it hedge-hopped from one end of the base to the other.

Then the guerillas opened up from the watch towers that they had by now occupied and the chopper was forced to climb higher. Suddenly its pilot spotted a woman scurrying around frantically amidst the clouds of bellowing smoke and flame. The only woman at the base was the colonel's wife who had come for a fortnight's visit.

He sent his machine down. At hedge-hopping level his gunner, pressing the triggers of his machine guns with one hand, slid the hatch open with the other and tossed a rope ladder out. The woman clutched at it and held on for dear life. As the pilot slowly ascended, the woman moved and snaked up the swaying ladder. The gunner reached out a hand, caught her under the armpits and dragged her inside. At that very moment he keeled over and slipped out, his body riddled by a burst of machine-gun fire from the ground. The pilot slammed the hatch and zoomed up.

After a farewell circle above the blazing base, he headed for the shore, where a mammoth, nuclear-powered aircraft carrier rode at anchor, amidst an escort of smaller guard vessels.

The guerillas were already butchering the base's last defenders. Again and again the pilot and the woman turned their heads to watch the circle of fire and flame that for long blazed through the night.

Running out of fuel before they had reached the shore, the pilot had to crashland his machine in the swamp-infested jungle. The two, a tall husky chap of twenty-five, and a petite society lady, who had seen her husband decapitated before her very eyes, found themselves stranded amidst a sweltering mangrove miasma inhabited by horrid scaly crabs and a species of swamp fish, whose saucer eyes stared vacuously at them as they pushed on. The woman shrieked endlessly, seeing slimy snakes at every step. And when the slippery fungi, pocked by squashy snails, brushed her, she shrieked again. Several hours later she bitterly bewailed her lot when the patch of skin touched became inflamed and swollen. In short, she behaved like any society matron lost in the jungle. However the pilot could not shake off a haunting suspicion. A fortnight's visit to a top-secret, strategic base was hardly ever granted, he knew that. And so he watched her every move round the clock, as if trying to catch her out in some horrible crime.

His suspicions mounted with every day. He certainly had reason. The woman had begun to treat him as if not she but some totally different person had but a few days earlier watched, from her hiding place amidst the empty petrol tanks, her husband's severed head being carried past on top of a bamboo stake. True, from time to time he himself seemed to sink into waves of oblivion, when, completely forgetful that her husband had been one of his best buddies, he thought she had always been his and had come to visit him and none else for that fortnight. At moments like these he was prepared to stake his life to a red cent, that she thought the same.

In between though, like a soul in hell, racked by torment, he savagely questioned her. Now and again he beat her cruelly, yet a minute later to beg her forgiveness and caress the tears away from her eyes with his lips. Tears that were indeed of a bitter saltiness. Once he bloodied her mouth and with morbid curiosity watched the crimson rivulet drip off her chin and stain her sylon blouse a rusty red.

The next day he tenderly kissed the crusted, swollen upper lip and wept in happy contrition, only to demand an hour later that she tell him whether her blood always clotted so quickly.

Meanwhile, weighted down by heavy rucksacks, they stumbled on through the boondocks with but compass for guide. They had taken with them all the stores they had managed to shake up from the abandoned chopper, but though with every day the burdens they carried grew lighter, there seemed no end to their fatiguing trek. She meekly submitted to the most vituperative insults—which only exasperated him more still.

More and more often now he was seized by fits of madness. With beatings and entreaties, he sought to wrest admission from her. "Who are you?" he screamed. And there was so much soul-wrenching torment in his inhuman cry, that the beasts of the jungle for long growled and whined in response. But she did not seem to understand what he wanted of her. It cost her little to switch from tears to laughter as she eyed him devotedly with her large, violet-tinged irises and showered him with kisses.

Then one night, when the fungi blazed forth like the burning eyes of tigers and the beasts slunk through the jungle along hidden trails to the water's edge to drink, he, seemingly bereft of all reason, croaked: "I must know who you are! I can't stand this any longer! You must tell me! Tell me!"

He shook her awake, but she still could not understand what he wanted of her—or pretended not to. Then he caught at her throat and compressed his fingers, aware that he was doing something frightening and irretrievable, but unable to stop, as if he was both Jekyll and Hyde at the same time. When she quivered for the last time and fell back limp in his hands, he cried out like a child. He sprang up, to find himself enmeshed in the parachute silk that he had rigged up for tent. Blinded, he lashed about stupidly, then broke out and rushed away, completely oblivious of the wet, prickly burrs that tore at his skin. As he ran, he stared wonderingly at his hands— seeing nothing, though, as it was pitch dark. He still couldn't understand that what he had done had failed to either answer his question or allay his suspicions. He kept blundering forwards, crying out to her, and trying to inspect his hands. But only lemurs flitting by overhead, now and again answered his cry.

He came out of the jungle, filthy and hairy. His eye-balls rotated wildly in their sockets, set within two deep grey circles that stood out quite distinctly against the greenish, unhealthy pallor of his face. He looked like a crazed lemur, they said—if indeed lemurs can go mad.

He was taken to a mental hospital, where, with the judicious use of chemotherapy, his sanity was slowly restored—though, I for one, think him mad as ever. No wonder, some take the story he tells for the ravings of a lunatic. The only survivor, he had wandered for so long amidst the boondocks. But . . . quien sabe? No other man—or woman—had lived to tell the tale.

But for some reason I believed him. And at once I imagined us. Denise and me. My blood seemed to curdle. I began to think that it had been us two wandering out there in the swampy jungle, and that Denise had forever been left behind there, in the darkness. Fungi dangle a luminescent white before the eyes and damp cobwebs brush the face. But the hands are not to be seen. Even though the fungi glow. From time to time something blurs the fungi, presumably hands. That's all.

It was then that I solemnly pledged to myself that I would not permit them to take Denise's molecular chart. For neither love or money! And it's a good thing I did that. I'll forever remember her as she was that night on the beach. She stood on her knees before the hole in which the flame burned, shielding it between her cupped palms, as if genuflecting to some mysterious divinity. Her elongated shadow reached out darkly across the crimson-tinged sand towards the pitch-black ocean.

That's how I'll remember her, and that's all I need. Nothing else. After all, nothing will help. How so terribly mortifying, so painful. Why did it have to happen to me, of all people? And I'd been so stupidly certain that all woes and miseries would pass me by. How did this come to pass? When? And where? But what difference does it make if I know the answer or not? That will change nothing! How long will it all take? I can't just lie here and think, think, think. It's too painful, too agonizing. Surely there must be something I can do? But why am I so sure that I will die? Why do I know that I will die? After all there have been other cases. . . . Could, by chance, the dose not be lethal? No! No! I don't want to think about that! Nothing gnaws at the heart so bitterly as hope.

AUG. 3. Hospital Staff Room

"Well, how d'you find him today?" The MO looked some ten years younger. He had given his silvery grey hair a neat crew cut. His close-shaven cheeks even glowed slightly.

"A long way to how I find you, at any rate," Tawolski smirked, as he helped the MO don his hospital coat.

"Do tell, now? Any changes for the better?"

"Serum sodium showed lower radioactivity than could be expected."

"Don't pin too much hope on that," the MO said with a wave of his arm, again thrusting out his nether lip in his habitually peevish manner. "Don't kid yourself. That still doesn't mean a thing. Not a thing! What's the blood count today?"

Tawolski put a lilac-coloured form before him.

"I see. Lymphocytes, neutrocytes, monocytes, thrombocytes," he mumbled, his voice gradually losing itself beneath his nose, as he swayed as if in prayer. "Red corpuscles," his voice suddenly acquired a tartness, as he jerked up his head, "the deviation seems to be really not so very much! And though white corpuscles number more than twenty five thousand, even that doesn't yet mean a thing! A relaxation, I'd say. Unfortunately, the picture'll change soon. Are you recording the blood coagulation time?"

Tawolski nodded.

"Good. Keep it up. What about the spinal cord?"

"If you remember we did a puncture the day before yesterday. The picture's rather vague. We'll again need some time, I expect."

"Sure. As soon as the white corpuscles start to run down,

begin exchange transfusions. Inject intravenously 20 mg of thiamine hydrochloride and half a million of heparin."

"What about bone marrow grafting?"

"Not now. Let's first see what's affected. After all, we don't even know roughly the number of Roentgen equivalents. Apparently, the gastro-intestinal stage is near-critical. We've gotta be on the lookout. Still, I wonder if the stomach's affected or not?"

"Cowan'll be arriving the day after tomorrow."

"Fine! Still, try to find out about the stomach."

Tawolski shrugged.

"It's ten soon. Time for our daily round," he said going towards the wash-basin.

AUG. 3. 19**. 10 A.M. Temp. 99. Pulse: 76. BP: 130/80

"Morning, Alan. Have a good night?"

"Thanks for asking, but I must say I couldn't get to sleep for quite some time what with all sorts of thoughts running through my mind, y'know. But I didn't wake ones."

"The more sleep you get, the better. See that he gets sleeping pills," Tawolski added, turning to the nurse. Then: "I've brought along the SF you asked for. A collection of stories. Now let's have a look at you."

The nurse gently withdrew the coverlet. Barton shivered and turned to the window.

Tawolski intently peered at his stomach, lightly touching the skin with his cold tapering fingers. His finger tips were stained yellow as he had the habit of smoking non-filters almost down to the very end. He looked long at a pale pink splotch just below the tanned portion of Barton's body. Then he drew a circle round it with a nail and asked:

"Does it hurt here?"

"No," Barton said. He was feeling cold and his skin had covered with goose pimples.

Tawolski again touched the spot with a shiny instrument, whose cold metallic touch caused Barton to tremble.

EVERYTHING BUT LOVE

"Everything's fine," Tawolski said. "I'm quite pleased with your progress, Alan. Well, wish you joy with your SF. As for me, I can't stand the stuff. See you later."

The nurse drew the coverlet back over Barton. But quite some time passed before he got warm again.

He took up the book Tawolski had brought.

" *'Oh, it's you. Come on up', Davis said, the moment he noticed Peter Baker. Then he whispered something into the ear of the man with the shaved head.*

" *'What can I do for my precious sister's lord and master?' he added, rising from the dilapidated, weather-beaten deckchair and pumping Peter's plump and clammy hand.*

" *'Ellen would like to have the powder you promised,' he rattled out rather hastily, as if afraid of being turned away.*

"*His brother-in-law threw up his hands. 'There,' he said to the man with the shaved head, 'you see a typical representative of the microworld. He intrudes into the microsystem, demanding his rights and not caring a damn for the great things taking place before his very eyes.'*

"*The man with shaved head smiled shyly and gave a barely perceptible nod.*

"*Peter felt discouraged. Again microworlds, again systems. He wanted to say that he, on the contrary, cared very much for the great things that were happening. But he just couldn't understand what great things were meant. Perhaps there were indeed some great things that were not worth a damn.*

" *'Now don't feel put out, my dear relation, I was only joking,' Davis said. 'However, you'll have to wait a bit. Of course, that'll put off for a little while the hour of doom for your bedbugs, but that's the way the world's made. Somebody's always bound to lose.*

"*Peter nodded in agreement and perched himself gingerly on a camp stool. He drank in deeply of the exhilarating air, and, with crinkling eyes, looked up at the skies overhead. They were of an amazingly bottomless blue. Tender wisps of* cloud played tag with one another, taking care though, to steer clear of the glaring, yellow eye of the sun.

" '. . . the sun,' Peter heard his brother-in-law say in his typical jerky voice. 'So, this is, perhaps, the ideal model of a process ever made by man.'

"And Davis poked a finger at the night-lamp standing on the frail, wickerwork table.

" 'The cutest thing about it is that it's perfect. Get what I mean? This perfect model is rigidly bound with the original system. Understand what that means?'

" 'That's exactly what's got me guessing,' the man with the shaved head intoned melancholically with a quizzically raised brow.

" 'Still, it's as I say,' Davis said succinctly, with a smile. 'Inside this is the sun, that honest-to-goodness luminary that's bondsman to the goddess Aurora. In the miniature, of course. But all the rest's as should be, inclusive of temperature', and he patted the semi-translucent cylinder.

" 'But the main thing, let me note once again, is the rigid bond with the initial object.'

" 'You've certainly got something there,' the man with the shaved head uttered.

"There was a pause.

" 'But,' said Peter's brother-in-law, suddenly remembering. 'Let's get back to the microworld. I'll go and look for that powder. If you care to come along,' he turned to the man with the shaved head, 'I'll give you some more details.' "

Barton stuck a finger between the pages to mark the place and closed his eyes. He breathed in slowly and exhaled still more slowly, to a count of three. He repeated this procedure several times. Then he began to hum. In this way he kept the nausea down. When he felt his condition had eased somewhat, he resumed reading.

"The two had gone and Peter was left to his own devices. He adjusted his hat and curiously examined the container that stood on the table. This was a piece of tubing of some *unidentifiable plastic that had been sealed at either end by lids of some dark material which sprouted a host of multi-coloured, shellacked wires. In its lustreless depths he was able to make out a spark the size of a pinhead.*

" *'So that's a model of the sun,' he thought to himself and moved his chair up.*

"*For a few more minutes he peered at the faintly glowing spark inside and to himself:* " *'A fine sun, indeed! Shear bull!' "*

"*Suddenly it seemed to him as if he was imagining things. There was a barely discernible flicker inside the cylinder as if the spark had grown brighter. He looked intently, and it appeared to him as if the spark had dilated and was blowing up, at first to the size of a pea and then to the size of a one-cent coin.*

"*Scared, he jerked his hat off his head and plunked it down over the cylinder.*

"*At first he couldn't even realize what had happened. Then his knees turned to jelly. A pall of darkness had descended all at once. The park was enveloped in complete gloom. Stars twinkled against the canopy of black overhead.*

"*Everything, house, trees, grass and flitting butterflies, had dissolved in the inky murkiness.*

"*Peter was petrified with horror, unable to either move or even breathe.*

"*With that shred of his mind which for some reason was still able to function, he cooly analysed the catastrophe. What particularly struck him was that the darkness was complete. The viscous blackness that he rather surmised than saw around him possessed an odd bottle-green tint, as if a ten-volt lamp had been lit in the depths of a big fish-bowl.*

" *'Imbecile, moron!' he heard his brother-in-law's cry, and the sound of hasty footsteps.*

"*An object fell at his feet, and a dazzling, explosive brilliance caused him to squeeze his eyes tight. Day had returned.*

With quivering, twitching fingers Peter picked up his green hat. . . ."

AUG. 4. 19**. 10 P.M. Temp. 99.5. Pulse: 90. BP: 140/85

Do I like this story or not? Rather does it disquiet me. In it the thesis of unity has been pushed to an absurd extreme—though, for the first time, it has been concretely expressed in terms comprehensible to the middle-class Babbitt. This is no mystical incantation of an ancient Egyptian high-priest, no hocus-pocus of the mediaeval alchemist, nor even the abstract computations of some armchair physicist from Berkeley. As Ramakrishna has it, when the Universe terminated, bounded and unbounded space became one. That is exactly what is meant. The inspired prophecy of a crazed Cassandra, the incoherent, delirium-shot utterances of an oracle. From times immemorial man has ever hoped for such fusion. A crimson dust, a black whirlwind threaded with atomized stars, fills my eyes. The idea comes from the conical-hatted Chaldean mages, the panther-skin-clad priests of Toth, the awesome, bearded biblical prophets. It is an idea which has turned the brain, an idea which, an elusive will-o'-the-wisp, radiates the eerie blueness of endless, phantom might.

The serpent devouring its own tail is indeed wisest of alchemical symbols. At some point the infinitesimal joints with the infinitude, the big becomes the small, and madness becomes common sense.

With me this has been a persistent fixation, even though on an almost forgotten note. For me science's triumph has been my personal defeat. Theoreticians have computed the diameter of Friedmann's model of the Universe. Collaboration between Berkeley, CERN, Dubna and Cambridge resulted in the experimental detection of primary quarks of matter. The infinitesimal and infinitude had both ends lopped off. The world was still inexhaustible, but now it was bounded. And I realized that I had been born to bring the two together.

After getting my Ph.D. at Columbia, I joined the staff of the Cavendish centre and worked at Gottingen and Copenhagen.

I took for my point of departure the highly controversial cosmogonic hypothesis of Lemaitre and Zeldovich as to a proto-Universe that had been compressed into one fantastic atom. There had been nothing anywhere except for a queer clot of matter. Then, at a moment which may be conventionally designated as zero time, it exploded into matter, space, and time. Tick-tock . . . tick-tock. Space loses its curvature, the fantastically enormous pull gradually slackens, and the diameter of the new-born Universe increases with the velocity of light. Tick-tock, tick-tock. By now there appear the first distinguishable elementary particles, which associate in the first unstable atoms of the lightest elements. A black bottomless void. Galaxies . . . stars . . . planets. Tick-tock . . . tick-tock.

Somewhere on the fringe of a run-of-the-mill galactic spiral, within the system of a run-of-the-mill yellow star, on a run-of-the-mill planet, life is born. The evolution of an aqueous solution of slime brings into being the brilliant brain in the head of an unassuming clerk at the patents office in Berne. Thus does nature acquire a self-awareness, to discover in amazement that the expanding galaxies are the still continuing consequence of that initial big bang. But this still does not come the entire logical circle. The paradox lies elsewhere. We are witnessing the disintegration of that oneness which man craved while still in infancy. The bounded and the unbounded had been compressed within that primaeval blob, that had been both atom and universe simultaneously. That elementary particle and endless mass to whose superpull time had called a stop.

But the world exploded to become the dichotomy of the infinitely large and the infinitesimally small, the bounded and the unbounded. Matter broke away from field, and space separated from time. Rather did our intellect accomplish this division. It divided the indivisible, analysed it and re-combined it through brilliant mathematical synthesis.

"They tell me there's a frontier
On skyline gleaming bright.
A flying saucer shadow,
It dances out of sight."

I essayed my hand at a poem which I called "Dreams of a Lost Oneness." But where the integer fails to score, the anapest will get nowhere either. Incidentally, as trivial and invariant is the no-talent thesis too.

In my poem I had conceived of a chapter called "Monuments to Oneness"—the super-dense neutron and hyperon stars, which, in effect, represent simplified models of the proto-Universe. With as much ground can a neutron star be dubbed a giant atom, as in it particles are as closely spaced as nucleons within a nucleus. Or differently. A star in gravitational collapse is a type of quark comprised of particles spaced at distances less than their own diameters. In this fashion does the large come within the small, while the infinitesimal is fraught with the infinite.

Who knows, perhaps some day we shall encounter the monstrosity of the infinite in our strivings for the infinitesimal? There surely ought to be a point where the yardsticks of "larger" and "smaller" must vanish. Nature is ignorant of them. The Sun is larger than an electron, the Galaxy is larger than the Sun. This is axiomatic. But what if, by some sudden quirk, we shall fail to say which of the two is larger, the meta-galaxy or the quark? Suppose the closing up of particles in super-powerful head-on beams in an accelerator affects the entire Universe? Shall we not then be plunking a hat down over the Sun? If we do, nature will wreak dire vengeance!

Were I a writer, I would write a story about the following. A physicist uses an accelerator to bring up particles within the distance of the elementary quantum of length, according to Heisenberg, and suddenly—bang! a hyperstar explodes. Could it be that the fantastic inexplicable phenomenon we call a quasar is but the result of experiment by some antediluvian physicist somewhere in Andromeda or Cygnus? Or, perhaps this. A rocket works up to the speed of light and again—bang! the Universe springs back into an elementary particle.

Christ, the things that come into one's head! Here am I delving into infinitudes and infinitesimals, into distances of the order of billions of light years, when all I have left to live are a few more days. I wonder, though, how far I would be able to get in this time, were I able to take off with the speed of light?

Suppose I have ten more days left. That gives me 864,000 seconds. Multiplied by 300,000 this amounts to roughly 250,000 million kilometers. How little! How so very little left! Only now do I see that so clearly. I will barely manage to break away from the solar system. No stars for me!

But supposing death too is stellar flight at light velocities? At such speeds, time stops, which means it will stop when I die. What whistlers in the dark we humans are! All that is vile in us and all that is miserable come from that. The truth is a thing which one must accept without prejudice, without bias.

Emotions comprise an excessive response to a truth that makes one kid oneself. In my salad days, being keen on Hinduism, I had the idea of becoming a neophyte of Yoga. I idolized Ramakrishna and Vivekananda. We are deluded by the maya, which, devoid of beginning and existing out of the framework of time, makes us take for eternal reality what is but a stream of transient images.

The illusion of immortality is both the oldest and most persistent of all illusions we ever labour under. It provides the bedrock for all religions. Hence, he who knows he is mortal is indeed great and worthy of greater veneration than any god or deity. But he does not seek veneration, as he is a plain ordinary mortal, despite which, or, contrariwise, because of which, he works for the future that is to come. The cream of mankind worked for us and our time, though they well knew they would never live to see it.

How come, then, that I am here? How come that I, who know everything and can attain everything, found myself working for death? When did that happen? Where was that last roadside warning, which I failed to notice?

And now the price is leukaemia. Still, this is but pure accident. Not leukaemia, but the burdensome, searing thoughts of the past few days represent the price I am called upon to pay. I could think of but universe, of pure, eternal depths, where iced time is frozen still. My mind is razorsharp, as never before. I could have grasped that elusive point in the ring, where past and present, beginning and end fuse. Instead, I am doomed to search for the explanation of my own fall from grace. That is the hell I have to go through here on earth. It has opened its gates even before I have appeared before the great god Osiris, who weighs in his balance all our sins and transgressions with literally scrupulous accuracy.

Thus did there once die like me, that young and handsome brilliant scientist Lewis Slotin, who at Los Alamos put together the first A-bomb with his own hands. Sixty-three times he brought together and scattered the blocks of uranium to ascertain the critical mass. Sixty-three times. On the sixty-fourth, the chain reaction began. He scattered the blocks and interrupted the raction. He died to save the others. Even the gold crown on his tooth became a source of beamed irradiation and blistered his lip.

He died an anguishing but brave death. How'd I like know what he, the man who put together the world's first A-bomb, had thought and reflected on at the time. The race they had run then to beat the nazis! But the Bomb cast the deciding vote. I wonder what occupied his mind to the last? What, indeed?

I think I'd be able to comprehend that, were I to retrace the elusive chain of compromises and deals with my own conscience that brought me here. He, Slotin, was a hero. But who am I?

Who am I? Who are we? Where do we come from? And where are we going?

Denise, too, sold out both me and herself. When I signed the contract, she did not ask why. Because she knew or guessed. However, death, like war, foots the bill for a multitude of sins. Behind that black door, there is neither vileness, treachery nor crime. The great equalizer, it breaks down the microbodies into the primary particles. It's a 168-hour week, with not a day off. Non-stop. No liabilities accepted and no contact with the outer world. Still worse than in this compound.

So why the pangs? Why? While Denise has not the slightest inkling of what I feel.

Here comes the doctor. He thinks I'm asleep. He feels gently for my pulse and mutters beneath his breath "One, two, three, four, five. . . ."

One . . . two . . . three . . . four . . . five. . . . I count the shooting stars. The usual August shower. Trails of fire in the nightbound sky.

So make a wish, Alan, hurry up and make a wish!

What a pretty little girl is with me up on the roof! So much ribbon and lace! So much white and sky blue! The blue is reflected in the dusty panes of the dormer, along with the black humped silhouettes of cats and the twinkle of innumerable stars.

Meanwhile I gaze steadily at the brightest star in the skies, which hangs suspended above the Smiles's chimneystack. I'm casting a spell on it, and, as if in answer to my hopes, it seems to shine ever brighter and brighter.

How much time will pass before it falls? How long? I burn with eager impatience. To see such a big star like that fall would be most exciting. It's none of your two-cent starlets that vanish with a plop, like so many soap bubbles! When this star falls the sight will be fantastic, perhaps even better than a Mardi Gras fireworks display.

"It's gonna fall rightaway," I mutter through clenched teeth without tearing my eyes away from it. "That big one," she cries in wonder. "Do such stars fall?" "Of course they do," I say, "and that one's certainly gonna fall! I've hypnotized it!"

The little girl cries and begs me to spare it: "They've also got little boys and girls with their Mummies and their Daddies up there! Let the little ones fall! They've got nobody on them! But that big one, it must go on shining! Do have pity on all the little children up there! And on all their Aunties and Grannies too! Please don't look at it like that! Just imagine, suppose somebody up there's looking at us right now, just like we're looking at them? So have a heart! Indeed, aren't you ashamed of yourself!" I'm no longer gazing at the star. But Denise doesn't know that and she keeps begging and entreating.

Forgive me, Denise, for the tears you shed then! Forgive me, Denise! I certainly didn't want to do any harm to the little boys and girls with their Mummies and their Daddies on that faraway star. I'd simply been wondering how it would fall and what would happen if, and when, it did. Just plain boyish curiosity. They say that the geniuses—or is it genii?—among the scientists retain that curiosity all their born days. Some, like Einstein and Bohr, do give thought to the little boys and girls with their Mummies and their Daddies. Others don't. It never enters their heads.

I and many of my colleagues come within that second group of "others." True, we're all rather nice people. It's simply we don't give thought to many things, for some reason. There's something very important that eludes us. The triumph of any new scientific discovery is nearly always an iconoclasm, sheer intellectual despotism. But it must on no account be irresponsible. Thought must always be given to the little boys and girls on the faraway star. Especially on days when stars fall on rooftops. How many, Denise?

"Ninety, ninety-one, ninety-two," the doctor lets my hand drop.

Ninety-two. Evidently my temperature's gone up a bit.

Why do the nights bring so much pain? The mornings, they bring a cool calm, lighting up the darkest corner, and gently unravelling Gordian knots. I wish morning would come sooner. I always doze off towards morning. And I sleep well then.

AUG. 4. 19**. 10 A.M. Temp. 99.2. Pulse: 84. BP: 130/85

The power the sandman has over us! I saw Denise in my dreams and it was much more agonizing than if I'd seen her in the flesh. I remember long ago, when I used to see blue ladies in my dreams and the memory haunted me for long.

Like all of real art, dreams have their own conventions. In dreamland, one is not only spectator and actor, but also, subconsciously so, script-writer, director and photographer. There are dreams that one will remember till dying day and as clearly as in a good movie.

What is born within us then comes to lead a life of its own. Here we have that same peculiarly instinctive human urge for oneness, for unity, or rather purposeful harmony. The harmonious unity of form and content rises in sunlike glory on art's horizon. Throughout all of my brief life I sought harmony in the physical world. In the chaos of disintegrations and interactions, in the stars of annihilation and transmutational paradoxes I conceived visions of complete, well-patterned forms of a theory that could explain everything.

I remember somebody at the university suggesting the rather amusing game of tagging each elementary particle with the colour one thought best suited it. This, mind you, was among physicists, people, who know better than all else that particles can have no colour—just as they can have no form, and no orbit. Curiously enough, seven out of every ten, including myself, coloured the proton red. Indeed a nut for the psychologist to crack. Why I suggested red, is still something I'll never understand.

This was my world, a world whose every inhabitant I could recognize. Now I am dying, riddled by a hail of particles, each of which I had mentally painted a different colour.

De-nise . . . Do and re. . . . Red and yellow. Purple and gold. The ire of the gladiator and the sheen of the lionskin. Invisible bridges of associations exist everywhere. I told Denise once that I visualized her name as a combination of proton and mu-meson. She laughed in that half-hearted way polite people do when they hear a corny chestnut told.

How did it come to pass that in my attempts to explain all causations in the microworld I overlooked the simplest of connections between cause and effect. I sowed dragon's teeth, heedless of what would spring up. It seems hardly plausible, but a person well versed in Hinduist mysticism, and familiar with Karma, did not pause one solitary instant to reflect on the likely consequences of one's own actions. When did I sell my soul to the devil? And how? Why, when signing that contract, didn't I remember the story of the crazed flier?

The whole point is that this story has no climaxes of betrayal. Nothing but the quiet evolution of a smugly complacent "I'm all right, Jack". It is simply not enough, when one knows about molecular copies, to prevent such a copy from being made of one's own fiancée. One should shout out about it from the housetops or grab at a BAR and fire that special ammo. It is simply not enough to never betray, to never commit oneself. One must resist, tooth and nail. The resister would never be here, even if he wanted to. His "reputation" would be guarantee enough against that. But I have an absolutely clean security clearance. And so it comes to pass that we act out our Karma in our own lifetimes. Why wonder then?

In so many plain words, I simply sold myself for a certain sum. And with myself, three years with Denise. All my contrite thoughts are nothing but the gripes of an unlucky gambler. I staked my own life, the ball rolled into zero, and my stake was swept up. Goodbye roulette, so much like the cyclotron. And goodbye cyclotron, with your tinsel targets. I myself have been the target that has been bombarded by particles with super-high energies. For the chemist this is but the radiolysis of a colloidal solution of protein in H_2O. Though this process attacks only one out of every ten thousand molecules, that is already more than enough. There is a symbolic meaning in my dying on the eve of the jubilee of the first atomic test. However, that is but an echo of Karma. Anything, however accidental it may appear to be, may be tied up with any other thing. A dunce-hatted atavism of theories of the occult. For some reason there comes to mind the creation of a surrealist painter whose acquaintance I made in Paris. If my memory's right, it was called "Cheviots Playing Snooker". One fanatical billiard buff had thought up a theory of elastic collisions. Suckers will ever look only for meaningful associations so as to win the prize at all costs. Don't be a cheviot—even in a case of the post-irradiation syndrome. It's utterly senseless to trail along with the herd to the slaughterhouse. One of the De Montmorencys demanded that he be borne on shoulders to the guillotine. There was some meaning in that, a meaning that neither the cheviots nor the merinos would understand.

There, the door has opened. It's time for the daily round. I must encourage Tawolski and show a cheerful optimism.

AUG. 6. Hospital Staff Room

With a cursory glance at the dermatologist's diagnosis, the MO stuffed the slip into his waistcoat pocket. Grimacing, he removed his eye-glasses, rubbed them with a piece of shammy, and massaged with his fingers the red indentations on the bridge of his nose.

"Sure it's erythema?" he inquired of Tawolski. "Definitely," Tawolski nodded. "The dermatologist thinks so too. He thinks there'll be ulcers."

"That's bad."

Tawolski shrugged with a snort.

"We must prepare for a sternal marrow transplant. That's the last hope. We can't expect any miracles."

"How about the blood?"

"Deteriorating."

The MO kept nodding, as if delighted with what Tawolski had to communicate.

"Monocytes and reticulocytes are diminishing. But swollen platelets are increasing in number."

"Toxic granulation of neutrophils is likely," the MO interjected.

"We're expecting that."

"What about the white corpuscles?"

"Diminishing too, but at a much slower rate than could be expected. Cowan advises a full transfusion prior to transplantation."

"Well, he certainly knows what he's talking about. What does he have to say about the slow decline in white corpuscles?"

"A good thing as such, but gives no grounds for optimism," Tawolski smirked.

"That's something we could've guessed for ourselves," the MO irascibly muttered. "What else does he say?"

Tawolski again shrugged and, flicking his cigarette butt into the wash-stand in the corner, proceeded to suck at his burnt finger.

AUG. 7. 19**. 10 P.M. Temp. 98.6. Pulse: 88. BP: 120/75 N. B. WBC down to 800 mm^2

Nurse Beata Travatti tramped up and down the corridor several times to shake off the feeling of drowsiness. The glass ward-doors yawned like so many black cavities. She took down a jar of instant coffee and lit the spirit burner. The minute, flickering purple flame was barely discernible in the shadowless light. Her emblazoned green smock assumed a bluish tinge. She pulled out her powder compact to look at herself in its mirror. The almost black lips and colourless cheeks evoked wry irritation with a lighting that muted every gay colour and clearly aged her. She pressed a button and the cold ceiling light flickered and faded. The black eye-pits of doors had now turned grey. The windows could be guessed at through the airlon curtains. Dawn was breaking.

Beata drew the curtain back and pressed her forehead to the glass. What she next saw in the gray light of dawn caused her to gasp and dart into Barton's room.

AUG. 7. Hospital Staff Room

Tawolski's telephone call awoke the duty doctor. Not quite realizing where he was, flustered and only half-awake, he blundered about the room, his heart pounding in his breast like a loose valve in a Diesel engine. Finally, he managed to find the telephone, and licking his dry lips, whispered something incoherent into it.

Tawolski: Hi, there. That you, Tony?

Doctor: That you, Abe? You crazy or summat? So dawn early?

Tawolski: Why, did I wake you up?

Doctor: No . . . But why aren't you in bed? It's not your watch.

Tawolski: Just can't get to sleep. How is he? We're operating today, y' know.

Doctor: Well, why not get a good night's rest, then. There aren't any changes. He's asleep. Temperature's steady, and I think it'll drop a little by morning. Go back to bed, Abe.

He was about to plonk down the receiver, when the door was suddenly flung open and Nurse Beata rushed into the room. He dropped the receiver like a hot potato and, jumping up, overturned the desk lamp. All this proceeded without a word said, as if in dumb show. They rushed out into the corridor to glimpse a figure wreathed in white at the other end. Not a footstep was heard. It seemed as if a spook was coming straight at them. When his eyes had grown a little more accustomed to the grey gloom, the doctor made out Barton slowly but surely coming up toward them. His eyes were wide open and gleamed in the flame of the burner. Barton softly turned the knob on the door of his room, and the corridor emptied.

AUG. 7. One Hour Later. Hospital Staff Room

Tawolski turned up in slippers on stockinged feet. Indeed,

in his service fatigues he cut a still more ridiculous figure at that moment than he was wont to, as he stood there shaking, as if with the ague, and frantically rubbing his palms. Meanwhile, the MO, his greatcoat thrown around his shoulders, continued to pace up and down the room.

The duty doctor, who had been sent out, drummed on the window and whistled tunelessly, as if to show that this was no concern of his. Nurse Beata sobbed silently into a damp crumpled napkin, also of the regulation green.

"Please explain, Major Tawolski, how come you gave but scant attention to the case history?"

Tawolski held his tongue. When the MO assumed that tone, there was no point in offering any explanation or excuse, as he would not be heard anyway. And, moreover, what could he, Major Tawolski, the physician directly in charge of Barton, say?

"I realize that irradiation's a special case that has no connection with the patient's past history. But I must say that a strained or broken ankle or even appendicitis are similar special cases. And in all such cases we never start treatment, unless it's extra urgent, before we know enough of the patient's past history. How come that you, a medic with years of experience, couldn't take the pains to check up on Barton's case history, which states in black and white that in childhood he walked in his sleep? How come, Major? How come?"

Tawolski continued to hold his tongue.

The MO dumped his greatcoat on the floor, sat down, at once jumped up and again paced up and down the room.

"This'll kill him, for sure! And what's still worse, it had to happen just before the transplantation, of which we'd had such hopes!"

He abruptly broke off, however continuing to tread the carpet much like a caged panther. The desk lamp still lay tipped over, unrighted. The sickly light of daybreak filtered slowly into the smoke-filled room, in which a stale hush pressed painfully on the eardrums.

At last the MO sat down. With annoyance he jerked the lamp upright and turned the switch. Tawolski squeezed his eyes for a brief moment.

"Find out at once where he went," the MO said drily. "First that. Only then do we take any further measures. Clear?"

"Yes . . . only . . . only how are we to find out? Somnambulists never remember where they've been or what they've done."

"Never? He's no ordinary somnambulist, don't forget that! He's radioactive and is sure to have left a traceable trail."

Tawolski wearily realized that the MO was taunting him and that he really shouldn't stand for it. But the chief was right, a thousand times right, and so he continued to hold his tongue.

"Get through to the control post and tell them to detail a man with a Geiger counter. Trace the entire route and report your findings."

Tawolski was about to pick up the receiver when the MO put a restraining hand on his arm.

"From the corridor, please. There are certain matters I need to discuss."

Tawolski rose hastily and, stooping, made for the door.

A sharp pang of compassion pierced the MO's heart, when he noticed that stooping back, which so eloquently showed Tawolski's weariness.

"Take a tranquillizer, Abe . . . and go back home. Tell Dr. Weiss to accompany the radiological monitor."

AUG. 7. 19**. Capt. Tony Weiss

The radiological monitor at once spotted the tracks and we confidently advanced. Barton had meandered and zigzagged as if circumventing a series of invisible obstacles. With the somnambulist the subconscious never sleeps. Which is why their environmental responses are much quicker than when awake. For that is the only explanation one can find to show how Barton managed to cross and recross the entire compound without being noticed once. He had passed our small golf links, had crossed over the concrete footbridge spanning the pond, and had then swerved sharply into the rose garden. However, just before getting to Sector Four, he again swerved, this time toward the fire station. Next, he climbed over the fence and crawled up the drainpipe onto the roof, reaching by this devious route the road in Sector Seven, onto which he jumped down from a tree. He further bypassed the PX, approached the radar towers and, sneaking into the radio station grounds, made, as the bee flies, for the ploughed perimetrical swath bounding Sector Zero. He took the barbed-wire entanglement right beneath the second sentry tower, evidently escaping the watchful eye of the guard on top.

As special permits were needed to get into the range, we had to return to Sector Seven, from where I telephoned the commanding general for permission, which was granted at once. We donned protective garb and entered the range. Here we soon found Barton's trail again, which showed that he had headed for the biological zone. Background radiation increased in volume at every step. Soon, at about two hundred yards in, it damped the trail entirely. We had to go back and ask the guard commander for a sleuth hound. He was dead set against it. "It means murdering the poor dog," he said. We had again to call the general, who at once gave the respective order. The guard commander cradled the receiver with livid face, but, nevertheless, immediately summoned handler and dog. The man quickly put on the protective suit and was about to set out, when the dog-loving guard commander demanded that he bring in the respective paraphernalia for the animal too. This was absurd, as the hound would never pick up the scent unless its head were left unguarded.

The dog picked up the trail confidently, but when we reached the Bingo Bess test area, it gave a long drawn-out whine and refused to budge. Indeed, further on the grass was burnt, to a frozzle except for a few tufts of sage. Squatting back on its haunches, with nose pointed at the sky, the whining dog looked so human, that I felt my flesh creep. As the dog was doomed and was of no further use, we put it out of its misery with a well-aimed shot behind the ear. Why on earth had the guard commander kept us waiting for the dog to be garbed? No doubt he's president of some SPCA local.

I scanned the field through my binoculars and at once deduced where Barton had gone. There was nothing but rotting plain right up to the horizon and on it a lonely A-tank stood silhouetted like a sore thumb. That was the only place he could have gone.

Background irradiation was up the full pitch and remained steady. Inside the tank frontal irradiation jumped sharply due to the intensively contaminated mass of metal.

Barton, as one of the members of the Bingo Bess project team, knew where the sheep would be during the test. His subconscious mind had directed his steps this way during last night's sleep-walking. It was quite likely that he had received his first dose during a similar nocturnal trance—about which he had not the foggiest notion upon awaking next morning. A thorough inspection disclosed the imprint of ungloved fingers on every lubricated spot both inside and outside the tank. As nobody else had received any radiological dose in the post-test period, except Barton, it was only logical to assume that these were his fingermarks. Hence, there was no need for dactyloscopic analysis. And as far as I, in my capacity as forensic and army physician, could judge, the fingermarks had been made quite recently, not more than a few days ago. Accordingly, I had enough ground to go upon to believe that Barton had got his first dose in precisely this manner.

I now considered my assignment discharged. There was no earthly reason for me to stay any longer inside the tank, all the more since the remains of the dead sheep presented a most gruesome sight. The rotted fleece, teeth and bones floated in a repulsive plasma. For a moment I imagined a town, its buildings and other structures completely untouched, but with all its people overtaken by this invisible and intangible neutron bombardment while they had been attending to their customary daily affairs.

God forbid that this ever take place. We climbed out of the tank and retraced our steps. For a few moments we stood in silent homage by the body of the dead dog. The poor creature had had not the slightest notion that its life would end in this squalid fashion. Barton had signed its death sentence. Ah, those physicists! They themselves don't realize what they're doing! First the A-bomb, next the H-bomb, and now Bingo Bess.

No doubt they have quite a burden on their consciences. For otherwise, why these nocturnal rambles? And where did he get the strength? After all he's dying. I'm no physicist and have had no part in the invention of all these horrors, but I bet I'll have nightmares for long after everything seen inside that tank.

It's a good thing, though, that I'm no physicist and no soldier either. My mission is to relieve human suffering.

AUG. 8. Hospital Staff Room

The MO strode in with his customary loping gait. He removed his slicker and shook it free of the raindrops. The smell of fresh rain at once filled the room.

"Most odd," he said, nodding a hello to Tawolski. "How come the weather's gone rotten so suddenly? Never expected it! Well, what's cooking?"

"I've cancelled the transplantation."

"Correct. He's absolutely hopeless. You can put him on drugs from tomorrow. What's he like now?"

"In a delirium. Keeps on calling for a girl who, he says, lives in Medan."

"How's his temperature?"

"Still at 99.8. The blood pressure's likewise the same. As for the blood, we'll have to wait, I suppose."

"Yes, but it's bad, in fact, couldn't be worse. Indeed, che sara, sara. Who'd ever thought of it? Poor chap. Abe, I was a bit overwrought this morning. So don't take it all so much to heart. And . . . the general's asked us to keep the entire case under wraps."

Tawolski nodded.

"Good! As for Nurse, I'll handle her. So, we don't mention any second irradiation, okay? How much is it now?"

"Four hundred."

The MO shook his head. "The end's in sight," he said. "What about Cowan?"

"Not in the picture so far."

"That's good. Find some excuse to send him away. No, I'll better do that myself."

"Cowan expects the skin to shed and all hair to fall out. We've got to do something to sustain the water in the tissues. And one more thing. I'd like to make a complete transfusion."

The MO shrugged and moved off to the window.

It seemed to Tawolski as if he could read the MO's mind like an open book.

"What for?" he seemed to intimate. "He's doomed and you'll only be prolonging his agony. Why did God have to ordain such an end? Let him at least die in peace."

"Well, if you insist," the MO said succinctly, emphasizing the last word. "I won't object."

"Well, then," Tawolski said dully, "we'll do the transfusion and also try hypothermia."

The MO did not reply. Then, with an abrupt gesture, he removed his eyeglasses.

"Do anything you think necessary, Abe," he said. "But keep these two things in mind. First," and he bent a finger, "don't make your compassion harrow either yourself or him. Second," and he bent one more finger, "I'm sanctioning drugs, in short am acting in contravention of regulations. However, he deserves a more or less peaceable end. Please understand! It's not of you or me that we're thinking about, but only him. Only! Or perhaps you think there's a thousand-to-one chance, a shred of hope? If you do, tell me, and I promise I'll do all that's humanly possible. Well?"

"I don't think there's any hope at all. Several hours ago, perhaps. . . . But not now. Nothing'll help. . . . But . . . but there's something . . . well, I don't quite know how to put it. You see, over these past few days I've come to understand him. He's a genius. If we could give him one more hour, even should nobody ever hear his thoughts, it'll be better for all of us. Do you understand?"

"I can't say I do. But I'm giving you a free hand. It's all up to you, and to you alone. I can't give you orders."

"Thanks!" Tawolski rose slowly, instinctively trying to smooth the creased back of his tunic with one hand, and holding a loose button in his other.

The MO tried to tear his eyes away from Tawolski's hunched back as the latter went out. With all the force his will could command he kept his head turned towards the window. However, at the very last moment, he swivelled round again to catch sight of the narrowing crack of closing door.

An idea flashed through his mind, and for some reason he thought he was seeing Tawolski for the last time. But then the usual plethora of routine cares eased the constriction he felt in his chest.

AUG. 8. 19**. 10 A.M. Temp. 100.6. Pulse: 96. BP: 150/110

"Miss R. was greatly surprised when she saw her brother seated at her bedside. 'How come', she thought, 'when he lives across the ocean?' She tried to speak, but could not get a sound out. When, at last, she regained self-possession, and said something, he rose, went towards the electric fireplace, and melted into the air like a ghostly wraith. Next morning Miss R. told her family about what she had seen when she had so suddenly woken up in the midst of the previous night. She seemed to be in deep confusion, reiterating again and again that she was greatly concerned for her brother's health. The family did their best to console the girl, assuring her that she had no doubt dreamed it all.

"However that evening a cable came, saying that Miss R.'s brother had given up the ghost that very minute she had seen him at her bedside."

The book dropped out of Barton's limp fingers, but he was of no mind to bother Nurse about it.

How trite it seemed. Items of that nature, appearing in books, newspapers and scholarly communications dealing with para-psychology, had been legion. Miss R. was probably as dumb as they make them, a typical Pollyanna who was liable to swoon at the slightest provocation. Back in the 1930's what they'd called necrobiotic rays had made a sensation. But then everything had died down. The enigma remained, though. Kindred souls did seem to be in empathic rapport, despite distance. There seemed to be no reason to doubt that. But what about the millions of good citizens lacking this gift? Or, perhaps, curse? What am I to do if I can't feel Denise? And what is Denise to do, when she doesn't even suspect that I'm dying? It is certainly tempting and easy to blithely dismiss it all. Pure bunkum, nothing more. But supposing it isn't? Supposing I do have a very real chance of communicating a last farewell to her?

What a cannily insinuating thing hope is! It steals up by hook or by crook, under any guise. Begone self-solace, begone sweet opium. It's senseless, and only drains me of my last meagre resources of time and strength.

But if? Well, let's presume it does exist. But let's forget about it, or rather about how to turn it to use. I am about to die. Let's better see, on this day of the 8th of August how we can study the possible physical methods that may exist for the propagation of the "psi" effect. That is the most essential thing.

Let us start with paradoxes. Neither distance nor the laws of cause and effect affect the signal. In a nutshell, there are a number of controversial cases when effect precedes cause. Can such a thing happen? In principle, yes. The neutrino, for instance, so feebly interacts with matter that, to all practical intents, it experiences no impedimenta even when passing through millions of suns. If telepathic information is carried by the neutrino or other similar particles, it will not tend to scatter within the earth's biosphere. In short Paradox No. 1 is easy enough to explain. The others are tougher. Only if we forego the accepted notions and conceptions of time and space, can we presume to find the answer.

What a life-saver mental gymnastics is! Cogito, ergo sum! No! I exist because I think! The idea has gone on the instant, like the shutter dropping in a camera. You fly far away from the earth. Not you really, but something, or rather, nothing. All else remains. Only you go, never to return, only you crumble to dust and lose the accumulated memories. Death is amnesia complete. The body may live on, but if memory is lost, everything is lost. Death is when you are not aware that you are dead. At first, your voice is forgotten, and then . . . My voice, did I say?

"Nurse, do me a favour and bring me a dictaphone. I can't write, you see."

If we take the results of telepathic experiments for granted, we find ourselves obliged to note three paradoxes.

Item: telepathic communication is not affected by distance, with communication over two thousand miles proving as successful as over twenty yards.

Item: such communication is not effected by any of the senses or through the propagation of mental electromagnetic waves. Indeed, electromagnetism generally cannot carry such information—which seems to have been amply demonstrated by experiments conducted within metal cabins that were impervious to radiowaves.

Item: some recorded cases of spontaneous telepathy and clairvoyance conflict with the laws of causality.

I shall neither uphold or debunk the truth of these paradoxes as I have neither the necessary empirical data nor dicta that need to be defended from natural encroachment. What is far more important and interesting is to see how well the cited paradoxes accord or conflict with the basic laws of the modern natural sciences.

To begin with, paradox No. 1. It is possible, should: a) the material carrier be a type of energy that will not tend to scatter in space, and, b) all humans be linked by a special "telepathic" field. In the first case, the neutrino may serve as such a carrier, as matter practically fails to absorb it. At any rate, in the earth's biosphere such absorption is negligible and can be discounted. In the second case, we may presume that not only inductor and percipient, but also an unknown number of other people are involved, in which case the signal may be amplified, as within a photo-multiplier, for instance.

Naturally, the first explanation is simplest. Even for the ordinary reason that it does not introduce any more unknowns into the physical environment and describes the given phenomenon by means of tangibly existing objects.

Paradox No. 2. In effect, it is removed from the agenda by the explanation we have provided for the preceding paradox. Accordingly, we may even suggest an experiment to verify the explanation provided. If the neutrino is indeed the material carrier, then the value of the neutrino background may influence the telepathic intensity. In short, experiments analogous to those conducted within the metal cabin may be staged in the vicinity of an atomic reactor, where large quantities of neutrinos are emitted in the process of beta-decay.

However, the neutrino hypothesis has several obstacles that need to be overcome. In the first place, it is not always clear as to which of the four neutrino types carries telepathic communications. True, in principle, this is of no particular significance. Except for its putting added complications in the way of the experiment.

Finally, before we end with paradoxes Nos. 1 and 2, we may postulate a combined hypothesis to presume that all humans are linked by a neutrino field. True, though there is apparently no need for this hypothesis, we must set it out if we do not wish to transgress upon the laws of logic.

Paradox No. 3. This is the trickiest and the most vulnerable to opponents of telepathy. To explain it we must either discard established, basic conceptions of time and space, or at least enlist the most original and daring ideas and theories that physicists are putting forward nowadays. The first alternative leads us onto the dubious path of nebulous hypotheses as to the existence of more than three dimensions and the like.

Meanwhile, as for the original theories now being suggested, they are, for the most part, unconvincing. Still we shall have to equip ourselves with them too.

One is the theory of what is called closed time cycle, which turns such notions as past and future into relative concepts, even outside the context of the special theory of relativity. If we espouse this idea, it will be logical to assume that the human brain will be able to chart the future with the aid of the neutrino. However, we can dispense even with this theory. Some postulate, of course, absolutely out of any connection with telepathy, that the specific aspects of the neutrino's behaviour stem from its moving from the future into the past, not vice versa, as is the case with all the objects we are accustomed to. Incidentally, this has been brilliantly confirmed mathematically. For us it is of interest, insofar as it provides an adequate explanation for paradox No. 3.

We may also take the more formal approach, based on the law of the conservation of combined sequence, from which it follows that all interactions are invariant relative to the time inversion. Which implies that the description of an interaction will not change if we replace 'future' by 'past'.

"Nurse, please switch the thing off, I have no further need for it."

The sensation is most odd. I've never had so much spare time as now. I'm in a position to bring any idea to its logical conclusion. I can trace the entire route from the obscure, winding sources to the thundering waterfall, when it, realized and anaemic, splashes down into memory's depths or fades into the purring of the recording tape.

Then comes a moment when a flash breaks away from this flow to notch its way into the heart. By itself it is nothing, but it is able to evoke associations.

Man charts the future. No frog-eyed clairvoyant, mind you, no croaking Cassandra, no mescaline-doped medium. Just a nice young Ph.D. in an up-to-the-minute lab, at Princeton, say. He turns a knob, and sees himself projected several years into the future in the reflected neutrino ray. No hallucination this, but a doubly and trebly checked experimental result, one that arouses not the slightest doubt. Hence, if he sees his own reflection, he will be prepared to run risks for the sake of science. Since he exists in the future, he cannot die at this moment. So he pulls out a pistol, cocks it and brings it up to point at his forehead. Then he squeezes his eyes, and pulls the trigger. Nothing happens. He pulls the trigger again, and again nothing happens.

If I were a writer, that's the kind of stories I would write.

Denise! Do you remember that green patch of light and the splashing of the tide and the invisible black shore, and the swaying fish? Like a spellbound fish he rides with the waves, up and down. Do you remember that night on the pier, Denise? That last ray of light, that last smell of freshness and then the plunge into the cold of darkness. Do visit me in my dreams, Denise! At least for one last time to say goodbye. It seems as if it was only yesterday, that starry night and the frothing tide.

A dust-specked bluish ray slips by beneath the water. Somewhere a ship's bells clang midnight. Phosphorescing crabs crawl ashore to conspire against their deep-sea president. Overhead, the blue dust of the Milky Way whirls and luminescent stars come scattering down. I'll spare that big star. Do you remember that night on the roof, Denise? Where has it all gone? Into what bottomless barrel has it all vanished? Does the past really just simply disappear into emptiness, into a cold and bleak nothingness? But time is one, eternal. Otherwise, would it be time? Could it be that past, present and future are but the transmuted condition of a oneness, of a three-faced, unfathomable entity? I have now within me past, present and future, all at once. They have blended into one present of the second order. It's just that we cannot take it all in, just as we cannot take in the Metagalaxy. Man is not meant to comprehend substance all at once, in one swoop. He gains an awareness of it gradually, through various phenomena. This is the combination of analysis and synthesis. Face and reverse. One phenomenon, and then the next. Oh, past, present and future! But diverse reflections of one single substance, whose name is time. We have come the full circle to no purpose. The intellect sinks in the black, plague-infested waters, with no hope, with not a single ray of light left. It may be that time stands still, that it is merely our mind that moves, glides, and envelops it.

But what if, subliminally, we are already aware of that? Most likely the day will come when the most sacrosanct mysteries of the Universe and with them the uniform system of particles will open up to us in the processes that occur within the dark depths of the brain. Because it is there that we record in finalized form the processes that are played out in both macro- and micro-worlds. The brain was created in conformity with the selfsame laws that governed the making of the Universe, and it is quite able to comprehend it in its fullest possible state. Thus, the sequence $1/2 + 1/4 + 1/8 + 1/16 + \ldots$ approaches unity without ever reaching it. And it could be that our brain has already comprehended the universe, only is so far unaware of that. Not I, but one French physicist said that. But I too think that. Only I have not yet brought the idea to its logical conclusion. People, bestir your brains from their lethargy! Physicists of the future, dig into your own minds, for they are your laboratories.

The analytical method of attaining the truth is practically

exhausted. With every day we are gaining more and more, but with every day too, we are losing more and more. We are advancing through selection up a ladder, whose rungs consist of alternatives. From manifold substance, the investigator extracts the axiomatic pearl and passes it on further. Thus, there emerges for but an instant a oneness from the contradictory dichotomy of dialectics. Then it, too, divides into opposites to tempt the next investigator with the choice of alternative, leaving in its trail a whole graveyard of shattered contradictions. Who is to rummage in the cast-up heaps where lie brilliant ideas unnoticed by those who came before us, where branches of learning we never knew were created of their own accord, where interred are whole realms of forever forgotten knowledge?

What a fine thing it would be if we would be able to descend to the source! If we would be able to retrace the landmarks, to revise the choice, and to forge together the links of rejected truths.

It is because we always choose but one of the opposites, that we advance along a spiral and that the morrow which we rejected yesterday returns today. We row now with the left, now with the right oar, for which reason our boat now strikes the swampy, now the rocky, bank. How are we to keep on course? How are we to avoid a mistaken choice and attain the truth in one go?

We must look for fundamentally novel approaches. But are they possible? And isn't the road that we have taken the one and only road that man could possibly take?

AUG. 9. Hospital Staff Room

"Has Cowan already gone?" The MO turned off the tap and wrung his hands above the washstand.

"Yesterday, already," Tawolski said handing him a towel. "But before he left, he wanted to have one more look at Barton."

"And what did he say?"

"The final phase seems about to commence. There are already several small spreading hemorrhages."

"Oh. And what about your hypothermy?"

Tawolski shrugged and reached for his attache case.

"We've received the roster of fortnightly visits from the head office. It requires your signature. They say you may introduce any changes you like, but within the set estimates."

"Let me have it. Who's on the list?"

"Senior radiological monitor Schultz, Lt. de Friez, Dr. Scott, Srgt. Heathaway, Maj. Salk, Dr. Goodow, Driver Peck, Sr. Fireman Balaguer, Dr. Barton and Pte. Tracy."

"Delete Heathaway! We don't want any more scenes like the one he staged last time! And also one of the doctors. Egg-heads take it harder than the others. When there's just one, he manages to conceal his feelings somehow, but if we'll have two on the visiting list, I really don't know what might happen! I hope you see what I mean. So, strike off one of them till the next time."

"But we've got three of them down here."

"Oh, you mean Barton too? No, it certainly wasn't him I had in mind. Do your best for him. Only, as far as I remember, you said there wasn't anyone?"

"That's so, but. . . . Please have a look at this. I drew it up and if you have no objections . . ." his voice tailed off.

"All right, let me have it." The MO read the paper, and then turned a vacuous stare to the ceiling. "Very well," he said a little later, "Let's try it. I'll okay it."

AUG. 9. 19**. 10 A.M. Temp. 101. Pulse: 96. BP: 150/105

"We've come to see you, if you don't mind, Alan?"

"Why, Mike! And Lee! And Ted! Just grand! Come on in. Make yourselves comfortable. How funny you look, Lee, in that smock. Yellow on green. Just like a lemon."

"I see you haven't changed, Alan," Lee said with a quiet smile as he cautiously sat down at the foot of the bed.

"Only not there!" Nurse Beata cried. "Further off, please! All of you!"

She switched off the ultra-violet and let the screen down.

"Just like a mummy," Barton smirked. "They keep me spotlessly clean. Well, what's new, you germ-carriers?"

"Nothing much," Mike, a small dark mercurial man, said, gesticulating wildly as he jumped up and marched up and down the ward. "Everything's much the same. We're all looking forward to seeing you." He broke off, unable to continue.

"Forget it, Mike," Barton said coldly.

"Yep, forget it Mike," Ted Wygand, an enormous, imperturbable giant of a man, a nuclear physicist by profession, repeated with a nod.

"Y'know, there's a little present we've brought along for you," Mike exclaimed, darting towards the door.

"Hold your horses there!" Wygand cried, but the other had already gone out.

"I'm afraid this isn't any too enjoyable for you," Barton continued with the same fixed smile. "I very well know what all of you feel and can quite sympathize. Honest, I'm ashamed of myself. But you've gotta understand me too. There's nothing we can do about it. So none of that false heartiness and maudlin sob-sistering. It just makes me boil! Let's talk business and part in peace. I know what you're all thinking. If it could all end sooner!"

At that moment Mike returned with a plexiglas box under his arm. A spotted guinea-pig crouched inside.

"This is for you," he announced solemnly, as he cautiously set the box on the bedside locker. "It's from the guys in the biosector. When they heard what'd happened they gave it a dose of fifteen hundred roentgens. Then they began to give it the same sort of treatment you get, asking Tawolski a hundred and one questions every goddam day. And whaddaya know? The day before yesterday its blood count showed improvement, and by now it's out of danger. So, if you don't mind we'll leave it with you."

He picked up the box and was about to deposit it on the coverlet, when Nurse Beata intervened.

"What do you think you're doing? Put it in that corner. We'll all take care of it. What a funny bunch!" She tapped on the lid, but the animal did not respond.

"Poor thing," Barton muttered, sinking back onto the pillow. He felt feverish. "Gimme some water," he said.

Nurse picked up the water jug and cautiously lowered the spout to the patient's lips.

"It's time you fellows went," she said, without turning her head towards them. "Look how excited you've made him!"

"Let 'em stay a little longer, Nurse." Barton licked his cracked and inflamed lips. "Thank the biologists for me, but let me tell you for your own information that they're just a bunch of dopes. Still, let the animal stay, it's not in my way. Well, what's the latest gossip, Ted?"

"Nuttin' much. 'Cept that Scott's dame's here."

"His missus?"

"Yep. For a fortnight."

"And?"

"He's doing his best."

They laughed.

"It'd seemed to me," Barton said, "as if I'd been lying around here since the world began and that you'd all been having fun. Now I see that nothing's really been having fun. Now I see that nothing's really been happening all this time. Or you're just no good at telling things, Ted?"

"Well, I dunno. But, it's quite true that nuttin's bin happenin'. Just ask Mike. Or Lee."

"All right. I'll buy it. You were always a Demosthenes who'd accidentally put too many pebbles in his mouth."

"Whaddaya mean?"

"Nuttin'. Forget it. Just tired, that's all. Suppose I ought to have a rest. Not used to talking much, y'know."

They at once made to go, but not before spending quite some time mussing around as if looking for something and then standing in the doorway, muttering and grinning idiotically.

Barton did not attempt to detain them. He thought to

EVERYTHING BUT LOVE

himself that lips sometimes seemed made of elastic, that they'd stretch out from ear to ear in a fixed grin and quiver helplessly. At such moments, people fib unconsciously out of a compassionate shame.

Mike was first to run. He suddenly wrinkled up like a sick monkey, and, barely able to hold back his tears, slunk out. Barton noticed Wygand's broad back shrink to pitifully eject those same miserable utterances, which the back's owner himself was unable to force out. However Barton had no sympathy for them. He was amazed to realize that he felt nothing for them at all. They'd just buried him alive, but he didn't feel a thing. He was neither sore, nor upset. Perhaps this wasn't him, but a complete stranger who was lying here?

He suddenly distinctly realized the borderline that his approaching death had drawn between him and everybody else. He was across, on the other side. They didn't know what he knew. His was a knowledge that completely changes outlook and character. No wonder they took quite a different view of one and the same thing. He looked down from the peak of what he knew. The others looked out of the dark crannies of ignorance and instinctive horror.

"I'll have to ask the doctor to bar all further visits," he thought.

I don't seem to be able to relax, to get it off my mind. What concern is it of mine, after all? It's high time I did relax. What I ought to think about now is the most crucial things, things about which I had never had time to think during that other previous and now distant life. The tasks are different. And the yardsticks are also different. Out with all that comprised the substance of the fuss and bother of my life before. Only those thoughts that came to mind last night should make up the substance of my present life. When the misty multiplicity of years still lay ahead I gave heed to but trifles. But now with only two steps to go to nothingness, I wish to think about what is eternal. What a funny creature man is!

Scientists say that today's babies are immortal. Perhaps, man indeed stands on the threshold of immortality? What a pity to die on the eve of that! But it has always been so, that someone dies on the eve, killed by the last bullet fired on the last day of war.

However, is it for me to talk of immortality? I must be terribly confusing and morbidly exaggerating things! So little remains, so little!

I wonder what vicious hate and stupid anger will turn into then? The immortal needs so very much more. But if death cannot check this now, what will check it then? When people talk about immortality, I myself think about the absolute reverse.

People have learned of the taste that the industry of death has. That is an invidious memory, which does not pass without trace, indeed cannot do so. We shall have to go on footing the bill without cease. Like a hot sponge, it will suck up blood without end.

So what lies at the root of it all? Is man indeed wicked by nature? If not, then whence this fearfully irrational mental defect? Though it happened before I was born, the alien memory of those who perished somehow came my way. So was I killed, was I slain for the first time. All that came after happened before I was born, the alien memory of those who perished somehow came my way. So was I killed, was I slain for the first time. All that came after happened only because I was already dead. With some, this fearful memory roused to struggle and pointed to a bright, though distant future. With others, the crime was accepted and carried on further. The future. With others, the crime was accepted and carried on further. The sole thing that I grasped was that one must not think about it. I wondered how to live on further, and found no answer. It was impossible to live on further. One could but yell at the top of one's voice, spatter windows with a hail of bullets, and dive into the water. That was how I saw it then. I shall never forget that day when in the cruel light of morning there dawned on me the realization of what had happened to those long since gone and to all of us. They had caught up with me, struck at my solar plexus, and had killed me. So when and where could I have caught the lethal dose?

Only now do I see how the distant inexorable wheel has come the full circle. The crime that others had perpetrated broke me like a reed and I ceased to think. And then I imperceptibly set foot on the path to one more crime. How it is all so cruelly clear now!

After all, the inventors of the death camps also started off from a certain point of departure. They too had ceased, at a certain moment, to think. And that is the crux of the matter. The moment we cease to think, we ourselves become potential murderers and accomplices in dastardliness. Throughout all the ages tyrants and despots tried to get people to stop thinking. The disease of intellectuality must never sap the strength of the workman and warrior. One must work and fight, not think. The road to fascism ever begins with this naively pragmatic jingle. How easy to ensnare man in these coils! Is it really only one's personal debacle that enlightens one?

> Where has it gone, that greasy smoke,
> The senseless stench of human fat?
> Perhaps, on roofs it sits a furry soot,
> Or, perchance, is scattered to all four winds?
> After all, this happened so long, long ago,
> While smoke, we know, soon comes to rest.
> The more so smoke that heavy is and stinks of fat,
> And filled is, too, with glow of fearful fire!
> It has indeed now come to rest,
> Stagg'ring thru' the scraggy pines
> Across the frozen, swampy soil.
> In tufts 'twas caught upon the barbs of wire
> To blur that piercing shaft of light
> Which, coming from the gloom, thru' shades of
>   years long by,

Stabs and cuts and wrenches at the heart.
But can we say that all has come to rest,
Or, dissolved in rainfall, has seeped

Thru' bitter loam and dust-dead leaves?
Can we say that?
It belched forth day and night, non-stop,
As train did follow train,
And more trains came,
Chugging to a rendezvous with death
'Cross miles of swamp, as sun went down behind.
No, not all, it seems, rests on roof and field.
Part, borne aloft by winds of time,
Still sweeps thru' pearly sky
To fall in open mouth,
Saliva'ed into stomach drips,
Thence to seep into the blood,
Down roads and routes first charted
When God made man of dust and clay.
And, thus, the last link's forged
In chain that earth and sky unites.
But what care we for that,
When smoke, as fulsome as before,
Which time alone could blind us to,
Still seeps into our blood?
This smoke's contaminated us,
Indeed everthing around.
How are we to live?

AUG. 11. Hospital Staff Room

"How's tricks, today?" the MO grinned as he rubbed his hands.

"No doubt had no trouble with his liver last night," Tawolski thought. "Yes, that's what it is. Had a good night's rest. Even those pouches aren't so much in evidence. Not like me. Couldn't sleep a wink, hardly. Which is why I feel so damn lousy. How simple!"

"So, how's tricks?" the MO repeated, as he raised the window, stuck his head out and drank in deeply of the warm air. Then he divested himself of his regulation jacket and loosened his tie.

"The latest serum sodium test produced appalling results. The dose must have been somewhere between ten and twenty hundred roentgens. The decline in monocytes and reticulocytes is catastrophic."

"Not more than three or four days, I suppose?"

"Perhaps even less. What about that paper?"

"The general passed the buck to the big wheels and it's been okayed."

"Thanks, prof!"

"What for?"

AUG. 11. 19**. 10 A.M. Temp. 102.4. Pulse: 102. BP: 160/110

So you've come, Denise! How did you get to know? Happen to see me in your dreams? Or perhaps suddenly caught sight of me in the crowd, rushed forward to catch me, elbowing and shoving everyone aside, and suddenly saw me melt away into thin air? Was that it, Denise? Why don't you say something. . . . Or will you too melt away into the air this very moment and leave me? Thanks, darling, though, for coming. For at least a few moments. I'm in a fever, true, and only think I see you here. Still, thanks, darling.

Do you remember our star, Denise? I didn't tell you then that I knew all about that star, not in this life, true, but in another, in a different time and, perhaps, place. The savage Indian tribe of the Cherente, who live in the basin of the Amazon, have handed down from father to son the tale of the youth and the star, a story that you know, only did not recognize as having taken place with us in those far-off times.

One night I looked up at the sky to see a blue star. It shone with serene brilliance, and its sad rays plucked at the heart strings. Enamoured of it, I fell on my knees and beckoned to it. I gazed long and hard at the heavens, yearning for that cold, bright star. In tears, I returned to my tepee to sink on my mat and dream of the beautiful star. Suddenly, in the midst of night I woke up out of this dream of sweet languish, feeling a gaze fixed on me. In the dark shadows I discerned a fair maiden with eyes of dazzling blue.

"Who are you?" I cried out in terror. "Begone!"

"Why bid me gone?" she asked in tones of soft suppliance. "I am the star you coveted for your gourd. Stars are maidens too and cannot live without the warmth of love."

Frightened, I lay tongue-tied, barely able to see her through the mist of tears before my eyes.

At last, stretching out my arms to her, I cried: "But there won't be enough room for you in my gourd."

She shook her head and flashes of blue glittered on the reed walls.

"But there won't be enough room for you on my bike. Why, I can hardly hold on myself. There's certainly not enough room for both of us."

But you shook your head, and climbed on without a word. How old were you then, Denise? Twelve? Or thirteen?

I opened my gourd and let the star-girl in. Now I had a little sky of my own, with the loveliest of all the stars in the universe shining inside.

Ever since I knew no rest. For days on end I wandered in the jungle. My heart and head were full of the star-girl, whom in a moment of pixilation I had beckoned down to me from the skies. At night she would step out of the gourd and let her shining loveliness glow till daybreak.

One night she invited me to go out hunting with her in the jungle. For hours on end it seemed, we followed the spoor. Living festoons of glow-worms glimmered above the red, baleful eyes of alligators that stared at us malevolently from the miasmic backwaters.

Then we came to a tall slender bacaba.

"Climb it," she said.

I meekly obeyed, overcoming my fears, but risking every

moment to fall. When I reached the very first ribbed palm fronds, she cried from below: "Hold on tight!"

Like a blue-streaked colibri, she shot up to the very top and struck the trunk of the palm with a branch. Up it grew and grew until its top touched the sky. She tied it fast and stretched out a hand to me. Cautiously I set foot on the sky, my head in a whirl from the dizzying height.

Suddenly I heard strains of music, the boisterous tune of that rollicking dance which is performed after a successful tapir hunt.

"Only don't look at the dancing", she warned me and glided away.

"Wait!" I cried, but she had gone.

So I stood there, facing the emptiness, while behind the music grew louder and stronger and I heard gay laughter.

Bursting with curiosity, I turned round to see . . . skeletons dancing in the starlight. Chunks of meat still hung from their bones, jaguar fangs clicked against their ribs, and hollow eyepits gleamed faintly.

A neutron beam of high density brings about the complete destruction of protein colloids.

Horrorstruck and scarcely able to breathe, I rushed headlong into the empty void. At this moment she returned and severely berated me for having disobeyed her. Then she brought a basin of warm water and washed my body free of the putrescent white patches that had erupted during the dance macabre.

A bleak hollowness opened under my heart. I eyed the heavens blindly and suddenly dashed towards the top of the bacaba, lashed its trunk with a twig, and went hurtling back to earth.

Sadly she looked after. "Why run away?" she said. "You'll never be able to forget."

The star was right. Down on earth I was ravaged by a fearsome, incurable disease.

And now I lie dying, Denise. Blinding tears fill my eyes and I am unable to forget.

Go down to the Amazon, Denise, and look for the Shinga River in the heart of the jungle. Seek the small but proud tribe of the Cherente and you will learn the end of our story. Because I did not tell the entire story that night. Do you remember? My grandmother was a Cherente Indian, Denise.

"And thus did the Indians learn, that it is not bliss which awaits them up there, even though stars shine down so luringly," my grandmother would conclude the story.

Why that look in your eyes, Denise? They're absolutely empty. Like the sky. Why don't you cry. No tears? Or you haven't been taught to?

So that's what it is. I wonder who I'm indebted to for this good fortune? To Tawolski? Or to the general? Or to the chief of the army office? Or perhaps to you, Denise? You must have registered and let them have your molecular chart. Why did you have to do that? Why?

I understand, of course, that you were dying to see me, and didn't know that I lay here dying, that I will die inevitably. You couldn't stand the loneliness. Denise.

No, don't touch me. No, not you, but Denise, who couldn't stand the loneliness and is now sobbing her heart out at home. You don't know how to cry. Second-class stuff, I suppose. I guess my benefactors sought to economize. Why go to all that expense, when it's only for a couple of days.

So you just couldn't take it any longer. Denise. Poor girl, I pity you. We've been terribly unlucky. We certainly didn't deserve it!

But, Lord, why this agony? Why all this muck at the very end of the road? Of course, they had best of intentions. Tawolski's a fine fellow, but how can he be such a moron! Whom are they out to kid? Me?! I wouldn't wish you, Major Tawolski of the Medical Corps, an end like mine. On no account. To so irredeemably spoil the few last moments. Respect death at least! Ersatz love and ersatz death. A sick joke in the worst of taste! All of society, of civilization must be sick to take such a liberty.

Take her away from me! Take her away!

AUG. 11. 19**. 10 A.M. Temp. 104.4. Pulse: abnormally fast and arrhythmic.

In coma.

Capt. Tony Weiss: Will you step out, Miss. There's something very important that I have to tell you. (Denise follows Weiss out of the ward.) Try to forget everything seen and heard here. Alan . . . took you . . . for somebody else. Our psychiatrists, who are wizards at their job, will help you to understand. You're young and all your life lies before you. Modern science is able to work miracles. You must forgive me. I'm feeling so terribly awkward. You see, I'm not quite prepared for this. Actually Major Tawolski would've explained, but as he's . . . well . . . worn out, he asked me to do it for him. For the time being, that is. You see, your fiance did the nation a very great service. Dr. Barton was . . . rather, is . . . a national hero! So the government has gone to every length. . . . In short, you'll be able to see for yourself. But first take this pill. Oh, it's quite harmless. It's to ward against too great an emotional . . . well . . . shock. And now please, would you be so kind as to go into this room?

(Capt. Weiss opens the door and lets Denise enter in front of him. She makes two steps and stops. With arms outstretched a smiling Alan Barton comes toward her. He is perfectly hale and hearty, in no whit changed since the day she saw him off at the airport.)

Denise: How unspeakably vile! How unhuman!

Weiss: Please, Miss . . . Wait, please. What . . . what are we to do with . . . him?

Denise: Send him back where you got him! And may you burn in hell!

Weiss: What?!

Denise: May you and this age burn in hell!

Nurse Beata (She has just rushed in and is frantic): Captain, please do something! Professor Tawolski has just taken an overdose of morphine. Please, doctor, hurry!

TO HOWARD HUGHES: A MODEST PROPOSAL

Joe Haldeman

Born in 1943, Joe Haldeman belongs to that generation which has never known a world free from the menace of nuclear weapons. And to him, war is not what it has been for too many science fiction writers, a thrilling fantasy for the indulgence of escapist heroics. When he was drafted in 1967, his college degree in physics and astronomy earned him a position as combat engineer in Vietnam, where he was seriously wounded.

In 1969, the year he got out of the army, Haldeman published his first story, "Out of Phase," in *Galaxy*. *War Year* (1972), his first novel, is set in Vietnam; he calls it "a fictionally extended version of my own combat diary." Then in 1974 came his magnificent novel *The Forever War*, which won the Hugo award of 1975 and has since been recognized as one of the very greatest of all the innumerable science fiction works about war. *The Forever War* extrapolates and projects the Vietnam experience to interstellar and millennial dimensions; it is certainly one of the finest novels yet published about the Vietnam War and its effects on American society.

Haldeman has continued to develop as a major figure in contemporary science fiction, winning a second Hugo for his short story "Tricentennial" in 1976 and a Galaxy award in 1978 for his novel *Mindbridge*. He now has a large audience, and there are even hints that he is gaining recognition as a major writer without the usual qualification "science fiction."

Somehow and someplace in his experience, Haldeman seems to have come up with the curious idea, expressed in "To Howard Hughes: A Modest Proposal," that it is "our *leaders*" who make wars, "advancing their own political aims" by sending others out to kill and die. So he offers his modest proposal as we contemplate what to do about this predicament.

1. 13 October 1975

Shark Key is a few hundred feet of sand and scrub between two slightly larger islands in the Florida Keys: population, one.

Not even one person actually lives there—perhaps the name has not been attractive to real estate developers—but there is a locked garage, a dock and a mailbox fronting on US 1. The man who owns this bit of sand—dock, box, and carport—lives about a mile out in the Gulf of Mexico and has an assistant who picks up the mail every morning and gets groceries and other things.

Howard Knopf Ramo is this sole "resident" of Shark Key, and he has many assistants besides the delivery boy. Two of them have doctorates in an interesting specialty, of which more later. One is a helicopter pilot; one ran a lathe under odd conditions; one is a youngish ex-colonel (West Point, 1960); one was a contract killer for the Mafia; five are doing legitimate research into the nature of gravity; several dozen are dullish clerks and technicians; and one, not living with the rest off Shark Key, is a U.S. Senator who does not represent Florida but nevertheless does look out for the interests of Howard Knopf Ramo. The researchers and the delivery boy are the only ones in Ramo's employ whose income he reports to the IRS, and he only reports one tenth at that. All the other gentlemen and ladies also receive ten-times-generous salaries, but they are all legally dead, and so the IRS has no right to their money, and it goes straight to anonymously numbered Swiss accounts without attrition by governmental gabelle.

Ramo paid out little more than one million dollars in salaries and bribes last year; he considered it a sound investment of less than one fourth of one per cent of his total worth.

2. 7 May 1955

Our story began, well, many places with many people. But one pivotal person and place was 17-year-old Ronald Day, then going to high school in sleepy Winter Park, Florida.

Ronald wanted to join the Army, but he didn't want to just *join* the Army. He had to be an officer, and he wanted to be an Academy man.

His father had served gallantly in World War II and in Korea until an AP mine in Ch'unch'on (Operation "Ripper") forced him to retire. At that time he had had for two days a battlefield commission, and he was to find that the difference between NCO's retirement and officer's retirement would be the difference between a marginal life and a comfortable one, subsequent to the shattering of his leg. Neither father nor son blamed the Army for having sent the senior Day marching through a muddy mine field, 1953 being what it was, and neither thought the military life was anything but the berries. More berries for the officers, of course, and the most for Westpointers.

The only problem was that Ronald was, in the jargon of another trade, a "chronic underachiever." He had many fascinating hobbies and skills and an IQ of 180, but he was barely passing in high school, and so had little hope for an appointment. Until Howard Knopf Ramo came into his life.

That spring afternoon, Ramo demonstrated to father and

son that he had the best interests of the United States at heart, and that he had a great deal of money (nearly a hundred million dollars, even then), and that he knew something rather embarrassing about senior Day, and that in exchange for certain reasonable considerations he would get Ronald a place in West Point, class of 1960.

Not too unpredictably, Ronald's intelligence blossomed in the straitjacket discipline at the Point. He majored in physics, that having been part of the deal, and took his commission and degree—with high honors—in 1960. His commission was in the Engineers, and he was assigned to the Atomic Power Plant School at Fort Belvoir, Virginia. He took courses at the School and at Georgetown University nearby.

He was Captain Ronald Day and bucking for major, one step from being in charge of Personnel & Recruitment, when he returned to his billet one evening and found Ramo waiting for him in a stiff-backed chair. Ramo was wearing the uniform of a brigadier general, and he asked a few favors. Captain Day agreed gladly to co-operate, not really believing the stars on Ramo's shoulders; partly because the favors seemed harmless if rather odd, but reasonable in view of past favors; mainly because Ramo told him something about what he planned to do over the next decade. It was not exactly patriotic but involved a great deal of money. And Captain Day, O times and mores, had come to think more highly of money than of patriotism.

Ramo's representatives met with Day several times in the following years, but the two men themselves did not meet again until early 1972. Day eventually volunteered for Vietnam, commanding a battalion of combat engineers. His helicopter went down behind enemy lines, such lines as there were in that war, in January, 1972, and for one year he was listed as MIA. The North Vietnamese eventually released their list, and he became KIA, body never recovered.

By that time his body, quite alive and comfortable, was resting a mile off Shark Key.

3. 5 December 1959

Andre Charvat met Ronald Day only once, at Fort Belvoir, five years before they would live together under Ramo's roof. Andre had dropped out of Iowa State as a sophomore, was drafted, was sent to the Atomic Power Plant School, learned the special skills necessary to turn radio-active metals into pleasing or practical shapes, left the Army and got a job running a small lathe by remote control, from behind several inches of lead, working with plutonium at an atomic power applications research laboratory in Los Alamos—being very careful not to waste any plutonium, always ending up with the weight of the finished piece and the showings equal to the weight of the rough piece he had started with.

But a few milligrams at a time, he was substituting simple uranium for the precious plutonium shavings.

He worked at Los Almos for nearly four years and brought 14,836 grams of plutonium with him when he arrived via midnight barge off Shark Key, 12 November 1974.

Many other people in similar situations had brought their grams of plutonium to Shark Key. Many more would, before the New Year.

4. 1 January 1975

"Ladies. Gentlemen." Howard Knopf Ramo brushes long white hair back in a familiar, delicate gesture and with the other hand raises a tumbler to eye level. It bubbles with good domestic champagne. "Would anyone care to propose a toast?"

An awkward silence, over fifty people crowded into the television room. On the screen, muted cheering as the Allied Chemical ball begins to move. "The honor should be yours, Ramo," says Colonel Day.

Ramo nods, gazing at the television. "Thirty years," he whispers and says aloud: "To *our* year. To our world."

Drink, silence, sudden chatter.

5. 2 January 1975

Curriculum Vitae

My name is Philip Vale and I have been working with Howard Knopf Ramo for nearly five years. In 1967 I earned a doctorate in nuclear engineering at the University of New Mexico and worked for two years on nuclear propulsion systems for spacecraft. When my project was shelved for lack of funding in 1969, it was nearly impossible for a nuclear engineer to get a job, literally impossible in my specialty.

We lived off savings for a while. Eventually I had to take a job teaching high school physics and felt lucky to have any kind of a job, even at $7000 per year.

But in 1970 my wife suffered an attack of acute glomerulonephritis and lost both kidneys. The artificial dialysis therapy was not covered by our health insurance, and to keep her alive would have cost some $25,000 yearly. Ramo materialized and made me a generous offer.

Three weeks later, Dorothy and I were whisked incognito to Shark Key, our disappearance covered by a disastrous automobile accident. His artificial island was mostly unoccupied in 1970, but half of one floor was given over to medical facilities. There was a dialysis machine, and two of the personnel were trained in its use. Ramo called it "benevolent blackmail" and outlined my duties for the next several years.

6. 4 April 1970

When Philip Vale came to Ramo's island, all that showed above water was a golden geodesic dome supported by massive concrete pillars and arm-thick steel cables that sang basso in the wind. Inside the dome were living quarters for six people and a more-or-less legitimate research establishment called Gravities, Inc. Ramo lived there with two technicians, a delivery boy and two specialists in gravity research. The establishment was very expensive, but Ramo claimed to love pure science, hoped for eventual profit, and admitted that it made his tax situation easier. It also gave him the isolation that semibillionaires traditionally prefer; because of the delicacy of the measurements necessary to his research, no airplanes were allowed to buzz overhead, and the Coast Guard kept unauthorized ships from coming within a one-mile radius. All five employees did do research work in gravity; they published with expected frequency, took out occasional patents, and knew they were only a cover for the actual work about to begin downstairs.

There were seven underwater floors beneath the golden dome, and Dr. Philip Vale's assignment was to turn those seven floors into a factory for the construction of small atom bombs. Twenty-nine Nagasaki-sized fission bombs.

7. August 1945

Howard Knopf Ramo worked as a dollar-a-year man for several years, the government consulting him on organizational matters for various secret projects. He gave as good advice as he could, without being told classified details.

In August, 1945, Ramo learned what that Manhattan Project had been all about.

8. 5 April 1970—3 February 1972

Dr. Philip Vale was absorbed for several weeks in initial planning: flow charts, lists of necessary equipment and personnel, timetables, floor plans. The hardest part of his job was figuring out a way to steal a lot of plutonium without being too obvious about it. Ramo had some ideas, on this and other things, that Vale expanded.

By the middle of 1971 there were thirty people living under Gravities, Inc., and plutonium had begun to trickle in, a few grams at a time, to be shielded with lead and cadmium and concrete and dropped into the Gulf of Mexico at carefully recorded spots within the one-mile limit. In July they quietly celebrated Ramo's 75th birthday.

On 3 February 1972, Colonel Ronald Day joined Vale and

the rest. The two shared the directorship amicably, Day suggesting that they go ahead and make several mock-up bombs, both for time-and-motion studies within the plant and in order to check the efficiency of their basic delivery system: an Econoline-type van, specially modified.

9. Technological Aside

One need not gather a "critical mass" of plutonium in order to make an atom bomb of it. It is sufficient to take a considerably smaller piece and subject it to a neutron density equivalent to that which prevails at standard temperature and pressure inside plutonium at critical mass. This can be done with judiciously shaped charges of high explosive.

The whole apparatus can fit comfortably inside a Ford Econoline van.

10. 9 September 1974

Progress Report
Delivery Implementation Section

TO: Ramo, Vale, Day, Sections 2, 5, 8.

As of this date we can safely terminate R & D on the following vehicles: Ford, Fiat, Austin, VW. Each has performed flawlessly on trial runs to Atlanta.

On-the-spot vehicle checks assure us that we can use Econolines for Ghana, Bombay, Montevideo, and Madrid, without attracting undue attention.

The Renault and Soyuz vans have not been road-tested because they are not distributed in the United States. One mock-up Renault is being smuggled to Mexico, where they are fairly common, to be tested. We may be able to modify the Ford setup to fit inside a Soyuz shell. However, we have only two of the Russian vans to work with, and will proceed with caution.

The Toyota's suspension gave out in one out of three

Atlanta runs; it was simply not designed for so heavy a load. We may substitute Econolines or VW's for Tokyo and Kyoto.

Ninety per cent of the vehicles were barged to New Orleans before the Atlanta run, to avoid suspicions at the Key Largo weigh station.

We are sure all systems will be in shape well before the target date.

(signed) Maxwell Bergman,
Supervisor

11. 14 October 1974

Today they solved the China Problem: automobiles and trucks are still fairly rare in China, and its border is probably the most difficult to breach. Ramo wants a minimum of three targets in China, but the odds against being able to smuggle out three vans, load them with bombs, smuggle them back in again and drive them to the target areas without being stopped— the odds are formidable.

Section 2 (Weapons Research & Development) managed to compress a good-sized bomb into a package the size of a large suitcase, weighing about 800 pounds. It is less powerful than the others and not as subtly safeguarded—read "booby-trapped"—but should be adequate to the task. It will go in through Hong Kong in a consignment of Swiss heavy machinery, bound for Peking; duplicates will go to Kunming and Shanghai, integrated with farm machinery and boat hulls, respectively, from Japan. Section 1 (Recruiting) has found delivery agents for Peking and Shanghai, is looking for a native speaker of the dialect spoken around Kunming.

12. Naming

Ramo doesn't like people to call it "Project Blackmail," and so they just call it "the project" when he's around."

13. 1 July 1975

Everything is in order: delivery began one week ago. Today is Ramo's 79th birthday.

His horoscope for today says "born today, you are a natural humanitarian. You aid those in difficulty and would make a fine attorney. You are attracted to the arts, including writing. You are due for domestic adjustment, with September indicated as a key month."

None of the above is true. It will be in October.

14. 13 October 1975

7:45 on a grey Monday morning in Washington, D.C., a three-year-old Econoline van rolls up to a park-yourself lot on 14th Street. About a quarter mile from the White House.

The attendant gives the driver his ticket. "How long ya gonna be?"

"Don't know," he said. "All day, probably."

"Put it back there then, by the Camaro."

The driver parks the van and turns on a switch under the dash. With a tiny voltmeter he checks the dead-man switch on his arm: a constant-readout sphygmomanometer wired to a simple signal generator. If his blood pressure drops too low too quickly, downtown Washington will be a radioactive hole.

Everything in order, he gets out and locks the van. This activates the safeguards. A minor collision won't set off the bomb, and neither would a Richter-6 earthquake. It will go off if anyone tries to X-ray the van or enter it.

He walks two blocks to his hotel. He is very careful crossing streets.

He has breakfast sent up and turns on the *Today* show. There is no news of special interest. At 9:07 he calls a number in Miami. Ramo's fortune is down to fifty million, but he can still afford a suite at the Beachcomber.

At 9:32, all American targets having reported, Ramo calls Raykjavik.

"Let me speak to Colonel Day. This is Ramo."

"Just a moment, sir." One moment. "Day here."

"Things are all in order over here, Colonel. Have your salesmen reported yet?"

"All save two, as expected," he says: everyone but Peking and Kunming.

"Good. Everything is pretty much your hands, then. I'm going to go down and do that commercial."

"Good luck, sir."

"We're past the need for luck. Be careful, Colonel." He rings off.

Ramo shaves and dresses, white Palm Beach suit. The reflection in the mirror looks like somebody's grandfather; not long for this world, kindly but a little crotchety, a little senile. Perhaps a little senile. That's why Colonel Day is co-ordinating things in Iceland, rather than Ramo. If Ramo dies, Day can decide what to do. If Day dies, the bombs all go off automatically.

"Let's go," Ramo shouts into the adjoining room. His voice is still clear and strong.

Two men go down the elevator with him. One is the ex-hit man, with a laundered identity (complete to plastic surgery) and two hidden pistols. The other is Philip Vale, who carries with him all of the details of Project Blackmail and, at Ramo's suggestion, a .44 Magnum single-shot derringer. He watches the hit man, and the hit man watches everybody else.

The Cadillac that waits for them outside the Beachcomber is discreetly bulletproof and has under the front and rear seats, respectively, a Thompson submachine gun and a truncated 12-gauge shotgun. The ex-hit man insisted on the additional armament, and Ramo provided them for the poor man's peace of mind. For his own peace of mind Ramo, having no taste for violence on so small a scale, had the firing pins removed last night.

They drive to a network-affiliated television station, having spent a good deal of money for ten minutes of network time. For a paid political announcement.

It only cost a trifle more to substitute their own men for union employees behind the camera and in the control room.

15. Transcript

FADE IN LONG SHOT: RAMO, PODIUM, GLOBE
     RAMO

My name is Howard Knopf Ramo.

SLOW DOLLY TO MCU RAMO
     RAMO

Please don't leave your set; what I have to say is extremely important to you and your loved ones. And I won't take too much of your time.

You've probably never heard of me, though some years ago my accountants told me I was the richest man in the world. I spent a good deal of those riches staying out of the public eye. The rest of my fortune I spent on a project that has taken me thirty years to complete.

I was born just twenty-one years after the Civil War. In my lifetime, my country has been in five major wars and dozens of small confrontations. I didn't consider the reasons for most of them worthwhile. I didn't think that any of them were worth the price we paid.

And at that, we fared well compared to many other countries, whether they won their wars or lost them. Still, we continue to have wars. Rather . . .

TIGHT ON RAMO

. . . our *leaders* continue to declare wars, advancing their own political aims by sending sons and brothers and fathers out to bleed and die.

           CUT TO:

MEDIUM SHOT, RAMO SLOWLY TURNING GLOBE
     RAMO

We have tolerated this situation through all of recorded history. No longer. China, the Soviet Union, and the United States

TO HOWARD HUGHES: A MODEST PROPOSAL

have stockpiled nuclear weapons sufficient to destroy all human life, twice over. It has gone beyond politics and become a matter of racial survival.

I propose a plan to take these weapons away from them—every one, simultaneously. To this end I have spent my fortune constructing 29 atomic bombs. 28 of them are hidden in various cities around the world. One of them is in an airplane high over Florida. It is the smallest one, a demonstration model, so to speak.

CUT TO:

REMOTE UNIT; PAN SHORELINE

RAMO

VOICE OVER SURF SOUND

This is the Atlantic Ocean, off one of Florida's Keys. The bomb will explode seven miles out, at exactly 10:30. All shipping has been cleared from the area and prevailing winds will disperse the small amount of fallout harmlessly.

Florida residents within fifty miles of Shark Key are warned not to look directly at the blast.

FILTER DOWN ON REMOTE UNIT

Watch. There!

AFTER BLAST COMES AND FADES

CUT TO:

TIGHT ON RAMO

RAMO

Whether or not you agree with me, that all nations must give up their arms, is immaterial. Whether I am a saint or a power-drunk madman is immaterial. I give the governments of the world three days' notice—not just the atomic powers, but their allies as well. Perhaps less than three days, if they do not follow my instructions to the letter.

Atomic bombs at least equivalent to the ones that devastated Hiroshima and Nagasaki have been placed in the following cities:

MCU RAMO AND GLOBE

RAMO

TOUCHES GLOBE AS HE NAMES EACH CITY

Accra, Cairo, Khartoum, Johannesburg, London, Dublin, Madrid, Paris, Berlin, Rome, Warsaw, Budapest, Moscow, Leningrad, Novosibirsk, Ankara, Bombay, Sydney, Peking, Shanghai, Kunming, Tokyo, Kyoto, Honolulu, Akron, San Francisco, New York, Washington.

The smaller towns of Novosibirsk, Kunming and Akron—one for each major atomic power—are set to go off eight hours before the others, as a final warning.

These bombs will also go off if tampered with, or if my representatives are harmed in any way. The way this will be done, and the manner in which atomic weapons will be collected, is explained in a letter now being sent through diplomatic channels to the leader of each threatened country. Copies will also be released to the world press.

A colleague of mine has dubbed this effort "Project Blackmail." Unflattering, but perhaps accurate.

CUT TO:

LONG SHOT RAMO, PODIUM, GLOBE

RAMO   RAMO

Three days. Good-by.

FADE TO BLACK

16. Briefing

"They didn't *catch* him?" The President was livid.

"No, sir. They had to find out what studio the broadcast originated from and then get—"

"Never mind. Do they know where the bomb is?"

"Yes, sir, it's on page six." The aide tentatively offered

the letter, which a courier from the Polish embassy had brought a few minutes after the broadcast.

"Where? Has anything been done?"

"It's in a public parking lot on 14th Street. The police—"

"Northwest?"

"Yes, sir."

"Good God. That's only a few blocks from here."

"Yes, sir."

"No respect for . . . nobody's fiddled with it, have they?"

"No, sir. It's booby-trapped six ways from Sunday. We have a bomb squad coming out from Belvoir, but it looks pretty foolproof."

"What about the 'representative' he talked about? Let me see that thing." The aide handed him the report.

"Actually, he's the closest thing we've got to a negotiator. But he's also part of the booby-trap. If he's hurt in any way . . ."

"What if the son of a bitch has a heart attack?" The President sat back in his chair and lowered his voice for the first time. "The end of the world."

17. Statistical Interlude

One bomb will go off if any of 28 people dies in the next three days. They will all go off if Ronald Day dies.

All of these men and women are fairly young and in good physical condition. But they are under considerable strain and also perhaps unusually susceptible to "accidental" death. Say each of them has one chance in a thousand of dying within the next three days. Then the probability of accidental catastrophe is one minus .999 to the 29th power.

This is .024 or about one chance out of 42.

A number of cautionary cables were exchanged in the first few hours, related to this computation.

18. Evening

The Secretary of Defense grips the edge of his chair and growls: "That old fool could've started World War III. Atom . . . bombing . . . Florida."

"He gave us ample warning," the Chairman of the AEC reminds him.

"Principle of the goddamn thing."

The President isn't really listening; what's past is over and there is plenty to worry about for the next few days. He is chain-smoking, something he never does in public and rarely in conference.

"How can we keep from handing over all of our atomics?" The President stubs out his cigarette, blows through the holder, lights another.

"All right," the chairman says. "He has a list of our holdings, which he admits is incomplete." Ticks off on his fingers. "He will get a similar list from China: locations, method of delivery, yield, Chinese espionage list from China: locations, method of delivery, yield, Chinese espionage has been pretty efficient. Another list from Russia. Between the three, that is among the three, I guess—" Secretary of Defense makes a noise. "—he will probably be able to disarm us completely."

He makes a tent of his fingers. "You've thought of making a deal, I suppose. Partial lists from—"

"Yes. China's willing, Russia isn't. And Ramo is also getting lists from England, France and Germany. Fairly complete, if I know our allies."

"Wait," says the secretary, "France has bombs too—"

"Halfway to Reykjavik already."

"What the hell are we going to do?"

Similar queries about the same thing, in Moscow and Peking.

19. Morning

Telegrams and cables have been arriving by the truckload. The President's staff abstracted them into a 9-page report. Most of them say "Don't do anything rash." About one in ten says "call his bluff," most of them mentioning a Communist plot. One of these even came from Akron.

It didn't take them long to find Ramo. Luckily, he had dismissed the bodyguard after returning safely to the Beachcomber, and so there was no bloodshed. Right now he is in a condition something between house arrest and protective custody, half of Miami's police force and large contingents from the FBI and CIA surrounding him and his very important phone.

He talks to Reykjavik, and Day tells him that all of the experts have arrived: 239 atomic scientists and specialists in nuclear warfare, a staff of technical translators and a planeload of observers from the UN's International Atomic Energy Agency.

Except for the few from France, no weapons have arrived. Day is not surprised and neither is Ramo.

Ramo is saddened to hear that several hundred people were killed in panicky evacuations, in Tokyo, Bombay and Khartoum. Evacuation of London is proceeding in an orderly manner. Washington is under martial law. In New York and Paris a few rushed out and most people are just sitting tight. A lot of people in Akron have decided to see what's happening in Cleveland.

20. Noon

President's intercom buzzes. "We found Ramo's man, sir."

"I suppose you searched him. Send him in."

A man in shirt sleeves walks in between two uniformed MP's. He is a hawk-faced dark man with a sardonic expression.

"This is rather premature, Mr. President. I was supposed to—"

"Sit down."

He flops into an easy chair. "—supposed to call on you at 3:30 this afternoon."

"You no doubt have some sort of a deal to offer."

The man looks at his watch. "You must be hungry, Mr. President. Take a long lunch hour, maybe a nap. I'll have plenty to say at—"

"You—"

"Don't worry about me, I've already eaten. I'll wait here."

"We can be very hard on you."

He rolls up his left sleeve. Two small boxes and some wiring are taped securely to his forearm. "No, you can't. Not for three days—you can't kill me or even cause me a lot of pain. You can't drug me or hypnotize me." (This last, a lie.) "Even if you could, it wouldn't bring any good to you."

"I believe it would."

"We can discuss that at 3:30." He leans back and closes his eyes.

"What *are* you?"

He opens one eye. "A professional gambler." That is also a lie. Back when he had to work for a living, he ran a curious kind of a lathe.

21. 3:30 P.M.

The President comes through a side door and sits at his desk. "All right, you have your say."

The man nods and straightens up slowly. "First off, let me explain my function."

"Reasonable."

"I am a gadfly, a source of tension."

"That is obvious."

"I can also answer certain questions about that bomb in your backyard."

"Here's one: how can we disarm it?"

"That I can't tell you."

"I believe we can convince—"

"No, you don't understand. I don't know *how* to turn it off. That's somebody else's job." Third lie. "I do know how to blow it up—hurt me or kill me or move me more than ten miles from ground zero. Or I can just pull this little wire." He touches a wire and the President flinches.

"All right. What else are you here for?"

"That's all. Keep an eye on you, I guess."

"You don't have any sort of . . . message, any—"

"Oh, no. You've already got the message. Through the Polish embassy, I think."

"Come on now, I'm not naive."

The man looked at him curiously. "Maybe that's your problem. Mr. Ramo's demands are not negotiable—he really is doing what he says, taking the atomic weapons away from all of you . . . strange people.

"What sort of a deal do you think you could offer an 80-year-old millionaire? Ex-billionaire. How would you propose to threaten him?"

"We can kill him."

"That's right."

"In three days we can kill you."

The man laughs politely. "Now you are being naive."

The President flips a switch on his intercom. "Send in Carson and Major Anfel and the two MP's." The four men come in immediately.

"Take this man somewhere and talk to him. Don't hurt him."

"Not yet," Carson says.

"Come on," one MP says to the man.

"I don't think so," the man says. He stares at the President. "I'd like a glass of water."

22. 15 October 1975

The only nuclear weapons in the United States are located in Colorado, Texas, Florida, and, of course, San Francisco, Washington, D.C., and Akron, Ohio.

23. 16 October 1975

2:30 A.M.

The only nuclear weapons in the United States are located in Colorado, Texas, Florida, San Francisco, and Washington, D.C. There is no Akron, Ohio.

Of the 139 who perished in the blast, 138 were very gutsy looters.

10:00 A.M.

Only San Francisco and Washington now. The others are on their way to Reykjavik.

The man who was named Andre Charvat walks down a deserted 14th Street with a 9-volt battery in his hand. A civilian and two volunteer MP's walk with him.

He walks straight up to the Econoline's rear bumper and touches the terminals of the battery to two inconspicuous rivets. There is a small spark and a click like the sound of a pinball machine, tilting.

"That's all. It's controlled by Reykjavik now."

"And Reykjavik is half controlled by Communists. And worse, traitors," Carson said huskily.

He doesn't answer but walks on down the street, alone. Amnesty.

In a few minutes a heavy truck rumbles up, and men in plain coveralls construct a box of boiler plate around the Econoline. People start coming back into Washington, and a large crowd gathers, watching them as they cover the box with a marble facade and affix a bronze plaque to the front.

The man who owned the parking lot received a generous check from the Nuclear Arms Control Board, in kroner.

24. Quote

"NUCLEAR WARFARE . . . This article consists of the following sections:

I. Introduction
II. Basic Principles
   1. Fission Weapons
   2. Fusion Weapons
III. Destructive Effects
   1. Theoretical
   2. Hiroshima and Nagaski
   3. Akron and Novosibirsk

IV. History
   1. World War II
   2. "Cold War"
   3. Treaty of Reykjavik
V. Conversion to Peaceful Uses
   1. Theory and Engineering
   2. Administration Under NACB
   3. Inspection Procedures

1 (For related articles, see: DAY, RONALD R.; EINSTEIN, ALBERT; ENERGY; FERMI, ENRICO; NUCLEAR SCIENCES (several articles); RAMO, HOWARD K.; VALE, PHILIP; WARFARE, HISTORY OF."

—Copyright © 2020 by Encyclopaedia Britannica, Inc.

DAW

The really great fantasy books are published by DAW:

Andre Norton

☐ LORE OF THE WITCH WORLD	UE1750	$2.50
☐ HORN CROWN	UE1635	$2.95
☐ PERILOUS DREAMS	UE1749	$2.50

C.J. Cherryh

☐ THE DREAMSTONE	UE2013	$2.95
☐ THE TREE OF SWORDS AND JEWELS	UE1850	$2.95

Lin Carter

☐ DOWN TO A SUNLESS SEA	UE1937	$2.50
☐ DRAGONROUGE	UE1982	$2.50

M.A.R. Barker

☐ THE MAN OF GOLD	UE1940	$3.95

Michael Shea

☐ NIFFT THE LEAN	UE1783	$2.95
☐ THE COLOR OUT OF TIME	UE1954	$2.50

B.W. Clough

☐ THE CRYSTAL CROWN	UE1922	$2.75

NEW AMERICAN LIBRARY
P.O. Box 999, Bergenfield, New Jersey 07621

Please send me the DAW Books I have checked above. I am enclosing
$_____ (check or money order—no currency or C.O.D.'s).
Please include the list price plus $1.00 per order to cover handling costs.

Name _____

Address _____

City _____ State _____ Zip Code _____

Please allow at least 4 weeks for delivery